THE SUN WORSHIPPERS
YELLOWLEG

TWO NOVELS BY
A. S. FLEISCHMAN

Stark House Press • Eureka California

THE SUN WORSHIPPERS / YELLOWLEG

Published by Stark House Press
4720 Herron Road
Eureka, CA 95503, USA
griffinskye3@sbcglobal.net
www.starkhousepress.com

THE SUN WORSHIPPERS
copyright © 2012 by Sid Fleischman, Inc.

YELLOWLEG
Originally published by Gold Medal Books and copyright © 1960
by A. S. Fleischman, registration #A436177. Copyright © renewed 1988
by A. S. Fleischman, registration #RE 397-731.
Reprinted by arrangement with Sid Fleischman, Inc.

"The Lure of the West" copyright © 2012 by Paul Fleischman

"An Interview with A. S. 'Sid' Fleischman" copyright © 2001 by *Paperback Parade*. Reprinted by permission of editor Gary Lovisi.

All rights reserved

ISBN: 1-933586-40-0
ISBN-13: 978-1-933586-40-3

Book design by Mark Shepard, www.shepgraphics.com
Proofreading by Rick Ollerman

PUBLISHER'S NOTE
This is a work of fiction. Names, characters, places and incidents are either the products of the author's imagination or used fictionally, and any resemblance to actual persons, living or dead, events or locales, is entirely coincidental.
Without limiting the rights under copyright reserved above, no part of this publication may be reproduced, stored, or introduced into a retrieval system or transmitted in any form or by any means (electronic, mechanical, photocopying, recording or otherwise) without the prior written permission of both the copyright owner and the above publisher of the book.

First Stark House Press Edition: September 2012

THE SUN WORSHIPPERS

Gamage is on his way to Thebes, the Southern California desert town that Colonel Martinka built-up with his date plantations. Now the eccentric Colonel is building a pyramid in the desert and the land boom is ready to begin. Gamage is an ex-newspaperman-turned-film-writer who's burned a few bridges in Hollywood. He's been hired to write Martinka's story for the family and prepare the world for the coming land grab. How was he to know that Ginny would be there, married to the Colonel's son Frank. He thought he'd seen the last of her in Europe, the night she ran out on him. How could he know he'd meet Conny, who would become his Girl Friday, and perhaps something more. And how could he know he would find respect for the old recluse himself, trapped behind the layers of family fear and fabrication. Thebes is waiting like a desert mirage and Gamage is on his way to find it—and himself.

YELLOWLEG

Yellowleg rides into town with Turk and his sidekick Billy. He's got a bullet in his shoulder that needs tending—he can barely shoot straight. But Yellowleg carries more than a bullet—he's got the scars from a scalping he received from a drunken Confederate soldier, and nothing but hate in his heart. Turk and Billy are there to rob the local bank but another group beats them to it, and that's when Yellowleg accidentally kills a young boy thanks to his bum shooting arm. Now, filled with guilt, Yellowleg is on a journey through Apache country with the beautiful widow, Kit, who is determined to bury her son next to his father. Turk and Billy have other plans. Turk wants the bank money. Billy wants the widow. And Yellowleg still wants his revenge. It's going to be a long, hard ride.

A. S. FLEISCHMAN BIBLIOGRAPHY

NOVELS
The Straw Donkey Case (1948)
Murder's No Accident (1949)
Shanghai Flame (1951)
Look Behind You, Lady (1952)
 [aka Chinese Crimson, UK, 1962]
Danger in Paradise (1953)
Counterspy Express (1954)
Malay Woman (1954)
 [aka Malay Manhunt, UK, 1966]
Blood Alley (1955)
Yellowleg (1960) [aka The Deadly Companions, 1961]
The Venetian Blonde (1963)
The Sun Worshippers (2012)

SCREENPLAYS
Blood Alley (1955)
Goodbye, My Lady [as Sid Fleischman] (1956)
Lafayette Escadrille (1958)
The Deadly Companions (1961)
Scalawag (1973)
The Whipping Boy [as Max Brindle] (1995)

As Sid Fleischman
FICTION
Mr. Mysterious & Company (1962)
By the Great Horn Spoon! (1963)
Ghost in the Noonday Sun (1965)
Chancy and the Grand Rascal (1966)
McBroom Tells the Truth (1966)
McBroom and the Big Wind (1967)
McBroom's Zoo (1969)
Longbeard the Wizard (1970)
Jingo Django (1971)
McBroom's Ear (1971)
McBroom's Ghost (1971)
The Wooden Cat Man (1972)
McBroom Tells a Lie (1976)
Kate's Secret Riddle Book (1977)
Me and the Man on the Moon-Eyed Horse (1977)
Humbug Mountain (1978)
Jim Bridger's Alarm Clock and Other Tall Tales (1978)
McBroom and the Beanstalk (1978)
The Hey Hey Man (1979)
McBroom and the Great Race (1980)
The Case of the Cackling Ghost (1981)
McBroom the Rainmaker (1982)
McBroom's Almanac (1984)
Whipping Boy (1986)
The Scarebird (1987)
The Midnight Horse (1990)
Jim Ugly (1992)
McBroom's Wonderful One-Acre Farm (1992)
The 13th Floor: A Ghost Story (1995)
The Abracadabra Kid: A Writer's Life (1996)
Bandit's Moon (1998)
The Ghost on Saturday Night (1999)
Here Comes McBroom!: Three More Tall Tales (1999)
A Carnival of Animals (2000)
Bo & Mzzz Mad (2003)
Disappearing Act (2003)
The Giant Rat of Sumatra: or Pirates Galore (2005)
Escape! The Story of the Great Houdini (2006)
The White Elephant (2006)
The Entertainer and the Dyybuk (2007)
The Trouble Begins at 8: A Life of Mark Twain in the Wild, Wild West (2008)
The Dream Stealer (2009)
Sir Charlie: Chaplin, the Funniest Man in the World (2010).

BOOKS ON MAGIC
Between Cocktails (1939)
Ready, Aim, Magic! (with Bob Gunther, 1942)
Call the Witness (with Bob Gunther, 1943)
The Blue Bug (with Bob Gunther, 1947)
Top Secrets (with Bob Gunther, 1947)
Magic Made Easy (as Carl March, 1953)
Mr. Mysterious's Secrets of Magic (1975)
The Charlatan's Handbook (1993)

7
THE LURE OF THE WEST
BY PAUL FLEISCHMAN

9
THE SUN WORSHIPPERS
BY A. S. FLEISCHMAN

141
YELLOWLEG
BY A. S. FLEISCHMAN

245
AN INTERVIEW WITH
A.S. 'SID' FLEISCHMAN
BY GARY LOVISI

THE LURE OF THE WEST
AN INTRODUCTION BY PAUL FLEISCHMAN

A writer's fiction, said Isaac Bashevis Singer, needs an address. For much of my father's first decade as an author, that address was in Asia, which he'd toured as yeoman on a destroyer escort during World War II. But in the late 1950s, like a homing pigeon, his fiction returned to the West he'd grown up in, where both he and it would stay—other than for a handful of excursions—for the next fifty years.

"Every author wants to try a Western," he once declared. Cowboys and Indians thundered constantly through books and across movie screens during his youth. Growing up in San Diego, the mythic West of dusty trails and bouldered canyons was just a few miles inland. He'd gotten a taste for history while at San Diego State College and gradually filled his book shelves with the books that I passed at eye-level in my own youth—*Thirty Years a Cowboy, Yuma Crossing, The Earp Brothers of Tombstone, Thirty-Three Years Among Our Wild Indians*. A writer's research sets in motion an exciting push me-pull you effect: you go looking for facts, but those facts give you new ideas for fictional characters and situations.

This is what occurred when my father discovered that the Indians may have learned scalping from Europeans. From that germ grew *Yellowleg*. Though the story takes place in the 1870s and the spoken English is Western instead of Pidgin, the book bears a family resemblance to his Far East suspense novels: an honorable man in a dangerous world, double-dealing, secrets, an alluring woman. With its tale of at-odds traveling companions, the book foreshadowed *The Whipping Boy*, the children's book that won him the Newbery Medal twenty-five years later. I recall my father equating the hero's yellow-striped cavalry pants with the yellow stars forced on the Jews by the Nazis. I suspect that the book was a reworking of my parents' courtship, which crossed religious lines, as well as being a post-war revenge story transposed back to the Civil War.

Fast-forwarding nearly a century, *The Sun Worshippers* is set in the California desert of the 1950s, with the Apaches replaced by real estate developers. The book's inspiration remains a mystery, though the idea of a man recreating the Great Pyramid of Gizeh has a whiff of Turk's dreams of empire in *Yellowleg*, the folly of mortals setting themselves up as gods. After my father finished the book, truth bested fiction yet again when news broke that falling-apart London Bridge would be sold and rebuilt over the Colorado. Las Vegas's historical fantasias followed. *The Sun Worshippers* is a Raymond Chandleresque tale set in a West unmoored from history, where anything seems possible, the West that offered pioneers new lives but that also nurtured crackpots and megalomaniacs.

For reasons unknown, my father's agent couldn't find a buyer for *The Sun Worshippers*. This was a blow. My father had put a lot of effort into the book and was proud of the result; the experience might have helped steer him toward writing for children. It was, to my knowledge, his only finished novel not to appear in print. That Stark House Press is at last restoring his perfect batting average would give him the greatest of pleasure.

Aromas, CA
June 2011

THE SUN WORSHIPPERS
BY A. S. FLEISCHMAN

CHAPTER ONE

1

Gamage, an ex-newspaperman, could sleep anywhere. The Greyhound bus out of El Centro was rolling north into the California desert; the seats were filled with Mexican stoop laborers in straw hats and shirts buttoned at the neck. Gamage slept. He slept in a $300 Italian silk suit with his collar open and his tie pulled loose.

He was an unhurried man, a bird of passage, with reddish brown hair and dark eyes. He wore heavy sunglasses. His cheeks were acne-scarred (he referred to his face as wormy chestnut), but he had an easy smile and good white teeth. He was tall and sinewy and gave the impression at any given moment of knowing where he was going.

He was going to Thebes, a small town further up the desert, where some eccentric was building a pyramid.

When Gamage awoke the lettuce and alfalfa fields of the Imperial Valley were gone. Salt, heaving up through the desert, lay over the ground like unmelted patches of snow. The sun hovered overhead, burning a hole in the sky. Gamage lit a Mexican cigarette and passed the time reading highway literature.

STOP! LOOK! BUY!
GET IN ON THE LAND BOOM!

He looked as far as the eye could see, but the boom was over the horizon. Clumps of greasewood and cactus speckled the landscape. It was just the place, he thought, to settle down with a bad cough. Thebes, 34 miles. Fresh Grapefruit 600 yards. Come to Mecca. Cactus For Sale. Another Martinka Development Going in Here. Send a Box of Dates Back Home. Salton Sea Property — Free Literature Ahead. Every Home with a Swimming Pool. Oasis Savings & Loan. Try a Date Shake.

HELP STAMP OUT REALITY

The graffito stood out in flaking white paint on the side of an abandoned roadside produce stand. Gamage returned the smile. It was a sign of intelligent life in the desert, he thought. When it came to stamping out reality, Gamage was an old pro.

He was a film writer. He had been brought out to Hollywood several years before after picking up a Pulitzer Prize in news reporting. Success had brought with it its own imperative clichés; he was soon living at the beach and taking his meals at Scandia and Perino's. He slipped into the gilt obscurity reserved for screenwriters. His name flashed on the screens of the world unnoticed, like fine print. The money was easy and pleasant and he spent it effortlessly. His sense of whimsy gave way to restlessness and boredom. For reasons that were now obscure to him he slugged an actor, breaking his nose and causing the picture they were shooting to shut down. He was sued for personal injury, fleeced by studio lawyers and barred from the lot. He decamped for Mexico.

He had always supposed he could return to the newspaper business, but when the time came he found he couldn't go back to the city room in a $300 suit. Hollywood had wired him in.

Mexico was a ball while his bankroll held out. His agent scratched up a job out of left field—some desert rat in the Coachella Valley needed some literary day labor done—but at the time Gamage was too busy chasing a long-legged Texas girl and betting on the cock fights. Finally, he woke up one morning in Taxco and discovered the girl was gone and he was Tap City. Broke. Was the desert job still open?

It was.

Across the aisle of the bus a man was cracking salted sunflower seeds between his yellow teeth. Outside, a streak of blue was rising on the horizon like watercolor—the Salton Sea. Gamage fished the clipping out of his billfold and studied it again.

PYRAMID TO RISE IN
CALIFORNIA DESERT

Date King to Pay Cost
Of Gizeh-Like Structure

THEBES, CALIF., Feb. 16 — This date-growing desert community, which claims to hold an option on the sun, will soon find itself in the rising shadow of a life-size pyramid to be constructed 28 miles northeast of town.

The Gizeh-like structure is being built by Col. Jesse Martinka, 74, wealthy real estate developer and pioneer in desert agriculture.

The pyramid will reach a height of 455 feet, exceeding by some four feet the Great Pyramid of Cheops in Egypt, according to plans revealed yesterday. The tomb will cover 12 square acres.

"With heavy machinery and modern construction techniques we expect to complete the job in slightly more than 18 months," said John H. Glendon, of the Los Angeles architectural firm of Glendon, Stuart & Petrie, designers of the desert monument.

"It will become the showplace of the desert," Mr. Glendon added.

Like it's ancient model, the California pyramid will have two royal chambers which will be opened to the public.

Cost of the project was not disclosed. Col. Martinka could not be reached for comment.

The announcement is expected to set off a real estate boom in the immediate area, a barren waste of creosote bush and cactus.

Col. Martinka was among the first to envision large scale commercial date gardens in the low California desert with its North African climate. He is widely known as the Date King of the Coachella Valley. Today, except for limited acreage in Arizona, this remains the only date-producing area in the United States.

With the growing popularity of this desert as a sun-lit playground at the smoggy back door of metropolitan Los Angeles, Col. Martinka has been a leader in the development of residential tracts from Palm Springs to the Salton Sea.

A native of Boston, Martinka aspired to become a grand opera tenor in his youth. Ill health brought him to the desert in 1907 and he remained to become the valley's first citizen. Villa Martinka, his home outside of Thebes, stands among the greenery of his original date palm plantation. At one time he was the largest importer of offshoots of the Deglet Noor palm from Tunisia and Algeria, which today comprises the major date crop of this inland valley.

Gamage gazed out the window at the hot blue Marrakech sky; he could easily imagine the pyramid rising out of the burning sands. Maybe a string of camels on the horizon, he thought, and a few imitation Bedouins hired as set dressing. A pyramid. What kind of flummery was that? My name is Oxymandias, king of the dates. Look on my works, ye mighty, and despair.

Martinka—the name had a rachet-like sound. Gamage folded up the clipping. Grab the money and run, he told himself. He had been hired to write the date king's biography. For private publication.

2

Welcome to
THEBES, CALIF.
"City of the Sun"
If You Lived Here, You'd Be Home Now!

The bus pulled in before the Queen of Sheba café and Gamage stepped out into the shimmering desert heat.

He made for the shade of the café and waited for the driver to dig out his luggage. His entire life, it seemed to Gamage, had been a series of entrances and exits. He hadn't let the Martinka family know when to expect him and there was no one to meet him. Just as well, he reflected; it was a shabby entrance.

He wanted a cold beer and a shower. It was too hot to bother with a cigarette, but he lit one anyway. He looked the town over and it struck him as a mouldering stage set. False fronts were held aloft like civic bric-a-brac, gathering dust. There was a plaza with a clutch of aging date palms in the center and the sidewalks were shaded by pink stucco arcades. The colors had an unfamiliar intensity. The sky was bluer, the sun closer, the shade darker. If he lived here, he'd be home now. Thanks, but no thanks, he thought. He wondered why anyone would live in the City of the Sun for more than ten minutes at a time. You could get a bad sunburn just crossing the street.

The bus pulled out for Indio, Palm Springs and Los Angeles (a hundred miles away on the coast), abandoning Gamage to the municipal silence. He threw his coat over one shoulder, took a grip on his bags (spotted with abraded hotel labels, like fading memories, of London, Paris, Athens and Singapore) and crossed to the arcades. Here and there farm hands hunkered together, taking squatters' rights on the shade, and viewed him from under the soiled brims of their hats. He inquired about the best hotel in town, if there was a choice. He was directed to the Plantation House further along the block.

The lobby had the effect of an atrium with polished wooden galleries supported by white barber pole columns and a hand-painted blue sky overhead. The floor was a patchwork of Indian throw rugs over blue and white Mexican tiles. Paintings of desert smoketrees, sandy wastes and hazy blue hills hung from the walls in place of windows. It was clear to Gamage that the Plantation House had once been very grand and maintained an aging, defiant air. It was not air-conditioned, except for the bar, and it was apparently offseason. He signed with a feeling that the place was a warren of empty rooms, had his bags sent up and stopped in for a drink.

He ordered a bottle of beer. The bar was a long darkwood affair with a pair of steer horns mounted above the cash register. "Do the nights cool off around here?"

The bartender was a pink-faced man with a whispy bald head. "Why, it ain't even started to get hot yet. You new in the valley?"

"Brand new."

"Your blood'll thin out."

"How long does it take?"

"About twenty years."

"I don't think I'll wait," Gamage said. The cold beer brought him back to life. "I guess the Martinka pyramid is causing a stir around here."

The bartender nodded. "Six months ago you couldn't give that land away by the section. You got to hand it to that old desert fox. I understand he's going to ask three-four thousand a lot now—and he'll get it."

"What are his drinking habits?" Gamage asked. It seemed to him as good a place to start as any.

The bartender reclaimed a cigarette stub from the top of the cash register. "I guess I've served everybody in the valley, one time or another. But the Colonel, he never drinks anything stronger than artesian water, at least during my time. But Frank is another story."

"Frank. Is that the son in Martinka & Son?"

The bartender nodded. "I'll tell you about Frank. He ain't exactly backward when it comes to making a dollar, either. Everything that family touches, it turns to gold. Frank just built himself a new house and I hear the bathtub handles are pure gold. Him and the wife probably use gold leaf for toilet paper."

Gamage paid for the beer. "What the hell," he grinned. "That's the American Dream, isn't it?"

3

From his third floor window Gamage watched a bulldozer in the distance staining the air with dust and he supposed that would be Martinka, the desert alchemist, turning base metal into gold. Closer in he could see a baking landscape of billboards and date gardens, a sham Araby tucked away behind the bare California hills. He would be here for weeks; it was a dismal prospect.

The room had a tile floor, white plaster walls, a high ceiling, a ceiling fan and an iron filigree bed. He took a shower (the tub had claw feet) and then, with a towel around his hips, he lit a cigarette and put in a call to Martinka.

"Martinka & Son."

"The Colonel, please."

"Who's calling?" the girl said.

"Gamage. Bill Gamage."

"Oh, yes, Mr. Gamage. We've been expecting you. You want to talk to Frank Martinka. He's not in at the moment, but I think I can reach him. Can I have him call you back?"

"I'm at the Plantation House."

"I know he's anxious to talk to you. I'll have him call you right back."

The phone rang while Gamage was dressing. It was the girl again. Frank wanted Gamage to come out to the house. It was south of town, in the hills overlooking the Salton Sea. Gamage said he would find it, and hung up. He looked at his watch. It was four-thirty.

4

The raw, newly carved road lay like an open wound. Gamage could see the house above, a sun-glazed pink box perched in the barren brown hills.

The taxi leveled out on a large motor court and swung around a rock garden set with barrel cactus and thorny bursts of ocotillo. A Japanese girl who spoke almost no English led Gamage through the house, her feet mute against the wheat-colored marble floors. It was a long walk and a splendid house, he reflected, a splendid house. Real estate peddlers knew how to live. They came out along a Moorish colonnade to an airy loggia, marble everywhere, and there in the pool was Frank Martinka talking on the phone.

He waved Gamage in without interrupting his monologue and Gamage seated himself in the shade of the loggia. Even though the sun itself had fallen behind the hills the sky remained a rich, oppressive blue. Gamage helped himself to a cigarette out of an ormolu box and tried to tune out Martinka's conversation, but the man's voice carried several miles.

"You're not going to stop us with that flat bed press of yours," he was saying. "You run a chickenshit newspaper, John. You always have. The pyramid means progress in this valley. You can't stop it. Listen, you've been taking gas down there for years. You're dead. I could put you out of business in twenty minutes, but it's just not worth the effort. But keep printing that puke of yours and I may decide to get nasty."

He gave Gamage a conspiratorial wink, hanging onto the pool coping with an elbow and the phone in a wet fist. Eternal sunshine had roasted Frank Martinka to a leathery brown, like the surrounding hills. His eyebrows were bleached to a kind of coarse gold and his blue eyes were so faint as to be almost colorless. He had a large, slack frame like a lifeguard letting himself run to beef.

He bobbed out of the pool a moment later and lit a cigarette with wet fingers. He threw a towel around his neck and joined Gamage on the loggia.

"You're Gamage," he said.

"You're Martinka."

"Let me get you a drink."

"Bourbon," Gamage said.

"When can you go to work?"

"I'm working."

"You're pretty expensive, do you know that? Twenty-five thou. Christ! I figure you're going to cost us about four bits a word."

"I'll use long words and give you your money's worth."

Frank laughed. "To hell with it. We go first class. I'm just talking." He turned to the bar and began fixing a pair of drinks. "Bourbon. You're my kind of guy. How was Mexico?"

"Mexican."

"One of these days some smart gonifs are going to go down there and open that place up. It's a sunny piece of real estate. That's what people are buying around here. Sunshine. We throw in the lousy land for nothing." He had a quick, volatile laugh. After passing Gamage his drink he settled himself on the edge of a charpoy. "Well, amigo, what do you need to get started?"

"The Colonel."

Frank grinned, appraising Gamage with his aspic eyes. "That's out."

"What's out?"

"The old swindler left for Italy two weeks ago."

"I can hop a plane," Gamage said.

"Over my dead body, amigo. I went to a lot of trouble to get him out of here. He wouldn't stand still for it if he knew you were poking around in his past—not that there's anything to hide. When I put the Life of Colonel Jesse Martinka in his hands—then he'll know." Frank laughed again and flipped his cigarette into the pool (Estate Size Lots, Gamage thought—Every Home With An Ash Tray). "Strictly a surprise. For his 75th birthday in November. I've gotten his papers together. I can give you all the facts you'll need. All I want out of you, amigo, is the four-bit words."

"It would help if I could meet him anyway," Gamage said. "For flavor."

"Screw the flavor. Don't give us *War and Peace*. I want something we can stick in the libraries and hand out to our enemies. You'd be surprised how many people around here think the Colonel wears horns."

Gamage watched the cigarette butt float away on the surface of the pool. "Then what you want from me is a dehorning job."

"But class. It's got to have class. Your name is class, isn't it? The Pulitzer Prize is class."

Gamage gave an inward shrug. Grab the money and run, he thought. "How did you get my name?"

"Amigo, I never heard of you. My wife met you at a party on the coast a couple of years ago. She said you had class so we hunted you up. Virginia Martinka. A tall blonde with the best pair of knockers in the valley. You probably remember her."

"No."

Frank grinned at him. "Don't put me on, amigo. You probably laid her. Everyone else does."

"That's your problem," Gamage said. He wondered how he would be able to put up with Frank Martinka for the next several weeks.

"Have you had your nose bobbed?"

"No," Gamage said. "Why?"

"You could be a hooknose in disguise. My old lady has a thing about the Hebrews. She wouldn't want the family epic written by a sheeny."

Gamage stared at the man. He began to rise. "Amigo, I've got a great idea."

"It's about time."

"Why don't you take this job and shove it up your keester?"

Frank Martinka threw back his head and laughed. "Sit down and keep your hair on," he said finally. "We're just getting squared away on the ground rules. Now you know the family. There's nothing in the contract that says you have to like us. Just make with the words."

Gamage squinted out at the desert heat. His instinct was to blow the deal. But he had been living on Martinka money for weeks. After signing the contract he had been wired an advance of $2500, but he had lingered on in Mexico trying to double his bankroll on the cockfights. The poultry had failed him and when he was down to $1200 in traveler's checks he had decided to catch a bus. From the first he hadn't liked the idea of writing a book-length puff. But now that he was on the scene he didn't want to walk away from the story. The old man was already beginning to fascinate him. It wasn't every day you ran into a pyramid builder. And Gamage couldn't fault the terms. He didn't have to like the Martinkas.

A click of heels sounded along the marble gallery. Gamage turned, and supposed that would be Virginia Martinka.

She made a smart entrance. She wore a black linen skirt with a tight hemline and a pink blouse. The hemline shackled her legs, making her take two steps for one, and on the black spiked heels she came on like the rattle of machinegun fire. She had short, tousled hair and earrings that dangled like wrecking balls. Gamage searched his memory, but came up blank. He had never seen this girl before in his life.

"Don't get up," Frank muttered. "It spoils these broads."

"Your wife is pretty."

"That's not my wife. Virginia flew out to some goddam horse show." He waved the girl in. "Conny, meet Bill Gamage. He's on the payroll now. A writer. Pulitzer Prize."

"How do you do," Conny said, barely seeming to notice him.

"Fix yourself a drink, Conny," Frank said.

"It might be poisoned."

"Then get me a refill. How about you, amigo?"

"I'm just leaving," Gamage said.

She rattled away with Frank's glass and Frank bent closer to Gamage. "Do me a favor," he murmured sourly. "Get her out of here."

Gamage gave the ice in his glass a slow shake. He was on the Martinka payroll now—was he supposed to sweep out Frank's left-over dames? He hadn't given Conny a last name, as if he were half-denying her existence. She returned after a moment with Frank's drink.

"I've never met a writer before, Mr. Gamage," she said. "The people I know can't even spell."

Frank laughed. "Go home, Conny. Bill said he'd give you a lift back to town."

Gamage let it pass. Conny interested him. He liked her eyes—violet, with dark lashes that seemed to open and shut on a smile she wasn't making public. She was small and slim, but tough as wire, he thought. And she was playing games with him. She was yet to look directly at him, but he sensed that she was interested. And she had sense enough to let him do the groundwork. He looked at Frank.

"Why a pyramid?"

Frank shut one eye and scowled. To Gamage he seemed to be making faces in order to conceal the one he had. "Listen, you sound like that chickenshit newspaper. Why the pyramid? Why the hell not?" He got up. The desert air had dried his skin and left his hair in yellow strokes across his forehead. He had the sudden, contentious air of an executive who had inherited the vice-presidency of the firm, but still bites his nails. "Here's your answer. This is a great piece of country. It's been good to the Colonel. He came out in 1907 with nothing to his name but a bad cough. He built himself a little lean-to west of town and figured he was dying. But that sun up there, that brought him back to life. Old man sunshine is a member of our firm. This is my dad's way of saying thanks. The Martinka pyramid is going to put this valley on the map. It's his gift to a great little valley, a great state and a great country." He laughed suddenly. "You ought to take that down, amigo. It's not bad. You can use it."

Gamage emptied his glass and set it down. Frank was going to be a pain in the ass. "Where are the family papers?"

"I'll get 'em on your way out."

"I'm on my way out."

"You just came."

"I work fast."

"Conny, call Bill a cab."

She went to the poolside phone, sitting on her haunches and making a thing of beauty of her skirt and legs. Frank gave Gamage a wink. "You can tell that broad's been calling cabs all her life, can't you?"

Gamage crushed his cigarette in the tray. It seemed to him that Frank was betraying a certain pique; maybe Conny hadn't come across. "How long will the Colonel be away?"

"Months. No one comes home in the summer if there's any excuse to stay away. I put the two of them, him and the old lady, on a plane straight for La Scala. His hearing is going, you know. He's got to grab all the opera he can while he can still tune it in. He had a voice once, a real voice, but the lungs went bad. TB thickens the vocal cords and that finished him off before he got anywhere. Now he could buy and sell La Scala—and it wouldn't surprise me if he did."

The desert fox might be human at that, Gamage thought. "Tell me," he said. "Is it true you Martinkas use gold leaf for toilet paper?"

Frank boomed out laughing. "Is that what they say?"

"That's what I heard."

"Of course we do. Doesn't everyone? Listen, you'll hear all kinds of crap about the old man. Keep checking with me. Sure, maybe he has tobacco stains in his union suit—don't we all, amigo—but don't put that in the book. Remember what I said. If we wanted *War and Peace*, I'd hire Dickens."

5

It seemed a long ride back. Shadows were reaching out like cobwebs across the valley. Gamage glanced at the pigskin attaché case on the seat between him and Conny and wished he could make it go away. The Colonel interested him, but Frank had hired him to elevate the desert fox to sainthood. He wanted a typewritten halo.

"Frank's not so bad," Conny said, "if you don't get to know him."

"Where can I drop you?"

"He's afraid of you."

"That's interesting."

"You made him nervous. He laughed too much. He's usually more of a crud."

She put a cigarette between her lips. He reached for his lighter, but she struck a paper match and lit it herself. The liberated female, he thought. She inhaled deeply as if she had been through an ordeal. Her pink blouse had a high, open collar, which set off the dark, sleek shape of her head and looked good on her. "Do you always light your own cigarettes?" he asked. "First thing we know you'll be wanting the right to vote."

She gave him a smile. "I can imagine what he told you about me."

"He spoke highly of you."

"I'll bet."

"How did you get mixed up with him?"

"Just luck."

Gamage smiled back. She knew the answers. "What's your last name?"

"Sargent."

"Conny Sargent."

"Yes."

"How did he find a bright girl like you?"

"In the yellow pages. I'm a public stenographer." She shrugged. "I guess

I've known Frank for about three hundred years, on and off. It's a small town. He keeps firing his own secretaries and I fill in sometimes. Sometimes he'll call whether he needs me or not. He'll dictate for an hour, not making sense but just looking at me and dictating every four letter word he can think of, expecting me to react. I'm used to it by now. I just take them down and type them up in triplicate and send him a bill. All very businesslike."

"Do you have to do it?"

"Don't get me wrong. I have a great deal of respect for Frank. A man with money can't be all bad."

"Where does it say that?"

"In the Bill of Rights, I think." She adjusted one of her earrings. She looked at him. "Are you really a Pulitzer Prize winner?"

"A previous incarnation," he said. "Can I buy you a drink?"

They stopped in at the Plantation House. She looked good on a bar stool, he thought; she was decorative and easy to be with and they sensed in each other a certain guilty rapport. Frank had bought them both, they were members of the same firm. She had come through with her virtue intact (a condition which seemed to threaten Frank, Gamage thought). She had discovered Gamage's own great ethical touchstone: Grab the Money and Run.

She ordered a marguerita and he asked her about Frank's wife.

"Don't tell me," she answered. "He never said he had a wife."

"Conny, you're not fooling me," Gamage said. "Beneath that hard exterior I think there's a hard interior."

"Thanks for noticing."

"How about dinner?"

"Not tonight."

He decided not to press it. "How long have you lived around here?"

"I grew up in Thermal."

"Do you know the old man—the Colonel?"

She gave him a dismal smile. "Of course. I remember him even when I was a kid. We thought he was some kind of a kook even then. He always wore one of those Hoover collars no matter how hot it was—and believe me, it gets hot in Thermal. He looked about ten feet tall to me then, all arms and legs, and eyes like God. I was afraid of him. He always had his coat pocket full of dates and he'd pat you on the head and give you a date—like Rockefeller handing out dimes. He made a big thing of being the Date King. He was always saying that a man could live forever on dates and goat's milk. All the while he was buying up land. Nobody else wanted it then. He had a thing about land, like some guys play cards or chase women. With him it was land. When the desert boom hit, he was ready for it. Boom. You know what BeJesus John says about him, don't you?" She gave him a half-smile, as if to remind herself that he was an outsider. "No, I guess you wouldn't."

"Who's BeJesus John?"

"John Amador—*The Thebes Weekly Sunset*. Scourge of the Martinkas. He says if Colonel Martinka gets to heaven he'll try to subdivide the Green Pastures."

Gamage laughed. She stayed for another drink and before putting her in a cab he decided if he met no one else in the valley he'd like to meet BeJesus John.

6

When Gamage stopped for his room key there was a message slip in the box. Frank had called. Gamage picked up a copy of *The Thebes Weekly Sunset* and took the elevator, a brass birdcage, to the third floor gallery and his room. He didn't return the call. He stripped off his coat and tie and smoked a cigarette at the window, looking at the lights of town. The man was right: the valley didn't cool off at night.

It was dinner time, but he wasn't hungry. He supposed he ought to lay off the booze in this heat. Finally he opened the attaché case on the bed and shuffled through the assortment of papers and letters. There was an old penny tablet, a diary, dated 1907, and he flipped through it. Fragmentary. The Colonel's wife had written an endless tribute on page after page of rose-tinted stationery. Gamage would read it later. There was a Karsh-like photograph, probably meant to be the frontispiece. The Colonel stared at the camera with a falconer's look in his eye and a fist on his hip. He had a thin face and a beakish nose. His hair was white, thick and cropped short; in contrast, his skin was darkened and toned by half a century in the sun. He had the air of a man who intended to live forever. Gamage put it all aside (there would be plenty of time tomorrow) and stretched out with the paper.

The Thebes Weekly Sunset was a frail four pages, almost bereft of advertising—it was taking gas, as Frank had said. The close set columns were designed for a reading glass. There was the usual scattering of newsless local news, some boiler plate features ("How To Work Plywood"), police items, a few sports pieces and no acknowledgment of the world outside the Coachella Valley. Gamage was not long in finding the Martinka name, on the editorial page.

STOP THE BULLDOZERS!

Excuse me if I am not my usual bilious and offensive self today. I have been dieting on the milk of human kindness for several weeks—ever since Col. Jesse Martinka unleased his bulldozers. The dust is flying. When it settles, behold! A bonafide, gosh-almighty Egyptian pyramid! You'll be able to see it from miles around—if you care to look.

If I have written unkind things in the past about our renegade date king, I beg to be forgiven. He is going to put this backward stretch of the valley in the public eye, no question about it. The time is coming when a man won't be able to run out of gas anywhere on the desert, and that's progress. Why, the good Colonel is going to pave our streets with gold. He's going to march at the head of his Grand Army of weekenders and Cadillacs. We'll be invaded and colonized. In no time at all our cactus will be growing in flower pots, where it belongs.

That's progress. As you know, I have long been opposed to the splendor of our barren acres. They were never good for anything but peace and quiet and a spring flush of wild flowers. Plow 'em under, boys! Bring on the bulldozers!

Let us all genuflect toward our village Pharaoh, pouring over his glorious blueprints.

Now there may be a few ungrateful citizens who will look upon the good Colonel as a mere real estate butcher knocking together a pyramid in order to sell a patch of worthless, sun-burnt acreage.

I have no patience with such untidy mutterings. Of course, it may be true.

We have already seen, during the last few years, our desert cut into 40-foot lots and pitched like breakfast cereal over the Los Angeles radio and television stations. So many paper cities have grown up that it will take three large wastebaskets to hold them all when the bubble bursts—The Garden of Eden, Sun-Blessed Dunes, Sunshine City, Salton Acres, Sand and Sea, and others too splendid to mention. Now, it seems reasonable to suppose, we will have Pyramid City or Egyptian Dunes or Upper Bellydance, Calif.

The sun worshippers are coming. They come to brown themselves on the patio spits of eternal sunshine. Col. Martinka is their prophet. Tract cities are rising where shaggy grapefruit and orange groves once pleased the eye. The old date palm gardens are being hacked out to make room for slab floors and swimming pools. If the sound of the desert was once the rustle of a leaf it is now the scratch of a ball point pen.

The weekenders are stealing our backyard.

The prophet is making a fat profit.

Soon there will be a traffic jam from Palm Springs to the Mexican border.

That, at least, is the view of the disgruntled, the peevish, the backward and the sore-headed. Such views are hardly worth paying attention to.

Still, this newspaper has long championed unworthy causes and foolish crusades. As a service to our affronted readers who believe that certain chunks of nature's badlands ought to be left forever wild—preserved—just plain left alone—we are printing up a petition on the back page. This recommends to the County Board of Supervisors that Martinka's Pyramid be moved to a slightly different location. Say, somewhere in Afghanistan.

Stop the bulldozers! Preserve the desert! Sign it today!

The phone was ringing. That would be Frank. Gamage let it ring. He turned to the back page and glanced at the petition. BeJesus John didn't stand a chance, Gamage thought, but it was quite a piece of literary grapeshot and Gamage wished him well. He hadn't read any country journalism in years and he'd almost forgotten it existed. He thought about the small town weeklies that had taught him his trade years ago, but he'd put that far behind him. The past was a series of closed doors and to hell with it.

The phone stopped ringing. Gamage took another shower and went out for a bite to eat.

CHAPTER TWO

1

The phone woke him a few minutes after seven the following morning. That would teach him to ignore Frank's calls.

"Did I wake you up, amigo?"

"No," Gamage said. He reached for his cigarettes on the night table. "I never sleep."

"Is the broad there?"

"Just a minute, I'll look and see." He lit the cigarette. "No, I seem to be alone."

Frank laughed. "Don't kid me. I fixed you up, didn't I?"

"What do you want, Frank?"

"I left a couple of messages."

"I was just about to call you back," Gamage said.

"I have bad news for you."

"So soon, amigo?"

"My wife has decided to throw a cocktail party in your honor. Tonight. Show up around five. It'll give her a chance to show you off. You know how broads are." He laughed. "And I've got a great idea for you. I'm going to set you up. You'll thank me."

"Five o'clock," Gamage said.

"And amigo."

That word again. "What?"

"Don't bring that goddam chippy with you."

"Why not?"

"Are you kidding? Listen, when I sleep with a dame that doesn't mean I want to meet her socially, does it?"

End of message. The loud-mouthed bag of wind, Gamage thought. Five o'clock. He finished his cigarette in bed and supposed he would have to show up for the sake of Frank's wife. He had no overpowering urge to face another day in Thebes. Sunlight was seeping in through the shutters and the room was already hot. He had left the wooden ceiling fan on all night and he watched it now, an artifact, stirring the air in another century. The hotel was a museum piece. There was always the cool of the bar, he thought, but it was too early for that.

Gamage lifted the phone and put in a call to his agent, Paul Stack, in Beverly Hills.

"Did I wake you up?"

"Who the hell is this?"

"When Martinka is awake, nobody sleeps."
"Is this you, Gamage?"
"Yes, amigo."
"Where are you calling from?"
"The City of the Sun."
"What?"
"Paul, I've got a great idea for a picture. Are you listening?"
"I'm listening."
"You'll love this," Gamage said.
"I love it already."
"There's this guy—a desert rat. It's Cary Grant with tobacco stains in his boxer shorts. He lives on cactus apples and dates. Goat's milk to wash it down. A man can live forever on dates and goat's milk, did you know that? Anyway, he strikes it rich. There's a boom in horned toads and he has cornered the market. He builds himself a marble palace and falls in love with a goat girl. When she sees the joint she says to herself: a man who uses gold leaf for toilet paper can't be all bad. She marries him. On the wedding night—you'll grab this Paul—on the wedding night he makes a small confession. He says that he has lived in the sun so long that he is turning to cactus. He rips off his shirt and sure enough he's growing thorns and spikes all over. He's become a cactus man. A monster. Think of the exploitation angles. He tries to embrace the girl, but she runs screaming through the travertine halls. There's just so much a dame can take. She gets away in a passing Cadillac. Months pass. He roams the desert pouncing on broads. After all, he's human even if he is a bit prickly. Nobody knows who the cactus man is. The whole desert is aroused. But then the worst happens. Spring comes along and you know what happens? He breaks into blossom. You can't kid Mother Nature. The bees smell all that nectar and pester him wherever he goes. The local garden editor gets a hunch. You know the rest. But wait. There's a happy ending. The girl comes back from India. As they lead the cactus man away she rushes into his arms. 'Hold me closer, cheri,' she sighs. 'I'll be waiting when you get out of the clink.' They go into a final clinch. 'But doesn't it hurt?' he asks. 'Silly boy,' she replies. 'For six months I have been sleeping on a bed of nails.' Fade out. I tell you, Paul, they don't make love stories like that anymore. Can you sell it?"
"If I can't, there's something wrong with the business."
"Go back to sleep."
"Keep in touch."
Gamage hung up. He felt better. The Cactus Man—he laughed and went in to take a shower.

2

The Thebes Weekly Sunset was housed in a whitewashed adobe building on an unpaved side street. An old corrugated tin awning extended like a rusty eyeshade over the two scowling front windows. An iron hitching post lingered out front like a sullen reminder of the unburied past.

The front door was shut. Gamage paused in the shade and listened to the dry rattle of a linotype machine. The tarnished gold lettering on the window said John W. Amador, Editor and Publisher. Founded, 1912.

The door was locked and the green shades drawn against the low morning sun. Gamage walked to the rear of the building. The shop door stood wide open and he lingered for a moment gazing at the black machinery. Then he stepped on his cigarette and walked in.

The flat-bed press reclined in the smell of oil and old age. There were pigs of lead stacked near the brick forge like ingots of silver. Type cases, ink-blackened with the put and take of fingers, commanded one wall. It was, for Gamage, like a short walk through his own past. There was the burnt smell of melting lead in the air (the stable odor of the rural press, he thought) and light bulbs hanging on long, dusty cords from the ceiling. Nothing had changed except Gamage himself.

A linotype kept clacking away. A man with a dirty green visor sat hunched over the keyboard, pounding the machine with two stubby fingers. Steel-rimmed glasses hung low on his putty nose and the butt of a cigar looked as if it were burning an ashy hole in the corner of his mouth. The machine clattered with hot slugs: words being cast in lead and given a molten reality that could be weighed by the pound. The man had to be BeJesus John, Gamage thought, and he was from Central Casting.

He looked up and peered at Gamage over the tops of his glasses. "Who let you in?"

"The door was open."

"If you're looking to collect a bill don't clutter up the premises, sonny. Don't waste your time here."

"Are you always so friendly?"

"No. This is your lucky day." He let the machine idle and appraised Gamage. An outsider. A weekender. "You lost or something?"

"With a little luck I thought I might meet BeJesus John," Gamage said.

"He ain't in."

"I'll wait."

"I wouldn't do that. He might not show up at all. It wouldn't surprise me if he went out and got hit by a Cadillac. Just out of spite. He's opposed to the internal combustion machine, you know. You didn't run over the old crank driving up, did you?"

"Not this trip."

"Too bad. You could have done this valley a service." BeJesus John removed the cigar from his mouth and dropped it into a spittoon. He rose from the bentwood chair, its legs cut down and wired together. Coffee was boiling in a gray enameled pot on a hotplate and he filled an unwashed mug. "You trying to serve a subpoena or something?"

Suspicious old owl. "No, sir. As a matter of fact, I'm an ex-newspaperman."

BeJesus John peered at him again. "That won't get you any free coffee around here. Newspaper bums come through here all the time. You looking for a job?"

"I've got a job."

"This isn't a newspaper, anyway. It's a charitable institution. If I'd had any brains when I was your age I'd have got into something with a future, like chimney-sweeping. Folks look up to a good chimney-sweep. But I didn't have the education for it, so I ended up running a newspaper. No future. None at all. The machine is going to finish us off any day now."

Gamage recognized the cue for a straight line. "What machine?" The man seemed to be sizing him up all the while and throwing up a barrage of words while he decided whether to throw Gamage out or offer him a cup of coffee.

"What machine? Why, the most important advance in journalism since the invention of moveable type—the garbage disposal. It's the handwriting on the wall. The day has finally come when folks don't need a newspaper to line their garbage cans. That was always the primary function of newsprint, you know. Why, half my subscribers can't read and never could. Everywhere they put in one of them disposals I lose a subscriber. *Tempus omnia revelet.* That's Latin." He reset the visor over his matted yellow hair. "Are you always so quiet?"

Gamage grinned. "Silence is an answer to a wise man," he said. "That's English."

"What did you say your name was?"

"I didn't. It's Gamage."

"Don't just stand there, sonny. Help yourself to the coffee."

Gamage found another mug and blew out the dust. BeJesus John seemed to him a kind of artifact like the hitching post out front. He was a born talker, part stylist and part liar, who could run up two or three hundred words on any subject, no matter how ridiculous the premise, and almost make you believe it. It was a rural art, and going the way of blacksmithing.

Gamage filled the mug. "I read your paper last night," he said. "Among other things you have a good hand with a scalping knife."

"I get by."

"Have you had any response to your petition?"

"I have. Two old maids in Oasis and an illiterate Sweetwater Indian have signed. My most optimistic estimates have already been exceeded. What is it you're after, sonny?"

"I'm working for a friend of yours."

"Is that so?"

"Martinka."

BeJesus John squinted at him through the smudged lenses of his glasses. And then he smiled. "You'll excuse me if I don't face Mecca and kneel at the mention of his name. What did he send you over for? To take an axe to the place?"

"No," Gamage said. "Coming here was my own idea."

"Why?"

"I figure you must have known Colonel Martinka for almost fifty years."

"I ain't proud of it."

Gamage hesitated for only a moment. "Frank hired me to write the old man's biography. It seemed to me you'd want to be of some service in this great enterprise."

BeJesus John fixed him with a crotchety stare. "You're either crazy or you're out of your mind." He bit off the end of a Red Dot cigar. "So the old goat is going to get himself put in a book. By God, that's interesting. Why tell me?"

"You'd find out anyway."

"That's right."

"How far back do your back files go? 1912?"

"Nope. I was burned out in '37."

"I plan to do a lot of reading."

"This ain't a library."

Gamage took a swallow of coffee. "I'll be around. I can be just as cussed as you."

"I doubt it." BeJesus John scraped a kitchen match along the underside of a galley truck and raised a glow on the end of the cigar. "Are you going to tell the truth about him?"

"I doubt it."

"Then don't waste my time."

"What is the truth?"

"The truth," BeJesus John snorted. "The truth is there ain't no Colonel Martinka. He's a figment of Jesse's imagination."

Gamage shook his head. It was too glib. "BeJesus John, you could say that about almost anyone—even yourself, maybe."

"Maybe. But he raised the skill to a high art. Take his rank. Colonel. Ask him what army he was in."

"I'd rather ask you. I missed him. He flew to Europe for the summer."

"Says who?"

"Says Frank."

"Frank is a liar. Always has been."

"If he's not in Europe, where is he?"

"At home, as far as I know. He's a recluse. Has been for years. Locked himself in. Hardly budges from the place. But he's there and he's still running the show. Europe! That's a joke."

On me. Okay, Gamage thought, it was clear enough that Frank didn't want him to meet the old man. "What's he hiding from?"

"I wouldn't know. Maybe he's lost the ability to look a man in the eye."

"Wasn't he ever in the army?"

"I didn't say that. He was. For exactly three weeks. If you could call it an army. Him and Charlie Hastings decided to break the monotony by helping Madero fight the Federales in Mexico. That must have been 1910. Before my time here. Charlie told me the Insurrectos made Jesse a colonel because he was the only visiting rebel in the state of Chihuahua who knew the manual of arms. Where he learned it I don't know. If he'd known how to ride a horse I suppose they'd have made him a brigadier general. He was a handsome devil, you know. Just about the finest looking man in sight. It's my opinion he went down there to look over the ladies—that variety of citizen being in short supply here on the desert. *Ubi mel, ibi apes.* Anyway, it took just three weeks to knock the soldier of fortune out of him, but he's been *Colonel* Martinka for fifty years. He did lose a finger though and I guess that's a credit to him."

"I didn't know." But Gamage was reminded of the fist-on-hip in the photograph, as if to conceal the missing finger.

"Shot clear off."

Gamage finished the coffee and put the mug aside. "Is Charlie Hastings still alive?"

"He is."

"Here in town?"

"Over in Mecca. He's a retired banker."

Gamage rolled a cigarette between his lips and lit it. "I have a feeling that you and the Colonel must have been good friends once, BeJesus John."

"That's right. He had me fooled up until four-five years ago."

"What soured you?"

BeJesus John gave Gamage a harsh, measuring look. "The greed came out in him. Maybe it was always there, but he kept it out of sight. He sold out to the weekenders. They come out here to tan their asses in the sun. It's a waste of good sunshine. It used to be so quiet you could hear a Mexican ground cricket scratch himself five miles away. Since he began peddling his sunburnt real estate the voice of the desert is getting to be the flush toilet. I'm against it. That Egyptian eyesore of his is going to finish us off. I'm not saying I can stop him, but I intend to try. Good day, sonny."

3

Gamage installed a rented typewriter in his room and began shopping around for something to drive. He ended up with a vintage jeep. It's fenders had turned a kind of verdigris, like old bronze, and the tires were smooth, but it would do for getting around the desert. He bought some khakis, a pair of brown desert boots and a straw hat. All he had to do to pass for a native was hunker in the shade.

It was late afternoon when he drove out to see the pyramid-under-construction. He turned off the highway and headed east along a freshly cut dirt road. He raised a six miles umbilical cord of fine dust. When he reached the site he was disappointed not to find a scene out of old Egypt, as rendered by The National Geographic. The pyramid was going up under the hammers of carpenters. A spider's web of studs and rafters rose from a poured concrete foundation. There was a kind of malaise about the operation, Gamage thought, as if Martinka hesitated to reach the top. He had a long way to go. Almost as far as the eye could see fifty-foot lots had been laid out with bright red rags tied to stakes. Beyond, a pair of earth-movers were clearing even more land.

Gamage got out and wandered along the base of the pyramid. The foreman came over in a tin hat.

"You looking for something, mister?"

"The Egyptians would have done it differently. They would have used stone."

"What do they know? We're doing it with stucco. If you're looking to buy a lot, the sales office ain't open yet. Don't hang around here. Something may fall on you."

"What have you got in mind? An ancient curse?"

Gamage started up the jeep. As far as he could tell all Martinka was building in the desert was a firetrap. The pyramid was as phony as a set on the back lot of a studio.

On the way back to town he ran out of gas. He got out and looked up and down the highway. He'd never seen it so deserted. In ten minutes, he supposed, the sun would melt him down to a grease spot. He kicked one of the tires for the sheer pleasure of it. Finally a lettuce truck came along and gave him a push down the highway to a two-lung gas station. It sold a jackleg brand Gamage had never heard of—Caravan Gas. It would probably bolix up the carburator and make the day perfect, he thought. Beyond stood a couple of low adobe buildings, one with a sign over the door that said CANTINA, and an auto wrecking yard half buried in drifting sand. Gamage honked the horn, but nobody came.

It was too hot to sit there and wait. He found the water hose and doused his head and the water almost scalded him. Stupid bastard that I am, he thought—a natural born outsider. He let the water run and tried again. Finally he unhooked the gas hose and filled the tank himself. He leaned on the horn, but gave it up and walked over to the adobe beer joint.

He couldn't see anyone at first. It was dark and a good deal cooler inside. The thick adobe walls were set with a couple of windows hung with wet gunny sacks. "That you making all the noise?"

As Gamage's eyes adjusted to the gloom he made out a bald-headed man in washed out Levis and an undershirt seated in a wicker chair at the back. Gamage supposed he had been asleep. "I was looking for someone to take my money."

"You found him."

"I'll have a beer."

The man got up heavily, scratching his overhanging gut, and walked behind the short bar. His arms were a gallery of old tattoos—kewpie dolls, a bleeding heart with fading drops of blood, a ship's anchor, snakes coiled around his wrists and the word MOTHER on his forearm.

"You need some help out front," Gamage said.

"I got help. The boy's out back rabbit hunting."

"In this heat?"

"He's part Indian. He don't know the difference." The barkeep looked Gamage over with dour little eyes. "All I got cold is Mexican beer. Tecate and Dos Equis."

"I'm not particular," Gamage said. "Just thirsty."

The man uncapped a dark brown bottle. Behind him on the plastered wall hung framed photographs of various navy ships at sea, several boxing poses and a tinted enlargement of a navy chief and a girl in a ricksha. "Most of my trade is greasers and Indians. Their money's as good as anyone else's. You want a glass?"

"Don't bother."

"You can't get a white man to work the crops out here. Everything's greasers and Indians. They get thirsty like anybody else."

Gamage looked at him. The man had a kind of arrogant stupidity that made the day seem a little hotter. "What do you call this place?"

"Morejohn's."

"Are you Morejohn?"

"That's right. Chief watertender. Retired." He indicated the photographs behind him with a backward jerk of the head. "Used to be fleet champ. Eight years China duty. I speak it. She's a White Russian girl. That's her in the ricksha. Moved out here eleven years ago."

"Kind of far from neighbors, aren't you?"

"A man with a pretty wife don't want neighbors." He let the point sink in, as if even Gamage were a threat to him. "I own this whole lash-up, what the sand ain't covered over. Started out to be a town. We get a cross-wind here and have to keep digging ourselves out."

"What's the population now?"

"Two. Me and the wife."

"What about the Indian?"

"He don't count." Morejohn slapped a fly on the bar with the flat of his hand and scooped it off on the floor. "What business you in?"

Gamage held up his empty bottle. "You got another one of these?" He didn't care to hang around, but the beer was cold and it was a furnace outside. "That pyramid is going to crowd you, isn't it?"

"It ain't built yet." Morejohn uncapped another bottle and fixed his heavy, dull eyes on Gamage. "What business you in?"

"Me?" Gamage put a twenty on the bar. The man was asking to be put on. "I'm a salesman."

"What are you selling?"

"Sun lamps," Gamage said.

"Sun lamps."

"That's right. I'm breaking in this territory. The Jim Dandy Instant-Tan Helio Light. You've probably been reading about it. We're bringing the sun inside where it belongs, like the flush toilet."

"You're going to starve to death out here, mister."

"You're wrong. I just placed an order for 400 Helio Lights with Martinka & Son. With air conditioning and the Helio Light a man never has to go outdoors—except to be buried. It's real progress, Morejohn. The coming thing."

"Sun lamps, huh?" The man licked his thumb and counted out some bills. "Them weekenders will buy anything. In another five years this valley won't even be fit for Indians anymore."

Gamage finished his beer. "Maybe it never was."

He picked up his change and braced himself for the heat outside. Morejohn told him to hurry back and returned to the shadows, settling himself slug-like in the wicker chair.

When Gamage reached the gas pumps he saw a young kid leaning against the fender. "How about a lift?"

"Which way are you heading?" Gamage asked.

"Which way are you going?"

"Thebes."

"Suits me."

"Get in."

He might have been fifteen or sixteen. He wore a bright Hawaiian sport shirt and a silver chain around his neck. He had well-packed shoulders that made him look almost stocky. It was only after he stood away from the fender that the fit of his trousers came into view. They took a skin-tight, leotard grip on his rear. This kid's vanity, Gamage thought, had located itself in the seat of his pants.

There was a scuffed brown guitar case at his feet. He stowed it, together with a bundle of soiled shirts, in the back of the jeep. He traveled light.

"Where did you come from?" Gamage asked.

"I work here. Only I decided to quit."

Gamage gave him a second glance. The face under the straw hat was almost fair. If he was an Indian he had to be some kind of a mixture, and a pretty good mixture at that.

Only the nose had a tribal look. His lips were thin and almost dimpled at the ends. His teeth were perfect and his eyes were as blue as faded denim. A well-laundered kid, Gamage thought, looking for someplace to go. The brim of his hat was curled like a pair of leaves, coming almost to a point in front.

Gamage started up the engine. "You don't look like you were rabbit hunting to me."

The young Indian grinned a little and cadged a final glance at the adobe bar. "That old ghee believes anything."

"Did you let him know you were quitting?"

"Naw. I'll write him a postcard." He lit a cigarette and slumped down in the bucket seat. He smoked Wings. Gamage rolled back onto the highway and shifted gears. When he glanced in the rear view mirror he caught the figure of a woman in a yellow dress hurry out to the gas pumps and then stand there, straddle-legged, watching the jeep disappear.

"Is that the chief's wife back there?"

The kid didn't bother to look back. "Must be. Sweet Mother of Jesus, is she going to miss me."

Gamage wondered if he had clouted the cash register, but he didn't look that simple. "Why quit a good job?"

"Who said it was a good job?"

"Then why quit a bad one?"

"That beetle was beginning to bug me."

"The what?"

"Irena. The wife. She's got a houseful of cats. She must have fifty of 'em. A regular cat house. She ain't so bad looking. In fact, good looking. She must be twenty years younger than him—one of those. It bugs him. It bugs him to have anyone look at her, except the cats, and maybe he's not too sure about them."

The kid seemed well schooled on the subject. The edge of the road was scalloped with sand and Gamage found himself driving on the center line. "How long did you work there?"

"Couple of weeks. I can tell you anything you want to know."

"That's less than nothing."

"We were on the bedsprings when you drove up."

Gamage turned to give him a one-eyed glance. Either this kid was reading him an old copy of Spicy Stories or Morejohn's wife was cradle-robbing. The Old China Hand may have buried her in the sand dunes, but forgot to watch out for kids. "How old are you?"

"I forget."

"Fifteen?"

The kid grinned, breathing smoke. "About that."

"Are you in school?"

"Naw. I quit. I got tired of weaving baskets."

Self-assured little savage, Gamage thought. He had a sense of personality and you had to like him. "What's your name?"

"Barbachano." His blue eyes scanned the empty desert and the hills with an attitude of ownership. "Mario Barbachano."

"Where's your family?"

"My mother's working down in Calexico."

"Do you play that guitar?"

"Yeah. The beetles go for it. A guy with a guitar makes out."

"What the hell is a beetle?"

"A dame. A broad. A beetle. It's all the same thing. But they've got to have the heat built in. I used to think when you turn a beetle upside down they're all the same. I always heard that. But that's dumb. Maybe 80 percent, they're all the same. But that other 20 percent—that's what makes it worthwhile. Like Irena. She's got the built-in heat. You can spot 'em. Strictly thyroid. The eyes pop. Not much. Just a little. And the hands. The fingers, they got to taper and they got to be a little fleshy at the third joint. Sweet Mother, when you've got that combination—the hands and the eyes—you've found a live one."

Gamage waited a long time before saying anything. This adolescent Aztec was a little disturbing, as if merely listening to him was contributing to the delinquency of a minor. It seemed clear enough that he had collided with the facts of life at an early age and made himself something of a scholar on the subject. He was wonderously mature, but the acne was there in his speech. The Indian within him was standing on stilts. "Where did you pick up all that?"

"Just cutting up touches," Barbachano grinned, withdrawing behind the barrier of argot. "It passes the time."

"You're a little startling," Gamage said. They were coming into town and he slowed down. "Do you believe that penny arcade folklore you were handing out?"

"I don't know if I believe it," he said. "But it works."

4

Gamage slept for an hour and then went through the motions of putting on a clean shirt and tie and driving out to the Martinka place. He was late. There was already a clutter of tail fins and sports cars around the motor court. He had no great interest in meeting Frank's wife or Frank's friends, but he went in.

The cocktail party had been staged in the living room and the drinking was well under way. There was an acre of citron carpeting and the guests stood about like film extras under the gilded hanging lamps. Windows looked out over the valley in one direction and over the pool in another. Frank was on the phone with his back turned and Gamage made his entrance unnoticed. He found his way to the bar and a Filipino in a white jacket fixed him a drink.

He looked over the beetles. They sat around the couches in harem-like groups, giving off occasional decibels of laughter. A pretty lot, Gamage thought, married to the men smoking cigars. If he had ever met Frank's wife in the past he saw no one he recognized now.

A portly little man with a bow tie came over to him and said, "You must be the word mechanic Frank's talking about."

"It's possible."

"Earl Sunshine's my name."

Gamage tilted an eyebrow. "Sunshine?"

The man laughed. "That's right—I'm Frank's sales manager. With a name like mine he practically signed me up for life. What do you think of our little desert?"

"It's a good place to live," Gamage said. "But I wouldn't want to visit here."

"Ha. That's rich."

Gamage lit a cigarette. Mr. Sunshine. It was almost too much. "Mr. Sunshine," he said, "how is the pyramid business?"

"Call me Earl. Those lots aren't for sale yet. We won't kick off the campaign until the middle of next month. Radio. Television. Newspapers. By the end of summer I expect to have fifteen hundred lots sold. At five thou a piece, bottom, you figure it out."

Gamage gazed out over his head, looking for somewhere else to be. "You'll be lucky to have a paved road in by the end of summer," he muttered.

"You're new here," Sunshine laughed. "You don't know how it's done. The last thing I need to sell sand lots is a road. No one in his right mind is going to drive out here to look at real estate in the summer. We charter DC3s. Give the weekenders a free ride. They pick out the lot they want from the air. We make a picnic out of it. We package it. As Frank always says, you could sell the common cold if you could figure out a way to package it."

"He's a card."

"He's got more know-how in his little finger—"

"Point out Frank's wife to me."

"Virginia? She's standing right behind you."

Gamage turned. An ash blonde stood with an unlit cigarette waiting between her fingers. Her tanned shoulders were thrust up through a summery green dress and she held her head at a slight tilt like a Modigliani: beauty abhorring a straight line. She looked at him through heavily made up eyes, party eyes, half-smiling, and it was a moment before he recognized her. And when he did something inside him gave a sudden, violent lurch.

"Hello, Gamage," she said.

He stared at her. It was like walking into a door he had closed five years ago. "Hello, Ginny."

"You looked right past me."

"Did I?"

"Yes."

The party sounds became a kind of distant static. Ginny Bassett. The European summer. She had done over everything but that throaty, hushed voice of hers, he thought. Frank's wife. "The hair fooled me," he said.

"Like it?"

"No."

She smiled and raised the cigarette to her lips. "Give me a light."

Five years. He lit her cigarette and they gazed at each other through the smoke, remembering the same Genoa hotel room, the star-crossed comedy, the wild pursuit that ended in Athens. Ginny. Time had hardly touched her, he thought. She had taken on a high gloss. Expensive. Hand-rubbed. She wasn't Ginny Bassett anymore. She was a Martinka now, Frank's elegant wife. He felt betrayed. She should have been Gamage's wife.

"You look like you need a drink," she said.

"I've got a drink."

"You're getting gray at the temples, darling."

"I was always gray," he said. "It's just beginning to show."

"I'm glad you came."

His eyes narrowed, unblinking and angry. "What's going on in that lovely blonde head of yours, Ginny? You were crazy to set this up."

"I had to see you again."

"For Christ's sake," he muttered.

"I'd better introduce you to Frank's friends."

"Aren't they your friends?"

"No. Just you."

"Don't count on me," he said.

"Don't be angry, Gamage."

"Why not?"

"We can't talk now."

"What's there to say? You're the bored hausfrau looking for a little action on the side."

She gave him an imploring look. "That's cruel."

"Listen, I've written the part a dozen times. I know all the moves, all the bits of business. If there's a happy ending it hasn't been invented yet."

She forced a thin smile. "Write one," she said. "You're good at it."

"Sure. The best."

"We can't talk here."

"Let's try."

"Gamage." Her voice had a range of about two feet. "I've got to find out if I'm still in love with you."

"Of course you are. Unless you never were."

"That's not true."

"I asked you to marry me." His flaring anger surprised him. "Twice a day."

"I couldn't." She hesitated, staring up at him with her tinsel green eyes. "For God's sake, can't you guess? I was already married to Frank."

He felt a clap on the shoulder and knew it had to be Frank's heavy hand. Gamage girded himself. He looked at Ginny as if she had passed him a burning stick of dynamite. The Cactus Man was talking to him.

"What the hell kept you, amigo? You're late. Who's the whore-house blonde?"

Ginny didn't bat an eye. She had heard it all before, Gamage thought.

Frank passed Gamage a wink. "I can pick 'em, can't I?"

"You can pick 'em," Gamage said.

"Doll, this party isn't getting off the ground. Will you go over and show that rented Filipino how to mix a martini? Bill, I want to talk to you."

Ginny crushed her cigarette in a tray, grinding it in, and took the cue. Gamage managed somehow to keep his eyes off her as she walked away. Meeting her again after five years had raked through the old ashes and stirred up live coals. She had given him a violent shake. She had been a Martinka even then. He saw now that their affair had been a kind of imitation from the beginning, but it had ended up leaving its marks on them both.

"I'll tell you about dames," Frank chuckled. "You marry 'em, but you never own 'em. You just lease 'em for a while."

Gamage was no longer listening. He remembered meeting Ginny going down in the tiny elevator at the Excelsior Hotel in Genoa. He was in Italy gathering material for a screenplay which, as it turned out, he never wrote.

She was a very pretty girl in red shoes. It was raining out and he asked if he could buy her a drink and she said she would love a drink. It was her first trip to Europe and she was traveling alone. It began as an accident of time and place and mood, one of those passing love affairs that was meant to last a few days. But it lasted through the summer. They seemed to invent a lonely place in each other's lives. She was a skylark, full of nonsense and wit—and uncatchable. It was clear to him now that she had come to Europe for an affair and nothing more, but even that had a kind of integrity to it. Their last day together was gray and windy, with the first leaves of fall in it. The next morning he found a note from her calling it quits. He knew she was in love with him, but that hadn't stopped her from getting on a plane. She was gone. They never wrote.

"Amigo," Frank was saying, "how would you like to run a newspaper?"

Gamage remembered he had a drink in his hand and finished it off. "What are you talking about?"

"I'm tired of waiting for BeJesus John to blow wise. He's getting to be a real pain. I'll buy that fish-wrapper and you can run it. Hell, I'll give you a piece of it."

"You couldn't give me all of it," Gamage said. He saw Ginny across the room; their glances sideswiped.

"Don't be a sap. With your savvy that paper can make nothing but money. This boom is just getting off the ground. Get smart, amigo. Deal yourself in."

The Japanese girl was passing with a tray of drinks and Gamage exchanged his empty glass for a bourbon and water. He really ought to lay off the booze. "It's not my game of cards," Gamage said. If Frank couldn't get himself a good press he would buy it and buy Gamage in the bargain. "Anyway, BeJesus John won't sell to you."

Frank grinned. "But he'll sell to you. All I need is a front man. He's taking gas. He'll sell. By time he finds out it's Martinka money he'll be outside looking in."

"I'm not interested," Gamage murmured. He was sorry for Ginny. Whore-house blonde. It was as if she had stayed married to Frank to work off a kind of penance for being in love with someone else.

"Sleep on it, amigo."

"I just did. The answer is no."

Frank laughed. "You'll change your mind. You're on your ass and I know it. I checked up on you. You've been on the beach for a year. Get smart. I'm offering you a chance to make something of yourself."

Gamage transferred the drink to his left hand, thinking that he had to hit this man. But the instant passed and it seemed to him a marvel of restraint. "Frank," he said, "what gave you the idea that I want to make something of myself?"

"When do I see the book? You started writing yet?"

"Yeah. I wrote in all the commas today."

"Anything you want to know, ask me."

"I'll ask you," Gamage said. He'd have another drink and get out of here.

"There's nothing in the notes about Mexico and the Insurrectos in 1910. I checked."

"Are you kidding, amigo?" Frank grinned. "He went down there on a screwing expedition. Forget it. Who you been talking to? We want this book for family reading."

"I think you mean he joined the wrong side, don't you? A bunch of unwashed revolutionaries."

Frank chuckled. "Stick to the notes, amigo. Stick to the notes. What do you think of the wife?"

"Do you need my opinion?"

"I can pick 'em, can't I?"

"Yeah," Gamage said shortly. "You can pick 'em."

He hung around for another drink. Ginny kept at a distance, playing it safe with Frank in the room, and finally Gamage walked out. Dusk lingered in the valley, heated and silent and suddenly ominous. He was on the Martinka payroll and he couldn't afford to walk away from the money. The Colonel interested him—he felt as if he had caught a rabbit by the hind leg and he didn't want to let go. But if he stayed he knew he wouldn't be able to keep his hands off Frank's wife.

He stopped at an open convertible with a built in telephone on the dash. He stared at it for a moment and then unhooked it. He put in the call. After a moment the Japanese girl came to the phone and he asked for Mrs. Martinka. He waited and finally he heard Ginny's low-key voice.

"Yes?"

"Ginny, darling," he said quietly, "you're a dreamer."

There was a pause. "Where are you?"

Gnats were in the air and he brushed them away from his face. "Don't get me wrong, kid. It was nice to be remembered. You're a real kick in the pants. But retreading old love affairs doesn't work."

"I can't talk," she whispered.

"Then listen," he said. "You look marvelous. You could make a case of the measles look good. But don't play me for a sap. I know a piece of geometry when I see it. If you could walk away from Frank you would have done it five years ago. That leaves one corner of a triangle, but I don't make the same mistake twice. I'm pulling out. Goodbye, kid."

"Gamage—"

He hung up slowly. Lights in the valley were finally coming on. He found the jeep and started it up with a roar. Ginny remained fixed in his mind, but why kid himself? This had been the wrong place and the wrong time and the wrong mood.

5

Night in the City of the Sun was a small reprieve from the ground fires of the day. Crop hands gathered with their cigarettes along the neon-lit arcades and insects knocked along the shop windows. Gamage stopped in at the Plantation House bar and found Conny with her neat little rump on a bar stool.

"Are you waiting for someone?" he said.

She looked at him. "You'll do."

"What have you got in mind?"

She gave a wry little shrug and he ordered a couple of drinks. She was a pretty girl in a pretty flowered dress with a slit hem and his gloom began to lift. He was glad to see her. He was glad to have someone to be with and Conny had a sense of the moment that pleased him. "Have you had your dinner?"

"No."

"Where shall we go?"

"There's a Chinese place in Indio. It's real home cooking. If you happen to come from China."

"Sounds great."

They drove up the line to Indio and sat in a hard paneled booth with beaded curtains. They ate pressed duck and Gamage told her that he would be leaving the valley in the morning. She asked no questions as if, somehow, she sensed that he didn't want to answer them. "I'm sorry," was all she said.

They ended up in a small bar along the highway, not to get drunk, but just to wear out the evening. There was a jukebox and even though there wasn't room for it they decided to dance. It came to little more than holding each other and swaying to the rhythm.

"I don't suppose you have a husband standing in the wings," he said.

"Why?"

"I've been bugged by husbands lately."

"Hey," said the barman. "Are you two dancing?"

"No," Gamage said, glancing at the no dancing sign. "We're just trying to keep warm, amigo."

The man grinned. It was a slow night. "I guess that's okay then."

Conny was looking up at Gamage, her blue eyes making a kind of open secret, and her earrings picked up the bar lights. "You've been around."

"And around and around."

"Damnit," she smiled.

"Damnit what?"

"Damnit, I almost got to know you."

"The evening's not over yet."

"Don't make any plans."

Her hair fell casually across one side of her forehead, dark and stylish. The music had stopped and they stood there a moment, silent, half-smiling, and then he signaled the barman to freshen their drinks. The evening had developed a pace of its own, unhurried and without time; a series of impromptu moments strung together. She told him finally that she had been married to an ex-Marine flier. "He talked Marine Corps from the time he brushed his teeth in the morning to the moment he brushed them at night. He couldn't stand being a civilian. That first summer he sat around all day in the heat drinking beer and built a pile of empty cans in the back yard like the Halls of Montezuma. One morning I woke up and found him standing over me with a service pistol in his hand. He pulled the trigger and it went click. Big joke. He opened another can of beer and when he was good and tanked I loaded him in the car and drove him up to the air station at Mohave and dumped him at the gate. Return to the military womb. I've never had any luck with men. I seem to bring out the dull bastard in them." She looked up with a quick smile. "Present company excepted—I think."

"Don't count on it."

"Where will you go?"

"I don't know. It doesn't matter." He was trying not to think about tomorrow. He was in hock to Frank for the book advance, and that was a complication. "The world is wide and full of small hotel rooms," he said. "That's home to me. I grew up in hotel rooms. My old man was a traveling sign painter. He was kind of elegant—he even spoke in Old English script. We'd lay over in small towns and he'd letter their windows and we'd move on. Sometimes, when I'm in the midwest, I'll spot his dead hand on some old bank window. That's immortality the hard way, I guess. Let's get out of here."

"Yes."

Outside, at the jeep, he slipped his arm around her waist and pulled her against him. "Why don't we run away to Mexico together?"

"Thanks. But I've already been to Mexico."

"Do you want me to take you home?"

She didn't answer.

He kissed her lightly, on the lips, aware that she was a stand-in for Ginny, and that the evening had been a kind of fraud. But Conny herself kept coming through. She was light in his arms and unfamiliar, a small thing, with a style and a certain wattage of her own. She touched him with a sense of her own identity and the feeling of deception left him.

He kissed her again, more honestly, feeling the hotness of her cheeks. "Damn you," she said. He picked her up under the knees and deposited her in the bucket seat.

It was past eleven when they crossed the lobby. The place was a morgue.

The elevator seemed to take forever, and she looked at him with a nervous smile. "Is anyone watching?"

"No."

"To hell with it. I never liked skulking around anyway." She took his hand. It was a small act of commitment. Once inside his room she glanced around at the four white walls and the typewriter and the filigree bed. The ceiling fan gave a languid stir to the furnace of the room. "So this is how writers live," she said.

"Sure," he said. "The best of everything." The Martinka papers were spread over the bed and he gathered them up. "Do you want me to send down for some drinks?"

"And wake everyone?" She pulled off her earrings and seemed to relax. Their smiles met and then he took her waist in his hands and her fingers met around his neck. "It's almost too hot, isn't it?" she said.

"It's never too hot," he said. He felt, suddenly, that she was out of place in this dreary, small-town hotel room with a man she barely knew. It was as if she were trying to lose her reputation. Or make one. "I'm not sure I know what you're doing here."

She gave a little shrug. "You're a man. I like that in a man."

She had a nice feel for dialogue and he was amused. But he couldn't entirely locate her in his mind. A lay was a lay, but suddenly it wasn't that simple anymore. "Conny, I think you'd walk out of here if you could think of a good exit line."

She shook her head. "No. But thanks for asking." She kicked off her shoes, lowering herself. "Do you have a spare pajama top?"

"I think we can manage it."

"I'd like to take a shower."

He found a pajama top and she turned at the bathroom door, only half-shutting it on herself. "Mr. Gamage, I'm not sure I'd be here if you weren't leaving town."

"Miss Sargent, that's a hell of a reason."

"A girl needs a reason."

"Yes."

She gazed at him from the chink in the doorway. "Sometimes a guy comes along and any reason will do. Am I surprised."

She closed the door softly and he peered at it. He saw himself suddenly as a set character, the stranger in town, the guy who makes out with the pretty librarian or schoolteacher. Life imitates art, he thought, and budget pictures. After a moment he heard the shower come on and he stripped off his tie and opened his shirt. Then he picked up the phone and got BeJesus John out of bed.

"Yeah?"

"This is Bill Gamage."

"Who?"

"I was in to see you this morning."

"Do you know what time it is? What the hell do you want?"

"I thought that you'd be interested to know that I'm leaving town."

"What?"

"I'm pulling out."

"You got me out of bed to tell me that?"

"Yeah."

"What are you? Some kind of son-of-a-bitch?"

"Calm down and listen. The Martinkas are going to buy you out to shut you up."

"They'll have to outlive me first."

"Frank is going to work it through a blind."

"Is it okay with you if I go back to sleep?"

"BeJesus John, you're a genuine old fake and I like you. Hail and farewell."

Conny, in bare feet and the pajama top, came out of the bathroom. She kissed Gamage and he patted her slightly moist bottom. She slipped away, taking his cigarette with her, and got into bed. When the phone range Gamage thought that would be BeJesus John on a delayed double take, and he answered it. But the soft, husky voice was Ginny's.

"Gamage?"

He was silent for a moment. "You just missed him. He left town."

"I've got to see you."

He glanced at Conny watching him through her wet eyelashes.

"I'm downstairs," Ginny said.

"For Christ's sake."

"I'll wait for you in my car."

"Forget it."

"Out front, darling. We can talk."

"I said forget it."

"I'll wait for you."

She hung up. Gamage stood for a moment, gripping the receiver like a weight, wanting to rip it from the wall. He looked at Conny through the wire-work of the bed, the imperative shape and wonder of a woman; this was what the evening had been all about. He wanted her. He felt a deep response, charged and demanding. But Ginny was waiting; the past. He knew he had to go downstairs. He cradled the phone softly and tried to find an attitude. "The telephone should never have been invented," he said. "I knew no good would come of it."

"What do you mean?"

"I have to leave for a while," he said.

Conny stared at him. "You're kidding."

"I'm sorry, Conny. This won't wait."

He buttoned his shirt and put on his tie and she watched him with curiosity and reproach, as if she couldn't quite believe what was happening.

"I won't be long," he said.

"You're an utter bastard."

"Yes."

"You'll hate yourself in the morning."

"I hate myself now."

"If you try to kiss me I'll kill you."

He left. Outside, the arcades were deserted and he saw a green Thunderbird in the shadows. He came around to the driver's window and the coal of Ginny's cigarette was a small beacon in the darkness.

"You're full of surprises," he said.

"I came as soon as I could."

"Where's Frank?"

"Asleep."

"You live dangerously."

"I don't want to be seen. Get in."

"Once around the block," he said.

He moved around to the other side of the car and she started up the engine. She backed out and turned on the lights. He made her out in the soft glow of the dash with a scarf around her head: exquisite peasant face, he thought. She had changed into pants and thonged sandals, and her long slim legs stretched out in a kind of implied nakedness. His eye moved back along her thigh and then he looked away. Frank held the lease. He always had.

"Gamage, don't leave."

"I don't like to play games I can't win," he said. "And I don't like to be tricked."

"I didn't mean to trick you—it just happened that way." She looked straight ahead. "I wanted to help you. I heard you were out of work."

"I didn't know you had taken a scholarly interest in my affairs."

She passed him a green-eyed glance. "I saw you last year. We were in the same restaurant on the Strip. Scandia. You didn't notice me."

"I must have been blind."

"You were with a girl."

"Take the next corner."

She handed him her cigarette to put out. "I want you to stay, Gamage."

"What there was between us ended at the Grande Bretagne in Athens."

"Not for me."

He was silent for a moment. He couldn't quite make out what battlefield he was on. He wanted to hurt her, but maybe it was because he couldn't afford her anymore. "Just remember," he said. "I was willing to marry you for your money. Before I knew you had any."

"You're being cruel."

"What were you doing alone in Europe? Where the hell was Frank?"

"I had left him. And his mother."

"His mother?"

"Yes. She calls herself Madam Martinka—that will give you an idea. She thinks she's the Queen Mother. I had to get away from them. I had taken out a passport before we were married and it was still good so I used it. I didn't want him to follow me. I was glad not to have to use his name."

"You could have told me the truth," Gamage said.

He was aware suddenly that they were out on the highway, lighting up signboards and trees.

"I wasn't sure I knew what the truth was anymore. Or who I was. I guess I was trying to be somebody else for a little while. Anybody else."

"How did you get caught with a swell fellow like Frank?"

She gave a tired shrug. "That's where the money was. I thought I wanted it. My father had a small dairy in San Bernardino and I was sick of cows."

He looked down the highway. "Where are you driving?"

"Does it matter?"

"Yes." He thought of Conny back at the hotel. She was no doubt packing her traps and making an exit. Poor kid. He was sorry. "I don't suppose I could persuade you to turn this car around?"

"No."

"I've got a dame stashed in my room."

She brushed him with a smile. "You haven't changed."

They were heading south and the hot wind was rushing in across their faces. The desert night was barren, heavily-scented, North African. He looked at her long fingers on the wheel, red-tipped and suddenly charged with sex. It was a moment before his mind caught up with it, the tapered fingers, and then he realized that young Barbachano had put that nonsense in his head. Ginny had the hands and the moody sculptured eyes that betrayed built-in heat. It was a crock, of course, he told himself. But the images lingered.

"Gamage," she said, "I had to come back to Frank."

"Sure. He's a fine fellow."

"I was afraid not to."

"It may come as a surprise to you, Ginny darling, but Frank is not my favorite topic of conversation."

An oncoming car lit them up like a flash of lightning. "He told me he'd find me wherever I went," she whispered. "He's capable of that kind of thing. You can't spend your life running away from someone. I came back."

"Does that make sense?"

"I thought in time he'd let go of me. I'm not the only girl on the block."

"But you're the prettiest."

"He warned me that he'd never let me have a divorce—but I think now it was the community property talking. Lately, he's been putting almost everything into his mother's name. Even the house we live in."

"You don't have to stand still for it," he said.

"I don't really care."

Gamage found himself staring at her. Their dialogue was taking the shape of a nest of boxes and when they reached the inner box he thought he would find it full of built-in heat. That's what he came along for, wasn't it?

"When I walk out, Gamage, it will be with the clothes on my back."

This was more than he had anticipated and something inside him took a small leap. "Are you going to call it quits?"

"Yes."

"When?"

Her voice was steady. "I don't know. I've got to wait for him to make the first move. I've got to let him think he's walking out on me."

They left it there and then, after a few miles, Gamage told her to stop. He took the wheel. She lit a pair of cigarettes and handed him one. "You smoke too much," he said.

"Yes."

"Where does this road lead?"

"Mexicali."

He put the car in gear and she found some music on the radio. It was after one when they crossed the border. If the town slept it wasn't at night. Light bulbs were strung in garlands across the streets and the bars, honeycombing each block, were going full blast. He cruised along, looking for a place, and Ginny said, "There's a good motel on the road to San Luis."

When they reached the motel he parked and they sat for a moment in the dark of the car, gazing at each other, and finally she said in a quiet voice, "Is this hello or goodbye?"

He felt a sense of return. A violent longing to renew the past. "Ginny darling," he said, "let's go in and find out."

CHAPTER THREE

1

It was past four in the morning when Ginny dropped him off in front of his hotel. She left a green-eyed smile with him, a kind of lagniappe, and then he watched the silent red glow of the tail lights hurry away. Her slim body, sun-warmed and wonderously jeweled, lingered in his mind. In an hour Europe had fused with the present and all the years that had separated them seemed now outside the immediate drama of their lives, like an off-stage wait. Tonight had a kind of inevitability about it, Gamage thought, and Frank could go shinny up a tree.

He started into the hotel but stopped when he recognized a figure watching him from the half-blackness of a doorway further along the sidewalk arcade. He saw the bosom and hips of a scuffed guitar case and thought it had to be the young Indian.

"Barbachano?"

The kid didn't stir from the cement step, but he leaned out of the shadow. "Hi."

Gamage walked closer. "Don't you have a place to sleep?"

"Sure. But I got lost in the big city."

"You can't sleep there."

"Why not?"

"The cops will pick you up."

"They've got to see me first. I been keeping on the move. It's when you fall asleep that they find you."

"Are you broke?"

"Me?" He grinned. "I'm independently wealthy."

"Come on. I'll get you a room."

"Naw."

"Couldn't you find a job?"

"I wasn't looking." The Hawaiian sport shirt had a certain intensity even in the shadows. "You find yourself a beetle?"

"What?"

"In the T-bird."

Gamage peered at him. "Look, I'll get you a place and then you're on your own."

Barbachano shrugged and picked up his guitar case and followed Gamage into the hotel. They roused the clerk and Gamage told him to give the kid a room and put it on his bill.

When Gamage went up the light was still on in his room, but Conny was gone. He saw from the ashtray that she had hung around for a couple of cigarettes and it surprised him. He stood for a moment, coming face to face with himself, and not liking what he saw. He wished now that he could replay the evening.

He got undressed and realized that he had been waiting for Ginny, knowing that she would turn up before he left town. The evening had been a kind of poker game and he should never have let Conny sit in on it.

He left the fan on and went to bed, but he couldn't get to sleep. He saw now that he had never really planned on leaving. It was an attitude that had to be cast off. Ginny might be a trick of memory but he knew he had to hang around and find out.

After a while he realized that it was getting light out. He got up and lit a cigarette and looked for something to read. There was only the *Weekly Sunset* which he'd finished, and the Martinka papers.

He shuffled through the leather case, the fragmentary diary, the letters and assorted materials. He glanced again at the portrait, the lean Martinka face with staring eyes and a cross-hatched neck. Early American robber baron, he thought. When he came across Madam Martinka's sheaf of scented pages, tied up in a ribbon, he picked it up. He might as well meet the lady. He realized that Ginny had planted a certain hostility in his mind. At worst, the Queen Mother would put him to sleep.

2

Villa Martinka
Thebes, Calif.

COL. JESSE MARTINKA
A Love Letter By His Wife

I am seated in a wicker chair on the veranda of our home. The sun has set behind the hills and soft, quiet hues have settled over our beloved desert. It is a living water color. Nearby, pigeons have made a nest in an old palm tree. They have been there as long as I can remember.

I look up and see my husband walking with long strides in the lingering twilight on the road. He misses his collie, Sheik. They walked together for sixteen years. When I shut my eyes and conjure up a vision of my husband, I see him always walking with his fine head erect and a slight twinkle in his eye. He needs the feel of the bountiful earth under his boots. On the hottest summer day I have known him to go out with a wide straw hat and cover five miles. He is in the habit of picking up a dried ocotillo stick or a willow branch along the way; on his sixtieth birthday I made the mistake of buying him an English walking stick.

"Madam," he said, swinging it from the wrist with a grand gesture. "Madam, this is a fine walking stick. Certainly the finest I have ever seen. A gem of a walking stick. Look at the grain of the wood. Hickory. Stout as iron, Madam. I shall never be without it."

He set it on the hall table so as not to forget it when he went out in the morning, but he managed to overlook it. He has overlooked it all these years. It is still there, dusted but untouched; a family joke.

I came to Villa Martinka as a young bride in 1920. There is a story that the first time the Colonel set eyes on me he returned to Thebes and built this lovely home. When the last nail was pounded he traveled by horseback to Twenty-nine Palms and asked for my hand in marriage. The story is true.

I had moved my sainted brother, James Elliot Crighton, to the dry, salubrious air of the desert in the spring of 1919. We hoped for a miracle. James had been gassed in the trenches during the war and his lungs had become pitifully weak. But was there ever so gay and brave a heart, or a smile so handsome and mocking under those bright, melancholy skies!

We had pitched a canvas tent in the wilderness and there we lived, day by day and week by week, waiting for the magic touch of the sun. James, stripped to the waist, grew tan as an Indian and spent his days designing homes he might never build and bridges that might never span more than the sheet of paper before him. We were alone, and my heart was full of dread and fearing.

I shut my eyes and see my yesterdays. I see a spare gentleman in brown leather puttees leading a scrawny bay horse down through the Joshua trees. How like a young Don Quixote he seemed to me in that moment, with his courtly stride and bright eyes peering out of the deep shade of his brows. He tethered his horse and looked up with a sudden smile.

"No," said he grandly, "I am not quite mad, even though you find me strolling under the sun with nothing to shade my face but a pair of eyebrows. I have had a misfortune."

There was something at once arresting and entertaining about this stranger and it was moments later, as James stepped forward to shake his hand, that I suddenly realized I was standing in my bare feet. I had been attempting to scrub clean an Indian metate we had found that morning and wished I were suddenly magically transported to our tent so that I could make a fresh appearance.

"If you're lost," said my brother, with a smile of his own, "we're delighted to find you. Our name is Crighton. This is my sister Greta. I'm James Crighton."

"Col. Jesse Martinka," the gentleman said, with a curt and friendly nod. "And this beast," he added with a grin, "this noble animal ought to be shot at sunrise—or before. He has twice kicked me, so I advise you to be wary of that right rear leg of his. The day I bought him he bit me on the shoulder out of sheer ingratitude. And this morning," he went on, joining us in the shade, "this morning, while I was fixing my breakfast and made the mistake of turning my back, he ate my straw hat. It was pure meanness, you understand. It was quite an old hat, and not very nourishing, but it did keep the sun out of my eyes."

James invited him to stay for lunch and I managed to slip into the tent for my shoes and to straighten my hair. We had not had any visitors, outside of an Indian boy who occasionally showed up to stare at us from a distance, and I felt as excited as if the Prince of Wales had walked into our parlor. At the last moment I decided to change my dress and made a grand entrance carrying a Japanese parasol. But the gentleman hardly seemed to notice the difference—or so I thought at the time. Later, Col. Martinka confessed to me that that was the precise moment he decided he would someday marry me.

"Col. Martinka tells me we're practically neighbors," James said. "He lives in Thebes."

"How far is Thebes?" I asked.

"That depends on if you go by car or on horseback."

"Horseback," I said.

"Two days."

"By car?"

"Two days."

James threw back his head and laughed and I knew I loved this stranger for brightening the gloom that weighed on our lives. But a moment later, James broke into a fit of coughing and I saw Col. Martinka study him out of the corner of his eye with vast understanding and experience.

"You must have a milk goat," he declared finally, when James had recovered. "The goat makes a fine doctor. Goat's milk will remedy that chest of yours. Now tell me, how did you happen to chose this spot on the desert?"

"No one seemed to be using the view," I volunteered. "So we decided we would."

My answer seemed to please him, but it was only later that I learned why. I told him that we had come all the way from Baltimore, that I had taught in a private girl's school, and that James was launched on a promising career in architecture when the doctors advised him to seek the dry air and healing sun of the desert.

I remember that we kept moving our camp chairs around a scrub juniper to remain in its shade. After lunch Col. Martinka lit a cigar. "So you're an architect," he said with great interest. He swept his hand to the west. "Look out there and tell me what you see."

"I see a dead land," James replied flatly, for he had been sentenced to this place like a prison. "I see rocks that stand like tombstones and trees that raise their arms like grave markers. I see an inhuman, inhospitable and primordial wilderness!"

The outburst left his face flushed and his eyes shining. When Col. Martinka spoke, his voice was soft and his eyes were creased with a stranger, personal vision. "I see endless green orchards," he muttered. "I see vineyards. I see tall date gardens. I hear the laughter of children. I see roads and waterways. I see cities."

A silence settled over us as if we were in the presence of a great prophet. And we were. For today they are all before us—the orchards, the roads, the cities, and the laughter of children. But Col. Martinka was more than a prophet that day. He worked to make his vision come true. He is working today on his dreams of tomorrow. He never stops. He never tires. There is always another vision to chase, to tame, to master. That is Col. Jesse Martinka!

But returning to that beautiful day under the juniper tree. By midafternoon he felt he must leave us and I refused to let him face the pitiless sun without headgear of some sort. James owned only the soiled felt hat he had worn from Baltimore. But I had among my things a straw boater that would be ridiculous to offer him, but I did nevertheless.

"I'm deeply touched, Miss Crighton," he smiled. "But I couldn't accept this fine hat of yours."

"But I insist," I said. "I have no earthly use for it here. If we take off the band perhaps it won't look quite so stylish. Do try it on."

We prevailed upon him and in due time he set it on his head. It was, of course, several sizes too small, and we all had a laugh. He struck a truculent pose and said he would wear it home and hope not to meet any of his friends on the journey. In many ways, that hat is the real beginning of our marriage—the first of so many things to be shared in our lives.

"Now then," he said before he left, turning to my brother and digging an envelope out of his pocket. "Design me a house. On the back of this. And I will build it. In return, I'll send you a fine milk goat."

"Fair payment!" said my brother, and immediately set to work on the back of the envelope. With quick lines a home took shape. "Thick walls," he said as he worked. "The Spaniards had the right idea when they built their missions. Adobe brick, if you can get it."

"I'll get it," vowed Col. Martinka.

"A wide overhang and plenty of veranda. Do you want a second floor?"

"Why not," the Colonel replied with the merest flick of a glance at me. "A home is meant for a wife and family."

James sketched in the upper story, with fine long windows and handsome shutters, and within a moment he returned the envelope. Col. Martinka unbuttoned the breast pocket of his shirt, replaced the envelope and gave it a pat for safe keeping. He mounted his horse and lifted the hat off his head to wave us a goodbye. And then he rode off with my boater tilted over his eyes, like a knight of old wearing the colors of his ladylove.

In due time the milk goat arrived with a very old and wrinkled Indian, who staked it and disappeared. It was months before I unraveled the mystery of Col. Martinka's strange question to us. Why had we chosen that spot for our stay? Our having chosen it as the best of the wilderness reassured him in his own judgment! For I discovered, quite by accident, the true identity of this desert cavalier. He was our landlord! He had bought two sections of land and we were squatters on his property! He had come to investigate and stayed to befriend us.

The weeks passed and my dear brother seemed to grow stronger. We even began to make plans to return to Baltimore, and pick up the lives we had dropped so precipitously. A month, two months passed without sight of the strange man who had walked into our lives. I stopped thinking about him, for I had my books—my beloved Keats and Shelley. Another month and then a fourth! James and I had collected many artifacts in the desert, planning to box them and take them back to Baltimore with us, but I began to know in my heart that James would never go back. The bloom on his cheeks was false; the cough real and growing worse.

Our desert cavalier reappeared!

How quickly my melancholy vanished at the sight of him. He stayed only an hour, but warmed my life for months to come with just a few words. He asked me to marry him.

But I could not say yes. My life was with my brother, to nurse him, to love him, to coax him through each day so there would be another.

This was my life. There could be no other.

Early in November I came upon James burning his drawings and designs in a small ravine. A week later he passed on, and I "wept that one so lovely should have a life so brief."

I had written to the Colonel that I felt the end was near, and together we buried my dear, sainted brother under the praying arms of a Joshua tree. Over the grave I read these lines of Shelley on the death of his beloved Keats:

> From the contagion of the world's slow stain
> He is secure, and now can never mourn
> A heart grown cold, a head grown gray in vain:
> Nor, when the spirit's self has ceased to burn
> With sparkless ashes load an unlamented urn.

In my grief I refused to consider marriage, for all joy had gone out of my life. The sun and the desert had deceived us; they had brought death rather than life. I wanted never to return to the scenes of my sorrow.

But the regenerative powers of love were at work, in the person of my desert cavalier! In time my sorrow healed, and my joy was restored. And one day I returned to become the wife of a gentleman who had kept a secret. For it was as a bride that I saw for the first time the home, designed in jest on the back of an envelope, that had been standing waiting for me!

I open my eyes and see my husband returning from his walk. The last light is vanished from the sky and the pigeons are returning to their nests.

"Madam," my husband says, "I think we shall drive down toward Ocotillo Wells tomorrow. There's good land down there. We could clear the salt cedar and till the soil. Turn that into green country. We've just got to put our minds to it."

Tomorrow we will drive to Ocotillo Wells. And a city shall rise. And the laughter of children will be heard.

3

The phone woke Gamage shortly before noon. He scowled at it from the pillow and supposed that would be Frank. Frank and his goddam wake-up service. Gamage didn't feel equal to the encounter and let the phone ring itself out. There had to be a better way to start the day than with the cactus man.

He was awake. He got up and brushed the night out of his mouth. He ought to quit smoking, he told himself, but as soon as he had washed he lit a cigarette. What if it had been Ginny on the phone? He checked with the desk to see if there had been a message. The girl said no, but she knew the voice. It had been BeJesus John calling.

Gamage sat on the edge of the bed and asked her to get him. After a moment he heard an abrasive voice. "Hello."

"This is Gamage."

There was a spitting pause. "I figured you musta left town without paying your bill."

"I can't get my car started."

"You want to buy a newspaper?"

"What are you talking about?"

"I'm going to sell."

Gamage tightened his eyes against the daylight at the window. He'd better quit the booze too. In this heat. "I thought Martinka couldn't mint enough money to buy you out."

"I ain't offering to sell to him. I'm offering to sell to you."

"You sized me up wrong."

"You said you were a newspaperman, didn't you? Were you any good?"

"Sure. I was so good I aced myself right out of the business."

"I'll make you a kindly proposition."

"Save your breath."

"Hell, sonny, you can walk in here and put your name on the window."

"You're talking to the wrong man," Gamage said.

"It's small potatoes, huh? A big timer like you."

"I don't have investment capital. That's just for a start. What made you change your mind?"

"I'm getting old. It just occurred to me."

What had happened, Gamage wondered? "Let me come down and talk to you. But don't get any ideas. You couldn't sell me *The New York Times*."

He hung up and fished out the copy of the *Sunset* he had discarded in the waste basket. It was thin and sickly. A slow ride to the poorhouse, he thought. He'd be a fool to consider it. Still, it was a temptation. The paper might be built up, fleshed out and made to pay its way. Every newspaper stiff carried the dream of a country weekly in his back pocket. It was a temptation, but it wasn't for him, Gamage told himself. With a change in luck he could write himself a barrel of money in Hollywood. He'd need it. Ginny was going to be expensive.

He tossed the *Sunset* back into the waste basket. It would wire him to the desert and that was out. If Frank cut Ginny loose, the valley would be no place for them. That was that.

Madam Martinka's rose-scented pages lay on the floor where he had let them drop one by one. He gathered them up with the ribbon and put them back in the case. She was, he thought, a woman to be reckoned with. Her lacy composition was a morbid deception. It was a love letter to that departed brother of hers and the colonel had appeared like a supporting player. She seemed formidable. Gamage supposed he would be expected to pick up some of her pressed-leaf sentences. He had an idea that the courtship of Greta Crighton Martinka would fill a book, but not the one he had been hired to write.

He stopped downstairs for a quick cup of coffee and then moved along the oven-hot arcades toward *The Thebes Weekly Sunset*. The front door stood wide open as if the building were gasping for air. A dead silence lay over the shop. BeJesus John sat back in a swivel chair with his feet propped in the litter of his roll top desk. The grimy visor was pulled low over his eyes so that he had to lift his chin to see out. "It took you long enough."

Gamage glanced at the shop beyond the low office fence. The black machinery lay idle and the hanging light bulbs were turned off. There was a heavy gloom about the place, the linotype still, the fire out under the lead forge. "What happened to the roar of the press?" Gamage said.

"I'm retiring."

"It's kind of sudden, isn't it?"

"Nope. I've been thinking about it for a long time. Two or three hours. If you can find a chair, sit down."

"Your subscribers are going to miss you."

"I don't doubt it."

"What happened?"

"Do you indulge in bottled goods?"

Gamage pulled up a chair. "On social occasions."

"How social are you?"

"At the moment, mighty social."

BeJesus John pawed through the waste paper on his desk and cleared a half-empty bottle of Jim Beam. "I lean to sour mash whiskey myself."

"You believe in having the good things of life at your elbow," Gamage said.

"When you reach my age if it ain't at your elbow, it's too far to walk." He pulled the cork and decanted the whiskey into two Dixie cups with the concentration of a chemist. "You look like a bright young go-getter. For a small price I'll make you my successor. Put your name on the window."

It would not exactly be a giant step forward, Gamage thought. From the silver screen to the flyblown window of a small town newspaper. "I've been trying to tell you that I'm not your man," Gamage said. "I don't have enough money to buy all the spittoons in this place."

BeJesus John poured down the whiskey and crushed the paper cup in his hand. He gave Gamage a smile. "Why, you weekenders and suchlike always got money. How much will you give me for the place—lock, stock and good will? I'll throw in my enemies for nothing."

Gamage was beginning to think that BeJesus John only wanted someone to talk to. "What the hell happened around here?"

BeJesus John lifted the visor and ran a hand over his thinning head. "I run out of money, credit and friends. In short, the paper wholesalers have locked me out."

"How much do you owe?"

"I stopped keeping track a long time ago, sonny. That don't worry me. The trouble is I don't have enough stock on hand to print Friday's paper. I called two-three paper houses in L.A. this morning, but they're tired of keeping me in business. They want cash. Tell you what you do. You tell Frank to make me an offer. Just give me time enough to finish off this bottle and improve my sense of humor."

Gamage leaned forward and looked up. "How about the newspaper brokers?"

"First of all there ain't time. The moment this paper stops publishing it's a dead mackerel. You got nothing to sell except the machinery, and the bank owns that. I'm into them more than they like to admit. Second, the brokers couldn't give it away. My books ain't exactly a thing of joy and beauty. I guess I could have made more money printing business cards on a hand press. No, there ain't nobody soft-headed enough to buy me out except the Martinkas, and I'm going to let them have it. The *Sunset* ain't missed an issue in forty-eight years. I can't let it die. *Pro bono publico*. Folks around here have got to have a newspaper of their own even if I ain't running it. I've had a good life here, no complaints, but times has changed and I ain't kept up. I'm as out of date as that hitching post out there. I know it. I'm licked. I know it. I'm selling."

Gamage gazed at him in silence. The day BeJesus John walked away from *The Thebes Weekly Sunset* he would begin his dying. Frank would turn it into a land speculator's billboard. Gamage pitched his empty cup into the waste basket. If he did nothing it would be an act of commitment; he would be throwing in with Frank. "How long would three hundred dollars keep you in paper and ink?"

BeJesus John took a fresh purchase on his cigar. "Sonny, I'd look upon three hundred dollars as something of an insult."

"I'm not offering to buy the *Sunset*," Gamage said. "I'd just like to buy you some time. Maybe you can bail yourself out."

BeJesus John lifted his chin and studied Gamage as if he were seeing him for the first time. "Put your money away. I didn't ask you here to pick your pocket."

Gamage signed a couple of traveler's checks and handed them over and reminded himself that it was Frank's money he was spending. He hadn't yet written a line of the Martinka epic and he was putting himself deeper in hock. The advance was slipping through his fingers. "Take it."

BeJesus John dropped his character actor's face. He held the checks up to the light and stared at them solemnly. Finally his eyes shifted back to Gamage. "It's mighty handsome paper, sonny. I appreciate the sentiment. But I wouldn't advise you to advance me a sum like this with any hope of seeing it again."

"At the moment the only thing standing between this valley and the pyramid is you," Gamage said. "I'm a sucker for a good fight. Spend it and forget it."

BeJesus John squinted, putting his face back on. "Couldn't do that. It wouldn't be business-like. Tell you what I'll do. You've just bought yourself a piece of a mighty fine paper. Just what piece it is I'll leave up to you."

"How about the spittoons?"

BeJesus John's eyes lighted up. "Sold. They're dear to my heart, you understand, real antiques—must be worth a fortune. I'll write you out a bill of sale. You want to take them with you? Must be six or eight around here."

"No," Gamage said. "If I want to spit I'll stop in." He got up and stood at the window. He ought to get back to the hotel and sit down to the typewriter. But he didn't like the feeling of being expected to work under glass, in a vacuum. He wished he could get a better grip on Martinka, even though Frank had hired him for a rewrite and paste-up job. He spoke without turning. "What makes you so sure the Colonel is still here in the valley?"

"Did I say that?"

"Yesterday."

"Maybe he is, maybe he ain't. Was it Frank told you he flew to Italy?"

"Yes."

"He ought to know better."

Gamage turned. "What does that mean?"

BeJesus John snorted. "There's some men who won't get in an airplane and Jesse Martinka is one of them. I've seen it. I've seen him get weak in the knees on a ten foot ladder. He'd crawl to Europe on his hands and knees before he'd fly there."

Gamage moved away from the window. "Where is Villa Martinka?"

"Back in the hills. You can follow the road out front for about a mile and you'll see a big pepper tree. Turn off toward the hills and you'll run into the place."

"Check me out on the wife," Gamage said, wiping the back of his neck with a handkerchief.

"Which one?"

"How many were there?"

"Two."

Gamage scowled. The attaché case was full of omissions. "Who was the first one?"

"A Mexican girl. The most beautiful woman I ever saw in my life. Camilla. He built the house for her."

"Villa Martinka?"

"Yup. At one time that was the finest house around here."

"I was under the impression that he built it for Greta Crighton Martinka."

"It was for Camilla," BeJesus John said. "But she never lived in it. While it was still building she was thrown from a horse and killed. It stood empty until Greta moved in."

"She tells the story a little differently."

"She's a smart woman. Once she set her cap for him he didn't have a chance. She hooked him. But all that was a long time ago and at the moment I got a check to cash. Stop in anytime."

4

The big pepper tree was standing where BeJesus John said it would be. Gamage turned off along a private road. Jimson weed and desert verbena lay over the sandy hummocks like dried antimacassars. He drove almost a mile before a chain appeared across the road with a no trespassing sign hanging from the center. Colonel Martinka could do no more than run him off, Gamage thought, and that would be better than no meeting at all.

He lowered the chain and continued along a gravel road. He could see nothing ahead but the seared brown hills. Gravel struck the underside of his fenders with the rattle of hail as if to announce his arrival. He swung around a spur and came upon a wide draw, green, lush with vegetation. It was as sudden as new scenery lowered from the flies.

Tall date palms, in fixed rows, stood as erect as pilings. They held aloft a prickly canopy of fronds and created a box of deep shade. Gamage saw that the irrigation ditches were dry and in the burning silence the place seemed abandoned.

He could make out the house at the rear of the date garden and threw the jeep in gear. He startled a flock of pigeons out of the trees and he watched them with a sense of *déjà vu*. Finally he parked and sat for a moment gazing at the house. Villa Martinka was not quite a mansion. It was a two-story adobe with a white stucco wash. The upstairs windows had green shutters like an aging Mediterranean pension. A wide, sloping overhang shaded a veranda that followed the house around on two sides. Toward the rear he could see a poultry yard, deserted, and a kind of bunkhouse.

BeJesus John could be wrong, Gamage thought. The place had an air of being boarded up. It would surprise him now to find Martinka home.

He left the jeep and walked slowly up the wooden steps to the broad veranda. He rang the bell and brushed the gnats away from his face. The date garden seemed alive with them. Grapefruit and tangerine trees, with fruit hanging like Christmas ornaments, grew along one side of the porch. He tried the bell again and when he turned he saw Frank coming around from behind the house. "I thought I heard someone out here."

Gamage tossed away his cigarette. "I made as much noise as I could," he said.

Frank was in jeans and western boots and dark sun glasses. "Look at this goddam place. It's going to ruin. I had a couple of wetbacks looking after the trees, but they must have got homesick, if that's possible. What are you doing here?"

"I was hoping to get run off by your old man."

"I thought I told you. He's in Italy."

"You told me," Gamage said. "I didn't believe you."

Frank laughed and hunkered in the shade of the veranda. "You're a good man. But don't work so hard at it."

Gamage sensed that Frank, behind his smile and his sun glasses, was angrier than he was letting himself show. The no trespassing sign on the road chain meant anyone who could read. And now that he was here Gamage wasn't sure why he had bothered. He wasn't going to win any prizes for digging out a true likeness of Col. Jesse Martinka. But he persisted, out of habit and general cussedness, he supposed. "Did you say he flew to Europe?"

Frank looked him over silently. "I didn't say that."

"I thought you did."

"You heard me wrong."

"I also heard that the Colonel is a recluse. That he never leaves the place."

"Stop talking to the natives," Frank grinned. "They'll only confuse you. If they were a little smarter they'd be getting rich instead of us. Now what is it you want to know?"

"There's nobody home?"

"Nobody."

Gamage could see himself reflected in the dark surfaces of the sun glasses. "What about the recluse story?"

"There's something to it. He's getting old and most of his old friends have either died or turned against him. He putters around the house. He's got everything right here—the trees he started with fifty years ago, the house he built and my old lady to see that he changes his socks every day. And the telephone. Why go out? If he wants something done all he has to do is call me. That's what I'm for. It's Martinka & Son—don't forget that. He still runs the show. I'm just the office boy. See that flagpole? You can always tell when the old man is here by that."

Gamage squinted at the flagpole rising from a small clearing. "What do you mean?"

"Come hell or high water he's up at dawn to raise the American flag. At sundown he lowers it. When you see Old Glory up there, amigo, you know he's home."

Martinkiana, Gamage thought. He'd drop it in the book somewhere. "What can you tell me about his first wife?"

Frank fixed him with a long cold stare. "There was no first wife, amigo."

"Camilla."

"She doesn't even rate a mention. Savvy? They were never married. It was a shack-up job. She was nothing. She was a wetback, and wetbacks don't count, do they?"

"You tell me."

"Stick to the notes. Hell, you can't crucify a man for getting serviced once in a while. Take you, amigo. You made out last night, didn't you?"

Gamage stood perfectly still. He felt a beating at his temples, a kind of internal thunder. "Did I?"

"I called you."

"When?"

"Ginny turned up missing. She had too much to drink. I thought you might be laying her."

"Was I?"

"Conny answered the phone. You go for real broads, amigo, real broads."

The thunder subsided. "She's a doll," Gamage said. It surprised him that Conny had answered the phone in his room. She must have thought it was Gamage himself calling her and got caught with Frank on the other end.

Frank spat between his teeth and looked up. "If I'd caught Ginny in your room you'd be minus your balls right now."

"But you didn't and I'm not."

"She came home around five this morning. She said she couldn't sleep. She went out for a drive and ran out of gas. Would you believe that?"

"It sounds phony enough to be true," Gamage said.

"Yeah. Even when a dame is telling the truth they're lying."

The man was a natural-born cuckold, Gamage thought. He had been stupid to phone ("Yes, she's right here; I'll put her on."), but Gamage put it down to an excess of Martinis. Conny had been generous to Gamage and he silently thanked her. It alarmed him that the first place Frank had expected to find Ginny was in his room. Frank seemed almost disappointed to scratch him from the area of his suspicions. There was an implicit warning in his having called at all.

Frank stood up. "I got to get some water under these trees," he said. "I'm just a country boy, you know. Anything else you want around here?"

"Not a thing."

"As a matter of fact, my old man doesn't like to fly. Does that answer your question? I put the two of them on the train and they took a boat over. I had a letter from them today. You want to read my mail?"

"Forget it."

"I'll see you around."

Gamage watched him amble away with the straw hat pulled over his eyes. For a man about to cast off his wife he was giving a pretty good imitation of jealousy and suspicion. Maybe Ginny was kidding herself. He might not be going to cut her loose at all.

Gamage started up the jeep and glanced back at the house, half expecting to see a face behind one of the upstairs shutters. He watched for a moment and then the pigeons came back, clapping their wings. He left.

CHAPTER FOUR

1

Gamage stopped off at a gas station and called Ginny from the phone booth. She wasn't home. When he entered the hotel lobby he saw her waiting for him with her knees crossed and a cigarette between her fingers. She wore Mexican sandals and a pink summer dress. He came toward her and then noticed Barbachano in a nearby chair, flipping through a comic magazine. Gamage decided not to acknowledge Ginny in his presence. He stopped. The kid appeared freshly showered and with nothing but time on his hands.

Gamage held up a palm. "How," he said.

Barbachano looked up. He grinned. "Hi, Great White Father."

"You'll get musty sitting around this lobby."

Barbachano glanced at the wall clock. "Checking out time is two. I got another five minutes."

"Have you had anything to eat?"

"Sure. I scrounged a few acorns and grasshoppers."

Gamage held out a five dollar bill. "Go get yourself some lunch."

The kid got up. He smiled and shook his head. "I don't need any paper," he said. "Like I told you, I'm independently wealthy." He rolled up the comic book and walked away, leaving the money between Gamage's fingers.

Once he cleared the lobby Gamage turned to Ginny. She seemed enormously composed.

"Hello Ginny," he said.

"Hello, darling." She glanced toward the doorway. "What was that all about?"

"The kid? He saw you drop me off this morning. Your car, anyway."

"Oh."

"What are you doing here?"

"Waiting for you."

"It's kind of public, isn't it?"

"Does it matter?"

"Not to me."

"Can we go somewhere and talk?"

"There's only the bar," he said.

"All right."

Gamage half-expected to find Conny's lovely rear-end perched on a stool. But the bar was empty except for a couple of ranchers at the far end. Conny had to be sore as hell, he thought, and she would be less than happy to find out that he was still in town.

They took a corner booth and Ginny ordered a gimlet. They looked at each other for a moment, smiling without smiling, acting the part of strangers. The hours before came back to him and he wished he could advance time a few weeks or a few months and have her openly and frankly to himself. "You shouldn't be here," he said.

"When you didn't answer the phone I was afraid you might be—leaving."

"I suppose I'd better keep my hands off you."

"For a little while."

"Christ," he smiled. He struck a match and she dipped her cigarette into it.

"Frank was waiting up when I walked in," she murmured.

"I know. I just saw him."

"I took a chance. I told him I had been out with you."

"You what?"

"Don't be shocked," she said softly. "He didn't believe me. I knew he wouldn't. At a time like that he expected me to lie."

The drinks came and they fell silent for a moment. Gamage looked at her. If Frank hadn't believed her it was only because he was dead sure Gamage already had the night made. The bartender moved away and Ginny brushed a wisp of ash-blonde hair from her forehead.

"He had been waiting up hours to twist the truth out of me," she said. "When I mentioned your name he thought I was only trying to make him jealous. Finally I just told him I'd run out of gas. He wanted to believe something like that. He went out to the garage and checked the tank. Fortunately there was hardly any gas left. I told him I'd bummed that from a passing car. He believed it."

"I'm not so sure."

"Darling, you don't know him."

"That's not the way he talks."

"That's the way he thinks. The male ego is coming out his ears. But we'll have to be careful for a while."

"How long is a while?"

"I don't know."

Gamage stared at her. Her stunning beauty seemed to him stark and out of place in the beer-scented gloom. "Ginny darling," he said, "you're kidding me."

She glanced up through her darkened lashes. "Kidding you?"

"Frank isn't behaving like a man about to divest himself of his wife."

"Be patient, darling."

"Ginny, I think you're even kidding yourself."

"No," she said, and a kind of weariness came into her eyes. "When he's sure he's got me completely beat down he'll show me the door. And give me a push. And his mother will be right behind him."

2

Grab the money and run. Gamage spent the afternoon in his room trying to get down to work. He couldn't shake the feeling that his affair with Ginny was a first step into quicksand for them both. He regretted nothing, but he wasn't going to enjoy skulking around the desert. Without a bankroll there'd be no future at all.

Finally he sent down for some beer and stretched out under the fan to read through the Martinka papers. The earliest material he could find was a water-stained penny tablet, a journal in the Colonel's own hand, dated 1907.

Gamage was surprised to find that the entries were both literate and self-amused.

Nov. 5 — My plans have gone awry. In Boston Dr. Chapman said I had six months to live, give or take a few minutes, and the six months are up today. For a dead man I feel astonishingly lifelike. He meant well, I suppose, but he has sorely upset my own calculations. My coughing still keeps small animals away at night, but I had not counted on a prolonged residence here and it is going to be bothersome.

I arrived in Thebes last July, age 21, thin as a breadstick, wearing a pair of corduroy trousers (which I am still wearing), a suitcase in hand, a mandolin, funds in my pocket and my life behind me. I remember twirling a brownie cigarette and figuring I had arrived on the outskirts of Hades. A fiery wind was blowing and a man was driving a mule through the sandblast with a gunny sack tied over its head. They call this the American Sahara. Like the seasick man who is afraid he is going to die, after the first half hour in Thebes I was afraid I wouldn't.

There is a hotel, if you are not particular, with screened in rooms and canvas flaps. Meals are served by a buxom young maiden in bare feet who is called the Missouri Girl. The town boasts a barber shop, a mercantile, a machine shop and a pool hall. But the town is dry, whiskey dry, I mean, which shows that there is no limit to man's inhumanity to man.

For several weeks I put up at the hotel and spent my days at the pool table. In short, I pursued the life of a gentleman of leisure, which suits my temperament exactly.

But one begins to play games with the Grim Reaper. A man with nothing to lose has everything to gain. Emmet Pearson's wife has left him. They have been two years on the desert and she could not stand it another day. He has ten acres in cantaloupe west of town. He let the crop rot on the vines. Now he is around town and cannot give the place away. Land here is not in short supply. He wants to find his wife. He hasn't train fare out.

I go out there. It is in a pretty little draw, secluded, perpetually sunlit, silent. He has sunk an artesian well and the flow comes up like liquid crystal. But he has let the vines die, unwatered, curled up like paper, as if to take out a vengeance on the land.

There is a tent half-buried in sand, with a board floor and two flys. Inside, a pair of canvas cots, a table, a *Sunbeam* lamp, and more sand.

He keeps chattering about melons. They grow as easily as weeds in this climate. A man can make a fortune. But all the while he is cursing the desert. "It ain't fit for women or flies," he keeps saying.

I buy the place for cash. I don't fancy myself a truck farmer. I have other plans.

There is considerable local talk centering around the culture of the date palm. The land here, below sea level, is Biblical. It is Palestine. It is the Nile Valley (the river is underfoot).

Government men are experimenting with a date garden in Mecca, and another has been planted this year near Indio. They are importing offshoots from Algeria. I have seen the trees in Mecca, which are just beginning to bear, and they excite the eye and the mind. They are called the Tree of Life and little wonder. They will bear for a hundred years and stand for centuries more.

For a man who reckons his life in days, I am obsessed by this Methuselan, hot-house tree. "The Tree of Life must have its feet in water and its head in the fires of heaven," goes the Arab saying. I can supply both on my "ranch." I have seen summer temperatures of almost 170 degrees in the sun. The sun got to my mandolin and split it open like a watermelon.

I made a one-acre planting—fifty bristling green offshoots. One male to a harem of 49 females. The male, called the King Solomon tree, will pollinate the harem. I will not see them through their first year (I remind myself), but even the worst of us wants to build monuments to himself. Man fears most an unmarked grave. To a man of least imagination even a tombstone is immortality.

Now I find it somewhat awkward to be still above ground. I have outlived my funds. I am busted. And I have fifty trees on my hands, like mewling babies. I cannot decide whether I have outwitted the Grim Reaper or he has outwitted me.

It appears that I must put aside this life of the country gentleman and find gainful employment of some sort. I thought I was finished with such troublesome things.

Nov. 6 — No job. Prospects poor.

Nov. 8 — Ditto.

Nov. 10 — The bank will not make me a loan on dates as a money crop. Too speculative, and it will require another three years before my offshoots begin to bear. They advise me to plant melons or asparagus. That is beneath me, of course.

The shopkeepers, I am finding, do not want to extend credit to lungers. They have attended too many funerals with bills due in their pockets.

Nov. 14 — The Missouri Girl is feeding me. In exchange I am to give her two singing lessons a week. She has no voice, but one should not tamper with a woman's dreams. Of her past, nothing is known.

My voice, when I am not barking like a coyote, has taken on a raspy edge. There is no going back for me. I tell myself it is a blessing in disguise. I would have spent my life traveling with third-rate opera companies. The truth is that in the best of voice I was not good enough. One cannot build his life on a lie. For an artist, to be anything less than first-rate is a mockery.

A Mr. Clay Fenner, well digger, of Indio, presented himself on my property today. He is an Old Testament figure with a stained beard and slouch hat. He claims to have sunk the well for which he is still owed the sum of $300. He is asking for immediate payment. The man is a comedian.

Nov. 15 — I have taken a job (temporary) at the Elysian Feed Yard & Livery Stable, Geo. Wagenner, Prop. The work is not of an exalted kind. I accepted only out of reasons of health, as it is widely known that a good strong stable odor is beneficial to the lungs. Geo. tells me that Mexican women will sometimes appear with a sick child and ask to leave it all day in an empty stall.

Nov. 17 — I have fifty trees. An adult palm can be expected to yield at least 100 pounds of dates. The Arabs, I read, are known to harvest 500 to 600 pounds from exceptional trees. But I will content myself with the conservative figure.

Fifty trees times 100 equals 5000 pounds. Fancy grade, packed in confectionery boxes, may bring $1 per pound as desert dates. Lower grade (but not culls), perhaps 20-cents per pound. My acre should yield in excess of $1000 each year—*for the next one hundred years!*

A man could provide for his heirs to the fifth generation with a date garden.

Now, if my ten acres were planted, I could look for an annual crop of 50,000 pounds, or $10,000 a year. A fortune.

To do this I will need to buy 450 additional offshoots@$6.50 ea. (approx.). That comes to $2925. Monstrous sum.

But I must do this as soon as possible.

Nov. 18 — Gave the Missouri Girl her lesson today, plucking at mandolin (more or less glued back together). We are attracting crowds.

I am notified today that the Indio well digger has filed a lien against my property.

Nov. 20 — Offshoots. A man could save money by making a trip to Algeria and importing them himself. Might bring them in@no more than $1 or $2 each. Would require some capital though.

Dec. 3 — The Missouri Girl has disappeared. There is a big fellow in town, hairy-faced, frock coat, claims to be a preacher. He is inquiring everywhere about a woman named Jerusha Muller. He describes her as sturdy-built, blonde, blue-eyed. The Missouri Girl, no question about it.

When I return to my place and strike a match to the lamp a face appears like a spectre in the corner. It is the Missouri Girl. She has been hiding in my tent for hours, pale and frightened.

"Let me stay," she pleads.

"But you can't spend the night here," I reply. "Who is this fellow looking for you?"

She tells me then that he is her husband, a Bible-shouting brute of a man. He married her when she was thirteen.

He would thrash her like the child she was at the least infraction of his rules. She ran away twice, but in each instance he brought her back. Finally, a year ago, she made good her escape. Now he has found her again. The swine terrifies her.

I let her stay. I put a canvas cot outside for myself, and in the morning I see the preacher coming along in a rented buggy. He steps down and "Bless you, brother," he says, "I am told that you are friendly with the Missouri Girl, as she is called here."

"That's right," I answer.

He frowns suspiciously at the tent. "Do you mind, brother, if we go inside and talk?"

"We can talk out here," I say.

He gives me a flash of brimstone with his eyes.

"I intend to have a look around, brother," he scowls and takes a step forward. I pick up a shovel and block his way. "Would you strike a servant of God?" he declares.

"Only at His insistence," I say. "You are trespassing here, sir. I advise you to return to your buggy and drive off."

We stand there glaring at each other. His nostrils are flaring like bellows. I take a tighter grip on the shovel, thinking that I will make his skull ring for a week. Then he turns his back, mounts the buggy, takes the whip from its socket and stings the air.

When he is gone I enter the tent and find the Missouri Girl standing rigid with fear and her eyes flooded. She has hardly allowed herself to breathe. She looks at me and her gratitude needs no expression.

"Go up into the hills and wait," I tell her. "I expect he'll be back."

I fill a canteen with water and give it to her. She moves away along the draw and I walk into town. We must get rid of the fellow, I tell myself, and along the way I see how it can be done.

I tell Geo. my idea. We ride out to his house to talk to his maiden sister, Elsa Wagenner. We find her in the poultry yard—plump and blonde, although not as young as the Missouri Girl. She will do. When I tell her that the Missouri Girl is hiding at my place and describe her fear of the man, Elsa enlists in the cause. She returns to the hotel with us, angry as a hornet, and agrees to impersonate the Missouri Girl.

We pass the word through town. For noon lunch the dining room is packed and Elsa performs like a trouper. Sure enough the preacher strides in for his noon meal. From the look he gives me I can be sure he has already been back to my place. Now he hears shouts of, "Doggone it, Missouri, what's this gravy made of—sheep dip?" and "Missouri, we figured you run off with that traveling salesman yesterday."

The preacher looks like he's just been jabbed with a pitchfork. He glowers at Elsa, head to toe, but he's not convinced yet. He gets up and leaves. Five minutes later he's back with a fellow off the street. None other than Geo. himself, who was on the way over for the fun.

"Brother," he says, "who is that young lady with the milk pitcher in her hands?"

"You mean the one with the yellow braids?"

"Yes, brother."

"The sturdy-built one?"

"Exactly, brother."

"Why, that's the Missouri Girl. I heard she run off yesterday with a traveling salesman."

The preacher looks ready to swallow his own mouth, beard and all. That afternoon he packs up and leaves us, and the laughter hasn't died down yet. That was yesterday.

Dec. 5 — Am obsessed with plan to make trip to North Africa for offshoots. Deglet Noors from Algeria. The Saidy from Egypt. No one here can afford importers' prices. And even if he could, the offshoots can't be had in any quantity.

Geo. says he will advance $1.50 an offshoot and put in 100 trees at his place. Am talking to other ranchers. But would my health stand the trip? Hemorrhaged again last night.

The Indio well digger is becoming bothersome. He writes me notes full of foreclosure talk.

Dec. 25 — Christmas day. Sandstorm blowing.

Jan. 1, 1908 — The new year starts. Temperature, 82-degrees. I talk to Stenquist about putting in a date garden at his place. Too many here view it as little more than an exotic hobby. They are beginning to call me the "Boston Arab."

Jan. 25 — Have taken in a free boarder. A redheaded young fellow named Charlie Hastings. He is flat busted. Quit his job as bank teller to grow lettuce at edge of desert below here in San Diego County. Could ripen crop two weeks ahead of the market. Went in with a number of others on promise that So. Pacific was going to build a spur line to get produce out. Spur line never materialized. A crooked real estate promotion. Lost every cent he had, but regrets nothing. Considers it a first-rate education.

April 10 — Sheriff has been here and posted a notice of foreclosure sale. Have been on my back since early March. No hope of raising money. Am pale as a cadaver. Who can blame them? Geo. offers me $150 put aside for offshoots, but the Indio well digger demands full amount.

April 12 — Charlie returns around noon and rips down foreclosure notice. Says lien has been lifted. Somebody paid off the well digger in full. I suspect Geo. and go into town, but he denies it.

April 14 — The Missouri Girl. I am speechless. She says no, it wasn't her, but Charlie wormed it out of the Indio well digger. It must have taken every cent she had and then some. If I live long enough I'll make it up to her.

July 4 — Too hot to shoot off firecrackers, but we do anyway. I have orders for more than 700 offshoots, if and when.

Sept. 5 — A speculator from the Imperial Valley has got himself a carload of Khadrawi palms and is trying to peddle them here at $8.50 per offshoot. The price is outrageous.

Oct. 11 — Charlie left today for Middle East, to act as agent of Martinka Date Importers. I have orders (and cash advance) for 2500 offshoots. Balance to be paid on arrival—cost plus ten percent. Between us, we will turn this overheated valley into the Garden of Allah.

The remainder of the penny tablet was blank. Gamage found the old man, as a young man, fairly engaging. As his grip on life tightened Martinka had apparently lost interest in scratching out a daily obituary. There were several old letters from Charlie Hastings, written in Biskra and Port Said and Busrah, informing Martinka, finally, that he had bought three thousand off-shoots of several varieties—"The final batch is stacked like cordwood, waiting to be boxed and put aboard the ocean steamer for home." The buying trip was a success.

Hastings was still alive. Gamage recalled that BeJesus John had referred to him as Martinka's fellow adventurer among the Insurrectos of Mexico in 1910; a retired banker living in Mecca. Gamage got him on the phone and Hastings agreed to see him at ten o'clock the next morning.

3

When Gamage entered the hotel coffee shop he saw a girl in a crisp pink blouse and skirt seated alone with a glass of orange juice and a copy of McCall's. It was Conny. She looked up from the magazine and in a flash of her eyes he felt himself become invisible. She was a woman scorned and he couldn't remember a moment when he knew himself to be in worse odor.

He hesitated a moment, wondering if there was anything he could say to take out the sting. She looked pretty sitting there with her dark hair in a loose swirl along her cheek and her breasts giving a fine shape to her blouse. It seemed impossible to him now that he had behaved so indifferently toward her. He took a breath and came over.

"If looks could kill, Conny," he said, "I've had it."

She turned the page.

"Mind if I sit down?"

"On a tack would be fine," she said without looking up. "This table is taken."

"I can see that." He took a chair and stared at her for a moment. "Conny, I'm sorry for what happened. I'll bend over if you'll kick me. We'll both feel better."

He was talking to himself. The waitress came over and he ordered juice, toast and black coffee. Conny turned another page. He gazed at her, searching his mind for another gambit. He liked her. He realized that he wanted her to like him even though that seemed forever out of the question. "Good story?"

She lifted one eyebrow. "Yes. It's about a man who chases other men's wives. He's something like you."

"He couldn't possibly be such a goddam—cad."

"You're right. He isn't." She crushed her cigarette. "I thought you were leaving town."

Gamage's name burst from the wall loudspeaker like a raspy cough. He ignored the call. "Something came up," he said.

"You don't have to explain." She began gathering up her things. "And you don't have to apologize. You saved me from a death worse than fate."

"You look pretty in pink. Pink is your color. Sit down and finish your juice."

"I have to see a man about some dictation. I'm late. You can do me a favor, Mr. Gamage. Leave me alone."

"Don't go. You're for hire."

"That's a delicate way of putting it."

"It comes to me. I'm going to be in dire need of some public stenography."

"I'm busy."

"How about this afternoon? Say, around three o'clock."

"I'll send a friend."

"I'll expect you."

"Don't hold your breath."

She left. He wasn't sure that he'd accomplished anything, but at least they were talking to each other even if they weren't on speaking terms. He got up and went to the house phone and found Frank on the other end. It was like picking up a live wire.

"What are you trying to pull?" Frank said.

Gamage dropped his cigarette and stepped on it, his mind racing for an attitude. "Okay, Frank. Let's have it."

"You're a smooth article."

"Never mind the compliments."

"You're supposed to be working for me."

Gamage stopped. What was he talking about? "Why don't you say what you're trying to say?"

"Don't knife me in the back, amigo. Why the money to BeJesus John? I had his water shut off. What are you trying to pull?"

Gamage's stomach untwisted. But for a moment he was sorry it wasn't Frank's wife they were talking about.

He had had a guilty reaction and the prospect of more wasn't pleasant. "How much were the checks?"

"Three hundred dollars and no cents."

"Do you know everything that goes on in the valley?"

"God damn right. Look, if you're trying to buy that chickenshit newspaper for yourself, I'll help you. I told you that the other night, didn't I? But don't work behind my back, amigo."

"I'm not buying it."

"Then what are you doing? You dropped three bills. What's in it for you?"

"I bought some antiques."

"What?"

"Early American spittoons. Frank, it's not clear to me why it's any of your business how I spend my money."

"Look, amigo, you can collect early American barnyard manure for all I care, but don't cross me. If you don't like the smell of my money, I don't need you. Writers are a dime a dozen. Do you know what that two-bit Hearst is going to do with those three hundred dollars? Zing me with every one of them. What's your angle? Amigo, I haven't got you figured out yet so you've still got a job. But when you work for me you don't work against me. Comprende?"

"Comprendo."

He hung up. It seemed a marvel to Gamage that he had stood still for the assault. He'd come a long way in a short time. Hell, he told himself, a man scrounging for a buck has no character. He went back to his breakfast. It was beginning to look like another fine day in the City of the Sun.

4

Gamage found Mecca shielded behind a dusty windbreak of tamarisk trees as if hiding from sight. There were only a few scattered buildings and no one at all on the street. The town was wrapped in heat and silence and a kind of public scorn. He stopped in at the post office and got directions to Charlie Hastings' place.

He followed a dirt road giving rise to a view of the Salton Sea. The house sat in the airless shade of an aging date garden. A pump was tumbling water into the broad irrigation ditches and Gamage could see a couple of men on high ladders working like mechanics at the undersides of the palms.

The housekeeper, an Indian woman in carpet slippers, told Gamage that Hastings had gone out toward the help house. Gamage moved into the garden and a few moments later he saw a rangy old man coming toward him along the dikes. He wore a long-sleeved white shirt, buttoned at the neck, and a wide slouch hat. His face was narrow and mottled with scars; he had a turkey neck and the parboiled complexion of a redhead. He had to be in his seventies, Gamage thought, but he was as lean and sure-footed as a basketball player.

"Mr. Hastings?"

"Sorry to keep you waiting, sir."

"You didn't keep me waiting. My name is Gamage."

"I remember." He made an explanatory sweep with his hand. "We had a little excitement back there. The boys killed a sidewinder. You never met such a hot-tempered citizen. He had taken squatters rights on some shade near the help house. There's nothing more stupid than a sidewinder in my opinion, sir. He can't stand the sun, you know. Hates it. Fears it. If you put one of them devils in a box and set him out in the open sun for five minutes he expires. Dead. For sheer stupidity he's hard to beat. If he had any sense at all he'd move to a more hospitable climate. We're 197 feet below sea level and if there's anything we've got in over-abundance it's sunshine."

"I've noticed that," Gamage said.

"Of course, I'm not much smarter myself," Hastings said. His teeth were worn down to yellow nubs, like settings of dried corn, but they were unmistakably his own. "With this infernal skin of mine I've got to live in the shade like a grub. The doctors have to keep carving the sunshine out of my face. They warned me years ago to move off the desert, but I'm still here, sir, as you can see. To borrow an old saying, you can get a man out of the desert but you can't get the desert out of the man. Shall we sit on the porch and have some iced tea?"

"I'd like that fine." All the while Gamage felt Hastings' sable-lashed eyes on him, friendly but appraising, as if he had yet to decide to be interviewed about Martinka. Gamage decided not to hurry the subject along; he'd wait for Hastings to open that package himself.

As they walked back toward the house Gamage gazed along the row of exotic palms and the effect of the garden was lush and Oriental. "It's peaceful here," he said. "I'm not sure I'd want to leave it myself."

"Peaceful!" Hastings snorted. "I guess you haven't been around palms and that's to your credit, sir. Shows good sense. Why, these are about the worst-tempered trees in existence. They're either moody or lazy or just plain cranky. No two alike. You've got to treat each one as if she were a queen." He paused to give the nearest palm a kick. "Why, these are man-hating trees, sir. You work up there around the crown where the new growth is and you'll think you stuck your hand in a cat fight. The boys are dethorning them now. In a year we have to climb up each tree forty or fifty times for one reason or another. And how does the palm respond to our solicitation? She just keeps trying to grow out of reach. Ornery, you see."

Hastings paused to speak to one of the men aloft in Spanish, and then they continued on their way. Gamage felt that the old man enjoyed having someone new to talk to, and that his remarks were well-used and self-amusing.

"Ignorant, too," he went on. "You never saw such an ignorant tree. Mother Nature was looking the other way when she made the date palm. They never heard of the facts of life. When the harem comes in season we have to go up with a powder puff and pollinate them. If we leave it to the trees they don't know what to do. You can't even trust the bees. He'll find himself the King Solomon tree and get all pollened up, but he won't go near the female unless we've been there first. No, sir, there's only one thing that makes less sense than the date palm and that's the man who tries to grow them."

When they reached the porch the housekeeper had already set out a pitcher of iced tea on a table between two rattan chairs, and they settled themselves. Below the plantation, in the distance, the Salton Sea shimmered in the heat. Hastings began filling a pipe, watching Gamage out of the corner of his eyes. "I don't understand why Jesse sent you to talk to me. I can't guarantee to speak kindly about him."

"He didn't send me," Gamage said. "Neither did Frank. It was my own idea. As a matter of fact, Frank would be less than happy if he knew I was here talking to you."

"Frank!" Hastings snapped. "The only thing Frank knows about dates is that you buy them by the pound, and maybe he doesn't even know that. That boy is nothing like his father." He struck a match and sucked the flame into the pipe. "How is Jesse? Getting old like me, I suppose."

"I haven't seen him," Gamage said. "He's in Europe."

Hastings looked up. "Europe? Why, sir, one of the boys who works for me—I think it was Manuel—saw him out on the highway just a day or two ago."

Gamage put down his drink. "I only know what Frank tells me."

"Then you've listened to a lot of bosh. What is this book you say you're going to write?"

"The official family biography. At least, that's what I've been hired to do."

"It sounds like damned foolishness. Jesse never did anything worth putting in a book."

"Foolish or not, I'm going to write it."

"There's nothing I can tell you that he can't tell you for himself."

"He seems to be playing hide and seek with me, Mr. Hastings. You've known him a long time. With your help I might be able to keep the foolishness to a minimum."

"You want my opinion of him?"

"For a start."

Hastings tamped down the coals in his pipe. "Like son, like father."

"What does that mean?" Gamage asked.

"Jesse has turned his back on all his old friends, but I've been watching him. It hasn't been agreeable to see. He's getting more like Frank every day."

"In what way?"

"I guess I know Jesse Martinka as well as anyone in this valley, maybe better, and I know this. He's got no talent for money-getting. Frank's got no talent for anything else. Why, Jesse can't keep his check stubs straight. No sense of money at all."

"That's not easy to believe," Gamage smiled.

"Money didn't *interest* him. He never knew if he had ten cents in his pocket and he cared less. He could never remember to pay bills and if he had any money he couldn't remember to put it in the bank. He'd leave it in drawers or on the mantel—anywhere. I used to go through his place every couple of months and gather up all the bills I could find and put it in his account. When I first met him he was on the verge of losing his place because of some old lien he should have looked into before he bought it, but it was only when they tacked up the foreclosure notice that it occurred to him that he ought to try to hunt up some money to pay it off." He glanced at the glass of iced tea as if it were medicine waiting to be taken. "Jesse Martinka was the most impractical man in those days you ever saw. He was full of enthusiasms. By that time all he could think about and talk about was turning this valley into a date garden. And he did it."

"Yes."

"But now look what he's doing. He can't bulldoze those palms out of the way fast enough. Money-getting. Frank has educated him. Frank has turned him inside out." He took a swallow of iced tea and made a face. "That pyramid he's throwing up is nothing short of monstrous. If I didn't see what he was doing to this desert with my own eyes I wouldn't believe it."

"Maybe he doesn't intend to build it at all," Gamage said.

Hastings' eyes slid over. "What?"

"I have some diary entries he made in 1907. He says you invested in a lettuce field on the promise that the railroad would put in a spur line, which never materialized. I wonder if he's not up to the same thing. He'll sell off several million dollars worth of scrub desert on the promise of a pyramid which he never intends to complete."

Hastings' answer was instant. "No, sir. You can say anything unpleasant about Jesse Martinka and I'll agree with you, but there's one thing I know he's not and that's a swindler. If he says he's going to build a pyramid he'll build it."

Gamage was reluctant to scrap the idea. It seemed to him that Hastings was caught between his affection for an old friend and his contempt for what Martinka was up to. Gamage liked the man. For a banker his scorn for money-getting gave him the air of an eccentric, and Gamage was irresistibly drawn to the left-handed men of life. Despite the scarred motley of his face Hastings wasn't going to be put off the desert; he stayed on, defying the sun by living in the shade. He was as ornery as his trees and again the illusion of North Africa was so strong that Gamage turned to him and said, "Do you have to nail down the carpets to keep them from flying off?"

Hastings chuckled. "You'll get over that feeling. It's not quite the Arabian Nights around here, sir. There's a lot of hocum in the valley and always was. I'll say this for Jesse. He knows more about the culture of the date palm than the Arabs. For all we know he is an Arab."

"From Boston?"

"I never believed his name was Martinka. And I never believed he was from Boston. The accent wasn't quite right, you know."

"I didn't know."

"Martinka was his stage name. He fooled around in grand opera at one time. He could sing in three or four languages, I believe. Well-educated. At least, he gave that impression. When he drifted out here to the desert he kept his stage name and by now I don't suppose he even remembers what name he was born with. I never knew what it was. He was close-mouthed about himself."

Gamage lit a cigarette and felt suddenly that looking into Martinka's life was going to be like peering into a well without being able to see the bottom. If the man had assumed another name there had to be something in those years before he turned up on the desert. "Didn't he ever make a slip in conversation? Betray himself in some way?"

"Not in my presence, sir." He took another gulp of iced tea and scowled. "This stuff is for Englishmen and old ladies and we're neither one. Emilia! I'm not allowed strong beverages, you understand. Emilia! But I learned a thing or two from the Muslims about *that*. Their religion prohibits the use of intoxicating beverages, but show me an Arab and I'll show you a demijohn of laqmi. That's palm wine. They solve their moral dilemma by refusing to admit that laqmi is intoxicating—even though a demijohn is sufficient to guarantee a full assortment of brawls and broken heads. Man's great gift in coming to terms with a hostile environment is his remarkable ability to lie to himself, sir. Emilia! Run out to the help house and see if you can steal us some beer!"

In due time the housekeeper appeared with a quart of cold beer and for the next hour Hastings recalled the early days in the valley and his trips into Algeria and Egypt and Tripolitania to buy offshoots. Gamage made occasional notes on the back of an envelope. Since the local bank backed away from making loans to the desert ranchers and truck farmers for the purpose of growing dates, still an experimental crop, Martinka conceived the idea of establishing a bank expressly for that purpose. "Once Jesse got hold of an idea, no matter how fanciful, he went at it twenty-five hours a day. He knew no more about running a bank than he did about pearl diving in Japan, but a trivial detail like that didn't slow him down. Since I had once worked as a teller in a bank he made me president and floated a stock issue in Los Angeles. They looked upon it as blue-sky stock and wouldn't touch it, but there are always a few souls who can't resist a spellbinder. Jesse button-holed anyone who couldn't outrun him. In September of 1912 we opened the doors of "The American Date Growers Bank of Thebes" in a vacant store with a capitalization of $40,000. Any damned fool who wanted to grow dates could step in out of the sun and walk out with money in his hand. Of course, the bank down the street, long gone now, thought Jesse was a madman. There were times when I was willing to agree with them. After that first day of business I wouldn't allow him on the premises. We'd have had a bank failure in forty-eight hours. But in January of the next year—that was 1913— there came the big freeze. The temperature dropped like a plummet. It hit 15-degrees in Indio and 13-1/2-degrees in Thebes. That's cold, sir, when you're growing hot-house crops. When the freeze lifted about the only things left standing were the date palms. The money crops were ruined. It made a lot of date growers out of truck farmers. Jesse himself didn't know the palms could sit out a freeze—they can withstand anything above 5-degrees. About the only thing affected are the male flowers. The cold turns them sterile.

Now Jesse had had lumber for a house carted in from Los Angeles. When the freeze was at its worst he ordered his Mexican boys to drag that fine lumber into the irrigation ditches and set fire to it. That was the most expensive smudging operation in the history of California, I suppose, and those trees suffered more from the smoke and sparks than from the cold. But he figured he'd saved his plantation. Until the weather cleared and he found out that all the other date gardens around had come through without even a candle to shield them from the cold. All he said was that he never liked the house he was going to build anyway. He had the ability to laugh at himself. Before the year was out he had thrown up a long shed to fumigate and grade and pack dates under his Sphinx label. He had an instinct. Right from the first he sensed that the future of the valley was in the Deglet Noor. It's not the biggest date by a long shot and it's about the fussiest palm to grow. It needs so much heat to ripen that one of the biggest date growers in the

Imperial Valley dug up his entire plantation around 1915 and moved his trees up here. It just wasn't hot enough down there, if you can imagine that. As it turned out the Salton Basin here is the only patch of desert this side of the Sahara where you can coax the Deglet Noor into behaving, and your headaches are just beginning. The berries will mummify on the tree unless you irrigate every day during the ripening period. You have to give them the equivalent of about 120 inches of rainfall a year. The Arabs call it a hot date—they eat three or four pounds of dates a day and not much else and they call a date hot if it burns the stomach and cold if it doesn't. The Ghars is a cold date. But none of this bothered Jesse. For him, there was no variety but the Deglet Noor. If you were willing to coddle it along you had the noblest date of them all, sir—mild but sweet, none better. It's the nearest thing to growing candy on a tree there is. But Jesse hadn't the least idea of getting rich in the bargain. He'd found a mission in life, you might say, and that was to put Coachella dates on every table in the country. He was a man carrying the gospel. It was his religion. BeJesus John Amador dubbed him the Date King around 1920 and the title has stuck through the years. Until lately."

The housekeeper served lunch on the porch and Gamage noticed that Hastings had skipped over the early Mexico adventure. Finally Gamage said, "I'd like to back you up to 1910. That's the year you two got involved in the Madero revolution, isn't it?"

"No, sir. It was the spring of 1911."

"Is there any reason why Martinka wouldn't want to talk about it?"

"A man doesn't always like to recall the damned fool things he did as a young man."

"Like what?"

"Didn't Frank tell you?"

"No."

Hastings tucked a napkin into his shirt and grinned. "Jesse did some gun running, you might say."

Gamage's eyebrows lifted. He smiled. Martinka was beginning to seem altogether admirable. "You're not kidding, are you?"

"No, sir. The U.S. government had put down an arms embargo and it's a wonder Jesse wasn't put in the penitentiary. Of course, he was a rank amateur at it. But he was devilish clever."

"Why did he go? What lured him into someone else's revolution?"

"A lot of young fellows were beating their way to El Paso to get into the sport of shooting at the federales. It was close by and that made it handy. It was the nearest thing to a foreign legion we ever had around here. Díaz was dictator of Mexico, a first-rate tyrant, but the sentiment on this side of the border was for Madero—the odds were so much against him. Jesse woke up one morning and decided he was in the wrong place. He had to go, and I had nothing better to do at the moment. I thought at first it was a lark. Jesse had been locked up in the valley with one foot in the grave for four years, but now he had got it out, and I figured he was looking for a diversion. But I was wrong. He was dead serious. There was a dark place inside him and he suddenly found out that he had to go. It was as if he was uncomfortable to be inhabiting the same world with Díaz. When we got to El Paso damned fools like us were arriving on every train. They called us filibusters. The revolution was across the river in Juárez. You could watch the street sniping from the rooftops and that appealed to me, but Jesse couldn't wait to put his foot back in the grave. We crossed over to look for Madero. His insurrectos were grouping in the hills west of Juárez. The real battle hadn't yet got started. Madero was a saintly little man, a vegetarian, with no stomach for violence. It was his idea to bring the federales to their knees by speechmaking. His general staff kept begging to start the attack, but Madero was also a spiritualist and he was forever conferring with Napoleon on strategy. *Mañana* was always a better time to attack than today. We learned that his headquarters were in a one room adobe near the dam and Jesse and I started through the streets in that general direction. It was then that Jesse and I parted company. His theory was that the safest place to walk was right down the middle of the street instead of slinking along the walls from doorway to doorway. I disagreed. I took to the walls and he went strolling out in the open as if it were Sunday afternoon. He looked too simple-minded to shoot at and no one bothered him, but I got my hat shot off before I had gone a block. I beat my way back to the barroom at the Hotel Sheldon in El Paso. I didn't see Jesse for two days. The federales were holed up in the town cuartel, an adobe fortification used as a drill yard. They had plenty of machine guns and had brought up mountain cannons and Canet 75s. The insurrectos, being mostly farmers and vaqueros, had nothing larger than 30-30 Winchester rifles, and they were going to get themselves slaughtered. Now, in front of the El Paso city hall there was a patch of grass with a small brass cannon, a muzzle-loading relic from the days of the Alamo for all I know. I was sound asleep in the hotel when Jesse appeared around two in the morning and got me out of bed. He had commandeered an old touring car and rounded up a couple of husky American filibusters. We ended up in front of the city hall, got a chain around the canon and hauled it off the lawn. We threw a tarpaulin over it and snuck it through the dark side streets. When we got to the river there was a raft waiting. We secured the cannon and swam the raft over to the Mexican side. When we rolled it into headquarters Madero's aide woke him up and when he saw that lone piece of field artillery he got as excited as a chicken. He gave Jesse a field promotion on the spot. Made him a colonel in the Maderista army, which was about equal to corporal in any other army. The insurrectos had no uniforms—a man was lucky to have a few rags on his back. Madero wrapped a strip of Mexican tri-color around Jesse's hat, which designated him an officer. The next morning, while the city fathers of El Paso awoke to discover the lawn cannon gone, the insurrectos were swarming around it, rubbing their hands over it and cracking brave jokes. From the standpoint of morale, that brass cannon was worth a division. After that, you couldn't stop Colonel Jesse. Not far away across the New Mexico line there was a small detachment of U.S. troopers stationed with two machine guns that they kept under tight-fitting waterproof covers. One morning *they* woke up, unlaced the canvas covers and found two wooden dummies. Jesse had a flare for that kind of mischief. I think he began to fancy himself as the Robin Hood of the Maderista cause. Finally the insurrectos got tired of waiting in the hills for Bonaparte to sound the spiritualistic bugle and they began moving into Juárez to attack. Madero was furious, but it was a kind of spontaneous combustion and there was nothing he could do but order the attack that was already underway. The noise was fearful. Jesse and I were helping to move the brass cannon toward town when dust boiled up along the road ahead and a yell went up around us. The federale cavalry was charging us. There was no time to do anything but jump behind the nearest boulder, which we did in great numbers. However, that galloping dust cloud didn't turn out to be cavalry, sir. The rattle of machine guns and rifle fire and the smell of powder had panicked every dog in town and they were pouring through the streets and finally out along the main road, along the river, in one long mad pack. There were thousands of them, yelping and barking and yowling with their tails between their legs and their tongues hanging out like watch fobs. It was sad to see, but it was funny too. When we got the cannon to the outskirts it had about as much range as a faucet leaking water. But we loaded it with rocks and old nails and it made a powerful report and that pleased the insurrectos mightily. They would attack for a while and then retire to the hills to eat and siesta. Madero had some European filibusters on his military staff, men who had some experience at warfare, and this tomfoolery horrified them. But they couldn't get that rag tag army all fighting at once. Still, those Chihuahua peons and bandits knew how to fight a Mexican war. They'd return to the front refreshed and in jolly spirits while the federales, going by the book, stuck to their posts without sleep and wore themselves out to no purpose. Jesse and I returned to the Hotel Sheldon at night to sit around the barroom for a few hours and then get a good night's sleep. It was a highly civilized procedure in my opinion. The federales had been cleared out of the section around the international bridge and it was like going to work in the morning. Neither side had any medical help, but the federales had its camp followers who nursed the wounded. The insurrectos were too new at the game for that. Women from El Paso would come over in cars or taxis and bandage up the rebels. As the battle for Juarez proceeded Jesse made a bad discovery and it took the sap out of him. He found out he couldn't shoot another man, even a federale. He tried, but finally I saw him turn his rifle over to a nearby insurrecto, a twelve-year-old boy, who knew what to do with it. That was the end of the war for Jesse. He was too humiliated to go on with it. Then the federales collapsed and General Navarro surrendered. The town belonged to the Maderistas and they made the best of it. Jesse came across a couple of charos who had lassoed a pretty Mexican girl, a camp follower, who had been trying to escape across the river. She had her brother with her, a boy of ten or so with a soup-bowl haircut. She must have been seventeen or eighteen. The insurrectos dragged them back soaking wet with a good many coarse jokes. The dress clung and her long black hair dripped down her back like melted wax. She knew what was going to happen to her and so did Jesse. And he knew that the tri-color band on his hat wouldn't stop them. Jesse was wearing sleeve garters and he looked around for a stout twig. He got behind a boulder and fashioned himself a sling shot. The vaqueros had slipped off their horses and were cackling and laughing around the girl. Jesse loaded the sling shot with a sharp pebble and gave one of the horses a bee sting on the rump. And then the second. Those animals bolted. If a poor Mexican has to make a choice between a good horse and a woman he's going to go for the livestock. The charos began yelling and waving their big hats and running after the horses. When Jesse tried to approach the girl she and the boy began stoning him. They thought he was up to the same mischief. Finally he gave it up and walked away in disgust. El Paso was full of refugees. A couple of nights later he spotted this pair huddled together in a doorway. Federale or not, he was smitten with that girl. She was barefooted and clung to that boy as if he were a doll. But she was fine looking, black-eyed, and the smoothest skin you ever saw. He introduced himself, very courtly, and ended up installing them in our hotel room while we passed the night in the barroom. We were going home the next day. In the morning he took them around to the Popular Dry Goods Store and put clothes on their backs. Her name was Camilla. She and the boy had been camp following her husband and he had been killed a few days before. They had no people and nowhere to go. Nothing would do but that Jesse bring them back to the valley with us like trophies of war. And that's what happened. He made the boy go to school and put Camilla up with the Missouri Girl. The revolution still had years to go. Pretty soon the Maderistas were popping away at their former comrades the Orozquistas. And then there was Huerta and Carranza and Poncho Villa, but Jesse sadly followed it only in the newspapers. I don't know what he was really looking for among the insurrectos, but maybe it was nothing more than that strip of tri-color around his hat. He was Colonel Martinka from then on. There was a streak of vanity in him. Still is. But he was never fond of talking about those Mexican days. It was as if he had failed some manhood rite, sir. That was damned foolishness, of course. However, he had the satisfaction of seeing the Díaz regime go under and the insurrectos inherit the earth."

Hastings wiped his lips with the napkin and dug out his pipe. Gamage couldn't have hoped for a more openhanded interview and it seemed to him that those weeks in Mexico must have fixed certain elements in Martinka's character in the way that fire hardens clay. A man ambling down the center of a street asking for a sniper's bullet was fighting a different battle. He wasn't looking for death, Gamage thought, but a guarantee of life. He was testing his fate as if he wasn't at all convinced that the sun-cure had any permanence. If he needed a safe conduct pass to the future, Juárez had given it to him. Gamage stirred his coffee. "But Martinka had a finger shot off, didn't he?"

Hastings looked up from his pipe. "No. Not at Juárez."

"I'd heard that."

"You heard wrong. That finger was gone before he ever turned up here on the desert."

"Do you know how it happened?"

"He never volunteered that information, sir, and I never asked him."

"Do you think it's important?" Gamage asked.

"In my opinion, it's probably as important as anything you'd want to know about him if you're going to put him in a book. Losing a finger is nothing to be ashamed of, but he was downright unnatural about it. I was around Jesse for a week before I noticed it for the first time. He was crafty. He had a way of keeping the hand folded so you wouldn't notice it, or in a pocket, or he'd keep on his work gloves. I used to wonder about it. It was my suspicion, and still is, that Jesse was hiding a good deal more than a missing finger. If you could get him to tell you about it I think you'd be doing yourself a service."

Gamage shrugged. Chances of digging out anything prior to 1907 seemed remote unless he could bring himself face to face with Martinka, and maybe not even then. He lit a cigarette and the two men sat silently for a while watching the tree crew at work on the ladders. Finally Gamage asked, "Did Martinka ever marry Camilla?"

"He did."

"Frank seems to think they were just living together."

"There was always a little talk in that direction, but it wasn't true. The wedding took place in Mexicali in 1913. I was there. So was George Waggener and his wife and so was the Missouri Girl. But some folks around here looked upon Jesse pretty much as a squaw man. Mexicans were stoop labor, peons, and a gentleman didn't marry one. That's how the talk started."

"Is Waggener still alive?"

"No."

"The Missouri Girl?"

"Alive and kicking."

"Where will I find her?"

"In Thebes, where she's always been."

"Is she still known by that name?"

"No. There's hardly anyone left from those days. She married a man named Swanson, who's dead now. Jerusha Swanson. You won't have any trouble finding her."

Later they drove to the store for beer and it was four in the afternoon before Gamage left.

5

When Gamage stopped for his room key the desk clerk handed him a sealed envelope that had been left in his box and told him that Conny Sargent was waiting in the bar. He glanced at the clock and crossed the tile floor to the archway leading into the bar. Conny was seated alone and when she looked up she seemed even less happy to see him then at breakfast. "In another three or four hours I would have given you up," she said.

"I'm sorry I'm late, Conny," he said. The bar was crowded and noisy. "I didn't think you'd show up."

"I need the money."

"That bad?"

"I may clear out," she said. "Alaska, maybe. I need a change of climate. Shall we get to work?"

"Is my room all right, Conny?"

"It couldn't matter less to me. And the name is Miss Sargent."

"I'll try to remember."

Gamage left the door open, creating a faint, warmed-over breeze, and she took a chair with her back to the window. She stuck a spare pencil through her dark hair, crossed her knees and turned back the green cover of a shorthand tablet. Out of long habit he worked best at the typewriter, but he began to pace back and forth to collect his thoughts. Her presence in the room distracted him. She waited, pencil poised, with a look of cool efficiency. "Miss Sargent," he said, "I'm sorry to see you pursue this life of money-getting like the rest of us. I was becoming genuinely fond of you."

"I'll try to bear up under your disappointment."

"I'd like to think that you kept our appointment out of some nobler motive, Miss Sargent. Like sheer hatred or a modest affection."

"Shall we get on with the dictation?"

"Miss Sargent, you have very pretty eyes, but I'd appreciate it if you'd use them for something other than ice picks. I'm afraid to turn my back."

"Bully."

He ripped open the envelope the desk clerk had handed him, and found a piece of newspaper folded up inside. He unfolded it and saw that letters had been carved in it with a razor blade. He spread it open to read the message.

GET THE HELL OUT OF TOWN!
YOU ARE WARNED! I MEAN IT!

Gamage refolded the paper and stuffed it into the envelope. He moved to the phone.

"Will you be keeping me long?" Conny asked.

"As long as possible," Gamage said. "I'll have dinner sent up and we'll work through the evening."

He got the desk clerk on the phone and asked who had left the envelope. The man didn't know. He had simply found it in the box with the room key. Gamage thanked him and hung up.

Finally he tore it up and dropped it in the waste basket. His name hadn't been on it. It may have been meant for someone else. If Frank wanted him to leave town he wouldn't be so indirect about it. Or was it a message from Colonel Martinka? The thought startled him for a moment.

Gamage turned and began to dictate. "Working title," he said. "Make it— *The Fires of Heaven*. The Life of Colonel Jesse Martinka. Remind me to find out if there's a middle name. All right. Chapter One...."

CHAPTER FIVE

1

On two or three occasions that next day Gamage lifted the phone to call Ginny, but in each case he changed his mind. Her own silence seemed to him a warning and he made himself wait for some word from her. Late Friday morning she called. Could he come out to the house? She said that Frank wanted to see him, but that, it was clear, was for the switchboard.

He would have preferred to meet her somewhere else, but he went along with it. She was waiting for him in the doorway when he drove up. For a moment he didn't like it. He had a fleeting impression of a girl in the doorway of a crib, but the association, he felt, was malicious and out of place.

The house was in cool shadows. She closed the door after him and leaned against it, half-smiling. "Don't look so gloomy, darling."

He felt a quick, inner response to the timbre of her voice. "Where's Frank?"

"He had to fly into Los Angeles for a few hours."

"The housegirl?"

"I sent her away for the occasion. We're alone."

He drew her to him, alive to the touch of her body, and he felt as if he had been holding his breath for days. How had he managed to stay away? They lingered in each other's arms and for a few hours at least he was willing to pretend that Frank didn't exist.

They went outside to the loggia, where coffee was waiting, and he was glad that this wasn't going to be the hit-and-run affair of their hour together in the Mexicali motel room. A gull from the Salton Sea was floating in the pool. There was plenty of time and they sat in the marble shade, watching the seagull, and enjoying the unhurried luxury of being together. He found it easy to imagine what life with Ginny would be like. They had wasted five years fumbling around with strangers.

She asked him how the book was coming and he told her that he had the writing underway, but that Frank would not be entirely pleased with the manuscript. "I heard Colonel Martinka was seen in Thermal just the other day."

She dismissed it with a glance. "But that's impossible," she said.

After a while she left him to change into a bathing suit. He looked about him, intimidated by the marble splendor, and wondered what kind of future he could bankroll for Ginny. The book money would only last for a little while. Ginny returned, pulling on a bathing cap, and told him that she had laid out a suit for him.

She went out into the sun and stood for a moment on the coping. Then she dove in and the seagull went flapping away into the sky. She swam to the pink marble shell at the far end of the pool and returned underwater. She looked sleek and golden below the surface—a marvelous animal, he thought. She bobbed up smiling. "Come on in, darling."

"I'd rather watch you. You're beautiful, Ginny."

But after a moment he returned to the house and got into the swimming trunks. Their time together was setting a pace of its own, a beat, and he was with it. When he came out into the sun he saw that she had pulled off her cap. Wet hair clinging to her neck reminded him of Camilla years before they were born—that moment when Martinka had first seen her.

Gamage dove in, swimming through the cool underwater twilight, and it was only after he came up near the shell that he saw that Ginny had cast off her suit. She slid away from him, smiling; he submerged and went after her. He caught her ankle at the center of the pool and she came to him. They rose to the surface together and she threw back her blonde hair. They looked into each other's eyes, laughing softly, and after a moment returned to the cool privacy underwater. They swam around each other and he watched her tanned breasts exquisitely free and responsive to the currents of swimming. When they climbed out he wrapped a towel around her and they sat together at the coping to let the desert sun dry them.

Finally they went inside to the den where light filtered through the Moorish grillwork onto a charpoy with yellow cushions and gleaming bronze legs. They made love. The language of love was silence and afterward they watched the grilled shadows, somehow like butterflies pinned to the walls. When it was time for him to leave she dressed in gold pants and a sleeveless black top. She told him that Frank hadn't let her out of his sight and that they would have to be careful not to arouse his jealousy. If he thought she was in love with someone else he would hold onto her out of rage and spite. She gave the marriage another few weeks and then she would be free of him. Gamage left.

2

On impulse Gamage turned off the highway toward Villa Martinka. He let down the barrier chain and continued along the gravel road. When he reached the edge of the date palms he stopped so that the rattling against the fenders wouldn't announce him, and walked the rest of the way. He kept to the trees. He wasn't sure what he would find at the house, if anything, but Frank wouldn't be around to get in his hair. The plantation was heated and still. When he could see the house he stopped and looked at the empty white flagpole—nobody home. After a moment he realized that he was hearing the faint sounds of a radio. His eyes traveled to an upstairs window standing half-open. He listened for another moment and then stepped on his cigarette and crossed to the veranda.

He tried the door, but found it locked. He hesitated and then rang the bell. Almost instantly the radio went out. Gamage rang again, but he knew no one was going to answer the door.

Finally he walked along the veranda to the rear. He looked through a window and could see the kitchen faucet dripping. He opened the screen door and tried the knob. The door was unlocked. He convinced himself that the only way he could arrange a meeting with Colonel Martinka was to walk in.

It was a Mexican style kitchen with tiled counters and floor. He stopped, glancing at the fresh drip of the faucet, and shut it off. When he came out into the living room a golden oak stairway led his eye to the heavy stillness above.

"Colonel Martinka?"

There was no response. The furniture, under sheets, formed cadaverous shapes around him. He stared for a moment at a large oil painting on the wall, a woman in a blue cloche hat in the style of the twenties, with her hand touching the shoulder of a boy in a French sailor suit. It was Madam Martinka, he supposed, and Frank at the age of four or five. His eyes were as expressionless as a doll's, but she looked out over the room as if standing guard. Gamage turned from the painting and again glanced up the stairs. There seemed nothing to do but finish what he had started.

"Colonel Martinka?"

The upstairs hallway was attic hot. He found the room where the window had been opened and looked in. From the dressing table he took it to be a woman's bedroom, with the bedding stripped off and the carpets rolled back. The sheet covering a striped chaise had been thrown off and lay in a heap on the floor. There had been someone in there, he knew, and he thought he smelled cigar smoke.

"Who's here?"

He walked in and looked around. It was a large room with rose fleur-de-lis wallpaper. It was a moment before he saw the scuffed guitar case behind the bed and when he looked back at the door Barbachano was standing there grinning.

"I ought to notify the fuzz," the kid said. "You're breaking and entering."

"What are you doing here?"

"I live here."

"Since when?"

"Since a couple of days." Barbachano's eyes shifted in a cautious glance. "But don't let me worry you. I won't bleat on you."

"Thanks."

"As long as you don't bleat on me."

Gamage looked at him, angry at first, and then amused by the offer. Barbachano had a gamin-quick mind; to Gamage the situation seemed suddenly comic. "Pick up your guitar and clear out of here."

"How about a lift into town? It's a long walk."

Gamage took a last look around. His dark intuition about the house had yielded nothing but a teenage half-breed. "Come on."

They left, setting the lock on the back door, and started out along the gravel road. Barbachano snapped on a transistor radio in his shirt pocket and Gamage looked at him.

"Did you pick that up in there?"

"Naw. I don't go that route. I didn't touch anything. I bought this. I like to listen to the news."

"You didn't have that much money the last time I saw you."

"I got lucky." He tuned in a Mexican station playing mariachi music. "Look, I don't have the family silver in my hip pocket. I told you, I don't go that way. All I did was smoke some of his cigars. There's a closet full of them. Must be fifty boxes. White Owls. That's a cheap cigar. I figure I did him a favor to smoke 'em."

"Cigars." Gamage figured he was exaggerating for the sake of story. "It's a good thing I came along before you stunted your growth."

"Yeah. And I kept the toilets flushed. They ought to pay me. The donikers will dry up in the heat if you don't keep 'em flushed."

They reached the jeep and Gamage started it up. Barachano had a pleasantly defiant approach to the realities and a self-correcting conscience. "Aside from smoking cigars and listening to the news what were you doing around here?" Gamage asked.

"I told you. I kipped down in the place. No one was using it. The old ghee is gone. When the big heat starts the money leaves. They give the desert back to us natives. You can take your pick of empty houses. Live off the land, so to speak. But all I found to eat in there was some canned asparagus and some cat food. I was getting pretty tired of that diet. I'm hungry. I was just about ready to get gone when you turned up." He stretched out in the bucket seat and pulled the straw hat down over his eyes. "What's your story?"

Gamage looked over at him. "I'm Arsen Lupin."

"What's that?"

"Apprentice jewel thief."

"Is that what you're writing a book about?"

"Where did you hear that?"

"On the news."

"I'm writing about Martinka. Your recent host. Did you ever meet him?"

"I saw him once."

"When?"

The kid hesitated. "You going to put it in the book?"

"Sure."

"On the level?"

"Absolutely."

"I saw him take a leak once."

Gamage smiled. This kid knew his lines. "I'll devote a chapter to it."

"On the level. He didn't know anybody was around. It was up on the high desert. I got cousins up there. Mohaves. He just whipped it out and made a puddle in the sand. That was six-eight years ago. I was a kid. The Mohaves visit it twice a year now. Like a shrine."

3

When Gamage returned to town BeJesus John, with a pile of papers under his arm like an aging newsboy, was dropping off copies of the *Sunset* at the tobacco shop across the street. Barbachano thanked Gamage for the lift and ambled away with his guitar case. Gamage crossed the street and met BeJesus John along the arcade. "I see you're still publishing."

"That's right. I found a financial angel. Some damned fool giving money away."

"Can you take time for a beer?"

"It's a temptation," BeJesus John grinned. "I'll meet you after I drop these off. My readership, such as it is, has got to be served. Have one with my compliments."

"I'll be over at the hotel," Gamage said.

BeJesus John scurried on to the drugstore and Gamage paused. He looked back along the arcade toward the tobacco and magazine shop and decided to check out Martinka and his closet full of cigars. The only sense he could make of it was that Barbachano hadn't been talking sense.

The man behind the counter had a fresh copy of the *Sunset* spread out on the counter and looked up through bifocals.

"Let me have a pack of Camels," Gamage said. "Make it a carton. Does Colonel Martinka do business in here?"

"That's right."

"Do you mind telling me what he smokes?"

"Cigars."

"I want to send him a gift. What brand?"

"White Owls."

"You'd think he'd smoke dollar cigars."

"You'd think so. But he don't. He's been buying White Owls for the ten years I've been here. Regular."

"How does he buy them?"

"What do you mean?"

"A few dozen boxes at a time?"

"Nobody buys cigars that way. He gets 'em like everybody else—one box at a time."

"Is he a heavy smoker?"

"I wouldn't say so. A box lasts him better than a month."

"When was the last time he was in?"

The man glared at Gamage. "You're asking me a lot of questions."

"Yes."

"He was in about three weeks ago, I guess it was."

"I heard he rarely leaves the house."

"He keeps to himself. But he stops in, him or the Madam. She fetches for him a good deal."

"But he was in three weeks ago."

"I didn't say that."

"I thought you did."

"It was the Madam, as I recall. She had brought his shoes next door to get soled, and she stopped in here. Are you a detective or something?"

"No. Just nosey."

Gamage paid for his cigarettes and left. And then it dawned on him that if Barbachano had seen a closet filled with cigar boxes they had probably been empties. It made an eccentric collection, on a par with saving string, but it was human and until a better explanation came along he'd buy it.

He took a barstool by the window, ordered a bottle of Mexican beer and opened up the weekly. It was a skinny four pages, it would hardly line a garbage can, and he wondered why he had bothered to prolong its life. It would drop into Frank's hands. All he had to do was wait.

An item caught Gamage's eye. He recognized the name Morejohn. Gamage had run out of gas there. Morejohn. The retired Navy chief with the White Russian wife.

WIND UNCOVERS SKELETON
IN DUNES NEAR MOREJOHN

Sheriff's deputies yesterday reported the discovery of human remains that had been buried for several years in the dunes east of Morejohn.

Shifting sands, driven by the crosswind in that area, uncovered the skeleton.

Chief Walter Morejohn, U.S.N., ret., came across the bones two miles east of his gas station while out hunting a bobcat which had been coming too close to his place for comfort.

Deputies speculate that the man, identity unknown, may have been a victim of the desert. Possibly a transient, he may have become lost during the summer heat and perished. There was no evidence of violence. Items of clothing have yielded no information.

A search of missing persons records is being made.

BeJesus John found him and laid his hat on the bar. "Don't read it too fast," he said. "It's got to last you all week."

"I see that Morejohn got his name in the paper. I'll bet he's a big man in Morejohn."

"I write that story three or four times a year. There's always some damned fool who goes wandering off, rock hunting or something, and gets himself lost. Or if he finally makes the road he steps on a snake. The snakes like the highway at night. Asphalt holds the heat and they cuddle up like it was a feather bed. But it's getting so civilized around here now a blindfolded idiot couldn't lose himself. The only risk he'd run would be to step into a swimming pool and drown. Are you buying the drinks or am I?"

"You forget. I'm the last of the big spenders."

"In that case I'll have a small beaker of sour mash. It's that time of day."

"BeJesus John, you're going to have to find yourself another angel when the money runs out."

"Is that what you wanted to tell me?"

"No. But look. Newspapers don't sell for a nickel anymore. If it's worth publishing at all it's worth a dime. When's the last time you raised your ad rates? The first World War? I'll bet it costs you more money to print these ads, such as they are, than you charge for them."

"I wouldn't be surprised."

"A business manager is about the only thing that's going to save you."

"I can't abide those gentlemen. Adding machines for brains. Always sticking their noses into editorial matters." BeJesus John scratched the back of his hand like a man scaling fish. "Anyhow, no man with a business head would come to work for the *Sunset*. If he did it would be a guarantee that he had no business head."

"You're right," Gamage said.

"I'll muddle through. Don't worry about me. I haven't missed an issue in forty-eight years." He raised his glass. "Chin-chin."

Gamage wondered how he had believed even for a moment that BeJesus John and his sickly newspaper could stop Martinka and his pyramid. BeJesus John was dreaming. But the audacity of the proposition still appealed to Gamage. "How's the response on your petition? Any action?"

"Action? Why, it's set the valley on fire. We must have forty or fifty signatures."

"Anyone under seventy years of age?"

"I doubt it."

"Do you expect the Board of Supervisors to pay the slightest attention to it?"

"You've put your finger on the weak spot," BeJesus John grinned. "Only two or three members of the board can read. It presents a problem."

4

Gamage had some 10,000 words on paper. Conny was spending the mornings with him, taking dictation until two or three o'clock. She would return with the material typed up the following day.

But this was Sunday morning. She hadn't shown up, of course, and he was surprised that he missed having her around—cold-eyed, sharp-tongued and efficient. Someone to trade lines with. There was nothing to do but read the paper, and he tried, but the metropolitan news seemed as remote to him as the foreign news. He gave it up and stood at the window. On two occasions he had called the Missouri Girl, but she refused to see him. Then, yesterday, he had received a note asking him to call on her at four that afternoon. That left him most of the day. The hotel room bored him. The small hum of the fan was getting on his nerves. From the window he looked down on the deserted plaza with its dusty clump of palms. He could see the roofing over the pink arcade below with the black tar blistering and bubbling in the heat. The days were getting hotter, if that were possible, and the desert outside of town seemed rendered of color.

He thought of Ginny lounging about that marble hogan Frank had built in the hills. He felt violently lonely, as if he must be the only man alive in town, and turned from the window. He had to see Ginny. He'd call Frank and invent some excuse to run out there. But when he lifted the phone he called Conny Sargent instead. She was a long time answering and he looked at his watch. It was not quite ten o'clock.

"Hello," she said.

"Did I give you the day off?"

"Oh, it's you."

"What were you doing?"

"Sitting by the phone. Waiting for you to call."

"I'm sorry if I woke you."

"Sure you are."

"I feel like dictating."

"Fine. Get a pencil and talk to yourself. I'll be in tomorrow."

"What do you do on Sundays? Sharpen your tongue for the rest of the week?"

"What do you want?"

"Is there anything to do around here except wish you were somewhere else?"

"Why don't you collect potsherds?" she said. "It makes a nice hobby."

"How fast can you get dressed?"

"Why?"

"Either you come in or I'll run out to your place."

"Look, Mr. Gamage, I never mix socially with my employers."

"Then you're fired. I'll be out in ten minutes."

He hung up and smiled. He put on a shirt, beat the dust out of his hat and left. He needed someplace to go and Conny would do fine.

She lived in a subdivision called Sun Blessed Dunes outside of town. The remnants of a date garden could be seen, hacked through like a jungle, to provide homesites. He had never been there before and cruised the street looking at house numbers. He found her place at the end, a ranch-style house, lime-green, with a wide grapestake overhang for shade. A For Sale sign was hung on an old date palm near the parking. The air was dry and scented with mesquite.

Gamage rang the bell. The drapes were drawn, there wasn't a sound inside, and he wondered if he had the wrong number. But he stayed with it and finally the door opened and Conny looked out. She had on a robe and yellow mules and she had only one eye open.

"It's you," she said.

"Yes."

"You're not coming in."

"Suit yourself. I'll wait for you."

"I'd have told you not to bother, but you hung up."

"Don't close the door," he said.

"Can't you see that I'm trying to sleep?"

"It's a beautiful day. We'll go somewhere. It's not more than 105 in the shade."

"Goodbye, Mr. Gamage."

"You can't leave me standing out here in the sun. I may burst into flame."

"Beat it, Gamage."

"Is that coffee I smell?"

"Next door. Try there." She shut the door, but as he reached up to knock the door opened again. She glared at him. "All right, damn it, come in."

"Thank you, m'am."

"Haven't you got anything better to do than hang around here?"

"It's the best thing I could think of," he said. "You must have got in late last night."

"You'll find books, magazines and my ex-husband's lead soldier collection. Amuse yourself. I'm going back to sleep."

She left him standing in the living room and disappeared along a hall, the mules on her feet slapping lightly as she walked, and then he heard a door close. He rubbed his jaw. That, he supposed, was that.

He looked around. There was a fireplace with some colored bottles on it and a large cast stone coffee table. The room was pleasantly cool. Mexican rugs with the look of being hand-woven made an agreeable gallery of the floor. He saw an easel with a half-finished canvas on it and several paintings of the desert on the walls. She painted. He was surprised.

He ended up knocking around the small kitchen. He started a pot of coffee. He found an omelet pan and decided to try his skill with it. He broke a couple of eggs and stopped. He might as well go the whole route. Bacon. He rummaged through the refrigerator and then arranged the last slices in another pan and turned on the fire. He cut up a piece of cheese and dropped a lump of butter in the pan. He put bread in the toaster. When the butter had browned he poured in the eggs, added the cheese and in no time at all the coffee was boiling over, the toast was smoking and the omelet was sticking to the pan. When he glanced at the doorway Conny was standing there, arms folded and a shoulder against the jamb.

"What," she said, "are you doing?"

"Go back to sleep. I can handle this. I hold the Cordon Bleu."

She came over and turned down the coffee. "What are you cremating in that pan?"

"Bacon. I like it crisp."

She got out a couple of coffee mugs and set them on the table.

"This omelet pan sticks," he said.

The toaster delivered two smoking embers. She threw them out and loaded in fresh slices. She took the pan out of his hand and gave the omelet a half-flip, folding it over on itself. It began to puff up.

"Beautiful," he said. "I can't understand what I did wrong."

She slipped the omelet off on a plate and handed it to him. "Sit down."

"That coffee smells good, doesn't it?"

"All the way to the Mexican border."

"I didn't mean to disturb your sleep."

"Of course not."

He ground pepper over the omelet and she got his toast. Then she filled the coffee mugs, sat down and lit a cigarette. He glanced at her. She looked up. She made a slight concession to the moment. She smiled.

"Thanks," he said.

"For nothing."

"You've got a nice place here, Conny. What's the For Sale sign doing out front?"

"I'm trying to sell the tree."

"You don't want to give this up. I'm used to hotels, but that kind of living would give you cabin fever. I'm hardened to it. Never bothers me. But this is great."

She picked up her mug. "Okay, it's great. It's for sale. You buy it. I've had enough sunshine and cactus to last me the rest of my life. I was born here.

If I don't get out now I never will. It just dawned on me. So I put up the sign. I need a change of luck. If I'm not careful I'll meet some fast-talking desert rat and get stuck here forever. Make me an offer."

"How do you mean that?"

"On the house."

"Don't do anything hasty. You're in a mood. It'll pass. You didn't tell me you painted."

"You didn't ask me."

"I don't as a rule care for lady artists. They always smell of turpentine."

"You just haven't been close enough to notice."

"Do you always paint the desert?"

"I never start out that way," she said. "But they always end up looking like the desert."

He smiled and poured more coffee into his cup. "I'd like to have one of your paintings."

"Why?"

"I'm a sucker for talent. What have you got planned for today?"

She knocked the ash off her cigarette. "It looks like I'm stuck with you."

"How about a picnic somewhere?"

She gazed at him. "Don't you think we'd better wait for a sunny day?"

"To hell with it. If it rains, it rains."

5

She brought along her paints and easel. They drove out toward the pyramid site, following the fresh road to the end. Bulldozers and heavy equipment stood like abandoned toys waiting for the weekend to pass. Gamage tooled out across the desert floor to an old smoketree, an oasis of shade in the heat haze, and parked the jeep.

Conny, in Levis and sandals and a kind of Toulouse-Lautrec straw hat, set up a canvas stool and her easel. She stood for a moment, crimping an eye at the view in every direction and then opened her paintbox.

"Do you want to try?" she asked.

"A painter I'm not," he said.

"That hasn't stopped me."

He opened a can of beer and sat in the shade. An impenetrable stillness lay over the desert; a primordial quiet. He watched her. Her face was glossy in the heat and perspiration along her back turned her blouse transparent. She couldn't care less, he thought, because he didn't count anymore. He had blown his chances. He would never get to first base with her again. That was understood. Soon she had the handle of a brush clamped between her teeth and others stood from one hand like a pincushion.

"Why did you go to work for the Martinkas?" she asked.

"Don't talk with your mouth full."

"A man like you. I mean, the Pulitzer Prize and all."

"I peaked out early."

"You're wasting yourself here."

"Stuff and nonsense," he frowned.

She began dabbing in white paint. "The Martinkas aren't entitled to everything money can buy. Those first chapters have style. And wit. I mean it."

"I think we can manage to keep it a secret."

"That's just what I'm trying to say. It's a waste. Hardly anyone is going to read the book except members of the family and a few friends, if there are any left. You're dropping your talent down a well. You won't even hear a splash."

"What's with the white paint?"

"Clouds."

"There's not a speck in the sky."

"There ought to be. So I put them in."

"You're a magician."

"No. Just a liar like everybody else. Like you."

"Like me," he said.

"You're writing words into Martinka's mouth. Things he should have said, but didn't. You're the wizard. But I'm with you. The truth is either dull or ugly or both. Who needs it?"

"You're wise beyond your years," Gamage smiled.

"A lot that gets me. Beauty is a lie. I found that out. But if you're good enough, it becomes the truth. That's what Martinka hired you to do. And that's what you're doing."

"Your nose is shiny."

"I'm shiny all over."

"I noticed."

She glanced at him. "Will you be going back to the coast?"

"I never make plans." He studied her a moment, grimacing in the heat. "I've got no business interfering in your life, so don't pay any attention to me. But I'd say you belong here and I wish I had something like that going for me." He finished his beer. "Aside from that, the sun looks good on you. You don't look bad in the shade either."

She gave him a mild glance. "And all the while I thought you just needed a place to go," she said, "when you've got no place to go."

"Don't be ungrateful," he smiled. "If it weren't for me you wouldn't be sitting out here soliciting sunstroke."

After a while he stretched out and went to sleep. Around two o'clock they packed up and left. She had finished the painting and gave it to him. It had been done as swiftly and deftly as a watercolor. It surprised him to see the beauty she had seen in a hostile landscape. Looking at the desert, he decided, must be an acquired skill and if he wasn't careful she'd teach him how.

He drove back for the road and saw two men standing near a bulldozer with a large blueprint spread at their feet. It was Frank and his sales manager, Earl Sunshine. A dusty Cadillac was parked behind them a few hundred feet along the road.

Gamage slowed down and stopped. Frank came over with a two-hundred pound grin. "It looks like we can't keep the mobs away."

"Hello, Frank."

"What are you doing out here, amigo?"

"Playing Indian."

"Some hunk of real estate, huh?"

"I don't know," Gamage said. "It gets a little chilly in the afternoons."

"When we blow the whistle," Sunshine said, "it'll be the Oklahoma Land Rush all over again."

"When will that be?" Gamage asked.

"A couple of weeks."

"Hi there, Conny," Frank said, casting a gleam at her. "I hope you're taking good care of my friend."

"Sure," she said. "He has to fight me off."

Frank laughed. "You've got a real squaw there, amigo."

Gamage threw the jeep in gear. "See you around."

"Look in on the wife," Frank said. "She's sitting in the car. But I'll be honest with you, amigo. I don't think she likes you. You know how broads are. You've been around here for going on a couple of weeks and you haven't made a pass at her."

Gamage looked ahead and saw now that it was Ginny behind the wheel of the Cadillac. He was sorry to run into her now, but there was nothing to do but take the hurdles.

He glanced at Conny and she said, "Don't worry. I won't louse it up for you."

"There's nothing to louse up."

"I'll pretend to be your sister."

He pulled up and Ginny lowered the window. She looked incredibly cool and fresh. If she felt the slightest disappointment in Gamage it lay concealed behind her dark glasses.

"Hello, Mrs. Martinka," he said.

She smiled a little. "Hi."

"Have you met my aunt?" he said. "She's a maiden lady. Visiting me from Omaha, Nebraska."

Ginny looked over at Conny in the bucket seat beside him with her blouse wringing wet. "My God, Conny," she smiled. "What is this madman trying to do? Drown you?"

Conny smiled back. "Hi, Ginny," she said in the tone used by old friends who no longer have much to say. "You look marvelous, as usual."

"It's just air-conditioning. If I stepped outside I'd wilt." Her glance returned to Gamage, but the lenses of her smoked glasses were impenetrable. "I won't keep you. We'll get together, the four of us."

"That'll be fun," Conny said.

Gamage gave her a kick with his eyes and put the jeep in gear again. They exchanged goodbyes and Ginny let the window rise, putting herself behind glass. They stared at each other for a moment and then Gamage tugged down the brim of his hat and took off down the road toward the highway. Finally he looked at Conny.

"What's funny?" he said.

"Who's laughing?"

"You are."

CHAPTER SIX

1

The Missouri Girl came to the door. Gamage hadn't wanted to keep the appointment; he felt suddenly tired of the Martinka family and the questions accumulating in his mind. But he was curious about the Missouri Girl and he had come. It was four o'clock, always a bad time of day for him, and his face felt swollen with the lingering heat and the glare of the desert. The house was on a dirt street, a Spanish stucco with a red tile roof and a sharply-scented pepper tree crawling with ants in the front yard. His knock had brought several dogs barking at her feet and set up a yipping and howling from the back yard. Over the caterwauling he could hear a scratchy phonograph wailing inside the house.

"You would be Mr. Gamage," she said. "Come in." The friendliness in her voice surprised him and put him at ease. Over the phone she had been suspicious, cool and unresponsive to his project, but she had obviously had a change of mind. "You'll excuse the fuss," she said, quieting the dogs. "We don't have many callers and they do like to make the most of it."

He had addressed her as Mrs. Swanson over the phone, and had come expecting a stiff, formal interview. But he had an instinct for people and quickly shifted his manner. "I've been looking forward to meeting you, Missouri," he said.

She was startled for an instant and then smiled.

"I haven't been called that in years, young man." She picked up a Mexican hairless with bulging marble eyes and led Gamage into the house.

"Do they bite?" he asked.

"Only city folks."

The dogs convoyed him, sniffing at his legs. "I think they smell the city on me," he said.

"It'll serve you right."

They reached the living room and he saw the phonograph, an old morning glory with a cylinder record. The shades were drawn against the sun, but an incandescent glow filled the room. The floors were thickly overlaid with fringed oriental rugs, reds and blacks, and there was a rich clutter of carved chairs and screens and hammered brass pots and platters. The room smelled of cloves.

"How many dogs do you have?"

"I don't count them anymore. They're strays. Poor innocent fools." She seated herself on a straight-backed chair and arranged the Mexican hairless on her lap. "People from the city drive out here with pets they're tired of and turn them loose. Nothing can live on the desert if it doesn't know how. The Indian boys find them and bring them to me. Three or four days without food or water and a dog will go mad."

Gamage glanced over at the morning glory and listened to the scratchy tenor. "Is that Colonel Martinka singing?"

"Pagliacci," she nodded, sounding the g. "Joy, what a voice he had in those days. That's an old Edison he gave me years ago. He was going to throw it away."

Gamage stared at the antique horn. Despite the old mechanical recording and the popping of static, the voice sang out—a powerful, ringing voice. He listened. The familiar clown in white satin and pom-pom buttons rose in his mind. He had the feeling of listening to a voice through a spiritualist's trumpet. The voice had turned to dust; it was a part of Martinka that had died. The wax cylinder revolved slowly, like a time machine, and Martinka called out from the past, lifting his voice to the broken cry at the end.

The drum boomed like a toy, sounding a final doom, a foreshadowing of the operatic future waiting for Martinka. The recording ended and the room fell silent. She didn't stir for a moment and Gamage had the uncanny feeling that Martinka had been there like a spectre at a séance.

She got up finally and turned the machine off. "I'll return this to him one of these days. I'm sure he no longer remembers that I have it. Would you like some coffee, young man?"

"I'd like it fine."

The dogs kept an eye on him while she was gone. She returned from the kitchen with a silver tray and two steaming cups. "They're Spode," she said. "Mr. Swanson liked nice things. Do you have a cigarette? I recently took up smoking."

She passed him a cup and seated herself again, picking up the dog like knitting she had left on the chair. Gamage bent forward and lit her cigarette. It was not easy to see the Missouri farm girl in the woman with freshly-blued hair across from him. If she had once been plain and raw-boned, as he somehow assumed, she had had to wait for old age to beautify her. She carried herself with implicit poise, as straight-backed as the chair, and with an air of secret bemusement as if her life had turned out better than she had a right to expect. Her face was angular, with snapping bright eyes, and her skin was almost marshmallow-white and smooth.

A string of amber beads hung across the lace bosom of her dress; he was suddenly struck with his father's old phrase, palpitating lace. "Excuse me for staring," he said, "but I think I was expecting someone else."

"A lady desert rat, you mean."

"Yes."

She smiled. "When I was younger it was unfashionable for a woman to go out without her face covered. We all wanted a milky white skin. It's hard to break the habits of a lifetime. The girls today tan themselves like leather. Who told you I used to be called Missouri?"

"Colonel Martinka refers to you often in an old diary."

"I didn't know he kept one."

Gamage gazed at her. "Missouri, why did you refuse to see me the two times I called?"

She puffed the cigarette, smiling a little. "I couldn't think of any reason I ought to talk to you. My memories are private. They belong to me, not to him, not in a book—and you're a stranger."

"But you changed your mind."

"Yes."

"Why?"

"You could say I had it changed for me." She made a pass at the smoke with her left hand. "I was told not to see you, and a thing like that does make a person contrary."

Gamage felt himself frown. "Frank?"

"It might have been."

"Why wouldn't Frank want you to speak to me?"

She tried the cigarette again and then picked up her coffee. "As I remember he said he couldn't be rightly sure of your discretion. But I believe what worried him was mine, the snip. So I felt obliged to have a look at you and I might even answer your questions. What is it you want to know?"

"That's easy," Gamage said. "Missouri, were you once in love with Jesse Martinka?"

"That's an impertinent question," she said, and then smiled. "But I'll be pleased to answer it. I was."

"It was there between the lines," Gamage said.

"We were all taken with him. Jesse had a kind of electricity. If you walked into a room he'd just left you could tell he'd been there. I'd never met an actor before—especially a grand opera singer. Of course, he'd been everywhere. He was nothing like the other men on the desert in those days. He was worldly. As a very young man he'd run away to sea."

"I didn't know that."

"Yes."

"Do you know what his real name is?"

She put aside her coffee. "You've been talking to Charlie Hastings."

"Yes."

"Charlie is a suspicious old fool. I never believed that about Jesse. And even if it's true, I don't see that it matters anymore."

"It matters," Gamage said, "if he took on an imaginary identity—his stage name—and let his real identity disappear."

"You want more coffee?"

"No, thanks." It was apparent to Gamage that she wasn't going to be pressed into saying more than she cared to. He let it go. "Do you know how he injured his hand?"

She hesitated before answering. "I believe you must have a better memory than mine. I'd forgotten about that. It's something you get so used to you don't see it anymore."

"Did he ever tell you how it happened?"

"Did you ask him?" she answered.

"I haven't met him. I'm beginning to think now that Frank doesn't trust his discretion any more than yours or mine." Gamage leaned forward again. "He's managed to keep me at a distance from his father. His excuse is that the book is to be a surprise, but I doubt it. No, Missouri, I haven't asked him."

"He probably wouldn't remember anyway."

"What do you mean?"

"I believe his memory has been fading for years. It may be gone now. He's forgotten the good with the bad. And I don't think he would enjoy reading about his hand in the book you're writing. You'd be charitable to leave out the unhappiness." She regarded him gravely. "He hasn't dropped his old friends, you see. I don't believe he knows us anymore. He's forgotten."

"Have you tried to talk to him?"

"Oh, Greta won't let us get near him. She'd try to cover a thing like that up. But I know. Until a little bit ago he always sent me flowers on my birthday. They stopped coming."

"How long ago?"

"The last few years. I'm not sure Greta ever knew and I suspicioned she found out and put a stop to it. But he'd have found a way. Now I know better. I believe he's simply forgotten. I had a great-aunt in Missouri who was that way when I was a child. If she went to town alone she couldn't remember where home was. Poor Jesse. Old age is being hard on him."

Gamage felt that she had talked herself into an easy excuse for Martinka's behavior over the last years. He discounted it. It was more pleasant to accept the possibility that he had forgotten her out of a trick of the mind than to accept a cold and late-blooming indifference. Still, if she had stumbled onto the truth it put the biography in a new and strange light. It meant that Frank had hired Gamage to write a kind of artificial memory for the old man, filtering out what was unacceptable and even sweetening the role that Greta Crighton Martinka had played in his life. Camilla was to be eliminated.

"About his hand," Gamage said, finishing his coffee. "The finger was gone before he came here to the desert. He seemed to feel an intense embarrassment about it—a kind of mortification. Why? Did he tell you what had happened?"

"He told me he had had an accident while at sea."

"Anything else?"

She smiled and was silent, her fingers playing absently with the amber beads. She waited for him to change the subject and finally he gave it up. She could be pretending to know more than she did, Gamage thought, but if Martinka had revealed himself to anyone it had probably been the Missouri Girl.

"Can we talk about Camilla?" Gamage said.

"Joy, what a lovely thing she was. You've seen pictures."

"No."

A mouldering black album was waiting on a table beside her, as if she had rehearsed the interview in advance, and she began turning the pages. Finally she handed it to Gamage at an open page. The snapshots had turned sepia, the images fading, the past interred. The Missouri Girl had written dates and captions in a square hand with white ink. A photograph, marked Sept. 1912, showed three people seated on a spring wagon in the sun. The names were written under them—Jerusha herself, Camilla and Manuel.

"Was the boy her brother?"

"Yes."

Manuel, bare-headed, held the reins with solemn importance. The Missouri Girl held a picnic basket on her lap, but her face was lost in the shadow of a wide-brimmed hat.

Camilla sat between them with a dark rebozo around her head and the barest of smiles on her lips. Her nose was thin and the cheekbones smooth and narrow. She looked serene.

"We were setting out on a picnic when Jesse took that picture," she said. "I guess she was about nineteen then. You couldn't make her wear anything but black in those days. She had lost her husband, you know."

"Yes."

"She was staying with me, but she never would talk about him. I don't think she had liked him. But she would have worn black for the rest of her life I suppose if Jesse hadn't brought her here. The first six months she would hardly say a word to anyone. You'd think we were holding her prisoner. Even Jesse hardly could get her to smile. He'd found her in rags, but you know she was wearing little diamond earrings? Her ears had been pierced as a child, the way they do, and the earrings had probably been given to her by her godmother. I don't think they show in the picture, but she always wore them."

"She was beautiful," Gamage said.

"Joy, wasn't she? I was considered tolerable looking before she came here, there not being much to compare me with, but she made me feel like a mud fence. Oh, how I hated her those first few days when Jesse asked me to take her in. It's a wonder I didn't poison her. But I got over that. You couldn't be jealous of her. That beauty didn't mean two cents to her. She'd have given it to me if she could. What she cared about was the boy. She was a mother to him. All they had was each other. She would scrub his face, chattering away in Mexican, before she'd let him turn up at school. The first day he heard himself called a greaser. He didn't know what it meant, but he found out. Jesse had to order him not to fight after that. The boy adored Jesse and he listened to him, but it wasn't easy for him. Christians have never been fond of practicing Christian charity. Of course, Camilla was anxious for Manuel to get a schooling. She hadn't an ounce of education, but she was born refined. The way she carried herself! I was always trying to improve myself and I used to watch her, learning. She didn't know it, but she was my teacher."

"How did she feel about Martinka?"

Jerusha Swanson smiled. "She'd heard stories about the gringos I suppose. She was afraid of him at first. I could see it in her. She couldn't understand why he was being so kind to them, but she could guess. Still, if he'd come for her to live with him, she would have done it without a word. Because of the boy. She expected to have to pay the piper. I can remember the way she would comb out her hair at night as if listening for him. But he never came."

"He must have been taken with her right from the first."

"But I don't believe he knew he was in love with her until the day Manuel died."

"When was that?"

"A few weeks after the picture was taken. He was killed by an old bull that Will Burley had out at his place. He was coming home from school, roundabout, because of some older boys. Will shot the bull later that night. I didn't think Camilla would ever recover. She couldn't cry, not even at the funeral. Jesse would come see her every day. I don't know how he did it, but he finally got her to cry it out. She already was packing her things to go back to Mexico. He tried to talk her out of it, but she had her mind made up. The next day we all went down to the station and he bought her a ticket on the Sidewinder. That was the S.P. train that went through here to Calexico. When the train stopped she found herself a window seat. She kept fussing with the rebozo and I remember the little diamonds sparkling in her ears. They were like tears. Jesse didn't say a word. He just watched her against the red plush seat and she looked at him and suddenly the train started to move. They didn't even wave to each other. Finally he turned his back. He never expected to see her again."

"Did he go after her?"

"No. I never saw him so confused. I think he was stung by her wanting to leave. I don't know how far the train got before she stopped it somehow. She got off and started walking back. She turned up here late that night. The next year they got married."

"That would be 1913."

"February, just after the big freeze. Jesse had been planning to build himself a house, but he burned the lumber trying to keep his trees warm."

"I know," Gamage said.

"So they went on living in the old board-and-bat cabin he had. He did add onto it. At night he taught her to read and write. On Sundays he'd drive her in the hack to Indio for Mass and wait outside. In those days he was busy getting his bank started and the packing house going and always putting in more offshoots. He began to talk about building Camilla the finest house anywhere around, but he was always short of cash. He was always spread too thin. The years went by. He'd pick up a piece of land the way you pick up a stray dog or cat—because you can't help yourself. And once he had the land it had to be cleared of mesquite or whatever and a well dug and offshoots set out. Camilla was patient about the house. I don't believe it rightly mattered to her. She raised turkeys and the first time Greta went out there she saw Camilla in the poultry yard and took her to be a servant girl. Jesse was quite put out about it. Any slight toward Camilla was infuriating to him."

"That would be the spring of 1919."

"Yes. Greta and her brother stayed at the Plantation House for a few weeks—it was new then. They rented a tent and went up into the high desert. He had been gassed."

Gamage nodded. "I know."

"Jesse was finally cash ahead and he wanted to get the house built. When he learned that young Crighton was an architect he hired him to design something for him. Crighton was mighty slow about it and Jesse finally went out on the desert looking for him. He came back with some kind of plan and hired some carpenters and went to work. Soon after that we heard that Crighton had died, and Greta moved back to town."

Gamage raised his eyes. "Then the house wasn't built for Greta at all."

"Of course not. But she likes to let on that it was. Jesse was sparing no expense. He was considered the richest man in the valley then, even though he was mostly land poor. Greta would go out there and watch the building going on. It was the last thing her brother had designed and you'd think she owned it. She got friendly with Camilla. But before the house was finished, Camilla died. Jesse stopped building. He was going to let the place rot."

"How did Camilla die?"

Her hand returned to the amber beads. "Jesse had bought her a beautiful sorrel mare. One Thursday afternoon she went out riding with Greta. It was a windy day with a good deal of grit in the air. It makes a horse nervous and they should have had more sense. Camilla was thrown and hurt bad. Greta rode back for help. It was turning dark and they spent hours trying to find Camilla out on the desert. Greta was confused about the lay of the land and that didn't help. When they did find Camilla—she was almost dead. She had been lying out there for hours. She died the next day. After that, Jesse seemed to lose interest in everything. He talked of going away. Greta collapsed when Camilla died. She blamed herself for not being able to lead the men right to where Camilla had been thrown. Saving that time might have made a difference. I think Jesse hated her—he couldn't help himself. But that wore off. She was taking it so hard, you know. She seemed to be sharing his grief. I suppose it made things a little easier for him and he became attentive to her. That woman knew her way around men. He found out that she couldn't pay her hotel bill and he paid it for her. She seemed so helpless. And finally she persuaded him to go on with the house—Camilla would have wanted that, she kept saying. When the house was done it lacked a woman in it and we were not too surprised to see Greta become, as she calls herself, Madam Martinka. She wanted that house. She wasn't always so grand and proper—that came after she married him. The next summer Frank was born. There was some talk about that—the baby coming so soon—but you know how petty small town gossip can be. I know better. I know Jesse. He never looked at another woman but Camilla until the day Greta married him—and I don't think he took a good look at Greta even then. No, there was nothing to that talk."

And yet, Gamage thought, it had lodged in her memory. "What kind of married life have they had together?"

The Missouri Girl hesitated. "I'd have no way of knowing. I'm on the outside."

"How does it look from the outside?"

"I believe Jesse liked having a family. He took a lot of pride in Frank when the boy was growing up. But I don't believe Frank ever liked his father. Of course, Greta's a strong woman and Frank lived in her shadow. He still does. When Frank was grown Jesse finally took a long look at him, and after that the two of them never seemed to have much to say to each other."

"And Greta?"

"Jesse made the best of it, as he usually does. But there was a limit."

"To what?"

Her fingers were busy with the amber beads. "You know Jesse was arrested, don't you?"

"No."

"It was pretty well hushed up. I never did really understand what happened."

"When was this?"

"Four or five years ago in Pasadena. They say he was arrested, but I don't know for sure. I only heard it."

"Missouri, you dodged my question."

"Did I?"

"Is the arrest part of it? Their marriage, I mean."

"I always felt it was." She shrugged. "But I heard so many different stories, you understand."

"Did she have him arrested?"

"I don't know. Jesse's not a wife-beater, if that's what you're thinking. But that's not to say I would blame him if he did something like that."

"Why?"

She looked up. Gamage had a feeling that whatever it was that had made the Missouri Girl change her mind and invite him to see her was finally rising to the surface. "You don't know about Greta?"

"No."

"She got herself mixed up with one of those lunatic crusades over in Los Angeles. I forget what they called themselves. Greta had found a new religion—hatred. Especially the Jews. She was a big contributor. She'd go all the way to Los Angeles to attend meetings. Still does as far as I know. Of course, they have her marked down as a rich cow and they don't lose any time milking her. She has given them thousands of dollars by now, I guess. Jesse told me she just wouldn't listen to reason once the fever came over her. A thing like that was bound to make him short-tempered. He just naturally leans to the underdog, like in Mexico, he sided with the insurrectos. But he couldn't stop her. If you met her on the street she'd start raving about international Jew bankers and whatnot. I think living in the same house with a woman like that has cost Jesse his mind. His mind just went to sleep. Poor Jesse. I really think that's what's happening at their house and I have a feeling Frank doesn't want you to know, so I'm telling you. That woman needs a comeuppance."

2

Gamage ate a solitary dinner. Later he worked up some notes at the typewriter, wondering gloomily why he was bothering. Camilla's name would never see print and neither would Madam Martinka's gouty anti-semitism. Make her out to be a sweet old lady and to hell with it. But it ran against the grain.

He went to bed early. It was too hot to sleep and his mind was haunted by the past. In her heavily-scented prose Madam Martinka had neatly removed herself from any contact with Camilla. Her role in Camilla's death struck Gamage as mephitic. And then the hasty marriage and the sudden pregnancy. The Missouri Girl had spelled it out: Greta Crighton knew her way around men. The implications were clear.

Around eleven he gave it up and went downstairs for a nightcap. BeJesus John was on his way out the street door, but Gamage stopped him.

"You leaving sober?"

"Not by choice."

"Sit down."

BeJesus John returned and joined Gamage in a booth. He fished in his shirt pocket for a folded sheet of copy paper and his reading glasses. "As a matter of fact, I've been sitting here writing out an editorial on the evils of strong drink—for women, that is. Look at 'em there. Rear ends lined up like overripe figs. I've always regretted giving the ladies the ballot. The next thing we know they'll start using the men's room." He put on his glasses. "I'll read you what I wrote in a loud voice."

"I'll wait to see it in print," Gamage said. "I suppose you know the Martinkas are going to start peddling their pyramid lots within the next couple of weeks."

BeJesus John pulled off his glasses. "That don't leave me much time, does it?" He pursed his lips. "I was hoping they'd come to their senses and buy me off—I could use the funds—but Frank ain't noted for generosity. So I guess I'll have to marshal the full power of the press in my next issue. I'll give the matter some thought."

"BeJesus John, you didn't tell me that Madam Martinka is bankrolling a little harmless Jew-baiting on the side."

"You found it out for yourself."

"Have you ever printed anything on it?"

"No."

"Why not?"

BeJesus John relit the stub of his cigar. "I don't know," he answered finally. "It's kind of like discovering syphilis in the family. You don't like to print a thing like that about a woman. And it's caused Jesse just about as much pain as he could bear, you know."

"You suppressed the story of his arrest, didn't you?"

"Yes. But not because he asked me to. I was friendlier to him in those days. I couldn't see any value in making him a laughingstock in the valley. Wish I had now."

"Did he take a swing at her?"

"He didn't lay a hand on her directly. That would have made sense. What he did was kind of noble, but it was the wildest foolishness—almost childish. The old lady had gone to Pasadena to attend one of their wormy-eyed meetings. She had developed this warp about the Hebrews and nothing could take it out. Jesse just couldn't stop her—she's a willful woman if there ever was one. They had some speaker who was large in their circles and she wasn't going to miss him. I think he was going to raise Hitler's voice from a tea kettle or ear trumpet. Anyway, she went. And Jesse went too. They called themselves the Patriotic Daughters, as I recall. Their symbol was a broom. They were going to sweep out the Jews and maybe a few Catholics and Negroes so as not to appear unduly biased. There were a few goons on hand and they ushered Jesse out in short order after he attempted to entertain the group with a few humorous remarks—I believe he offered the opinion that he knew just the place for the broom, providing the guest speaker would bend over. Those folks had no sense of humor. Jesse told me he stewed outside for a while and then he noticed one of those colored boy hitching posts in front of the lawn. He located himself a bucket of paint and a brush. He painted that black face white. Then he noticed a few more of those hitching posts along the street. They're popular in Pasadena, I guess. He got a little carried away. He started along the street with his bucket of paint, painting those black faces a pearly white until someone saw what he was up to and called the police. That was fine with Jesse. He had to get that protest out of his system, but no one would listen. He was clearly a crackpot of some kind—maybe even a Communist. The police turned him out with a warning. They managed to keep the story out of the papers. A thing like that would make Pasadena look foolish—one of their expensive residential streets lined with black slaves in whiteface, and a group of nice old ladies in paisley dresses chipping in to buy gas ovens for local use. It just never saw print—none of it."

3

Conny showed up at nine in the morning and Gamage dictated more than 5000 words. When she returned the next morning with the pages typed up he didn't bother to read them over. He was being paid to write the book, not to read it.

He hadn't heard from Ginny and he kept waiting for a call, but when the phone rang it was inevitably Frank. There was another letter from his old man, this one mailed from Lake Como ("that's in Italy, amigo") and he was going to send it over to Gamage with several others. Gamage could finish off the book with Col. Martinka's European pleasure trip and bring his life story right up to the minute.

When the packet of letters arrived Gamage tossed them on the bed. He didn't get at them until after dinner. They were written in the same squarish hand that he remembered from Martinka's yellowed diary, but the old man had lost his capacity for wit. The coffee, he complained, was bad everywhere in Europe. The lake made a pretty view—too pretty; fine for women to look at. He preferred the Salton Sea. The opera houses were drafty and Madam Martinka had caught a cold. Two pieces of their luggage had been stolen. They'd eaten better Italian food at Ghio's right in Thebes. In fact, "as your mother tells me twice a day" she wouldn't trade all of Italy for an ant hill in the Coachella Valley.

For a man without a memory he had total recall for every minor misfortune of the trip. Either the Missouri Girl was wrong or Martinka had recovered his faculties—if he had ever lost them. Gamage struggled to reconcile this bitter, whining old tourist with the pyramid builder he was now writing about. In the more than half a century that stretched between the 1907 diary and these letters, Col. Martinka had forgotten how to laugh at himself.

Gamage put them aside. He was far from the end of the book and if he used the letters at all he'd have to rewrite them and give Martinka back his sense of humor in order to keep the character constant. If time itself hadn't changed the old man, Madam Martinka had.

4

At one-thirty in the morning the phone rang. After a moment he heard Ginny's soft, low voice from the receiver. She would meet him at Villa Martinka.

He got dressed with a vague feeling of resentment. Why didn't she get her lovely ass out of Frank's house so they could run this affair right?

When he reached Villa Martinka he found her green Thunderbird parked near the flagpole. The night air rasped and trilled in the heat. He could make out the house, a dark, baleful shape in the star glow. When he started up the steps the front door gave way and he saw Ginny in the opening. She had changed into something cool. A thin green wrapper hung loosely from her shoulders. She knew how to make an entrance, he thought.

The moment he was inside the door she shut it and turned on him. "God damn you," she said.

The room was pitch black and they couldn't see each other now, but he had a strong sense of her presence, perfumed and angry, a foot away. "That's not bad for openers," he said. "But what the hell are you talking about?"

"Don't play games with me, Gamage."

"Like what?"

"Like Conny."

"Well," he said. "For Christ's sake."

"You've got her staked out on the side, haven't you?"

"Not exactly. But it's an interesting idea."

"It's true, isn't it?"

"Ginny, we could have played this dialogue over the phone and saved the trip."

"You two-way bastard."

He began to smile. She had written the curtain to this scene, he thought, before he arrived when she slipped into the wrapper. "Ginny, darling, you're standing there in the rind. What have you got in mind?"

"What do you think?"

"Get dressed. I'll buy you a cup of coffee."

There was a moment's dark silence. Then he felt her hand reach out and touch his chest. "Don't," she whispered. "Don't laugh at me. I've been in a rage ever since I saw Conny with you. I'm jealous. I can't help it. It scares me to think I could lose you again after all these years."

"But you're seeing things that aren't there."

"Frank said—"

"Frank is peddling stories."

She was suddenly against him, holding tight. "You're all I've got left, darling, and I'm scared. I can't help it."

His hands moved inside the wrapper along the burning surface of her back. "Look, Ginny," he said gently. "I was in dead storage on Sunday. I needed someone to be with. I see Conny every day. She's typing for me. But Sunday afternoon was just what it looked like. Nothing."

"Okay."

"How did you get away from Frank?"

"He got up around one and took a sleeping pill. He's good until morning now."

"I don't like having to live under a rock this way."

"Be patient with me, darling."

"My God, you're beautiful. Even in the dark."

"Come on."

She took his hand and led him to the stairway.

The electricity was shut off. Upstairs, in a room across from Madam Martinka's, she lit a white kitchen candle and fixed it in an ashtray.

He looked around. The desk and chairs and bookcases, cobwebbed with sheets, stood like spectators in the room. The shades were drawn. "Is this the Colonel's room?" Gamage asked.

She nodded and let the wrapper drop from her shoulders. She gave it a toss over the massive rosewood bed and let it flutter down on the mattress, stripped for the summer. Her shadow shifted along the walls in the candlelight. She looked over, aware of his eyes on her, and smiled slightly.

"In the rind," she said.

"And not bad."

He opened his arms and she came to him. Her skin was humid to the touch. They were a long time together in the candlelight while the room filled with an ashen, waxy scent.

They let the candle burn. Toward three o'clock she thought she heard a sound outside. Gamage blew out the candle and stood at one of the windows, pulling the shade aside. He looked down at the two cars side by side near the flagpole. Nothing stirred. He watched for two or three minutes, listening, while she dressed.

"I'd better go," she said.

He went downstairs with her, leaving the door ajar, and walked her to the car. "You leave first. It'll be better that way," he said.

"Yes."

"I'll lock up and follow a little later."

She kissed him and slipped into the seat. She seemed a little frightened now and he was sorry. He hated to see her go; these meetings were always too short and hurried and she was beginning to jump at every sound. But it had been worth the trip. She started up the engine and their eyes met. "I'll call you," she whispered.

He nodded and she pulled away. After a moment she switched on the headlights. He stood watching. He could feel her scent and perspiration clinging to his skin; Ginny had built-in heat. It would always be worth the trip. The car lights swept the plantation trees and finally disappeared along the road. He was alone. The silence returned and with it the whine and chirping of insects. He returned to the house.

He struck a match and once at the stairs he went back to Col. Martinka's bedroom. He lit the candle and took a long look around the room. He found it easy to imagine the old man shuffling back and forth across the floor or standing at the window, a self-imposed exile from his friends and the valley.

Gamage stopped at the closet door wondering if this was the one, the closet with the cigar boxes. He opened it and looked in. The old man's suits were on hangers and there was the exhale of mothballs. Shoes were neatly lined up on the floor. Gamage lowered the candle, lighting up the rear of the closet, and he saw what Barbachano had seen—thirty or forty boxes of cigars stacked against the wall. Gamage frowned. He felt suddenly tired of the petty mysteries surrounding Martinka's old age. He hoped the boxes would be empty, putting an end to the matter in his mind, but he pulled one out and it was heavy and when he broke the tax seal it was full. The kid was right.

Gamage straightened and lit a cigarette with the candle. He didn't know what to think. He was aware that there were vintage years in cigars and that fanciers put them away like fine wines. Havanas, maybe, but not White Owls. It made no sense at all.

Well. Martinka was entitled to his eccentricities, but maybe he had lost his marbles at that. Gamage felt a sudden overwhelming desire to get the book written, collect his bankroll and clear out.

He took a last glance around the room, feeling that he and Ginny had profaned it by bringing their affair here, and walked out into the hall.

He had hardly cleared the doorway when he heard a quick, close flutter beside him and he thought for an instant that a bat had got into the hall; the blow fell across his neck. His vision jarred. The candle dropped from his hands and went out. The next blow cracked against his head—he could hear it—and staggered him to his knees. A walking stick or poker. Pain shot through him to his fingertips. He tried to reach out and then, on reflex, to shield himself. The blows rained down on him in a fury, beating him senseless, and he pitched forward against the carpeting, unconscious.

5

Gamage rolled over on his back. He stared upward, seeing nothing in the darkness, and listened to someone groaning. Slowly it came to him that the sound was breaking from his own lips. He stopped. His mind began coming back to him, and he raised himself against the wall. He saw a bright spot glowing at his feet like the eye of a cat. His cigarette; it was still burning.

He made the effort to pick it up. He listened. There wasn't a sound in the hall now. He lifted his hands; they felt broken, but he could work his fingers. Frank. It had to be Frank, he thought.

He struck a match for light and found the candle and lit it again. He looked up and down the hall and across at the open doorway of Col. Martinka's room. Or hadn't it been Frank at all? Frank would have killed him. Was the old man somewhere in the house?

Gamage's head was splitting; he could barely see. He worked his neck slowly and knew that he was scared. He wanted to get out of the house alive. He remembered now what he had managed to forget, the note warning him to get out of Thebes. Martinka. He felt he could sense the old man's presence.

He waited for his vision to clear and then started to move. His hands were already puffy and he knew he couldn't defend himself if he were attacked again.

He found Martinka's heavy walking stick on the floor at the head of the stairs; that was what had beaten him down. He bent for it, taking a grip, and looked around him again. "Martinka!"

Nothing. No one. The house was still. He braced himself for the trip downstairs into the living room.

He shut the front door after him, hearing the final click of the lock. The jeep seemed a mile away. He made for it and eased himself into the seat. He rested a moment, trying at the same time to remain alert, and then switched on the lights. He felt like a kid afraid of the dark and he looked at the house again. Instinct told him it had been the old man—never mind the letters from Europe—and he must still be somewhere in the shadows.

An immense rage caught up with him. He felt that he had been played for a fool and he didn't understand it.

CHAPTER SEVEN

1

A knocking at his hotel room door woke Gamage. It was morning and that would be Conny to begin the day's dictation. He lay there silently. He didn't feel like facing anyone, especially himself. Maybe she would go away.

"Gamage?"

He got up and then sat heavily on the edge of the bed. He felt hung over; his neck was stiff and his head ached. Conny knocked again.

"Are you awake?"

"I am now. Don't break the goddam door down."

"It's after nine."

He got to his feet and stood talking through the door. "We'll skip it for today, Conny." And then suddenly he changed his mind. "Wait a minute. I mean, go down and have yourself a cup of coffee while I shower. And bring me up a pot, good and black. Okay?"

"Okay."

He dug through his things for the aspirin and went into the bathroom. He looked in the mirror and was surprised that he recognized his face. He couldn't understand why his head wasn't as large and ugly as it felt. There was a welt over his right temple that disappeared into his hair and his eyes were bloodshot. His right hand was still puffy and raw; he supposed he ought to have it x-rayed for broken bones.

He gulped the aspirins and his rage of the hours before returned, but there was nowhere to go with it. To Frank? The police? He couldn't very well explain away his being at Villa Martinka, even trying to leave Ginny out of it; he couldn't ream Frank out for letting the old man run around loose with a blunt instrument in his hand. He'd be smart to mark it down to experience and let it go at that. At the same time he was angry with himself for having blown the chance to have a look at Col. Martinka—if, for Christ's sakes, that was who it had been.

There had been the note. That should have tipped him off that there was a silent spectator to his goings-on with Ginny. It had been kind of a senile communication now that he thought about it. And then the old man had been moved to violence at finding them together in the house (Gamage had to remind himself that Ginny was, after all, a Martinka—a member of the family), and like an avenging old patriarch he had tried to give Gamage an old fashioned caning.

He turned from the mirror and stopped. Either Martinka had suddenly returned from Europe, which did not seem likely, or he had never gone—a possibility that Gamage could not dismiss from his mind. In that case, who had written and mailed the letters from Italy—Madam Martinka?

Gamage faced a new and threatening possibility. If it had been the old man at the house all he had to do to open Frank's eyes was pick up a phone. The thought was chilling. Ginny. He looked through the open doorway to the phone and decided the time had come for Ginny to pack her bags. Frank would beat the hell out of her if she hung around. It was too risky. "Ginny?"

"Hello, darling."

"Are you alone?"

"Yes. Let me light a cigarette. I'm still in bed."

"You were right, Ginny. We had company last night."

She was silent for a moment and then her voice came through in a whisper. "Frank?"

"You tell me. Was he asleep when you got home?"

"Yes. I think so."

"Ginny," Gamage said. "I have a feeling it was the old man. I can't shake it."

"No," she answered flatly.

"Says who? Frank? For God's sake, Ginny, level with me. The Colonel is here on the desert, isn't he?"

She was silent.

Finally he said, "You too?" He was tired of this bluff. "Look, I've been conned before, but I don't buy this one. He was in the house waiting for me and he was goddam short-tempered about it. Take my word for it. But what worries me is you if Frank is put wise. Or maybe the old man wouldn't bother. You tell me. He's not overly fond of Frank, is he?"

"Gamage, darling," she answered. "I'm trying to level with you. There's nothing to worry about."

"What kind of an answer is that?"

"Frank won't find out. Not from his father."

Gamage scowled. What exactly did that mean? He felt that she was telling him more than he was capable of understanding. "Has the old man lost his memory, Ginny? Is that what you're going to count on—that he won't remember this morning what he saw last night?"

"We shouldn't talk over the phone."

"We're talking."

"I don't know who could have been out there. Are you sure there really was someone?"

"For Christ's sakes."

"Didn't you see him?"

"No."

"Darling, what happened?"

His anger was rising. "Go back to sleep." He hung up. What kind of sense did that make? She had jumped at noises at Villa Martinka and now she couldn't care less. Okay.

He returned to the bathroom and suddenly what should have been obvious to him before now crossed his mind. Of course. He had been talking like a fool. If Ginny thought for a moment that the old man was around she would never have arranged to meet Gamage at Villa Martinka. Well, maybe she was conned like everybody else. He took a shower.

When Conny showed up with a carton of black coffee she regarded his bruises and said, "You look like a door walked into you." She put down the coffee and her bag and looked at him again. "Hurt?"

"The pain is excruciating. Sit down and let's get to work."

"Is there anything I can do?"

"Do you know a good phrenologist? I'd like to get these bumps looked at." He opened the shutters and squinted out at the day. Ginny's reactions over the phone were off the mark and it bothered him. "Where did we leave off?"

2

Grab the money and run. He began putting in twelve and fourteen hour days. He felt as if he were writing his way out of bondage; he wanted to clear out. Why kid himself? Martinka was a footnote in his life and the book, when it was finished, would be so much waste paper. The days were getting hotter, one by one, and he was bored with the sun and the view from the window and the sense that he was playing the fool.

By the end of the week he had more than 40,000 words on paper. He was drawing heavily on the material Frank had provided. He pieced the story together from letters and newspaper clippings and when he was lacking a point of local history BeJesus John could usually fill him in. In 1929 Martinka's bank failed, but the date gardens went on blooming and bearing. During the winter of 1931 Martinka had run a full page ad in *The Thebes Weekly Sunset* inviting the hungry to live like Arabs on a healthful diet of dates and goats' milk. He threw his plantations open to the public and while no one in the valley starved (Conny said) there was a high incidence of diarrhea.

She would leave in the afternoon and type up the day's shorthand at home. Gamage's bruises were fading and when the pain in his hand eased he didn't bother having it looked at. He would grab a siesta once Conny left and then sit down at the rented portable and begin knocking out copy on yellow paper. He was in his element at the typewriter and did his best work alone. He distrusted dictation; it was too easy to be glib.

But he liked having Conny around and he looked forward to her arrival every morning—bright-eyed and sharp-tongued and always in a fresh, crisp blouse as if the temperature outside hadn't already broken a hundred. She had come to feel important to the project even though she despised it.

He returned to Martinka and the depression years. In the early afternoon the phone rang and Gamage found himself talking to Frank. "Listen, amigo, I don't like your friends."

Gamage glanced at Conny and sighed and sat on the edge of the bed; he supposed he was in for a long one. Frank was on his neck two or three times a day now; no excuse was too petty for Frank to pick up the phone. The book, now that it was being written, seemed to make him nervous. "Frank, what are you talking about?"

"I'm talking about BeJesus John. He's your friend, isn't he? You subsidized the bastard. I got the paper right here."

Was today Friday? Gamage had forgotten to pick up a copy. "What's he written?"

"Do I detect your fine Italian hand, amigo? Did you put him up to this?"

"Frank, I haven't seen the paper and I don't know what the hell you're talking about. If you've got a complaint call him up. I'm busy."

"You could do me a favor and get his brains out of hock. He can't stop the pyramid and I hate to see that hard-headed old geezer make a public nuisance of himself. I don't want to get mean about it. It's not my nature, you understand. He won't sell and he won't die, so why don't you go down there and get your money back? I should have canned you when I found out what you were up to. As a matter of fact, amigo, what the hell are you up to?"

"Frank, climb down off my back."

Gamage hung up and looked at Conny waiting patiently with the shorthand pad on her lap. "That was Frank," he said.

"Frank who?"

He left her there and went downstairs. He picked up a copy of *The Thebes Weekly Sunset* and it didn't take him long to find what was bothering Frank. It was the entire front page. BeJesus John was calling on every old-timer in the valley to gather for a protest march on the board of supervisors seventy miles away in Riverside. "Get out your walking shoes and your liniment bottles," Gamage read. "The time has come to stand up or lie down and get run over by a steam roller. Tomorrow the desert will be under three inches of concrete. It's time to act—so follow me to Riverside! We'll rout the bulldozers! We'll chase off the cement mixers! Last chance! Save the desert!"

There were columns of it. He invited the old folks to bring their wheel chairs and crutches and meet at his office "a week from tomorrow"—Saturday morning at seven sharp. It might take them days to negotiate the seventy miles, but when they came straggling into Riverside the Supervisors would know they meant business.

Gamage returned to the room and began reading out loud. When he had finished Conny asked, "Do you think it'll work?"

"Of course not. The man is off his crumpet. All they'll get out of it is sore feet." He gave a dismal sigh. "Frank is laughing at him. He was putting me on just now. Nobody is going to show up for a seventy mile hike in this goddam heat."

Conny poked a pencil into her hair. "I may."

"You're under age."

Gamage folded up the paper. A march of the ancients. If anyone was crazy enough to show up they'd never get past the first shade tree. It was doomed.

3

The offices of Martinka & Son, Land Development, consumed a sleek modern building on the northern shore of the Salton Sea. On either side of the entry a matched pair of palms shot skyward. Gamage parked and got out and ducked into the shade of the overhang.

It was Tuesday. His contract called for another payment with the first batch of copy and Gamage had stuck a hundred pages in a manila envelope. He and Conny had worked through the weekend. Gamage had talked himself hoarse and, as it seemed to him, to no real purpose but to sweat out exit money. As biography it was a slick illusion; it was Col. Martinka in pristine white-face, unblemished and unlined.

A secretary looked up from a copy of *Vogue* as he entered the air-conditioned world of Martinka & Son. She had been selected as part of the decor. She was quite thin and quite blonde. Swedish modern, he thought. There was a grouping of angular chairs with striped fabric and on the wall behind her hung an antique banjo clock. She gave Gamage a melting smile. "How do you do?"

"Frank Martinka is expecting me," he said. "My name is Gamage."

She flipped a switch and passed the word along. After a moment Frank appeared in the doorway of his office and flagged Gamage in. "You're a fast man with the pages, amigo. You must write with your hands and feet. I learned a long time ago if you need a job done call in a pro. You know Earl Sunshine, don't you?"

The cherubic sales manager stood there in white shirtsleeves, a polka dot bow tie and a blazing smile. "Have a look at this page proof," he said. "It breaks in the L.A. papers Friday." He stretched the page between his hands as reverently as old parchment. "See? *Live in the Shadow of the Great Pyramid! Grand Opening Tomorrow! City-by-the-Nile, California.*" He winked and chuckled. "That was Frank's idea. The Nile. It says water, doesn't it? You think of houseboats and cool breezes. It's romantic. That's what we're pushing. Romance on a fifty foot lot. Right, boss?"

"Is there a river out there?" Gamage frowned.

"Do we say there is?" Frank laughed. "Look, if they want to see water all they got to do is turn on the faucet. Sit down, amigo."

Gamage lingered for a moment over the proof. A half-tone of the Pyramid of Gizeh, the real article, filled the page. *Homesites, where the Past meets the Future! Get in on the ground floor on the Greatest piece of ground in the West. Free flights from Los Angeles! See it from the air! Don't miss this once-in-a-lifetime Opportunity to live like a Pharaoh in the shadow of the Great Pyramid now under construction! Come to City-by-the-Nile, the jewel of the desert. Phone now for reservations!*

"By next sunday night," Sunshine said, "we'll sign contracts on a hundred homesites. And that's a conservative guess, boss. In six months we'll be selling that real estate by the square inch."

"Earl," Frank grinned, "clear out."

Gamage laid the manila envelope on the desk. "You've got everything going for you but Cleopatra."

"I may dig her up for a door prize," Frank said.

"Here's the first hundred pages. Make me out a check."

"How do you know I'll like it?"

"There's nothing in the contract that says you have to like it."

Frank laughed. He riffled the pages of the script and then flipped the intercom. He told someone named Middleton to write out a check for five thousand dollars and then he looked up smiling. "How's your friend?"

"BeJesus John? He tells me he's going to shoot down your air force over the weekend. I guess he means it."

Frank laughed. "With what? Spitballs? I guarantee you those old codgers won't get a mile out of town before hardening of the arteries sets in. I may send out a couple of ambulances to pick up stragglers as a public service."

Gamage found Frank's cock-sureness oppressive. He wouldn't walk around the block to save the desert, but maybe he'd show up on Saturday morning just to be cussed about it.

He picked up his money and left.

4

By Friday Gamage could see the end of the book. He began stitching in the letters from Europe, doctoring them to take out the conceit and petty rancor ("The opera houses are drafty—your mother caught a cold during the second act of *La Traviata*. She was sitting too near the tenor."), and Gamage stopped again to compare the handwriting with that of the 1907 diary. The penmanship matched, but Martinka's style and outlook had corroded. A forgery? But why? "If I weren't a man of character," he told Conny suddenly, "I'd flush this whole project down the tubes."

"Frank liked it."

Gamage paused at the window. The day was clouding over and the heat could be weighed by the pound. Another fifteen or twenty pages and the book would be finished. "You know what I think of Martinka?"

"You're just tired."

"I like the old bastard. I mean it. He commands respect. Up to a point when he begins to turn himself inside out. About five years ago. Everything collects around that time in his life. He started to go against his own character. That's what stops me. He'd gone at real estate like a stamp collector. And then suddenly he rolls out of bed one morning and starts hacking up the valley and cuts himself off from his friends and grows horns and a tail. Here's a visionary gent who never chased a five-dollar bill in his life and suddenly he can write the book on the fine art of money-getting. He practically invented the American date industry and then he turns the bulldozers loose on his own trees in order to grow spec houses. Here's a nine-fingered country gentleman whose only act of vanity was to hang onto a half-assed military title and now he breaks out in twelve acres of pure egomania. I'm talking about the pyramid. 'Look on my works, ye mighty, and despair.' That's Shelley—but is it Martinka? I don't buy it. He's been out of character for five years. What the hell happened? He's acting like he thinks he's Frank. Frank is doing his thinking for him. Either Frank or the old lady or both. I have this bilious feeling that I've been walking through an elaborate piece of stage machinery without being told the name of the play. Come on. I'll buy you a drink."

They took a break and went downstairs to the hotel bar. "Do you think we'll finish tomorrow?" Conny asked.

"I don't know. I thought I'd join BeJesus John and the old folks for a quarter of a mile or so. I need the exercise."

"I suppose you'll pick up your shoes and leave next week."

"As soon as I collect my money, I'm gone. I'm tumbleweed."

"Is Ginny going with you?"

He turned slowly and eyed her. "That's a crazy question."

"Then give me a crazy answer." And then she dropped it. "I mean, forget it."

5

When Gamage stopped by the newspaper office he found a military camp of one. BeJesus John was on his hands and knees, with a cigar burning like a fuse between his lips, tacking printed placards to long wooden pickets. *Save the Desert! Stop the Bulldozers!* BeJesus John looked up over the steel rims of his glasses. "You come to enlist?"

"Don't get anxious."

BeJesus John got up and tried a sign out on his shoulder like a rifle. *Pyramid Go Home!* He walked back and forth and stopped with a grin. "How does it look?"

"It looks like damned fools are in season around here."

BeJesus John chuckled. "I may not have enough pickets to go around. Come early."

"Who's going to show up?"

"Oh, I got the desert rats stirred up."

"BeJesus John, don't you ever look at a calendar? It's the middle of June. That's summer."

"The heat's a little late this year. It's hardly noticeable. Anyway, we're used to it." He returned to his hands and knees and began tacking again. "I never could make out you weekenders. You come out here looking for the sun and then sit around playing pinochle in air-conditioned motel rooms."

Gamage picked up a sign and looked at it. He was sorry he had come. The battle lines were drawn, but BeJesus was deluding himself. He wasn't going to win. He was a local Don Quixote tilting at the pyramid with a picket.

6

Gamage was awakened at eleven o'clock that night by a heavy pounding at the door. He lurched to his feet, unsteady for a moment, not sure what was happening. Was the goddam hotel burning down? He jerked the door open and Frank was standing there.

"Is she here?"

"Is who here?"

"Don't get cute with me!" His face was so fiercely red it looked sandpapered. He pushed past Gamage and his eyes raked the bed. Was the man roaring drunk? He glowered back at Gamage and rushed into the bathroom. Then he was back looking for the closet.

"Stop acting like a low comedian," Gamage said. "Get out."

Frank shot him a murderous glance.

"Who do you think you're going to find?" It was a stupid question, but Gamage felt that the occasion was stupid. Frank was puffed up like a blowfish; rage was strangling him.

"That slut."

"Get the hell out, Frank."

"She's gone."

"What are you talking about?"

"She's been putting out to some son-of-a-bitch and I figured it was you."

"That's a good guess. Maybe she's trying to tell you something. Now clear out. She's not here."

"She left me."

"What?"

"Got herself a meathound. Run off. Left."

Gamage didn't move a muscle. "Calm down. You don't know what the hell you're talking about."

"Did I ask your opinion? I'll break her neck. She's done this before." Frank went roving around the room in a kind of dazed abstraction; he wasn't drunk but he wasn't entirely sober either. "I'll find her."

"Not in here." Not so stupid, Gamage thought. What had happened? Ginny wouldn't leave. Not yet. Frank had to have it wrong. "She'll turn up. Go home, Frank."

Frank glared at him. "I had you pegged. Is she meeting you someplace?"

"There's the door."

"Some son-of-a-bitch has been calling the house. He hangs up when I answer. It should have wised me up."

"You're wise now."

"That goddam alley cat." His eyes flashed around the room again as if he ought to make the rounds once more. Then he glowered at Gamage and was gone.

Gamage shut the door and dug out a cigarette. He couldn't figure out what had happened. It wasn't possible that Ginny had checked out on him. But maybe it was. He hadn't been calling the house and hanging up. He smoked the cigarette down, trying to figure out where he stood, if anywhere, and then got dressed. He didn't know what he was going to do, but later, outside, he started up the jeep. Maybe something had happened to Ginny; or maybe it was happening to him.

A few minutes later his headlights flashed around the flagpole at Villa Martinka, but there was no sign of Ginny's car. He waited, gazing at the place, at the upstairs windows, and then turned back. He hesitated at the crossing, looking at the black highway, the road to the border. There was Mexicali and the motel on the way to San Luis. Ginny had seemed to know that road by heart.

Gamage turned south.

CHAPTER EIGHT

1

He had to stop for gas in Calexico and then crossed the border. A spider web of light bulbs hung over the streets, glowing in the dusty heat. He crept through the Mexicali night traffic, past the bars and curio shops; he crossed the railroad tracks and located himself by a great corrugated tin cotton gin he remembered from before. He shot out along the highway.

After a few miles he saw the motel on his right. He hoped he was wasting his time. If he found Ginny he didn't want to find her here.

There were half a dozen cars and at the rear of the motel, opposite a lighted room, he saw a Thunderbird and it was green.

So what? There was more than one green Thunderbird in Mexico. He pulled in beside it, letting the engine idle for a moment, and then killed it. He held out a fragile hope until he checked the registration slip.

He straightened and gazed at the lighted room. Ginny. He felt a violent urge to walk away from it. She wouldn't come to a place like this to be alone. She had played him for a chump right along with Frank.

The door opened an inch and Ginny looked out at him. They stood for a moment, their eyes locked, and then she opened the door a little wider. She backed away, leaving it open, and a sad anger possessed him. He tossed away his cigarette and walked in.

There were several magazines spread over the bed and a Mexican station was playing softly on the radio. She was alone. But she had been expecting someone. He watched her, tall and blonde, in the same wrapper he remembered from their hours together at Villa Martinka. She snapped off the radio. "I wasn't expecting you."

"I get the idea."

"I'm sorry you found me."

"No, you're not," he said. "You wanted me to find you. That's why you came here."

"I wanted to tell you, Gamage."

"Tell me now."

She picked up her cigarettes and Gamage's glance fixed itself on an object reflected in the dressing table mirror across the room. He turned slowly, seeing it now in a corner near the door—a scuffed brown guitar case.

Barbachano. He was stunned. His mind wouldn't accept it. And then he looked back at Ginny and realized that he was seeing her now for the first time in his life. All right, they were through. What was he hanging around for? "So Frank had it right," he said. "You had another bull in the pasture."

She gave him an imploring look. "Please, Gamage."

"He's a goddam kid. He's fifteen years old!"

She ran her hair back with her fingers. "I love him, Gamage."

"For Christ's sake, you're out of your mind."

"I can't help myself. I love him. It's been that way for months."

"Get your clothes on and clear out of here."

"No."

"Where is he?"

"His mother lives in Mexicali. He'll be back."

He eyed her solemnly. "Do you know what you're doing? You're flushing yourself down the toilet. Even Frank won't take you back. Do you think you can spend the rest of your life on bedsprings with that overheated Aztec? You're just another beetle to him. He collects them like scalps. In six months he'll be passing you around to his friends."

She sat with her knees close together as if she were cold. "I love him. I'm going through with it."

"My God, you don't know what you're saying. I'll drive you back."

"I didn't want this to happen," she whispered. "It just—did." She avoided Gamage's eyes. "Last February. The landscape man sent Mario out to put in some plants along the parking. I found myself watching him."

"Look," Gamage said. "Don't tell me about it."

"He'd strip off his shirt and I could see his muscles working. Shiny in the sun. He was around for two or three days and then he was gone. But he turned up a couple of weeks later, at the door, asking if there were any odd jobs he could do. I was alone and in a hell of a mood. I felt as if I had been waiting for him." She made a hopeless little gesture with her hand. "I let him in. I was fairly sluttish about it. I let it happen. I wanted it to happen. There was no love in it, Gamage. It was an act of hatred. I was hurting Frank. Humiliating him—striking back. I almost wished he'd walk in and find me fouling the nest. With an Indian. When you can't hurt someone, when you can't reach him, sometimes you settle for hurting yourself. It works. When Mario left I gave him ten dollars. He tore it up and flushed it down the toilet. Frank wouldn't have that much style. After that Mario began calling me. I tried to drop him, put an end to it, but after a couple of weeks—I saw him again. I liked him. Then he'd disappear for weeks at a time and I couldn't get him off my mind. I never knew where he was. Then the phone would ring and he'd say he was at some café or gas station on the highway and could I come down and pick him up. I always did. He's no fumbling kid, Gamage. Once Frank had the house full of people and Mario called. I just walked out without a word. I couldn't stop myself."

Gamage sat down. He hated listening to it, but he felt a compassion for her—the kid with his Svengali-like power over her would drop her along the way, a pariah, an outcast. She was letting him destroy her; she was destroying herself. "Ginny, you're going back."

"To Frank?"

"Frank needn't know."

She shook her head. "Don't, Gamage. It won't work."

"Why did you bring me to the desert? Why did you tie this can on me?"

She was silent for a moment. "We were in love once. I thought I could be in love with you again. I wanted to go away with you. I really meant to, Gamage. I saw what was ahead of me with Mario and I didn't want it to happen. I guess I was trying to save myself—but that didn't work either. I couldn't stop seeing Mario. It wouldn't end. I'm sorry if I hurt you."

"Look," he said. "That fire went out the moment I walked in here. Was it that goddam kid who invited me to leave town? There was a note like a plot turn out of one of those comic books he reads."

"He knew about us almost from the beginning," she said. "He was violently jealous of you."

"That day I found you waiting in the lobby of the hotel. He was sitting there. You weren't waiting for me. You were there with him, weren't you?"

"He was broke," she said softly. "I had to see him and help him. I was hoping you wouldn't walk in, but you did."

"Was it Barbachano hanging around Villa Martinka the night we were upstairs?"

"Yes."

"For Christ's sake, Ginny." It was clear to Gamage now that he'd even had the geometry wrong. It wasn't Frank in the other corner—it was Barbachano.

Ginny inhaled nervously. "He told me he'd kill you next time."

"He'll have the chance the moment he walks in." Gamage got up and turned, staring at the door as if he could see through it. He sensed Barbachano's presence and when he jerked the door open the kid was standing there.

His white shirt was tight and sweat-stained around his chest, open at the neck, and his lips were set in a scornful grin. "You heard the lady. Heel out. Your ass is wagging your ears."

Gamage shoved his hand in the kid's face and sent him pitching backwards into the fender of the Thunderbird. He was dimly aware of Ginny calling out Mario's name. He pulled Barbachano up by the shirt front. "Listen, you snot-nosed punk. You're gone."

The kid swung on him and Gamage sent him sprawling into the parking. The ringing of cicadas in the shrubbery stopped short. Barbachano wiped his lip and looked up at Gamage with sullen arrogance. He rolled to his feet and then, like a bullfighter showing utter contempt, he turned his back and slowly walked away as if daring Gamage to charge. He kept walking and for a long time Gamage stood there fighting down a murderous rage. Finally the darkness separated them and Gamage got the guitar case and pitched it into the parking. It split open and comic books scattered. There was no guitar. Gamage scowled for an instant; he had been taken in by an empty package, a piece of luggage the kid hung onto to separate himself from the herd.

Ginny was sitting on the edge of the bed with her head in her hands. Gamage shut the door. "Get dressed. I'm driving you back."

Her green eyes looked up with cold, immovable defiance. "To what? Frank? Why don't you leave me alone?"

"Frank suddenly looks good."

"You don't know what you're saying."

"You tell me."

"Frank was drinking last night and he tried to kill me. I mean, kill me." Her voice lowered to little more than a whisper. "I got the message."

"Because you were putting out? Frank had his nose in the wind."

"No. Because he wasn't sure I'd keep my mouth shut any longer. *It's been five years!*" She rose from the bed and went fumbling for another cigarette. It was five years ago that Ginny turned up in Europe—was that part of it too? The thought hadn't occurred to Gamage before. He watched her. She stayed across the room from him, facing the wall, and lit her cigarette. She lifted her head, exhaling deeply, and turned. "Frank's father is not in Italy."

"I guessed that."

"He's dead."

The statement left a profound quiet in the room. Gamage didn't move.

"He's been dead for five years," she said.

2

"Summer had started and the desert was almost empty." Ginny had returned to the edge of the bed. "Madam Martinka generally left for Los Angeles when the heat started and she had begun to pack. She had fallen under the spell of a balmy group called the Patriotic Daughters. The old man didn't want her to spend the summer sewing swastikas, or whatever it was they did. He'd been patient with her for almost a year and now he wanted her to get out. She was already beginning to see Jews coming out of the woodwork. She was terrified of them. Anyway, she was packing and they got into a real battle. I was downstairs and I'd never heard him raise his voice before. He was inclined to let people go their own way—even Madam Martinka—but he'd had enough of the Patriotic Daughters. It went on and on. After about an hour he came storming through the house and left. He didn't come home that night. The next day we were all out looking for him. The temperature was around 105. Frank found him. He had pitched an old tent out in the sand dunes a couple of miles off the highway and packed in some food. Frank couldn't get him to budge—if anything, Frank made it worse. They had hardly exchanged a dozen words in the last few years and this was no time to begin. Later we all went out there. He greeted us in a very courtly manner—even Madam Martinka. He seemed entirely happy where he was. He said he wasn't coming back. He'd come to the desert with next to nothing and he wanted nothing now but to be left alone. I really didn't blame him. He looked happy for the first time since I had met him. I was extremely fond of him and I think he was fond of me. We all stood out in the sun and the old lady began to rage at him. He *wasn't* going to cast her aside to live in a rotting tent on the desert like an Old Testament Hebrew. She cared about appearances and she didn't intend to let the valley laugh at her. She went on and on. I watched him and until that day I didn't realize how deeply he loathed her. He had been trying to keep it bottled up, but now his face turned beet red and finally, when it came out, it was like a howl of pain. He held up his left hand and spread his fingers. 'See that, Madam? Look at it! Four fingers! Don't tell me about the Jews!' He said that it had happened when he was sixteen. He had enlisted in the Navy in Boston and was put aboard a frigate. There were two Jews on the ship, Madam, he said, and the Navy in those days was no place for a Jew to be. They were hounded and tormented. At sea, after several months, one of them jumped overboard and drowned. The other got a medical discharge. 'He got hold of a meat cleaver and chopped off the index finger of his left hand, Madam. Look at it! You have been consorting with a Jew for thirty-seven years!'"

Gamage looked up. They were getting to the bottom of the Martinka nest of boxes. The old man had given Madam Martinka her comeuppance five years ago. He had used the Jew in him like a weapon.

"The old lady turned white," Ginny said. "I don't know how he had managed to hold it back so long, but he had finally decided to let her have it. She had been torturing him for all those months with the Patriotic Daughters and their frothing bigotry, and he had tried to warn her off. He had been through that house of horrors once before and had had to pick up a meat cleaver to get out. He had spent his life running away from himself only to run smack into himself again. I think he was relieved. I think he was glad to make his own acquaintance. The old lady was struck dumb, but not for long. She let loose. She turned the air blue. Frank stood there stunned by the whole thing. That meant *he* was part Jewish and it seemed to daze him. You'd think he was going to grow a hook nose on the spot, and I think I first began to hate Frank at that moment. And then his mother stopped short and seemed to notice Frank for the first time. 'Thank God, *you're* not tainted!' she said. 'He's not your father! Frank, he's not your father!' The veins were standing out on the old man's neck. He looked at Frank. It didn't matter that Frank had disappointed him in so many ways. Frank had grown up as his son and now Madam Martinka was going to take even that away from him. At that moment he did Frank a kindness. He gave Frank a father. 'You'll find him under a Joshua tree on the high desert,' he said. And then he faced the old lady and he couldn't help himself. He cut her to ribbons, even though the words literally choked him. 'I have not been fooled all these years, Madam. No, Madam. You posed as James Crighton's sister and lived with him like a common strumpet. I'm sure he was the only man you ever cared for. Why he refused to marry you I can guess. Did he already have a wife, Madam? He died leaving you to find a husband, and soon, and I made the mistake of feeling sorry for you. Madam, I have lived to regret it.' His face was terrible. He was in pain. He hardly got the last words out. He began to gasp. He was having a heart attack."

The air was streaked with cigarette smoke. Ginny got up, and now almost seemed to be acting out the moment. "They just looked down at him, the two of them. I tried to shade his face and finally Frank helped me get him into the tent. The old lady just stared. We were a long way from the road—a couple of miles. I told Frank to run for help, but she stopped him. She said it was too late. She knew the look of death. Maybe she did, but the old man was still alive. I got up and started running toward the highway. I can still remember the feel of hot sand between my shoes. I must have gone almost a mile when Frank called to me. He caught up and told me the Colonel was dead and not to get anyone. He took my keys and told me to wait at the car. I went on ahead. They buried him and packed up the tent. It took hours. When they got back to the car they just glared at me. They told me no one must know yet. Madam Martinka's eyes were piercing. She said that their affairs were a house of cards. The Colonel was no businessman. Everything was spread too thin, he had bought too much worthless land and there were mortgages on everything. He had been holding things together on the strength of his reputation. If it got out that Colonel Martinka was dead everything would collapse around us. The tax men and creditors would move in like blackbirds and pick everything clean. A fortune would slip through our fingers. We'd be left with nothing. No, his affairs had to be straightened out first. We had to provide for ourselves. As long as no one knew he was dead there was power in his name and it would prop everything up. It would only be a matter of weeks. They'd transfer as much of the estate as possible into our names. Later, we could report him missing. It would be years before he could be declared legally dead. Meanwhile, we could make ourselves very rich. I kept my mouth shut and hated myself for it. But it wasn't a matter of a few weeks. It became months. Frank began to worry that the old man's body wasn't deep enough in the sand—he used to go out there with a shovel. But there had been a sandstorm and he could never find the grave. It was like trying to locate a spot in the ocean. They continued to operate in his name. Frank learned to forge his signature and began to fly high. He started a subdivision. The boom had started and the money began to roll in. The only land that was any good, that was close enough in, had been planted in dates. Frank began tearing them out. Frank and the old lady were surprised at how easily everyone in the valley accepted the Colonel's presence. Why rock the boat? I couldn't stand it any longer. I left Frank. I thought I was through. I wanted out of it. That's when I met you in Europe. But Frank was afraid of me. I might talk. He turned up in the Grande Bretagne and just missed seeing us together. I realized then how tied to him I was. He'd see me dead before he'd let loose of me." She shrugged dismally. "But that's only part of it, Gamage. There was all that Martinka money. There was going to be millions now and I'm a girl who grew up with barnyard manure. If I went back with Frank it was for the money. I was bought and paid for a long time ago."

"So you left me standing in the Grande Bretagne."

"Yes. It was so easy to pretend the old man was still alive. Madam Martinka would send his shoes out to be repaired and Frank would grind them down again and scuff around in them and four or five months later back they'd go to the repairman. Madam Martinka would never let the cleaning woman upstairs. They'd quit on her. The house would make them nervous. They'd always come to believe that the Colonel was locked up in his room like a madman."

"And they didn't forget to buy him cigars."

"No. They had a bull by the tail and they were afraid to let go. And it was so easy. People thought they saw the old man down the street or driving past in the car. He's been dead all these years and yet he's still the most powerful man in the valley."

Gamage nodded. As a pyramid builder Frank couldn't have swung the financing for a project of that size, but Martinka gave the thing weight and importance. "Then the biography I'm writing is so much window dressing."

"Yes. They never planned for things to go on for years this way. And they no longer really need him. Once the big money starts coming in on the pyramid development, Frank is made. Really made. They've talked over a dozen different ways to lay him to rest. If they declare him missing the estate will be tied up for years. They've already transferred as much as they could into their names without arousing suspicion. They're going to end it once and for all this summer—as soon as Frank can get your book passed around. You're giving the old man five more years of life. They're not taking any chances. People believe what they read in a book—especially if it's written by a Pulitzer Prize winner. Once I mentioned you, Frank couldn't wait to get you. He's no fool."

"Then the letters from Italy are faked."

"Yes. Frank can turn out the old man's handwriting as easily as his own.

Everything he gave you from these last years is forged."

"Is Madam Martinka in Europe?"

"Yes. As soon as your book is printed they're going to slip off their own hook. She'll send Frank a couple of telegrams. The first will come from somewhere in Austria and say that the Colonel has had a heart attack. A few hours later there will be another announcing his death. Who's going to doubt it? Even BeJesus John will print it. Frank intends to fly to Europe like a grief-stricken son. When he gets back to the valley with his mother they'll say the Colonel wanted to be buried in the town where he was born. It's true too. They found it in his will. A little town in the Austrian Alps called Igls."

"They're home free."

"Yes." She pushed back her hair and looked at Gamage with a final spark in her eyes. "You still want to take me back to Frank?"

CHAPTER NINE

1

Gamage stopped for a cup of coffee across the border in El Centro. It was past three. His face shone in the heat and his eyes were solemn and tired. He had got the Martinka story, but he had no feeling of triumph. Ginny cast a heavy shadow across his mind. If she had been looking for a purgatory Barbachano would provide it. She had helped pick the Colonel's dead pockets by keeping her mouth shut and in the end she had parlayed a little greed into a rat-hole. Gamage saw now that he had never really been in the running; when she reached out for him she was grabbing at straws. Barbachano was made to order. But she was pasting the wrong label on the can. She called it love, and maybe it looked that way to her, but she was going the other way.

He hunched over his coffee. It was over for him. That door was closing tightly behind him. He thought of Martinka, a tall, angular Jew who had solved the equations of his life with the meat cleaver before he ever turned up on the desert. And then his life had come full circle. He found himself married to an anti-Semite. Reality was a poke in the eye with a sharp stick.

Outside, a wind was rising off the alfalfa fields. The highway was deserted and Gamage made time. In a few hours BeJesus John would march against the pyramid, but now he could save his shoe leather. He could bring down the pyramid with his flat-bed press.

Wind swept across the highway in long drafts. Gamage would lay Martinka's ghost and clear out of the City of the Sun. He could be gone by noon.

The desert was strangely dark and heated, starless under the low sky. A sand storm was kicking up and Gamage tried to outrun it. His headlights cut into the thickening haze ahead. Some forty miles above the border the jeep began to miss and sputter and finally the engine quit. Gamage rolled to a stop.

He couldn't be out of gas. He'd had the tank filled on the way down, in Calexico. He looked at the gauge for the first time. It said empty.

He sat for a moment, refusing to believe it, and then got out. He uncapped the tank. He had no flashlight to look in, but when he rocked the jeep and listened there wasn't a sound from the tank. It was dry.

He straightened. Grits of sand in the air struck his face like live sparks. He looked back, toward Mexico, and he could see Barbachano laughing at him. That punk. That geek. The goddam Aztec had siphoned the tank.

Gamage turned his back to the wind. He felt in the middle of nowhere. He couldn't remember the last gas station he had passed or think what was ahead. The sand storm began closing in around the beams of his headlights.

Another car was bound to come along. He'd flag it down. But twenty minutes passed and when another pair of headlights appeared they went by like meteors. Gamage shouted out at the driver and then swore at him.

He'd walk up ahead. There could be a town a quarter of a mile away and he wouldn't know it.

He left on the headlights as a beacon and started forward. Sand stung his eyes and fouled the air. If he didn't find something close he'd turn back. But once out of range of his lights, BeJesus John's warning called to him. The highway was no place to be on foot at night. Desert crawlers liked to warm themselves on the asphalt.

The thought slowed him down. All he needed now was to step on a snake. He stopped. The entire desert seemed on the move—sand and tumbleweed and an occasional flying branch.

He looked at the darkness around his feet and tried to hear through the abrasive wind for the rattling of snakes.

In the end he turned back. He wasn't going to accommodate Frank by risking snakebite in a goddam sandstorm. That would be Frank's luck. If Gamage was going to step on a sidewinder he'd do it after unloading the Martinka story.

He was a long time working his way back to the murky headlights. When he got there he saw a pickup truck parked behind the jeep and a man, with a handkerchief wrapped around his face, looking for him.

"You got trouble?"

"I ran out of gas."

"Well, let's not stand around. I'll pull you into town."

2

At dawn the entire valley was under a great dust cloud. It was past eight when Gamage crept into Thebes. The jeep's paint had been sandblasted down to the raw metal. Across the way, palms were bent in the wind, banging and slapping their fronds.

Sand was spraying everywhere along the arcades and piling up in drifts along the doorways. Gamage stopped at the hotel and hurried inside. His skin felt rasped and raw and his eyes stung. He picked up his mail—a letter from his agent. A producer was interested in the cactus man story—they might be able to put together a deal.

Gamage tossed the letter on his bed. Fine. He'd head for the coast.

He stripped off his clothes, weighted with grit and dust, and took a long shower. He felt that he'd be spitting sand for a week.

He left the hotel for the office of *The Thebes Weekly Sunset*. He was sure that BeJesus John had called off his hike and expected to find him chewing a cigar at the window, glaring out at the weather. At least, the sand storm would ground Frank's air force, and that made it a draw.

Gamage could see lights burning inside, but when he walked in BeJesus John was nowhere in sight. Conny was there and she was pouring a cup of coffee for herself.

"What are you doing here?" he said.

"Waiting for you. You're late."

"For what? Where's BeJesus John?"

"He just left. On foot."

"You're kidding? Who the hell showed up?"

"He did. And I did. And I guess you make three. You want some coffee? You didn't think a little blow like this was going to stop him, did you? He's marching up the highway with one of those signs over his head and he's mad as a hornet."

Gamage sat down. Sand was striking the window like buckshot. The unused pickets, with their fresh signs attached, were stacked up like firewood. "You should have stopped him."

"How? With a brick?" She handed him a mug of coffee. "He'll turn around. He didn't bother to lock up. He just stormed off. He's got to get it out of his system." She sat on the office fence as if it were a corral; she wore Levis and a gingham shirt and a pair of desert boots. "What really hurt him," she said, "was that nobody even showed up to say they were going home. The weather be damned, nobody cared enough to get out of bed. He realizes now that he's been talking to himself. He knows he's licked and he's just got to thumb his nose at everybody."

Gamage sighed and finished half his coffee. "I'll head him off at the pass. He's got a newspaper to get out. Look, call the sheriff's office. That skeleton Morejohn found in the dunes a couple of weeks ago. Make like a newspaper woman. Find out if that stiff was missing a finger. If it is, tell them to stop looking in their missing persons file. It's Martinka."

Gamage found his way back to the highway, creeping along through the dusty gloom with his lights on. The wind was beginning to play itself out. He went a couple of miles and then turned around. Somehow he had missed BeJesus John. He decided that the man had walked off his peeve and gone back to the office. Well, it would wait.

3

Frank answered the door himself. His clothes were rumpled; his shirt was unbuttoned down his chest and his trousers hung around his hips. "What do you want, amigo?"

"Shall we go in or do you want to talk out here?" Gamage said.

Frank regarded him with morose, boozy eyes. "Look, forget what I told you last night. I got excited. Ginny was home when I got back. Yeah. She's in bed now. Forget it." He put on a smile, a ragged mask, and it was almost painful to watch. "I love that broad. You know how it is. A guy starts imagining things. So forget it, amigo."

Gamage eyed him. Pathetic bastard. "I'm glad to hear that, Frank. I know how much she means to you. But what I've got to say won't wait. Let's get it over with."

Frank shrugged and led the way into the living room. He picked up a half-finished drink waiting with a bowl of melting ice and a bourbon bottle on the coffee table. He stretched out on the couch where it looked as if he had spent most of the night.

"All right, amigo. What's eating you?"

Gamage stayed on his feet. This wasn't going to take long. "Thank me," he said. "I'm not finishing the book. It'll save you money."

Frank's eyes slid over. "You can't quit. We got a contract."

"Let's start with this. You couldn't pay me enough to keep me in this shell game you're playing. I know how it's done. I know all the moves."

"You don't say, amigo."

"I just said it. I was hired to paint a little stage scenery and that's not my line of work. You're not getting your hands on the rest of the book. But that's almost beside the point now. There are laws against fraud, but with a little luck and a good lawyer you might get off with twenty years."

Frank gave Gamage a shrewd, measuring look. "If I knew what the hell you're talking about, I'd throw you out."

"You know what I'm talking about, Frank. Your old man is dead."

Frank didn't bat an eye. "You chump. That horseshit has been cropping up around here for years. Hell, you want to talk to my old man? I'll put him on the phone."

The man was an actor. "He's dead, Frank. Stop trying to con me. He died just like Camilla. Your old lady knew a main chance when she saw it lying at her feet. She qualifies as an expert, and you took your cues from her. The two of you stood there waiting for him to check out. You might have saved him, Frank, but you didn't even try. He didn't have horns when he died. You hung them on him. You changed his spots. You've been destroying him, but by bit, and now he's hated up and down the valley. That Old Testament bastard had defiled your saintly mother—never mind that she let Camilla die in order to hook him. You settled the score. And then you dream up the idea of building a pyramid. A pyramid. A tombstone with his name on it. There was a message right from your skull, but I didn't stop to read it, and I don't think you did either. You're going to bury that spectre under one hell of a pile of rocks—at a nice profit, of course."

Frank's face had darkened and his eyes were mere, puffy slits. "You found Ginny."

"I found her."

"Where is she?"

"Don't waste your breath."

Frank's voice rose in a tormented bellow. "*Where is she!*" Gamage was silent. And then, suddenly, Frank thought his way through the booze. "Listen, amigo," he laughed. "What the hell do I care where she is? All I want her for is to throw her out. Get smart. You're smelling up the place with that crap. Nobody's going to believe it. She's sore at me and she's been blowing smoke up your rear end. What are you going to prove? Not a goddam thing."

"I'm going to try."

Then Frank almost smiled, like a seedy magician about to pull a trick out of his sleeve. "Maybe you ought to meet my mother."

"I haven't time for a wild goose trip to Europe."

"It won't take any time. She's home. Amigo, she's standing right behind you."

Gamage kept his poker face intact. He turned. A woman with yellowing hair stood at a far end of the acre of citron carpeting. Gamage knew at once it had to be Madam Martinka. She looked to him as if she had just stepped out of Grant Wood's Daughters of the American Revolution. Her thin lips were pinched and she glared at Gamage through faintly aloof, glacial eyes. All she lacked was a teacup between her fingers.

"My dear Mr. Gamage," she said bitingly. "I have been listening to your nonsense. I advise you to pack up your obscene lies and leave the desert. If necessary I shall cable the Colonel and advise him to come home at once."

"That'll make you look pretty stupid, amigo," Frank said.

Gamage watched Madam Martinka with a certain fascination. She held herself with the commanding air of a general who had finally ventured to the front lines.

"I'm sorry to disappoint you, Madam Martinka," Gamage said. "But I'm not ready to leave."

"Then we'll be obliged to file a slander suit against you."

"I'll have to risk it."

"We can crush you, like a common insect, Mr. Gamage," she said.

Gamage wasn't altogether sure now they would let him reach the front door alive. He decided to play out the rest of his hand. "I've got a call in at the sheriff's office. I think you've both been losing a lot of sleep over that stiff they dug up. It could be just a desert rat. But there could be a finger gone and that would be bad news. Is that why you flew home, Madam Martinka? Say the left index finger. Say Colonel Martinka."

Frank pitched the whiskey glass at him and then lunged. Gamage met him with a quick chop to the side of the neck. Frank fell in a wide sprawl to the carpet. Gamage got a quick flash of Madam Martinka watching without a visible flicker of emotion. Frank tried to rise to his hands and knees and peered helplessly at her as if Gamage ceased to exist. In that moment Gamage realized that Frank, dazed and half-drunk, was more in terror of her than him.

"You child," she breathed. "Frank, get off your hands and knees and throw this man out."

"Don't bother him," Gamage said, resurrecting a line from one of his old screenplays. "I'll throw myself out."

4

It was almost eleven when BeJesus John appeared in the doorway of *The Thebes Weekly Sunset*. The sign and picket was dragging behind him like a tattered rudder in a sea of dust. Gamage, waiting impatiently in the swivel chair, swung his feet off the desk. "How did you come back? By way of Omaha, Nebraska, for Christ's sake? You've got a paper to get out."

"I have been reviewing my life, sir, in a tavern of my choice."

"He's stoned," Conny said.

BeJesus John pulled himself up grandly. "*Sua cuique sunt vitia.* That's Latin, madam." And then, to Gamage. "A paper? A paper, you say. Why, sir, I have retired from the fifth estate. Or is it the fourth? This is indeed an occasion for rejoicing. I predict dancing in the streets. I intend to dedicate my remaining years to allowing the world to go to hell, and other good works." He took a step forward and fell flat on his face.

Gamage shot his cigarette at a cuspidor. He was angry. He wanted to clear out. He had stuck around to drop the Martinka story in BeJesus John's lap, and now he glared down at the man, a fuming heap on the floor.

He couldn't control his vexation. "Light a match," he glowered. "Maybe the old crank will ignite." He was tempted to walk out and give the story to the metropolitan papers.

Conny shut the door and bent down. "Poor man."

"Don't humor the bastard."

"He looks kind of sweet with his mouth shut. I never noticed that before. I'll make another pot of coffee."

"What for?"

"We'll sober him up."

"He's ossified. It'll take a week." And then Gamage gave a long, angry sigh. Why kid himself? The story had to break in *The Thebes Weekly Sunset*. But BeJesus John was through for the day. He'd wake up with a head full of broken glass. "To hell with him. He's cluttering up the joint. Let's get him out of here."

They loaded him into the jeep and Conny started up the engine. She'd take him home and find a neighbor to help get him inside. Gamage stood on the porch until the jeep disappeared into the dusty fog. The sun was beginning to burn through like an evil eye. He returned to the office and kicked over a bentwood chair. Then he went into the composing room and made his way to the linotype. He'd set the story himself. He turned on the machine and pulled up the runted, sawed-off chair and sat down.

He lit a cigarette. How had he got himself wired into this situation? It had been a long time since he had put out a newspaper. He switched on the light over the keyboard. He spit (the cuspidors belong to him, didn't they?) and then slowly, angrily, letter by letter, he punched out the slug line—MARTINKA.

He hunched forward, sorting his thoughts, and set his fingers over the keys. He got his lead. He began to write and the room filled with the harsh rattle and clatter of the machine.

It was an obit five years overdue. Col. Jesse Martinka had cadged a kind of immortality, living on while his bones mouldered in the dunes. Gamage struggled with a feeling that he was putting an end to the man and he was almost sorry.

He lost track of time and the slugs began stacking up in a lengthening column of lead. Martinka had put on an illusion show, escaping into a stage name, but when it came to stamping out reality, like the sign said, the old lady had no peer. She had been able to sit down and coolly compose a love letter to a man she hated, a pretense to be put on public view.

When Conny got back he interrupted himself. "Get back on the phone and start rounding up some local news to fill out the pages. See what you can pick up on the sand storm so far. There's bound to be crop damage. Get an estimate. And check with the sheriff's office again to find out if there have been any accidents on the highway."

She was game and he found himself looking her over as she ambled away.

He kept himself awake with coffee. Later in the day he showed her how to pull a galley proof and then made her sit and proof read it. He found some old wooden type that BeJesus John probably hadn't dusted off since the 1918 armistice. He set the headline in it. "Remind me to raise the price of the paper," he said. "I'll make a box on it. The locals have been cheating BeJesus John for years."

He didn't realize that the day had passed until Conny pulled him away for dinner. The wind was gone but the dust was still settling. They stopped in at the Queen of Sheba Café and the news getting around town caught up with them. Frank Martinka had shot his mother and then himself.

5

They worked through the night. It took seven columns of type to bury Martinka & Son. The paper was locked up late Sunday morning. Gamage had filled holes with set type he found in the galleys, and made up a few free ads to make it look like a newspaper. He inked up the press and soon the old flat-bed began banging out newspapers. Gamage pulled off a copy and Conny came up beside him to look it over.

"You're pretty good at this," she said.

They ran off all the newsprint they could find in the shop. Gamage, who hadn't been to bed since Friday night, was ink-smeared and smiling. There was a sense of achievement in getting out a paper that he had forgotten. BeJesus John came wandering in the back door and his eyes darted around the shop as if he were in the wrong place. What was going on here? The press was feeding out copies and Gamage was bundling them up. BeJesus John scowled and plucked a wet newspaper from the machine and walked forward to his swivel chair in the office. He was a long time reading it.

Finally he came wandering back to the composing room. "So old Jesse is dead."

"That's what it says."

"I can't say I was glad to read it. Buried in the dunes all these years."

Gamage nodded. He had a sudden sensation of being asleep on his feet.

"Poor old bastard," BeJesus John said. And then he spit. "Never saw so many typos in my life."

"Break his arm," Conny said.

"But, by God, this will stop the bulldozers."

"For a while," Gamage said.

"I'll just get some of these papers around town." He said, loading up a pile under his arm. He loosened the cigar from his teeth and held it for an instant poised over a cuspidor. He glanced at Gamage. "Okay if I use the spittoon?"

"Be my guest."

"What are you going to do with that masterpiece of fiction you've been writing?"

"It's yours. You can cut the fiction and I'll fill you in on the rest before I leave. Run it in installments. It'll sell newspapers and you might even be able to peddle some ad space."

"You leaving town?"

"I'm gone," Gamage said.

"That sounds a bit hasty. Your blood'll thin out. It takes a little while." He ran his hand over his lips. "I might be persuaded to sell you a half-interest in this place for a reasonable sum. Say, a dollar."

"BeJesus John, you're keeping me awake."

"Of course, that would be overcharging you. The *Sunset* ain't worth anything. But I'd kinda dislike to see it die off. How does a dollar strike you?"

"He'll buy it," Conny said in a casual voice.

Gamage shot her a tired glance.

"Cash, if possible," BeJesus John said.

"Thanks, but no thanks," Gamage said.

"He'll think it over," Conny said.

Gamage dismissed the two of them with a glance. A pair of con artists. He'd get some sleep and pack his traps and clear out.

By the end of the day *The Thebes Weekly Sunset* had settled over the valley like a sudden fall of leaves, and Gamage was sound asleep. He had dropped Conny off at her place and she had invited him in for a last cigarette together. He fell asleep on the couch.

He awoke the next day at noon and found himself alone in the house. He peered out at the day—the air was clearing, but the nearby palms were great shaggy pom-poms of dust—and turned on the coffee.

For a buck he could put his name in gold leaf on the window of *The Thebes Weekly Sunset*. It would be sheer lunacy. The money was in Hollywood, and his foot was back in the door. All they had to do was button up the deal on *The Cactus Man*.

There might be a whole series in it. *Return of the Cactus Man. Son of the Cactus Man. Return of the Son of the Cactus Man.* How could Gamage reasonably toss away a literary future like that?

Conny came in the front door with a bag of groceries and he looked her over. She was in shorts and a blouse tied at the midriff. "I'll fix you something to eat," she said, "and then you can get gone."

"Don't get anxious."

"The coffee is boiling."

"What's wrong with you is you get anxious."

She turned off the coffee and looked at him queerly. "You said you were heading back to the coast."

"I'm cogitating."

"Don't change your mind on my account."

"I just figured it out," he said. "What a man really needs is a place to put his name. You know, I used to be great once. The trustees of Columbia University said so. I had the document to prove it. I don't know what happened to it."

"I'll take your word for it."

"Is there a sign painter in town? I want the name in gold leaf. Gold is eternal, you know. I'll settle for a scrap of immortality. Conny, you look fine half-naked."

She regarded him with a blossoming smile. "I'm not half-naked. I'm half-

dressed. It's all the way you look at it."
He pulled her into his arms.

THE END

YELLOWLEG
BY A. S. FLEISCHMAN

CHAPTER ONE

The hat. The hat stood tall and straight on his head, never at a jack-deuce angle, and the two men riding with him had never seen a man who did so little fussing with his headgear. The morning sun was now hot on his neck, but that didn't seem to bother him any more than the biting midges drawn to his sweat.

They rode in silence, the three of them, along a dung-marked trail toward Gila City, New Mexico.

He sat in a McClellan hull from the war, a rawhide affair with hickory stirrups. His trousers, too, were from the war—long-faded yellowleg breeches. He carried a bone-handled jackknife in one pocket and a jangle of coins in the other—a couple of cartwheels, Mexican pesos and a single California gold piece.

He rode with his eyes tightened on the horizon, a man alone with his thoughts. He was tall and big-boned with a touch of gray at the temples. But his eyebrows were black, black and curly, and he hadn't bothered to shave in several days. He was a silent, rough-looking man; folks took him for a saddle tramp, and that suited him fine.

The early summer heat pressed down on them, three specks moving across the vast, bleached country. They had been riding together for five days, drifting toward the nearest town with a bank in it. The other men hadn't bothered asking his name. They'd begun calling him Yellowleg, and as a summer name it would do.

The short, big-eared man, the one who called himself Turk, pulled away and dismounted along a cutbank. He began humming a little tune and unbuckled his breeches in the area of some bunchgrass. He rejoined the others about ten minutes later.

The third man, Billy, turned to him in his young, loose-jointed way and grinned. "You got the natures or something, Turk?"

"Nothin' that a little whiskey won't doctor up," Turk said.

Yellowleg didn't waste a glance on them. In five days he'd learned that Turk had the talking talent and Billy had the shooting talent. And what Yellowleg didn't know, he could guess.

He knew they had come out of the Reb army together and he guessed they had deserted. Yellowleg reckoned Billy's age to be around twenty-two and, figuring back, it meant he had gone into the army at fourteen or so. "Just a big, overgrown Texas colt fibbin' on his age," Turk had said. "I took him under my wing and made a soldier man out of him. Why, he paunched himself three blue-bellies before he was able to shave."

But the war was long past now, seven years past, and they had welcomed

Yellowleg's gun hand. They had been in opposite armies, but that didn't matter when it came to hoorawin' the countryside. When you needed a man to fill in, a Yankee saddle tramp was as good as any.

They reached the rim overlooking Gila City late in the morning. They sat there a long time, gazing at the dusty street, the tarpaper rooftops and the narrow false fronts. It wasn't much of a town and there was no sound but that of a mechanical piano from one of the saloons. A fitful breeze carried the jangling notes to their ears in muted bursts of sound.

They gazed and wiped the flies from their faces. It was a long time before Turk spoke, and his tone was hushed and reverent. "Now look at that nice little bank down there," he said. "Just waitin' for us to come a-callin'."

Yellowleg felt Billy's young gaze turn on him. "You look a little peaked. Ain't you ever gunned a bank before, Yellowleg?"

"I'd say he looks more scared than peaked," Turk scowled. "You can never tell about Yankees."

"We could let him hold the horses," Billy said. "Break him in easy."

Yellowleg ignored them both. He sat hunched slightly forward on his claybank mare, and continued studying the town.

"Now ain't he the most unsociable gent you ever met?" Turk said. "Been ridin' with us goin' on a week now, and ain't lost his temper even once't."

"Turk," Billy said. "I don't trust a man that don't lose his temper now and again."

"You and me both, Billy boy."

Yellowleg tossed away the dead cigarette between his lips and spoke quietly, without looking at either of them. "We're not taking that bank."

There was a dead silence, and Yellowleg was aware of the hard glance that passed between Turk and Billy.

"You don't say," Turk remarked finally.

"The money'll keep."

"You givin' the orders now?"

"It looks that way, don't it?"

"It don't look that way to me," Billy grinned. He wore the brim of his hat low over his bleached-blue eyes and gazed at Yellowleg as if he were seeing him for the first time and couldn't help admiring the man.

Yellowleg pulled his last match from the horsehair band of his hat and fired it with his thumbnail. He lit a cigarette slowly, his eyes still fixed on the town below.

"Mister," Turk scowled, "maybe you better turn around and go back where you come from."

Yellowleg took his time. "Turk, your horse needs shoein'," he said quietly. "Billy, you and me need a drink. And then we're going to have a bath. A posse'd be able to follow us by the scent."

Turk spit and looked up again. "Maybe you didn't hear what I said?"

"Turk," Yellowleg said, "there're some men ain't worth listening to."

Billy burst out laughing. "Be john dog!"

Yellowleg pulled up on the reins and backed the mare from the edge of the rim. He hadn't expected Billy's laughter, but it told him what he had already sensed. Beneath their partnership lay a mutual contempt, and he was sure now he could handle them both.

"If we take that bank, we'll take it my way," he said. "If you ride with me, you'll ride my way—you'll drink my way, eat my way and maybe die my way. If that don't suit you, arguments are easy to settle."

Turk licked his lips, ignoring Billy's laughter, and decided against prolonging the argument. His eyes shifted to Billy. "The man's just askin' for a shallow grave, Billy boy. A shame too. We was gettin' to like him." He spit. "Reckon we'll have to kill him to get rid of him."

Billy leaned forward on his saddle horn and thumbed his hat back on his head. "It don't matter to me which way we take that bank. Yankees can be awful smart sometimes."

Turk's face hardened. "Paunch him, Billy."

"It is a temptation."

"You hear me?"

Yellowleg gave them a brief glance and drew the Springfield out of its boot. "When you make up your minds," he said, "I'll be waiting in town." He pointed the rifle toward the false fronts half a mile away and then took aim. He raised the sight high enough to be sure of clearing everything and then squeezed the trigger twice. "I'll be in the Davis & Davis Saloon. You can't miss it. Some damn fool has gone to the trouble of paunching the dots over the i's."

Yellowleg slipped the rifle back in place and didn't bother to check the expressions on their faces. He had dotted those i's almost a year before, at much closer range, and from here it didn't look as though the sign had been painted over. Unless he was wrong, he had made up Billy's mind at least. He touched the claybank's flanks gently with his spurs and without another word started down the hill into town. It meant putting his back directly toward Turk, and that, he knew, was taking a long chance. Billy was another matter. To Billy, Yellowleg thought, the rituals of death were sacred and the kid had too high a regard for himself to take advantage of a man's back. Turk was the man to reckon with. Yellowleg was careful not to low-rate this squat, bullnecked prairie derelict, and he waited for the first creak of leather behind him. He would have spun on it, but the sound never came.

"Billy," Turk scowled. "Get him smack between the shoulder blades."

"Ain't my style. And I kinda take to him. The man's a natural born damn fool. You know, that pi-anna is makin' me awful thirsty."

They walked their horses down the center of the wide street, the three of them.

Yellowleg's gray eyes scanned the boardwalks, but his mind was on Turk. The man, apparently, was gun-smart enough to know when he was outranked even by a man's rear. Yellowleg put him down for a shifty, all-around, second-rate criminal. When Billy had joined Yellowleg on the road into town, Turk had come scuttling after them. Turk lived in Billy's gun shadow, Yellowleg thought, and had no taste for playing a lone hand.

Still, Yellowleg rated Turk the deadlier of the two. Billy was as easy to see through as a barbed wire fence. He was a big, good-natured killer who lived by Turk's wits. What Turk lacked in pride he gained in cunning.

Yellowleg assumed there had been other Billys, before the war, and Turk had survived them all. Turk was like half a man, Yellowleg thought, who found trigger-happy kids to do his shooting for him—and, when the time came, to do his dying for him. Riding together, Billy made Turk a whole man.

As they passed the bank on their left, their six eyes held on it. For the moment, Yellowleg thought, Turk had been cut down to size. Now Billy would have to be cut down to his. Yellowleg led them on by and they stared at the warped false front of the Davis & Davis Saloon. The i's were dotted all right. You could see daylight through them. The wood was weathered through and through and at this distance it was impossible to say how fresh the holes were.

"Be john dog," Billy said.

Yellowleg wouldn't put any money on how long these two would stay fooled. But for the time being, it would do. And it had made gunplay out of the question. His shoulder had been acting up lately, and it was laming his draw, and that worried him. He had turned them off toward Gila City days before, tantalizing them with a rich account of that bank, but what Yellowleg had in mind was carved in a small oak shingle across the street, two doors from the bank, and his glance drifted back to it. Dr. Ramsey B. Caxton.

There was no putting it off any longer. The old slug in his right shoulder had to come out. And Caxton, in a manner of speaking, was an old friend. Yellowleg doubted if the ex-Tennessee Army doctor would even remember him, but he would know soon enough.

Turk gave Yellowleg a hard glance. "There's the sheriff's office."

"Kinda sleepy looking, like you said," said Billy.

"How long you figure on lettin' that money keep?" said Turk.

Yellowleg didn't bother facing him. "Couple of days, maybe. Maybe more."

Turk shifted his glance and peered at Yellowleg as if he had gone loco. "I shoulda knowed better than to let a Yankee throw in with us."

"You'll know better next time."

"Me, I'm kinda anxious to get over the line to Arizona. I ain't exactly well liked in these parts."

"I guess."

"It ain't good for the kid, neither. Gets town crazy. Kinda hard to handle when he gets the scent of some calico sage hen. I'm tellin' ya, we ought to hit that bank and light a shuck. The sooner the better."

"When I'm ready."

"Couple of days, huh?"

"About that."

"Mister," Turk spat, "that's a long time to let money sit. Just look at this town. Must be all of two people on the street and one of them so drunk he's lost the fine art of walkin'."

The doors of the livery stable were wide open and they could see the glow from the forge. Yellowleg nodded toward it as they passed.

"There's the blacksmith shop."

"I was kinda figurin' on havin' a drink with you boys," Turk said.

"We'll be around."

Turk hung on another moment, but when not even Billy invited him to join them, he reined over toward the forge. The other two continued on toward the hotel with its narrow windows and faded green shades, its cafe and barber shop. There was a sign in the barber's window that said BATHS and they pulled up to the hitchrail.

"Ain't you the one, though," Billy chuckled. "Leadin' Turk around by the nose. I never seen the old gent with so much arch in his back."

"He'll get used to it."

"Maybe we can get him to take a bath. He's the most water-shy gent you ever met. It gets kinda noticeable in town, don't it?"

Yellowleg dismounted and waited, with his reins, for Billy to climb down. But the kid lingered in the saddle and his eyes scanned the empty boardwalks. "Hope they got some pretty women in this town," he said.

"When you get this close to Arizona, all women are pretty."

Billy dismounted and gave a little whoop. "Two days of squaw chasin'. A thing like that always appeals to me."

Yellowleg handed his reins over to Billy. "Take the horses around to the stable."

Billy turned slowly and his eyes narrowed on Yellowleg. "You talkin' to me?"

"Your name's Billy, ain't it?"

"Maybe it is."

"Well, is it, or ain't it?"

Billy's face, in the desert shade of his hat brim, had turned cold and bloodless. The two men stared at each other, and Yellowleg thought for a moment this was more than the kid's pride could tote. Then Billy's glance traveled back to the tall false front of the Davis & Davis Saloon with its smartly dotted i's. When his gaze returned there was a grin in the corners, and the player piano behind the bat-wing doors started up again, making an absurd thumping and tinkling in the heat. "There's some men I just can't help likin'," he said. "If I didn't, I guess I'd kill you."

He took the reins of Yellowleg's horse together with his own, and walked away, a tall, thin-waisted youth with a gun on each hip and enough fighting tallow to go with them. Yellowleg watched him a long time. It had occurred to Billy, he thought, that Yellowleg just might nail him to an awning post. Some killer's instinct warned him to back down before it was too late. He was outclassed. And there was no longer any question who was running the bunch.

The piano played on.

CHAPTER TWO

Curls of flypaper hung inside the barber shop window, limp festoons of encrusted black flies and sage bees. The air was luxuriously scented with Bay Rum, which stung pleasantly at Yellowleg's nostrils. The barber looked like an old gristle-heel who saw the world through a green eyeshade and didn't care much for the view. He paused to size up Yellowleg in a long glance, and then resumed squirting the Bay Rum onto the sheared head of a boy of about six, who was all but lost under the folds of the dirty cloth.

"How about a bath?" Yellowleg asked.

The green eyeshade came up again. "We're a mite low on water," the barber said. "I'll have to charge you four-bits. In advance."

It was too hot to stand there arguing. Yellowleg dug out the money and found the boy gazing at him as if the dust of far off places clung to him.

"Howdy," Yellowleg said.

"Howdy."

"Straight through," the barber said, "in the back."

Yellowleg bathed in four inches of water with a square cake of White Rose glycerine soap. He lay there a long time sorting out his thoughts. He had brought both Turk and Billy into line without a fight. The next step was to get them drunk and into jail if possible. That would be the best way to keep them out of trouble and within reach. In jail. A week maybe. Until his shoulder healed up.

He sponged off the old wound, trying to ease the pain of the lead ball. It seemed strange after all these years to have it act up when he needed his gun hand the most. He couldn't risk it, and when the showdown came it had to be right. Perfect, even. He'd spent too many years planning it, thinking it, dreaming it, and when it came there'd be no time to fuss with a bad shoulder.

Yellowleg wrapped a towel around his lean hips and spent a little time beating the dust out of his clothes. He spotted the worst places with spirits of hartshorn he found on a shelf, and took his time dressing again. Turk, he knew, was the one to watch. Turk would be quick to ferret out a man's weakness and make use of it. During the last five days the pain had come often and Yellowleg had had to grit his teeth to keep from rubbing his right shoulder. Now he'd get the lead plum pulled, here in Gila City. When Billy and Turk walked out of the hoosegow, Yellowleg would be ready for them.

The long years of waiting were almost over.

When Yellowleg re-entered the barber shop, the towheaded boy was gone and the old man was dozing in his big chair. Yellowleg hung up his gunbelt and rapped the barber's feet to wake him. The green shade was lowered, but now he raised it for business.

"The best sleep in the world's in a barber chair."

Yellowleg glanced through the ribbons of flypaper at the sheriff's office across the street. "What kind of sheriff do you have?"

"A dead one. He wasn't much good anyway. The durned fool rode off a cutbank and broke his neck. All we got's a deputy. We figure on writin' away for a lawman. You stayin' long?"

"Just passing through."

Yellowleg took the chair and the old man found a shot glass among his bottles. He squirted it full of Bay Rum.

"Like a little drink, mister?"

Yellowleg shook his head.

"I always say it's a shame to waste good Bay Rum on a man's hair."

He poured down the shot and wiped his lips with the back of his hand. Then he picked up his scissors to get down to barbering, but he stopped when he saw Yellowleg sitting there with his hat on.

"Ain't no way in the world to get a haircut with your lid on, mister."

"Just shave me."

"You aim to keep that thing on?"

"Is there an ordinance in this town against a man wearing his John B.?"

"Nope." The barber put down his scissors and got a shaving mug. "Just his guns."

The player piano was still hammering away when Yellowleg and Billy entered the Davis & Davis Saloon. It was a barn of a place with a high ceiling and a long bar. The bar section was deserted. Off to one side, the card tables were stacked on top of each other and several townswomen were arranging chairs in rows on the dance floor.

The bartender, a short man with a clean collar, was standing on a ladder to get at three paintings, in heavy gold frames, of nude women. He was turning them skin to the wall.

Billy stopped short of the bar to admire the saloon art and then glanced over at the townswomen, as if to make comparisons. They wore starched sunbonnets and drab calico dresses with high necks and long sleeves. Billy held them in a steady gaze; they were a disappointing lot. He moved up to the bar, next to Yellowleg.

"None of 'em look pretty to me," he said, with an air of protest.

"You just ain't far enough west yet, kid."

"Old maids. At a hug social, they'd go two for a nickel."

"What's keeping Turk?"

"Maybe he's got the natures again. We was down in Mexico two-three years ago, and his stomach never got over it."

The bartender moved his ladder to the third painting and Billy spoke up.

"You out of your mind? Turn them females back around so a man can get acquainted."

"That'll have to wait, gents."

"What for?" Billy said.

"Church is about to start." The bartender got the huge painting flipped around. "The parson don't like lookin' at 'em during the sermon."

"You loco? This ain't Sunday."

The bartender finished and climbed down. "That's a matter of opinion in Gila City. We ain't seen a calendar in two years and folks has got a little mixed up. You know how it is."

Townspeople were beginning to enter, in twos and threes, ignoring the bar as they passed, and taking up seats on the dance hall. The bartender put away his ladder and returned to his customers.

"Some folks hold it's Monday," he went on, "but these folks hold it's Sunday, and they're right ornery about it. You gents lookin' for a drink?"

"Looking right at it," Yellowleg muttered softly, surveying the row of bottles and fancy labels. "What's in that one?"

"Best we got. Hand-made on the banks of the Cimarron. Guaranteed not to have more than six percent coffin varnish. The mayor drinks it regular."

"That'll do," Yellowleg said.

The bartender reached for the bottle, flipped the cork with his thumb and filled two glasses.

"How does the bank hold?" Billy asked.

"Bank's open. They're Monday folks."

The bartender drove the cork home with the heel of his palm, as if he was cutting off their credit.

"What do you think you're doing?" Billy said. "Keepin' the flies out?"

"Sorry gents. You got about one minute to do your drinkin'. The bar is closed when the parson walks in. No drinkin' in church."

Billy was losing his sense of humor. "Rules is easy to change."

"You gents carryin' hardware?"

"Kinda looks like it, don't it?"

"No gun-totin' inside the city limits. We got a new ordinance."

"You don't say."

Billy turned to give Yellowleg a wise glance, but Yellowleg had lost interest. He was looking toward the door and Billy followed his eyes. A woman was entering, a young woman with red hair and a pale, store complexion that had gone untouched by the New Mexico sun. She was wearing a bustle, in the latest style, and a green velvet hat.

"Now *that's* what I call pretty," Billy said.

Yellowleg said nothing. He just watched her from under the brim of his hat. She paused a moment in the doorway and glanced with a hesitant air toward the congregation that had filled up on the dance floor. It looked for a moment as if she would turn around and walk back out. But she didn't. She held a new prayer book in her hand, and she tightened her grip on the hand of the boy beside her as she came on in. Yellowleg had seen the boy before; the little tow-head in the barber chair. His hair was still slicked down with Bay Rum and his big lonely eyes gazed out over the dour faces of the congregation.

The gossipy chatter had stopped abruptly as the red-haired woman entered, but now it resumed in whispers. From where he was standing at the bar, Yellowleg could hear the voices of quiet outrage.

"That dance-hall woman. Imagine comin' in here, and bringin' her wood's colt with her. She wouldn't know his father if she met him again."

"Now, Sarah."

"I imagine this'll be as close as she ever was to a parson. Holdin' a prayer book, like she was respectable."

Billy turned to the bartender. "Who is she?"

"Kit Tildon. Didn't expect to see her in here. Maybe she's quitting the dance hall profession."

"Pretty as a picture."

"I wouldn't get any stray thoughts, mister," the bartender said, grinning a little. "She can be all horns and rattles."

Kit swept on by, so close that Yellowleg could smell the lilac fragrance of her perfume. She held tight on the boy's hand and the boy said howdy as they passed.

"Howdy," Yellowleg nodded.

The woman ignored him as if he were just another tall stick of furniture at the bar, and found a place for herself and the boy in the last row.

"Eeee-yow," Billy said quietly.

The boy peered at all the long, stony faces in the congregation. The men sat in collar and hams without seeming to breathe, as if it might be a sin to be comfortable in the preach house. The women were trussed up in their Sunday-go-to-meetin' clothes with their expressions quoting chapter and verse. The boy looked around for some friendly glance, and Yellowleg heard him turn to his mother with a whisper that was louder than it meant to be.

"If they're going to heaven, let's me and you not go."

There was a flutter of hand fans, and she shushed him and the parson walked in.

"Gents," the bartender said. "The bar is closed."

"Is he the parson?" Billy asked.

"Says he is."

The bartender closed down the piano and came back. "Used to be a chuck wagon cook, but he got religion. Maybe he ain't much, but he's the best we got at the moment."

He was a stocky man in a black serge gospel coat. He took up a position against the windows, which said Davis & Davis Saloon backwards, and in a hoarse voice led the congregation in a hymn. It was at this moment that Yellowleg saw Turk enter the batwings.

Turk's step faltered as he realized that a church meeting was going on, and he blanched a little, but then he saw Billy and Yellowleg at the bar and came on in.

"Never heard music like that in a whiskey mill before. Kinda throws a man."

"Makes a man feel peaceful inside."

"Speak for yourself, Billy boy. Speak for yourself."

"Always liked a good sermon. See the parson?"

"I can see and hear him."

"Started out a dough-belly. Maybe he's goin' to orate against sonofabitch stew."

Their voices cut into the hymn and Kit Tildon turned around to give them a glance. Billy tipped his hat.

"Howdy, m'am."

Yellowleg laid a cartwheel on the bar. "Let's find another place to do our drinking."

"Now you're talkin'," Turk grinned.

"I kinda like this one." Billy's eyes were still on Kit. "Look at that perky little hat she's wearin'. Bet it came all the way from San Francisco, or Paris even."

"Finish your drink," Yellowleg said.

"I just might hooraw this meetin'. Put a little life into it. Let that bit of calico there know who I am."

"Spare yourself the trouble."

"It won't be no trouble."

Turk cleared his throat. "If you got no objection I'll have a little drink while you two argue it out."

"Won't do you no good," Billy grinned. "The bar's closed for the church meetin'."

"I declare. And me dyin' a thirst." Turk looked over at the bartender. "Whiskey. The cheapest you got. I ain't particular."

The bartender moved a little closer and bent forward to whisper against the singing.

"Like your friend said—"

"Give him a whiskey," Billy remarked.

There'd be no getting Billy out of this place now, not with the Tildon woman sitting there, Yellowleg knew, and he eased his elbows back against the bar. One way or the other Billy would get himself thrown in jail before nightfall. The sooner the better. Turk would take a little more doing.

"I said give him a whiskey," Billy repeated. "Look, gents—"

Turk was grinning like a man offering to hold your coat. "Show him how fast you draw your guns, Billy."

Billy glanced over at Kit, but only the boy was looking at him. Nevertheless, Billy slapped out his guns and leveled them at the bartender.

"Now let's see how fast you can draw the cork out of that bottle."

"Yes, sir!"

Yellowleg studied the kid. Billy was fast and maybe as accurate as any man with a temper in his trigger finger. That could land him in a shallow grave. Too much temper didn't mix with too much trigger itch.

"The kid here's a real comer," Turk was saying. "Gonna make a rep for himself. Taught the boy everything I know. Ain't that right, Billy boy?"

The bartender filled a third glass, peered at the parson working his arms through another verse, and slid the glass toward Turk. Turk licked his dried lips and teased himself a moment just looking at the drink. "Nothing like a little psalm singing to make a man appreciate a drink. My, but ain't they makin' a racket, though?"

Turk reached for the drink, but Yellowleg's hand got there first. He flattened his palm over the lip of the glass and held it to the bar.

"Like the man said," Yellowleg muttered. "These folks got themselves a church. And you ain't drinkin' in it."

Turk's eyes flashed up as if he had been wounded. "Yellowleg," he said, "you're just a natural born trouble-maker, ain't you?"

"I said you ain't drinkin' in here."

Turk shifted his glance to Billy for some sign of support, but Billy let him down again and began to chuckle.

"Turk, I reckon you're just gonna have to look at that whiskey all through the parson's sermon."

The parson was in full voice.

"Oh, I was a bad'un in them dark, misguided days," he said, casting his hard eyes over the congregation. "But the Lord, he was awatchin' over me with his posse of angels. And he gimme the sign. I was sittin' there in the bunkhouse lookin' for paper to roll me a cigarette. And the foreman loaned me a book for the purpose and that's when I knew the Lord was lookin' right smack at me. That there book, folks, was the Bible. And that's when I quit smokin' and started preachin'."

The parson was looking right at them.

"Kinda stuffy in here, ain't it?" Turk said.

"Lord," the parson said, "I see you sent us some new faces today, male *and* female."

Yellowleg could feel Kit's discomfort at this remark, and like Billy, he found his eyes traveling over to her as if she were the only point of light in a dark sky.

"Lord, I thank ya. And folks, I welcome ya. There's plenty of room for all at His chuck wagon, and I'll be dishin' up the gospels in a minute. But first, I gotta say a word to you gents with your hats on."

Billy touched Turk with his elbow. "You suppose he means us?"

"I never took my lid off in a saloon in my life."

The parson's words began to gather like thunder.

"Tenderfoots to the Lord's rangeland, from the ugly look of ya. Maybe you're afeerd you'll get gospel grease spread on yur hair."

Yellowleg was sorry now they had lingered. "Let's go."

"I'm stickin'," Billy said. "Kinda reminds me of my paw. He was always hollerin' at me until I got too big to holler at. I beat him up with a fence post and he ain't hollered since."

The verbal thunder was rolling over them now.

"You'd look nice jinglin' your spurs at the gates of the Big Corral with yur hats and guns on. This here's a preach house, gents, and you'll take yur hats off to the Lord."

The townspeople were craning their necks now. Billy was the first to whip off his hat.

"Always glad to oblige the Lord," he said.

"Me too," Turk echoed. "Now get yur spurs in that sermon, dough-belly, before I die of thirst."

Yellowleg was standing with his hat still square on his head. Everyone's eyes seemed riveted on him, and his jaws set hard and tight.

He wasn't taking his hat off.

"Get on with the service," he said in a quiet voice. His eyes flashed to Kit, and for the first time their glances met. "I'm leaving."

"Mister," the parson scowled. "No man sets himself above the Lord. Whip off that lid of yours!"

Yellowleg ignored him and pushed himself away from the bar. In the heavy quiet his long steps jangled against the hemlock floor. Almost at once, behind him, Turk picked up the shot of whiskey and swallowed it. The congregation sat in a stunned silence, and even the parson was now struck voiceless.

"Mighty touchy about his hat, ain't he?" Turk declared.

"Never seen anything like it. Don't take it off even to sleep."

Yellowleg kept walking. Mighty touchy. The skin of his face felt tight and drawn, and in the taut silence of the saloon each stride seemed to leave a squeak and echo and jangle of spurs. Yellowleg held himself as straight as a poker and kept his eyes on the door. Mighty touchy.

"Folks," the parson thundered. "Have yourself a look. There's a man carrying a pitchfork in his saddleroll. There's a man walkin' straight to Hell!"

CHAPTER THREE

The batwing doors creaked behind him and Yellowleg's gray eyes tightened against the burst of desert sunlight. He pulled the hat down low over his eyes, set his jaws like a man looking for a dog to kick, and walked the quiet street. That dough-belly had more lip than a muley cow. A preacher ought to know when to mind his own affairs. But what did he matter? It was Turk and Billy that counted. Turk and Billy and the hat. The hat. He'd had seven years of it—a drifting purgatory of taunts and glances and barroom laughter. If Billy got drunk enough he might try to shoot it off. He wouldn't be the first man to try. But a man only tried a thing like that once.

And yet that sin-buster had almost been right. Only it wasn't a pitchfork in his saddleroll. It was a Bowie knife.

Sharp enough to scalp a man.

Yellowleg found himself making friends with the town dog, a mangy bitch half asleep in a shade pool of curled leaves under a live oak tree. And then he raised his eyes to the shingle with the carved letters and to the upstairs window with the name repeated in gold leaf on the glass. Caxton. Dr. Ramsey B. Caxton.

Yellowleg stood up and glanced back at the dusty windows of the Davis & Davis Saloon. Then he spit and decided to get on with it. He'd made up his mind days ago to see Caxton, and the time had come. He straightened his hat and ambled onto the plank walk. He felt sure Caxton wouldn't recognize him. There had been that moment, a year before, when they had come face to face in a Gila City bar and Caxton had taken him for a complete stranger. Yellowleg had almost spoken up then, but instead he had lit out of town. Now it was different. He could trust Caxton to mine that lead ball out of his shoulder, and he could trust Caxton to understand the Bowie knife in Yellowleg's saddleroll.

Yellowleg tossed away his cigarette and walked up the dark stairway.

"That lead's been in there a long time," Dr. Caxton said.
"I know that," Yellowleg nodded.
"Bother you much?"
"Now and again."

Yellowleg sat in the center of the bare, upstairs office, straddling a chair, with his shirt off and his hat on. Dr. Caxton had hardly changed at all. He was still a beanpole of a man with uncombed hair, a quiet Tennessee voice and a crusty look in his eyes. His coat hung like Spanish moss on an iron clothes tree; green garters held up his white shirt sleeves. He still took Yellowleg for a complete stranger and Yellowleg decided not to hurry him.

"It ought to come out," the doctor said.

"I figured."

"You got a room at the hotel?"

"Not yet."

"You take one for two weeks. Make it three."

Yellowleg peered at the man and reached for his shirt. "Thanks, anyway."

Dr. Caxton poured water into a tin bowl and washed his hands. "A thing like that won't heal overnight."

"I figured on a week."

"It's in smart and deep, right close to the collar bone." Dr. Caxton dried his hands and lit a panatella. And then his eyes narrowed. "Where have we met?"

"Take your time."

"You go over to the hotel, buy yourself a bottle and a small glass and wait. I'll be over directly."

Yellowleg tucked in his shirt and hitched his gunbelt back on. "I'll be out of town before you finish that cigar. Forget it."

"You ever do any fighting in Tennessee?"

"I fought for the North," Yellowleg said. "We fought in different armies."

Dr. Caxton seated himself with his long feet crossed on the corner of his desk. "Cavalry, huh? Private?"

"Sergeant."

"I had a field hospital in Tennessee." Dr. Caxton fixed him with a steady gaze. "That's the only time I ever saw you yellowlegs up close. They were Ohio boys, most of them. Twelfth Cavalry. Came raiding down into Tennessee and had to leave their wounded behind. You from Ohio?"

Yellowleg left the question unanswered. Knowing the Reb doctor was in Gila City had tantalized Yellowleg for a year, but now that they stood face to face Yellowleg wondered if he was being a fool. "I'll be going."

"I'd hang up that gun belt."

"What?"

"Either get that lead ball out or I'd advise you to confine your shooting to rabbits and the Fourth of July."

"I'll make out."

"Maybe. But there'll be no way of telling when the pain will come and go. And when it comes it's like a toothache, isn't it, and you'd better not be on a gunman's walk when it does. A thing like that is bound to foul your draw or jimmy your aim and land you in a shallow grave."

"I said I'd make out."

Dr. Caxton rolled the cigar between his lips and gazed half amused at Yellowleg. "You brush poppers are all the same. You'd have to be argued into drinking whiskey if you thought it was good for you."

"What do I owe you?"

Suddenly Dr. Caxton's feet dropped off the desk. There was an unmistakable gleam of recognition in his sun-wrinkled eyes and Yellowleg knew now it was coming. "Do you mind taking off your hat?" Dr. Caxton muttered.

Yellowleg stood there looking at him. There was no turning back now. Dr. Caxton had a glimmer and the rest would come in a rush of memory.

"Sure," the doctor murmured. "He was a fellow just about your size. A yellowleg sergeant. Wounded. We took him prisoner-of-war, only he was a little different from the others."

Yellowleg watched Caxton's cigar coil up a vine of smoke in the airless office, and he could hear a sage bee buzzing along a window. And then he took a slow breath and met Caxton's gaze.

"Some damned fool had tried to scalp him," Dr. Caxton said. "With a Bowie knife."

"I've heard the story."

"I was there too." Dr. Caxton stood up and came a little closer. "They carried in that poor damned Yankee half out of his mind. No Indian had done that to him. A white man had tried it—some soldier from our own lines with too much likker in him."

Yellowleg still remembered that blast of sour breath, and the taste of salt blood on his lips. He remembered the drafty field hospital near the Tennessee swamp and the doctor with the thin fingers and the grasshopper bones and the crusty, young voice.

"You could take off that hat and make me out a liar," Dr. Caxton said.

Yellowleg shook his head slowly, and the doctor settled back on the corner of his desk. Outside, the mangy bitch began to bark and it made the day seem hotter.

"We treated you pretty well for a Yankee. I spent an hour stitching you up, and I did a mighty fine job. Mighty fine. Some of our boys came out of the war with a lot more than a few scars. But a near scalping.... A thing like that sticks in a man's thoughts. Take off your hat. I'd be interested."

"I got kinda used to keeping it on."

Caxton gave him a sharper look. "Why? You've got nothing to hide but a few war scars."

"It's just my way. Let's leave it at that."

"I'd hate to think you haven't taken that hat off around folks since the war."

"I didn't say that."

"Then I'm askin' it."

"I tried."

I tried, he thought bitterly. At first. But how do you explain scalping scars? Three of them. A seam just behind the widow's peak, almost from temple to temple, and the stitches running like parts along the top. The doctor had stitched him up well, and the hair grew, but the strange scars were still there, and the memory, too. Do you explain them to a child laughing at you? And the Ross girl back home, the girl you'd always planned to marry, looking at you with horror the first time you take off your hat. And the ragging you take in any saloon with a couple of drunks in it. You try, but you begin living in your hat and you never forget the cold edge of that scalping knife.

"Never is a long time," Dr. Caxton murmured. "If a man's afraid to tip his hat to a lady, it must be a pretty lonely life."

"I've been busy."

"It's seven years since the war and I'd say those wounds of yours have worked their way down deep inside where no surgeon can get at them, and that makes me sorry for you, soldier. Did you find the man that did that to you?"

"I vowed I would."

"You were out of your mind."

"Maybe."

Dr. Caxton placed the panatella back between his lips and Yellowleg felt that the Tennessee doctor was staring at him as he would at a madman. "I've seen men with revenge in their eyes," Caxton went on, "but I'd say you take the cake. My hunch is you've got revenge worked out to a fine art. Why did you bother looking me up?"

"I figured you were a good enough sawbones to dig out that lead ball without laying me up for three weeks. I guess I was wrong."

"Not a chance. Mister, you'd be surprised how many times I wondered what happened to you. I hoped you'd go back to the plow like nothing had changed. I'm sorry I was wrong."

"Like I said, there was nothing to go back to. I made a different kind of life for myself, and I'm not complaining."

"What kind of a life? Combing through a scattered army looking for one man?" Dr. Caxton wrinkled his brows. "We never found out the name of the man you were looking for. The war's long over now, and I guess you're still looking."

"No," Yellowleg said. "I found him."

CHAPTER FOUR

Yellowleg stood at the upstairs window and looked across to the Davis & Davis Saloon below. The church meeting hadn't yet broken up, but he saw Turk come through the batwing doors alone. Turk hesitated in the raw sunlight. Then he jammed the hat on his head, set it at a fighting angle, and went looking for another saloon. He found one next door.

Yellowleg remained there gazing through the window. Dr. Caxton had known better than to ask more questions and Yellowleg was not going to volunteer more answers. Still, Yellowleg felt if he had a single friend out of the past, it was this Tennessee army doctor. He alone could understand. And Yellowleg thought of those bitter seven years, lonely and obsessed; the endless days of following trails and crossing towns, looking for a man whose name he didn't know and whose face he'd never seen in the black night. Revenge had been hard on Yellowleg, but it had given him something to live for. It had begun as a sort of madness and maybe it would end that way, but he had found that Reb and no mistake about it.

Even now there was that salt taste in Yellowleg's mouth, the taste from the war. He'd awakened in the swamp with the first cold touch of the knife and he'd sunk his teeth into the man's scalping hand. He remembered the sour blast of whiskey breath and his teeth locking in flesh and drawing blood until the knife fell and the Reb went squealing away in the dark. When the war ended Yellowleg had only two things to go on. He knew that Reb had come from the West, being so handy with a scalping knife, and he knew he had left deep teeth scars in the man's right hand.

He'd drifted from bar to bar asking about a drinking man with bad scars in his whiskey hand and over the years a name began to crop up which he marked well. And then one day he'd found the name on a wanted poster, with a picture, and the rest was only a matter of time. He knew the man's name, what he looked like, and that he had a scarred hand.

Unless Yellowleg was mistaken, that hand had a whiskey glass in it right now.

Turk was hunched over the bar giving heavy and educated concentration to the whiskey in front of him. He held the glass in his hand, and the deep bluish scars formed a ragged crescent near the fleshy part of the palm. Yellowleg gave the scars a reassuring glance as he came up to the bar.

"We're moving out," Yellowleg said.

"Now you're talking." Turk glanced up with a sly wink. "All that money just sitting across the street is enough to drive a man to drink."

It seemed strange to be standing next to the Reb after all these years. They'd been traveling together five days now and Turk hadn't the slightest glimmer, Yellowleg knew, that they had met before. That they had scarred each other for life in the nightmare of a Tennessee swamp. Yellowleg had a special purgatory picked out for Turk. He wasn't going to kill the man. And he wasn't going to sit in a hotel room for weeks waiting to patch up a bum shoulder. He'd take a chance on that lead plumb not kicking up when the moment came to dig out that Bowie knife and fix Turk to wear his hat the rest of his days.

There was no point in putting it off now. It was only a matter of getting out of town and getting Billy out of his way.

"Go next door," Yellowleg said, "and get the kid out of that church meeting."

"Not a chance," Turk croaked. "I tried all the while I was in there. I think Billy boy's gettin' religion. He won't budge."

Yellowleg left the bar and went out. He had never counted on Billy, but the kid had to be reckoned with. Once they got out of town he would have to separate the two of them. Billy was in the way.

Yellowleg stopped outside the doors of the Davis & Davis Saloon and peered in. He had no appetite to show himself in there, but he saw that Billy was no longer standing at the bar. The kid had taken a chair at the back of the congregation, seating himself with his hat on his lap and right next to the Tildon woman.

The sight of the two of them together set Yellowleg's jaws a little tighter. The woman had enough troubles without Billy's adding to them. And he sat there with his eyes fixed on her, as if staring would make her turn. But she was working hard at ignoring him.

Yellowleg caught Billy's attention, but Billy made it clear that he wasn't about to leave. Yellowleg had an impulse to pull him out by the scruff of the neck, but he couldn't make himself walk back into that church meeting. The parson was glowing with brimstone and hardly pausing for breath.

"And I'm asking you, my friends!" he said in a voice that must have carried his fervor to the Arizona line. "You got a choice, ain't you? Heaven or Hell? Make your choice! Oh, don't think old Beelzebub ain't wrangling souls right here in Gila City! If there's any man, woman or child sittin' here who reckons he wants to go to Hell, then I say let that man, woman or child stand up and be counted!"

An impressed silence held the congregation and Yellowleg felt like a fool standing there behind the doors. The parson had made his point and he stood like a statue letting his parboiled meaning sink in. And then, in the last row, Billy Short got to his feet.

"Parson," he yelled back. "Start countin'."

If Kit had ignored him before, she couldn't help looking at him now, and

Yellowleg saw at once that he was going to hooraw the meeting if only to let her know he existed. The entire congregation was gawking at him now, and the parson unlimbered his evangelical pose.

"You white-livered, whey-bellied coyote, you mean to stand there and declare you intend to go to Hell!"

"Shore do, Parson." Billy jerked his guns. "And every man here'll be goin' to Hell pronto if he don't jump to his feet and keep me company."

It only took a moment. First one and then another of the men rose from his chair, and then they began popping up like jacks-in-the-box. Billy began to laugh.

Yellowleg watched the scene and fought down the surge of temper. It was their affair, not his, and apparently there wasn't a man there with guts enough to face a square-shouldered punk with more show-off than sense.

But when Yellowleg saw Kit rise from her chair, he knew he wouldn't be able to stay out of it. She stood, facing Billy for a moment, and then she slapped him hard.

But Billy only smiled more broadly, as if a slap was better than nothing at all. "I been slapped before," he said. "Name's Billy Short."

"Get out," Kit muttered, with cold fury. "You've done enough."

"My, but your eyes do spark when you're mad," Billy said.

"Get out!"

Yellowleg stepped through the swinging doors. Billy tipped up his hat with the barrel of his gun and suddenly hugged Kit up close to him and kissed her. "Mighty glad to have met you, m'am. Mighty glad."

He holstered his guns and walked out—directly into Yellowleg's plunging fist. The smack sounded like a rifle crack. Billy spun around and fell—out cold. Yellowleg picked him up across his shoulder and walked out with him. It had been a lucky punch, nothing more. But it had hurt Yellowleg's shoulder and his hand felt almost numb from the blow.

He didn't look back at Kit, but he imagined she stood there wiping Billy's kiss off her lips. He heard a whisper that was louder than it should have been.

"Just lookin' at her—he could tell *her* kind, all right."

CHAPTER FIVE

Turk was waiting at the bar as Yellowleg walked in and dropped Billy in a poker chair. Turk came over with a bottle in his hand and a bemused look in his eyes.

"Glory be," he mumbled. "Looks like Billy boy got more preachin' than he could hold. That's strong stuff, when you ain't used to it."

Yellowleg took the bottle out of Turk's blue-marked hand and poured what was left of the whiskey into Billy's face. Turk watched with mild disapproval.

"Sure is a waste of bad whiskey."

Billy's head turned against the back of the chair, and then his eyelids fluttered and formed a squint against the raw desert sunlight that pressed through the windows. Then his eyes focused on Yellowleg, a long dangerous gaze, and Yellowleg thought he was going to have to hit him again. But maybe Billy didn't want to get hit again. He began to smile faintly.

"Lick your chin," Turk said. "You're sweatin' ninety-proof whiskey."

Billy straightened and rubbed the back of his neck and looked at Yellowleg again. "I ain't been hit that hard since I left Texas. You got a mean wallop, for a Yankee."

"I'll buy you a drink," Yellowleg said.

"You got that sage hen staked out for yourself?"

"I warned you to stay out of trouble."

Turk cleared his throat. "I hate to say it, Billy boy, but the Yank here's talking sense. We're movin' out and that pretty little bank's just waiting. Let's get that drink and attend to business."

Billy tested the shape of his jaw and began to grin. Yellowleg knew that the kid's pride was hurt more than his jaw, but he was doing a fair job of concealing it. Still, it would rankle, and Yellowleg would have to be careful how he played out his hand with Turk.

They moved to the bar and uncorked a fresh bottle. The best plan, Yellowleg decided, was to let them have their bank. But once out of town he'd order them to separate. Later, he'd double back on Turk's trail. That would get rid of Billy, and Yellowleg could finish out his hand with a Bowie knife.

The bartender moved away and the three men hunched over their drinks. They were silent for a moment and Turk was the first to pour down his shot.

"I'm ready," he said.

"Take it easy," Billy said. "The bank don't close for a couple of hours."

Turk winced a little, and glanced at Yellowleg. "You got the kid talkin' like you. Never saw such a patient man when he comes to standin' up a bank."

Yellowleg's glance flicked over the scars on Turk's hand. "That's all I've got left, Turk. Patience."

"Well, not me," Turk growled softly. "I like to get a thing over."

Billy poured himself another drink. "There never was a man so hungry for money," he said. "I think you must be savin' up to be a miser."

Turk laughed and then bent his head closer to Billy and his eyes hardened as his voice softened. "Me and you're goin' in the army business. It takes money to get started."

"You still dreamin' about that?"

Yellowleg made no effort to listen. He'd heard it all before, especially at night when they were bedded down. All of Turk's aging imagination had now coalesced around a single grand idea.

"It ain't so crazy," Turk was saying. "Set us up a whole republic if we want to. This is empty country and there ain't nobody to stop us. With that bank money growin' mossy across the street we could get the comancheros to sell us a hundred, two hundred slave Indians. Make us up an army, uniforms and all. And I'd drill 'em—right dress, left dress, about face. You can do things with an army of men—even Indians."

"If it was me," Billy said. "I'd buy squaws. Nothing but squaws—they're cheaper anyway." He glanced over to Yellowleg. "How'd you like in on a harem, Yank? Some of them moccasin sage hens ain't so bad."

"Let's go," Yellowleg said.

They wiped their lips on their sleeves and turned their backs to the stained mahogany bar. A quiet card game was in progress in a far corner of the saloon.

"I never saw such a town," Turk mumbled. "They see you're wearing guns, and no one'll play cards with ya."

"The way you play cards," Billy said, "a man needs his guns."

Yellowleg spoke to Turk without looking at him. "You bring the horses around to the hitch rail."

"And don't tie up," Billy added. "Except maybe your own."

"Ain't you funny, though."

Turk was a long time getting the horses. Yellowleg and Billy kept across the street from the bank, smoking cigarettes and watching the sights. Yellowleg noticed the town dog pick up and begin barking again at two drifters riding into town from the south, but then the church meeting let out and the boardwalk was suddenly full.

Yellowleg saw the young Tildon boy first. He ran across the street as if he'd just got a reprieve and began walking the hitch rail. A buggy or two pulled out and then Yellowleg glanced off to his left and saw Kit moving unaware along the boardwalk toward them.

When she did see them her step faltered for only an instant. Her skin looked amazingly pale under the wooden awning, as if she kept it somehow untouched by the harsh desert sun. This country was hell on redheads, Yellowleg thought, and he felt sorry for her. Her beauty struck him as a fragile, hopeless thing; out of place and unexpected in a dried-up little New Mexico town. It reminded him of the bloom of mountain cactus which opened its petals for a brief display in the night and then withered and browned in the next day's heat.

Beside him, Yellowleg saw Billy break into a grin as she seemed to straighten her shoulders, aware now of their eyes. She kept coming, and Billy whipped off his hat.

"Howdy, m'am."

She kept her eyes straight ahead and carried herself with a poise that was both dignified and relaxed. And then she was gone, leaving only the faint scent of her perfume.

"She sure does smell nice, don't she?" Billy said slowly. He took a long breath and held it as if to preserve the fragrance. "Kinda stirs up a man's blood."

Kit Tildon had cut them both to a shine, but it had no effect on Billy. "Put on your hat," Yellowleg said. "You're standing there like someone had a deck with the joker missing."

Billy pulled on his Stetson low over his eyes and watched Kit's receding figure. "Too bad we ain't hanging around. I kinda figured on addin' her to my war bag."

"Yeah."

"Them Sunday-go-to-meetin' clothes don't fool me. She's pure calico queen and just my style."

"Here comes Turk."

Billy thumbed up his hat and turned his mind to business.

It was an instant later that Yellowleg realized the two drifters who had just ridden in had gone into the bank. Turk was still in the middle of the street when the bank window was shot out.

The Tildon boy stood in a frozen balance on the hitch rail, but the street seemed to clear itself.

"There goes our bank money!" Billy snapped.

The two of them skinned their guns and leaped into the street. There was shooting going on inside the bank and the air sounded like the Fourth of July. The two drifters appeared in the doorway and then leaped for their horses.

Yellowleg squeezed out two quick shots and realized that Billy had chosen the same target. The drifter had one foot in the stirrup as the mustang headed down the street; he sunfished in the air and then plunged backwards, dead on arrival. His foot twisted in the stirrup and the horse pulled him through the dust of Gila City with the money sack emptying itself in the sun.

Out of the corner of his eye Yellowleg saw the Tildon boy come unglued from the hitch rail and start running down the boardwalk. The other drifter hit the saddle and kicked his spurs.

Yellowleg changed his stance and leveled his gun at the man's checked shirt. His finger tightened against the trigger, but at that instant pain grabbed at his shoulder and he faltered and the shot went out wild. It startled him, but in the next instant Billy dropped the gunman with a single shot. The fireworks were over.

Yellowleg cursed his shoulder and looked up again and saw for the first time where that wild slug had gone.

The young Tildon boy lay on the boardwalk and a crowd was beginning to form.

CHAPTER SIX

Yellowleg stood frozen in the heavy heat of the day. He had stopped breathing. He just gazed, incredibly, across the street.

Behind him he heard Turk come up to Billy with the horses in tow.

"Did you see that?" Turk said, in an astonished tone. "Something's haywire, with that Yankee's shootin' arm."

Yellowleg felt himself beginning to walk. He reached the boardwalk and the crowd spread for him. He bent down on one knee.

"Pore little shaver," someone muttered. "Paid for his maw's sinnin', looks like."

Yellowleg knew his hands were trembling. He tried to open the boy's shirt and then he found himself ripping it apart.

"Get the doc."

"A couple of the boys went out to find him."

He found the wound, and he saw that it had stopped flowing. He closed the ends of the shirt over the narrow cage of ribs and stared at the pale, breathless lips, and for a moment there wasn't a sound from the crowd. He touched the boy's cheek, and it was like touching a memory. The smell of Bay Rum was still on his hair.

Yellowleg stared and found himself filling with a helpless anger. He wanted to shake some life back into the kid; why hadn't he run like the others when the shooting first broke out?

"It wasn't your fault, mister. I seen it. The boy just got in the way."

Yellowleg looked up slowly and the old lead in his shoulder felt like a lump of fire. He gazed at the grim faces, almost as if they formed a vagrant halo around the boy, and hated the sight of them. Their bank money was safe now and that made the shooting all right. It was too bad about the boy, but he was a wood's colt anyway and it could have been one of their own sons on the street when the shooting started.

Sure, they had seen it. But only Dr. Caxton would understand it. Yellowleg dreaded the man's arrival and the look that would flash into his eyes.

But it was Kit Tildon the crowd opened for. Yellowleg turned and saw her stop, as if struck, and the boy's name came voicelessly to her lips. "Mead—"

"Bless his soul and memory," someone muttered.

A portly man in a frock coat took her elbow, as though he expected Kit to faint, but she shrugged off his touch and took another step forward. Apprehension had drawn the color from her face and now a wide-eyed disbelief settled like a haze in her eyes.

"Bless his soul and memory."

She settled slowly on her knees beside the boy and bent close, as if he were only asleep and she was trying gently to wake him.

"Mead?"

She said it so softly, so tonelessly, that Yellowleg barely heard it. She seemed completely unaware of him.

"Mead, honey."

"He can't hear you," Yellowleg said quietly. "He's dead."

"Let the doc through."

There was a rustling in the crowd and the doctor appeared. There was a quick moment of recognition when he saw Yellowleg, but he was already opening his bag and probing for a heartbeat. Finally he straightened and looked at Kit; tears had finally come to her eyes.

"I'm sorry, Kit."

"It was them outlaws, Doc," someone said. "You know how it is. They did a lot of wild shootin'."

"It wasn't them," Yellowleg said quietly. "It was me."

Until that moment Kit didn't seem to realize a man was there beside her. Dr. Caxton looked at him with a lowering of the brows and started to speak, but held his tongue instead. The crowd became very still and all the while Kit was fixing her eyes slowly on Yellowleg, and he could see a deep, burgeoning hatred begin to form.

What good would it do to tell her he was sorry; it couldn't make any difference to her—or himself. You couldn't undo a wild shot with words and he didn't try. But he was sorry. So sorry that his fists were still clenched to keep them from trembling, and it was a sorrow that he could never set right.

And still she looked at him.

And the voices returned, like vultures circling over the dead.

"We'll have the boy a good funeral."

"The best there is."

"The whole town'll come, Kit. I'll see to that."

Kit's green eyes, with all their silent hatred, suddenly whipped up to the townspeople crowding around. She looked from one to the other and when she spoke her voice had a stinging contempt. "Bury him here? Would that ease your consciences! You think I don't know all the whisperin' and the little jokes you made every time he passed! You and your gossiping wives with their pinched little faces and their noses in the air!"

"Now, Kit—"

"'That dance-hall woman with her tow-headed wood's colt.' Oh, I've heard it all! 'No tellin' who the father was.' Your wives put a brand on us the day we came to town and they smelled brimstone every time we walked by! They've hated us both, me and the boy!" Her eyes lowered to the six-year-old, and her voice softened. "Well, he's dead now. You can tell your wives there was no sinnin' and there'll be no funeral. Not here."

The portly man spoke up. "Now, Kit, you're all riled up—"

She cut him off with a clear, decisive voice. "I'll just trouble someone to help take him to Siringo."

Even the portly man held his tongue now, and Yellowleg saw Dr. Caxton look at her strangely. "You can't do that, Kit. The town's all boarded up now, and you know it."

"I'm taking Mead there."

"You just don't realize what you're saying."

"I said it and I mean it."

"You're rightly upset, and nobody blames you. Mead's entitled to a decent burial and maybe you said something that's needed saying for a long time. You was always too pretty to be welcome in a town like this. The married ladies were plumb afraid of you and they fought back the only way they knew how. But you ain't going on to Siringo. It's smack in the middle of Apache country, and you know it as well as we do. You'd need cavalry to get through, Kit, and then some, maybe."

"Mead Tildon's going to be buried in Siringo," she said firmly. "Next to his father."

CHAPTER SEVEN

A moaning wind came up with nightfall. The coal-oil chandelier in the Davis & Davis Saloon was lit and by nine o'clock the poker games were well underway. But a sombre quiet hung over the place. There was a clatter of chips, but the voices were low and restrained.

Yellowleg stood alone at one end of the bar. He had been drinking for hours, but he was far from drunk. He glanced occasionally at Billy and Turk deep in cards at a table near the piano. Turk was having a winning streak and one of the men dropped out.

"Don't go away mad," Turk grinned. "I ain't quite caught onto the game yet."

Yellowleg turned back to the bottle. Turk was cheating with a crude skill that would pass only in a saddle blanket game. Yellowleg could almost see the crimps in the cards from where he stood. He'd better watch Turk. It wouldn't do for Turk to get a halo before Yellowleg could settle up with him.

He forced himself to think about it, and it eased his mind a little. He thought of the Bowie knife he'd been packing for seven years and he wondered about the look on Turk's face when the time came. That would be worth the waiting. That would be the sweet end of revenge. The look on his face.

But Yellowleg's thoughts wouldn't hold on it, and he filled his glass again.

A deputy in levis came in and settled further along the bar. He gave Yellowleg a half-glance and then concentrated on the drink the bartender set up for him.

"Talk her out of it?" the bartender said.

"She ain't going to be talked out of nothin'. Me and the mayor tried—and you know what a good talker he is."

They spoke in low tones, but it was so quiet in the saloon that Yellowleg could hear the deputy rasp a hand over the stubble on his chin as he spoke. He looked about twenty-two and still growing.

"You asked everybody?" the bartender muttered.

"All the single men I could find. Wastin' my breath, Archy. Nobody in town's willing to make that trip—not to tend to a buryin'."

The bartender nodded and wiped the back of his neck. "Poor Kit," he said. "She's tryin' awful hard to make folks believe about the boy's paw."

"Almost believe it myself."

"You a single man, Cal?"

"Married."

"Didn't know that."

"Well—almost married, me and Emma. She won't let me go off with Kit that way."

"Not to mention the Apaches."

The deputy bridled a little. "You know as well as I do, Archy, there ain't much chance of gettin' through. Over seventy miles of it. Some folks are sorry for Kit, but not that sorry."

"It's bad country, all right."

"Even the mosquitos give it up."

They fell silent and Yellowleg put the cork back in his bottle. He realized the two men had glanced over, but he ignored them.

"Tryin'," he heard the bartender mutter. "Tryin', but just can't seem to get himself drunk. Some men are like that."

"I guess."

"That boy's leanin' awful hard on him."

Yellowleg walked out.

The boardwalk was deserted and the saloon lights cast long shadows into the street. A hump of tumbleweed was slowly drifting through town, like a maverick blown in off the desert. There was the lone sound of hammering from deep inside Scott & Mercer's shop, a combination furniture store and undertaker's parlor. Yellowleg tried to shut the sounds out of his mind. He'd ride out somewhere and bed down. He had to get out of Gila City, even though he hated to let Turk out of his sight.

But Turk wouldn't be going anywhere before morning. He and Billy would play cards until the bank doors opened. Yellowleg knew he could almost count on it.

A lamp was burning in the livery stable. Yellowleg began saddling up his claybank. He needed to be alone. The townspeople were careful to avoid looking at him and yet their eyes always seemed on him. Even the blacksmith, greasing up the hubs of a spring wagon, gave him a hesitant glance as he walked in.

"This is the best I got."

Yellowleg turned. "You talking to me?"

"I said this is the best I got," the blacksmith remarked, with a heavy chaw of tobacco in his cheek. "Nothing better than Wisconsin oak."

"Yeah," Yellowleg said shortly.

"Fisher Bros. They make a good wagon. She's sure got this town in a daunsy mood."

"What?"

"I said I never seen the town so daunsy. Everybody's wearin' his chin down around his instep."

Yellowleg said nothing, and the blacksmith spit a flash of tobacco juice into a pile of sweet-smelling hay.

"Folks think she'll change her mind by mornin'," the blacksmith went on.

"But I know better. She'll be long gone by sun up."

Yellowleg suddenly realized what the blacksmith was telling him. He left the saddle unhitched and walked around the wagon where the blacksmith was working under the lamp.

"Did she rent this wagon?"

"Kinda old, ain't it? But the wheels ought to stand up. You can't hardly bust Wisconsin oak."

"Is this for her?"

"That's right. Her and the boy."

The blacksmith walked around the platform and set to work on another wheel with the cup grease. Yellowleg hesitated, and then followed him around.

"How soon is she planning on leaving?"

The blacksmith straightened. "She told me to hurry. They fixed the body to travel in the heat and I heard them nailing the pine box just before you walked in. All they gotta do is seal it up good. I'd say she'll be leavin' just as soon as I finish greasin' this wagon, and I'm finished now. In other words, she's goin' tonight, mister, and goin' alone if she has to."

The blacksmith gave him a narrow glance, but Yellowleg turned away. He was sorry, but Siringo was out. He'd spent too many years hunting for Turk, and he couldn't walk away from him now. That was firm in his mind, a fact, and you don't argue with facts.

He cinched up the saddle and checked his bedroll, but then he stopped and looked again at the spring wagon in the flickering pool of light. It looked worn and troublesome, as most rental wagons were. The paint was long gone and the platform was in splinters, but the hardware looked all right. Maybe it would do, if Kit Tildon knew how to handle a wagon.

The blacksmith had already chosen a brace of horses and was hitching them up when the alarm triangle began to ring from one end of town. The blacksmith went to the door and looked out and transferred the wad in his cheek.

"It's the mayor. Goin' to make a speech, looks like."

Yellowleg took the bridle and led out the claybank. He was not interested in the mayor or speeches. But half-way out the door he saw that the triangle had attracted no one, and Yellowleg stopped. The mayor moved out into the middle of the deserted street and peered around. He was a burly man with a heavy watch chain that glinted out there in the night.

"Has every man in this town gone deef!"

The blacksmith spit almost at Yellowleg's feet. "Got quite a pair of lungs, ain't he?"

"Ashamed to show yur faces!" The mayor struck an arm toward the west and held it there. "That's bad country—no one's sayin' it ain't. But we can't let Kit go out there alone, can we?"

He looked almost foolish standing in the cross lights from the saloons. The plank walks and false fronts resisted his scorn with a dead silence. Yellowleg felt his anger rise. If these people had wronged Kit's reputation, as they now half-admitted, it was up to them to set it right. Yellowleg's going to Siringo wouldn't bring that six-year-old back to life, and Kit Tildon's reputation was none of his affair.

The mayor took another step and half-turned. "Well, come on out! I know I ain't just talkin' to myself! You can hear me!"

"They hear but ain't listenin'," the blacksmith said.

The mayor waited for a gust of wind to pass. "I ain't sayin' she knows what she's doin'," he shouted. "But she's a woman. And after the things this town's been sayin'—I say a couple of you boys should step out here and see Mead gets buried where she wants! Next to his paw!"

The town held its tongue. Yellowleg stepped on his cigarette and peered at the deserted street with a quiet rage. The blacksmith snorted and turned away. "The trouble is," he said, "she called this town a liar, and folks don't want her to prove she was right."

And suddenly Yellowleg knew his contempt was for himself. He led the mare to the rear of the wagon and tied the reins to the tail gate. Turk would keep. Maybe Siringo wouldn't. There were things a man had to do to make peace with himself, and this was one of them.

The blacksmith had hitched up the team and had one foot on the wheel hub when he saw what Yellowleg was up to. He smiled a little and Yellowleg took the reins out of his hand and climbed up on the warped oak seat.

"You'll find her at Scott & Mercer's," he said.

Yellowleg nodded and snapped the reins. The wagon sighed in all its joints and rolled slowly out of the livery stable.

The mayor was still haranguing an empty street. He had taken off his coat and carried it over one arm. When he saw the wagon at a distance he quieted down and then spat. He was through talking. He motioned the wagon over to the general store.

"Pick up supplies for her, Jeb."

In the dimly-lit street the mayor had mistaken him for the blacksmith. Yellowleg pulled around before Choteau's General Mercantile where a bearded storekeeper who could only have been Choteau himself was ready with supplies and a keg of fresh water. The mayor came over and gave a hand, and it was only then that he recognized Yellowleg on the wagon seat.

"I wondered why that claybank was tied to the wagon," he said. "I guess you know what you're doing."

Yellowleg said nothing. He leaned on his knees and stared off toward the undertaker's sign further along the street.

Choteau tossed a bedroll onto the wagon and turned to the mayor.

"She ought to have a shotgun along."

"I'll give her mine," the mayor said. "The least I can do."

After a moment Yellowleg snapped the reins and the wagon moved under the oak tree. They were ready at Scott & Mercer's. Almost at once Dr. Caxton and a rosy-faced man carried out the pine box and set it gently on the bed of the wagon. Yellowleg didn't see Kit at first. Then he realized she was standing behind the darkened window of the shop, a vague shadow watching the men ready the wagon.

The mayor came up with his shotgun and laid it along the footboard and handed Yellowleg two boxes of shells.

"Put those somewhere handy."

Yellowleg found a place for them behind the seat and Kit came out under the tree. Her face looked almost ghostly in the tree shade, and Yellowleg knew she had been crying. But she held her shoulders straight now; she had changed into a simple dress for traveling and seemed in full control of her emotions.

"I'm rightly ashamed of this town," the mayor said. "No one even showin' his face to see you off. I did my best."

"Thanks, Emil," she muttered softly. "I'm not blaming them."

Choteau came up with a black umbrella from his store. "I hate to think what all that sun's going to do to your face," he said. "You take this along. Hear?"

"No—thanks."

"You take it. Can't sell it anyway, it hasn't rained in so long. Imported all the way from St. Louis."

He slipped it behind the seat and Dr. Caxton took Kit's shoulders, gently between his bony hands.

"Listen, Kit," he said. "It's still not too late if you want to change your mind."

She shrugged loose of his hands. "Goodbye, Doc. Emil. Paul."

"Good luck."

She turned to climb up onto the seat and stopped. She met Yellowleg's eyes for the first time, and for an instant her resolute poise seemed to fall apart. She gazed at him and then at the others on a bewildered note, and then back at Yellowleg.

"I'm taking the reins," he said. "Climb up the other side."

She saw, now, that his horse was tied behind the wagon and her eyes whipped back with their former contempt.

"Get down," she said quietly.

Yellowleg only stared at her.

"I said get down from there!"

"I heard you," he said.

A puff of wind rustled the dead leaves at her feet. "Haven't you done enough?" she whispered harshly. A slant of light fell across her cheek, polished by the night heat.

"Someone's got to drive this wagon."

"Not you. You're not going along."

"Then I'm asking to go."

Her eyes burned into him and he wondered why he sat there like a fool. She turned suddenly and moved to the rear of the wagon. She untied his mare. When she returned there was little room for argument. She didn't want his pity, if that's what it was, and she wanted his company even less.

"Now get down," she said.

But still he sat there, in a sort of fit of stubbornness to match her own. "I said I was going."

Her eyes found the shotgun at his feet and she slid it out. "And I said— get!"

Yellowleg stared at the end of the gun and supposed she was choused up enough to squeeze the trigger.

"Kit," the mayor said, stepping closer. "That thing's not loaded."

But she held it point-blank as though it were, and Yellowleg got tired of looking at it. He pushed the barrel away and climbed down slowly and avoided the eyes of the men standing at the edge of the walk. She had more temper than good sense. He smarted a little at being talked down by a woman, but let it go. He picked up the reins of his horse and came to his own senses. What a fool he'd been to consider walking away from Turk. How could he so easily have turned his back on seven years? He glanced back with an anger of his own and saw Kit on the wagon seat give the reins a snap.

"Ha! Git up!"

She turned the team in the middle of the street and almost ran him down. His mare shied and he had to grab the bridle. He swore at Kit and then stood watching as the wagon passed beyond the flickering lights of town and vanished in the darkness.

And as he peered at her, he knew. He knew she'd never make it. He had a feeling she wasn't even fooling herself. She had a cussed streak a mile wide, but that wouldn't get her to Siringo.

He took a match from his hatband and lit the stub of his cigarette. Whether she cared for it or not, she'd have to put up with his company.

CHAPTER EIGHT

Someone started up the mechanical piano and the gloom began to lift in the Davis & Davis Saloon. When Yellowleg walked in he couldn't see Turk and Billy at first. A haze of cigar smoke hung in the air and the card tables were full. But he heard Billy's voice, just loud enough to carry.

"Never saw so many cowards in any one town."

Yellowleg turned and spotted them elbow deep in empty glasses and poker hands.

"It's them city ordinances," Turk said, sliding a pile of chips into the pot. "Breaks a man's spirit, givin' up his guns."

The other players huddled over their cards and their consciences; they were in no mood to argue the fine points of cowardice and let the barbs die in the air. Kit had left town, the pressure was off and give me two cards—aces, if possible.

"I'm buyin' the drinks!"

There was a minor stampede for the bar and the saloon found its natural voice—loud and woolly. Yellowleg cleared a path through the crowd and stopped short of Turk's back, not yet sure of just what he was going to do. The poker lamp was pulled low over the table and the teeth marks, as old as the war, showed up as clearly as a brand on Turk's dealing hand.

One of the players tongued a cigarette to the other side of his mouth and discarded three cards. "Bet she don't get twenty miles out before she turns around," he said. "Apaches don't exactly make nice traveling companions."

"Yankees is even worse," Turk said, Billy looked up and saw Yellowleg standing there. He grinned slightly and let Turk talk on. "I was kinda hopin' he'd leave town. Him and me were bound to have a showdown and I don't like drawin' on Yankees. It's too easy."

The man with the cigarette glanced up uncomfortably. "I imagine he's feelin' right poorly about that boy."

"Not him. He don't feel nothin'. Never met anyone like him. What ya got?"

The players laid out their hands and Turk flipped his cards over one by one. "Sorry, gents. I seem to be in possession of four aces."

Turk had a hand out for the pot when he became aware of Yellowleg standing behind him.

"Cash in," Yellowleg said, "We're leaving town."

"You don't say?" Turk passed a glance to Billy and then raked in the pot. "Now ain't that a mite premature, Yellowleg?"

"The horses are out front."

"I kinda figured on bankin' my winnin's in the mornin'. I was always the thrifty sort."

"Move!"

"Now? In the middle of a winnin' streak?"

"*Right* now."

Turk winked at Billy and shook his head. "Now ain't it a funny thing," he said evenly. "Me and Billy, we kinda took a shine to this town. Thanks for the invite, Yank, but I guess you'll just have to go alone. We ain't leavin'."

Yellowleg was in no mood to argue it out. He looped a boot under Turk's chair and kicked the seat out from under him. Turk's arms flew out and he dumped over backwards. He lit on the floor with Yellowleg standing over him, and Billy burst out laughing.

But the saloon fell quiet and braced for trouble. Turk raised himself to an elbow and stared at Yellowleg with murder in his eyes. "It wasn't me that shot the boy," he said.

"Get up."

"Billy, tell this Yank if he's lookin' for a dog to kick, it ain't goin' to be us."

But Billy only looked on and smiled. "You heard what he said, Turk. Looks like we're goin' to Siringo."

Yellowleg didn't bother glancing over. He wasn't surprised at Billy's easy compliance. Billy would give him trouble of a different sort. But Turk transferred his anger to Billy in a flash of pure frustration. "Listen, kid," he said tight-lipped. "You ain't old enough to give me orders."

"Not givin' 'em, Turk. Just backin' 'em up. Banker, cash me in." He tossed what was left of a long-nine into the brass cuspidor. "I'd kinda like to go to Siringo with that girl."

For the second time that day Billy had deserted Turk. It was hard to take from the floor of a saloon, but there was nothing for Turk to do but hold onto Billy as best he could, and he took it. He pulled himself up and reached for his winnings.

"Get your hands off that," the man with the cigarette said.

"What?"

"A man that gets four aces... twice in one night... he'd *better* leave town."

Turk peered at the silent faces and withdrew his hands from the table. He knew hemp fever when he saw it. Retreating in time had long kept him from hanging up to dry on a cottonwood.

"Just a friendly little game," he said. "No harm done."

Yellowleg and Billy went out and Turk pulled his hat down tight with more cockiness than he felt. A path cleared for him toward the door, and he took it. There was no point in arguing with a posse. No point at all—especially with the fifth ace that popped out of his lap when Yellowleg kicked over his chair.

They led their horses away from the hitch rail and the town dog followed them down the street to the edge of light. Then the dog turned and went back.

"That dog's got good sense," Turk said. "He ain't goin' to Siringo."

Billy carried his eyes straight ahead, almost as if he could see Kit off in the distance. "Sure is a pretty girl. Yes, sir."

Yellowleg said nothing.

Billy was going to give him trouble.

CHAPTER NINE

"There she is."

The three men had trailed through the night, dozing in the saddle, but keeping the dim bluish North Star off their right shoulder. Now dawn spread against a streaked sky and raised a sea of Mexican poppies at their feet. They were in a long, tilted valley, and a rolling cloud of dust stood in the distance like a marker.

"Goin' like the heel flies are after her," Turk muttered.

Billy beat the dust out of his hat and put it on again. He grinned across to Yellowleg. "Maybe they are, eh, Yank?"

"Let's go."

Yellowleg spurred his horse gently and led them along the slope of the valley. They had almost caught up with her in the night, but Yellowleg had held back. He had half expected her to ride out her anger and come to her senses before morning. Once she discovered they were trailing her, he knew she'd never turn back—and from the way she was driving that team he guessed she wouldn't anyway.

"Sure smells good," Billy said.

Turk looked at him quizzically. "What does?"

"Coffee. Take's a woman's hand to make a good pot of coffee. I can just smell it now."

"You got a lot to learn. The purtier a woman is the worse the coffee she makes. The best jamoka I ever drunk was in a parlor house in Wichita. That woman was so ugly her face belonged in a halter. But she had two talents, and one of them was makin' coffee. The coffee was free." He spit over the side in the sadness of memory. "Of course, I was younger then. The last I heard she was plyin' her trade on the Bravo and a bounty hunter took a shine to her hair. She'd made the mistake of dyein' it black—you listenin'?"

"I kinda prefer ugly coffee and pretty girls."

"Well, sir, that man ran out of money and she never would extend credit. You know how feisty some women are—like that one out there. Just won't listen to reason. It kinda annoyed him and durned if he didn't treat her to an Apache haircut. Sold the scalp in Arizona. They was offerin' a bounty in those days and give him sixty dollars in gold for it. By the time they found out it wasn't an Indian scalp at all, just dyed black, he was long gone."

Yellowleg found himself staring at Turk. "A friend of yours?"

"We was slightly acquainted, you might say." He scratched his back long and luxuriously. "Use to be good money in Indian scalps. Of course, it was a kind of risky profession."

"I think she sees us," Billy said.

Spires of soapweed bristled against the western horizon. They approached at an angle with the sun casting long shadows ahead of them, and caught up with her in the hollow of the valley. She had been driving the wagon with a blanket thrown across her shoulders, but now she let it drop and held the shotgun in the crook of her arm.

Billy lifted his hat just long enough to show he had the instincts of a gentleman and gave her a disrobing glance to disprove it.

"Mornin', m'am."

Kit regarded him with an icy calm. Her hair held bronze highlights from the sun at her back and Yellowleg wondered how she managed to look so fresh and clean after a night's steady travel. The wan cast was gone from her face and he saw gentle coloring there, as in a fine painting. If he had taken her for something hopelessly fragile, he saw now that he was wrong. She was a bigger-boned woman than he had realized—he could see it in her wrists—and her eyes had lost none of their burning hatred and cold resolve.

"You'll kill those horses, driving 'em that way," he said.

"Leave me alone—and stop following me."

"I think you'd better let me drive that wagon."

"I told you before," she said evenly. "I don't want your help."

Yellowleg dismounted. "You'd better get used to it," he snapped.

She let the shotgun slide off the crook of her arm and into her hands. "Get back on that horse."

For the second time Yellowleg found himself looking at the wrong end of that gun, and he had a feeling now that it was loaded.

"You shouldn't point a gun unless you're willing to shoot."

She cocked the trigger and stared at him.

"M'am," Billy broke in with a smile. "I'd be mighty proud to ride that wagon with ya. Now why don't we have us a pot of coffee and get better acquainted?"

"Leave me alone," she answered firmly. "Both of you."

"It ain't exactly safe for a woman out here," Billy added.

"It's not exactly safe for you either—any of you," she said. "Now—*get!*"

Turk leaned on his saddle horn and grinned. "Boys, let's head back."

Kit cracked the whip and the wagon lurched forward, leaving Yellowleg still on his feet. Who was she trying to fool? He hunkered down on his heels and watched the wagon hurtle off through the soapweed.

"That bank's probably just openin' up," Turk said.

"Yes, sir," Billy grinned. "That's a *woman*."

"Feisty. Like I warned you, there ain't no talkin' sense to a feisty woman. No point in standin' here gatherin' dust."

"Look at her go."

Yellowleg glanced over his shoulder at Turk reining his horse around. "We're not heading back to Gila City," he said slowly.

"What's that?"

Yellowleg caught the reins of his mare and put his foot in the stirrup. "We'll follow along behind and try to keep her out of trouble."

Turk stared at him and then spit. He glanced at Billy and saw that it would be a waste of good breath to argue and his avaricious hopes faded as quickly as they had come. "Feisty," he said.

"That's what I like," Billy grinned. "A feisty woman."

The three horsemen started through the wagon dust.

CHAPTER TEN

Their shadows traveled close underfoot, like timid reflections. Yellowleg brushed the heel flies from his face and peered at the badlands ahead. The distance was turning black with malpais. The lava stretched like a petrified hide, encrusted and broken, over the dry lands. Not a tree stood against the empty sky and, except for the banging of the wagon canteens half a mile ahead of them, not a sound broke the intense and heated silence.

"Ain't she never goin' to stop?" Turk mumbled.

"Don't look that way," Yellowleg said.

"That malpais'll slow her down. If she's got any sense at all."

The lava would give the horses trouble with their footing, and Yellowleg wondered if he would have to interfere to keep Kit from cutting her team's hooves to ribbons. But for the moment the trail was still sandy and they wouldn't be into the malpais for another hour.

He could feel the steady weight of the sun on his shoulders, and soon the sun would drop into their eyes. And yet Yellowleg felt a certain, dour sense of well-being. It was an inhospitable land, but whatever his own discomforts, he knew that Turk was suffering. Turk was not a good traveler. His stomach had been giving him trouble all morning, and it rankled him to be following a dead trail to a dead town because of the woman. Billy dozed in the saddle and only the heel flies kept him awake. Yellowleg found himself nodding as well, with the distant sound of the canteens in his ears. For a moment it reminded him of a cow bell they had back home, and he thought of Iowa and the green farmlands he'd never go back to. The Ross girl had ripened during the war, and waited for him, but he hadn't come home the lanky farm boy with the shy smile. Turk had fixed that. Yellowleg had heard that she married herself off almost as if afraid he'd turn up again to claim her. Occasionally Yellowleg wondered what his life might have been but for Turk, and then he'd put off thinking about it. The farm boy could never be resurrected from the cold ashes of his life.

He roused in the saddle as if to break off thinking about it. Turk had pulled somewhat ahead of him and he watched his horse raise silent puffs of sand. Yellowleg's sense of fulfillment was almost complete. Turk was close enough to spit on and these were the foothills of revenge.

The land lay like a giant shadow under them and the hooves of the horses grated and rang out against the lava. Colonies of porcupine cacti had taken hold in the malpais and they could see where the wagon wheels had split the growing things and left wet strains on the lava. They were leaving a trail that even a blind Indian could follow, Yellowleg knew. And yet, except for an occasional road runner and the heel flies, they had seen no signs of life around them.

"We're gettin' further and further from that bank money," Turk said. His voice was dry-mouthed and he kept blinking in the heat.

"We'd only spend it anyway," Billy said.

"Spend it on an army—that's what we'll do."

"You told me."

"I mean it."

Didn't Turk ever get tired of talking about his maverick army, Yellowleg wondered? Even Billy was bored with the sound of the man's voice and his crackpot daydreams.

"Buy up some housebroke Indians and put uniforms on 'em," Turk went on. "Teach 'em to salute us and polish our gold braid. A man looks like something in gold braid. Take you, Billy boy. Ever think what a figure you'd cut all dressed up in them kind of duds? With an aide to fetch and carry for you? And *yes sirrin'* you from hell to breakfast."

"She sure looks pretty, sittin' on that wagon, don't she?"

The wagon had dropped back against the rocky trail and they were trailing not more than five hundred yards behind. Yellowleg had seen her glance back only once, but some instinct had kept her from trying to hurtle across the malpais.

"You hear what I'm sayin'?" Turk spat.

"I always had a fancy for one of them bowler hats and a vest all sewn up pretty," Billy said. "My old man had a bowler hat. He used to wear it to funerals, and poker games and other important occasions. I always had a hankerin' for one."

A rim had begun to fall off toward their left and soon the trail took the wagon lurching southward off the lava mesa and along a shallow gorge. The horses had sensed water, lifting their heads against the reins, and now Yellowleg could hear the muted, drumming sounds from the split earth. There was water in the gorge and it was moving fast.

"It don't look like she's even going to slow down to water that team," Billy said.

"Waitin' for it to rain," Turk snorted. "Fool woman."

Kit kept urging the team on, despite their snorting and blowing and head-tossing against the reins. Yellowleg asked himself what she was trying to prove? That she could take all the punishment the desert had to offer without breaking stride? Did she feel that bringing her team to a halt would appear to them a first sign of weakness and conciliation? The mule-headed little fool. She must be bone-tired from the joggling that wagon was giving her, and that oak seat must have imprinted a firm distaste in her for the entire state of Wisconsin. But still she sat there, straight-backed with the reins fighting her fingers raw, and her eyes holding on the endless distance.

"Plumb crazy to pass up water," Turk said. "You'd think there was a posse on her tail."

Yellowleg gave her a final look and then reined off toward an eroded slope leading into the gorge. "Let her go," he said. "We might as well make use of that river."

"Fool woman," Turk snorted. "It just don't make sense followin' a bit of calico all over the desert. Especially in this heat. Now why don't we cool off and talk it over."

An hour later they came upon Kit. They had washed out and filled their canteens and let their horses graze on the tufts of river grass. Yellowleg hoped that by dropping behind they would give her an opportunity to stop further along the river. And for the first time she might be facing the loneliness of her position. Whether she had admitted it to herself or not, there had been a certain begrudging comfort, he knew, in being able to glance back and find the three men pacing her. But what if they had turned back? What if she were truly alone out here in the badlands?

But once they were back on the trail he realized that these questions had not troubled her. She had not stopped. The wagon tracks followed the rim of the gorge, with seeming indifference, and the sight of that resolute trail began to anger him. But then he noticed fluted marks in the right track and he found himself looking quickly at Billy.

"She's got a loose wheel."

They spurred their horses and came upon the wagon around a squat spire of granite. It had swerved off the trail and come to rest against a stunted cottonwood, one axle hanging raw and open under the wagon bed.

Yellowleg saw that the wagon seat was empty and expected for a moment to find Kit thrown to the ground. It was Turk who saw her first.

"Now look at that. Bet she's mighty glad to see us."

The wagon wheel had spun off down the slope and Kit was up to her knees in water trying to reclaim it from the gorge.

Billy straightened his hat and smiled. "Now ain't she a pretty sight? And ain't we a pretty sight? I'll just go on down and lend a hand."

"Stay where you are," Yellowleg said.

"She'll never get that wheel."

"Let her find that out."

She had seen them. She had looked up from below and stared for a moment, and Yellowleg expected the call of her voice. But instead, she picked up her skirts and waded further out into the rushing stream.

Stubborn as a muley-cow, he thought again. Maybe that river would wash some of the warpaint off her. She couldn't get to Siringo on three wheels and he'd keep Billy and Turk standing there until she called for help.

The wheel was floating with the river, revolving slowly in the gorge shadows, and she waded doggedly after it. For a moment it came to a stop against a boulder, but cleared itself before she could reach it. And then it hung up in debris and she made a rush for it, but again the current freed it. Yellowleg watched her with a faint grin on his lips as the water creeped up her skirts and destroyed her resolute air of poise and aloofness.

She began to look almost human.

"What we waitin' for?" Billy said, looking over at Yellowleg. "A printed invitation?"

Again she made a lurch for the wheel, almost within her grasp, but she lost her footing on the mossy rocks and plunged with a gasp into the stream. Her red hair instantly darkened into strands, and as she rose the wheel went slowly revolving down the gorge.

She stood now in a speechless anger, with the rive coursing between her legs, and her eyes flashed up to them. It was a long moment before her voice rose out of the gorge.

"Do something!"

Yellowleg glanced at Billy. "It ain't printed," he said. "But I guess it'll do."

They picked their way down the steep bank and the horses plunged into the stream. Yellowleg left Kit standing knee-deep, with hardly a glance, and led Turk further down the river. The wheel was already out of sight around a bend, and it was only then that Yellowleg realized Billy wasn't behind him. He turned and saw Kit still standing where he had ridden past, bent over as she wrung out her hair. And Billy sat his horse, staring at the figure she cut in the wet, clinging dress. Yellowleg had an impulse to turn back to them, but stopped himself. He couldn't prevent Billy from talking to her— and why should he?

Nevertheless, he found himself holding his horse at the bend as Turk went on after the wheel, and his eyes held resentfully on Billy's wide grin.

Their voices carried downstream, but still Yellowleg didn't turn away.

"Reckon you'll have to dry out that dress," he heard Billy say. "Won't take long in this sun."

Kit gave him a dark glance and Billy extended his arm to help her on his horse.

"Give you a hand back?"

"I'll walk."

The rest happened so fast that Yellowleg had hardly touched his spurs to the claybank's flesh when it was over. Billy caught her around the waist, lifting her out of the water and reined his horse around. But Kit became, instantly, a fighting handful and the horse reared. Yellowleg saw both Kit and Billy plunge into the river. Billy, finding himself in the water with her, grabbed her flailing arms and pulled her up against him and kissed her hard.

When Yellowleg reached them a moment later Kit had a good-sized rock in her hand and in another moment would have made a good try at braining him with it.

Billy winked at Yellowleg and reclaimed his hat from the water. "Never saw a dance-hall girl so edgy about gettin' kissed."

"If you touch me again," Kit muttered softly, "I'll kill you."

"Unhitch that team," Yellowleg said. "Get them horses watered."

But Kit didn't take her eyes off Billy and she still held the rock poised at her wet shoulder. "I'll kill you."

Billy grinned and picked up the reins of his horse. "M'am. I just naturally take to high stakes."

He mounted and walked the horse to the shingled bank and started up the slope. Then Yellowleg turned and picked his way down river again without looking back until he got to the bend. When he did, he saw Kit wringing out her hair again.

Turk was waiting for Yellowleg with a cigarette burning close to his lips and a strange little smile in his eyes. He just sat in his saddle, like a man of patience, with a joke up his sleeve, and waited for Yellowleg to see it.

The wagon wheel had come to rest. It had floated into an eddy and hung itself up on the water-logged boot of a dead man lying in the shallows.

"Dead as a door nail," Turk said.

Yellowleg said nothing, even though the sight of that submerged face raised the hackles on his neck. The face was bloated and only the man's clothing seemed to keep the body from bursting. Yellowleg dismounted and approached with his lariat. He made it fast to the wheel and freed the man's boot from the wooden spoke. He recognized body bruises that could only have been gathered from rolling along the bed of the river.

"Looks to me like that gent's been meanderin' downstream four or five days," Turk said.

Yellowleg nodded almost imperceptibly and busied himself with the rope, taking a dally around the saddle horn to drag the wagon wheel out of the gorge. Yellowleg knew Turk was waiting for him to say what was now on both their minds, but finally Turk said it himself.

"Appears to be some Indians north of us."

"Looks that way."

"Terrible," Turk said in a pious tone. "And in the prime of life, too."

Yellowleg touched the mare's flanks with his rowels and turned his back on the grim sight in the eddy. It had been hard for him to look at the poor devil, but during these moments Turk had filled him with a seething anger. Turk had sat his saddle staring openly with a casual but morbid fascination.

The dead man had been scalped.

CHAPTER ELEVEN

Billy sat under the cottonwood wiping out his guns when Yellowleg came up from the gorge, dragging the wheel after him. The wagon team was still waiting to be watered and the sight of Billy whistling softly in the dappled shade burned Yellowleg. But for a moment he said nothing. He didn't want to have to tell Billy again; it would have the effect of weakening his authority unless he put a bite into his voice—and he'd rather do that when it counted.

"What happened to you?" Turk said, knitting his coarse brows at the sight of Billy's wet shirt and levis.

"Horse threw me," Billy grinned. "That cow pony was born woman shy. Not like me at all."

"Your ammunition get wet?"

"All of it. And three cigars."

"That ain't so good. Indians up north of us—or were. No tellin' where they are now."

Billy absorbed this news indifferently and went on with his guns. Yellowleg had dismounted and was now rolling the wheel to the wagon axle.

"Throw me your makin's," Billy said. "I could sure use a smoke."

Yellowleg's eyes whipped over and the bite came into his voice. "I told you to get that team watered."

Billy's eyes narrowed with surprise. "You're givin' an awful lot of orders lately," he said slowly.

Turk looked between them and sparked to the sudden possibility of a showdown. "Yankees is all that way," he said.

"I ain't telling you again," Yellowleg muttered. "Unhitch that team. Now move."

Kit chose that moment to appear from below, the wet hems of her skirts heavy with sand. She struck a silence between them without meaning to, but Yellowleg was glad for it. He hadn't wanted to promote an argument with Billy here and now, and he had a feeling Billy himself had no stomach for it.

Billy turned and watched Kit hesitate, as if gathering her determination. And then she walked past him toward the wagon. The sheer bodice of her dress, clinging in wet highlights, revealed the firm shape of her breasts, and Billy was unable to hold back a hopeful grin. He walked over to the team, leaving Yellowleg standing as if words had never started between them or as if they might be finished up at some odd, casual moment. And Yellowleg too let them lie. He would need Billy. Billy was a touchy kid, but he'd be a gun hand if they ran into trouble.

Billy pulled down his hat brim and strolled to the team. "Your horses need waterin'," he said. "I'll be obliged, m'am. That is, if you don't mind."

So that was it, Yellowleg thought. Billy had calculated his moment and waited for Kit, as if it mattered. But Kit cut him cold, busying herself with a straw suitcase. Billy unhitched the team and Kit unfolded a dark blue calico dress from the suitcase.

"I'd change myself," Billy went on. "But it'd take a team of horses to strip wet levis off a man. I'll just have to live in 'em, I guess."

She climbed down off the wagon as Billy freed the team and led them along the bank. She started walking back along the trail, but Yellowleg decided she wasn't going to get off that easy.

"You know how to make coffee?" he said.

There was, he knew, a note of sarcasm in the question, but he felt she might have shown enough silent gratitude to start a pot going without his asking. He didn't wait for an answer; he began wrestling with the wheel to get it back on the hub. She returned and unhitched the coffee pot hanging with the canteens and got a fire going by herself.

Yellowleg was too busy to realize that for the first time he was alone with Turk. He'd got his Bowie knife and fashioned a wedge for the hub which set the wheel in tight. It had felt good to be doing something with his hands and it was only as he was rolling the knife back up in its oil cloth, like a sacred idol to be put away, that he saw Turk silently staring at him, and it occurred to him that they were alone. The coffee had not yet begun to boil and Kit had found privacy somewhere further back on the trail.

Turk hadn't recognized the Bowie knife after all these years, Yellowleg thought. He wondered, suddenly, if any man was worth seven years of looking. Maybe the trouble with revenge was the day you caught up with it. And the Reb, when he found him, seemed somehow smaller than life. Turk. A whining, bull-necked drifter who wasn't really worth spitting on. Still, this was the man who, with his breath smelling of sour whiskey, had come upon Yellowleg lying wounded in the night, gone through his pockets, and tried to collect his scalp lock.

Yellowleg hunkered by the coffee pot and lifted the lid. It let out a blast of flavor, simmering and pungent, and he saw that Kit had made the coffee good and strong. The aroma awakened his hunger, but the coffee would do until they made camp for the night. There were still three or four hours of daylight left, and he wouldn't hold Kit back if she wanted to keep traveling. He dropped the lid and met Turk's eyes. "Forget that bank money," Yellowleg said.

"There's somethin' fishy about you, mister," Turk scowled.

"You don't say."

"We've had enough."

"Yeah?"

"Me and Billy both."

"Forget it. You couldn't drag Billy back to Gila City. He thinks he's courtin' her."

"It's clear she don't want us along. I say we ought to accommodate her by leavin'."

"You can leave anytime you want," Yellowleg said. "Alone."

Turk, he knew, would squirm and bellyache all the way to Siringo, but he wouldn't light out alone.

The coffee began to boil and Turk didn't wait for it to mellow in the pot. He poured himself a boiling cup and began nursing it down his throat, but it didn't still the rumbling in his stomach.

"You deserted, didn't you?" Yellowleg said,

Turk looked up suddenly, both wary and surly. "What?"

"The Reb army."

"What you gettin' at?"

"I got a feeling you deserted."

"That's my business."

"What happened to that hand of yours?"

"That's my business too."

"Just tryin' to make conversation," Yellowleg said evenly. "Nothing personal."

Billy led the horses back up the slope and smelled the coffee boiling. He looked around, back along the trail, and then let the team graze in the cottonwood shade.

"She sure takes a long time to change her dress," he said.

"That coffee's about ready," Yellowleg said.

They filled their cups and Yellowleg tossed Billy his sack of tobacco. They sat and smoked, waiting for Kit, but when she didn't join them Billy tossed his cigarette in the fire and rose with a brooding temper.

"I hate a high and mighty woman," he said.

"And don't she take the cake," Turk added. "You'd think we wasn't fit company for her. She ain't much more than a parlor girl, when you come right down to it."

Billy peered off in the direction she had gone, his jaws working hard. Yellowleg watched him closely, wondering how he could head off the trouble he saw coming.

"I'll be back," Billy said.

Yellowleg caught his eye, and it was a warning. "I wouldn't do that."

"She's goin' to sit here and have a cup of jamoka with me if I have to pour it down her throat."

"Cool off, kid."

"You're just full of advice, ain't you, Yellowleg?"

"No point in gettin' ringey over a girl," Yellowleg answered quietly. "Especially this one."

"Shut up."

"Stay where you are. Leave her be."

Turk was quick to size up the suddenly developing situation and to widen the breech with a few well chosen words. "Looks to me like Yellowleg here has taken a real shine to that woman, don't it, kid? And all along we thought he only felt sorry about the boy."

Yellowleg didn't waste a glance on Turk. "Stay out of this." Billy's jaws were still working; the kid was looking for something to strike out at and now Yellowleg would do.

"Touchy, too, ain't he?" Turk went on, prepared to ignore Yellowleg's quiet warning. "Like he is about that hat of his."

"Yeah," Billy muttered.

"You know what I think he's got hid up there, Billy? Greenbacks. What do you think, Billy boy?"

Yellowleg recognized a softening at Billy's eyes, as if he had made a decision and it pleased him. Turk had provided him with an easy excuse, an outlet for his frustration over Kit.

"I know one way to find out," Billy said, standing motionlessly. "We could ask him. Yellowleg, take off your hat."

Yellowleg felt his face flush. "Billy, I'm not looking for a fight with you."

"I'm doin' the lookin'. Take off that hat."

Yellowleg stared at the kid and felt like breaking him in two. "Stop talking like a punk—" And then he saw Kit in the blue calico dress, approaching along the trail behind Billy. "There she is."

But Billy didn't turn; he only began to grin and held his ground.

Turk cleared his throat. "Billy, it looks to me like that Yankee's scared of ya."

Yellowleg knew Billy had begun to believe the same thing, and it was serving to remake his pride and confidence in an image larger than life. "Yellowleg—take off your hat or I'm going to shoot it off."

Kit grew larger in the background, but nothing—not even Kit—was going to head Billy off now. "If you want to talk that way," Yellowleg said, "you'd better strap on Turk's guns."

Turk was alive to a happy outcome, which, to judge by his sudden and cocky smile, he must have considered inevitable, Yellowleg thought grimly. "Glad to oblige, kid, bein' as how yours are wet," said Turk.

Kit seemed yet unaware of what she was walking into. Billy strapped on the belt and weighed the guns as if to adjust himself to the heft and feel of them. Yellowleg could feel the heat of the coffee fire on the back of his legs as he stood, feeling the unwanted tenseness, and waited. He had been able to forget his shoulder most of the day and he refused to think about it now. If the pain came and joggled his aim he had no doubt that Billy would kill him.

Billy twirled the guns and dropped them into their holsters. And still Kit came along the trail toward the wagon. But now as Billy's legs parted and his heels seemed to dig into the earth Yellowleg saw her stop. She stood frozen, as though her breath had stopped, and then Billy's hands flashed for his sides.

Yellowleg's reaction came in a burst of movement and he felt his fingers on the triggers and even before he could squeeze he knew he had won the draw. In that moment, he saw Billy clearly, and the kid was still elbows out and his feet in the grave. But in that same moment he saw the shimmer of blue on the trail behind Billy and it froze his hands. She was so close in the line of sight. That had been the way with Mead; an innocent bystander. There was no pain, only the memory of it, and the fear of it, but it kept him from squeezing the trigger.

Not a leaf seemed to move in the lengthening silence. Billy, staring certain death in the face, gaped with his guns half-drawn. And then it became clear even to him that there wasn't going to be a shooting. Yellowleg's guns were still leveled at him, but the unexpected silence was a reprieve, and he began to breathe again. And then his hands cleared the gun butts.

"Kid," Turk said, a quick grin. "You need more practice."

Billy turned away morosely. "Shut up."

Kit came on in and Yellowleg said, "Let's get moving."

Turk tipped his hat to her and seemed undaunted by Billy's sudden defeat and humiliation. "Mighty good coffee, m'am," he said. "Mighty good."

CHAPTER TWELVE

Yellowleg kicked dirt into the fire and hooked the coffee pot back on the side of the wagon. Kit's wet hair still clung to the back of her neck; she hadn't brought along a change of shoes and she settled herself on the wagon seat with her feet bare. It gave her an earthy look, while sun and the day's exposure were beginning to roughen her face. Somehow it made her easier to talk to.

"I ain't the best company in the world," Yellowleg said, "but I know how to drive a wagon."

She was gaining a begrudging tolerance for him, he felt, but still her voice carried the coolness of an armed truce. "That fight was because of me, wasn't it?" she asked quietly.

"You're a mighty pretty woman and Billy ain't blind."

"Keep him away from me."

"He's got a mind of his own."

"So have I." Her temper hardened. "All you know is murder, isn't it? Both of you. Animals all dressed up in leather boots and big hats and the touch of death in everything you do. Swelled up with your own importance and tearing at each other's throats to settle an argument. Well, don't settle any arguments over me. You can bury each other, for all I care, but don't set me up as any prize. I've got a shotgun and you both look the same in the sights."

She picked up the reins and he studied her in a crisp, rising anger of his own. It hadn't occurred to him before that she was judging him by the company he kept, but that didn't really matter. "Maybe you'd better get one thing straight," he said. "I'm not along because of you, and don't forget it."

"Ha! Git up!"

The wagon lurched forward, scraping a low-hanging limb of the cottonwood, and Yellowleg found himself standing there a little foolishly, not quite finished with his little speech. She was a strange one. High strung and fighting hard to maintain the illusion of rock-hard pride and independence. But she wasn't fooling him any more. She was afraid. She had sensed that only Yellowleg stood between her and Billy's stud-like conquest, and standing back there on the trail, as the two men faced each other, she had frozen with the vision of Yellowleg lying dead.

He smiled a little.

They rode into the sun on a vast, dead countryside. Even the tufts of desert grass cast shadows, like lengthening spider webs, and the horses paced heavily against the lingering heat of the day. Yellowleg rode with his neck bent to keep the sun out of his eyes. The sound of the wagon canteens clanked ahead of him in water-full tones. They had better pick out a spot to make camp soon, he thought. There was a thin veil of dust in the western sky and there would be a long, red dusk—another hour of traveling time at most. Kit ought to start looking around for a spot and make for it.

Billy and Turk had fallen a few paces behind and he could hear them mutter and argue in quiet tones.

"She's more woman than you can handle, kid," Turk was saying.

"That's your opinion."

"Me and you could go back fur that money. A town posse'd never foller us—not to Siringo. Never saw folks so scared of Injuns."

"Pretty feet," Billy muttered in a sort of parboiled reverie. He had shucked off his sullen mood and for long moments Yellowleg had the feeling of Billy's eyes on his back. The kid had been outdrawn to a fare-thee-well, but Yellowleg had frozen on the trigger, and Billy had obviously been turning that over in his mind. Either the Yankee had no lust for killing or Billy was too valuable to him on this trek, or both. At any rate, Yellowleg knew, Billy had rendered his humiliation into a sort of victory. It had given him the armor of a charmed life. "Mighty pretty. She's got about the prettiest feet I ever seen. All white and mighty pretty."

"Don't waste your thinkin'," Turk spat. "Yellowleg's already staked his claim, and you can't divvy up a woman."

"I don't plan to."

"You got her all choused up, kid. You gone about it wrong, and you got that Yankee choused up too. No, sir. You listen to me. There's enough money sittin' in that bank to burn a wet mule."

"Ain't you ever goin' to stop talkin' about it?"

"I'm talkin' about an army. We'll set up our own republic maybe—like that Edwards fella did back in Texas. Fredonia, he called it. Yes sir, the Reepublic of Fredonia."

"He was crazy too."

"We'll be smart. All this land out here—just waitin' for someone to come along with ideas. Why, you'd be walkin' around with so much yeller braid you'd assay like a gold mine. Think of it, Billy boy. We'd make all the laws we want, only they wouldn't apply to us."

"They don't anyway. Never did."

"I'm talkin' sense."

"All white and mighty pretty. Somethin' about a woman's naked feet—especially hers."

Turk's voice came up with mild exasperation. "Ain't you forgettin'? When it came to skinnin' your guns you came up with a big case of slow."

"I just wasn't used to your guns. Kinda slows a fella up."

Again Yellowleg had the cold sensation of Billy's eyes on his back. In the open silence Billy had gone to no trouble to keep his voice private and it seemed almost as if the kid were speaking directly to Yellowleg. And yet Yellowleg found himself only half-listening. Turk was a mouthy bore and Billy had an unerring taste for folly. He would destroy himself with it. He was already learning to talk too much.

The wagon was carving its wheel through a dry wash turned agate by the low-setting sun. Yellowleg lifted his eyes and saw that Kit was pouring canteen water into a handkerchief. She set about wiping the heat from her forehead and cheeks. He touched the claybank's flanks with his rowels. He caught up with the wagon and began to pace alongside.

"That water's for drinking," he snapped.

She gave him a brief glance and moistened the handkerchief again. The rouged sky cast her face in tones of heat and fatigue, and he knew she couldn't go on much longer. But still she managed that cool look of defiance and continued with the luxury of wiping her face with drinking water.

"It'll only dry out your skin and set it smarting," he said. He reached out for the canteen, took it from her hand and recapped it. Then he hung it back in place where it began to clatter against the other. He was aware that Billy and Turk were watching him now and decided to hold his ground.

"There's saltbush off to your right. Head toward it. We'll make camp."

"Make camp if you want," she said simply. "I'm going on."

"There's just so much you can take, and that goes for your team too." He took hold of the lines, heading the team northwest, and she didn't resist. Then he tossed the reins back into her lap. "Fool stubbornness ain't going to get you to Siringo."

Her bare feet were spread against the weathered and splintered footboard, but she seemed unaware of his glance. He found Billy's phrase rising in his mind like an unwanted memory. Mighty pretty. All white and mighty pretty. The phrase had the raw intimacy of parlor house talk and Yellowleg averted his eyes. She should have had more sense than to tempt Billy with the sight of her skin. And what of himself? Did she think he was any different? Did she think he'd never held anything but a squaw with her back to the sun-warmed earth?

He rode alongside, his eyes scanning the vast distances around them, and knew somehow that he wasn't unwelcome. Loneliness was a worse companion.

"I guess you used to live in Siringo," he said. When she didn't reply, he added: "Not that it's any of my business. Sure quiet out here, ain't it?"

She remained silent and he thought again of Billy and Turk watching him.

"Look," he said. "I'm not blaming you for the way you feel about us—and me in particular. But it just might be a good idea to pretend we was getting along."

She turned her head; she wasn't giving an inch. "I'm not very good at pretending."

"I've noticed that. You're not used to being out in the sun, either. Better get under the umbrella."

"You might stop telling me what to do."

"You might start using your head."

They were getting nowhere fast, but Yellowleg felt a surge of mule-headedness and hung on.

"I didn't invite you along," she said crisply. "Any of you."

"I've been thinking about that," he said.

"Good."

"Anybody else would be glad of company on a trail like this."

"I'm not anybody else."

"You made your point a long while ago. I can't help wondering if you really figured on going to Siringo at all."

It stopped her cold for a moment and then her eyes began to blaze. "Just what are you trying to say?"

"There are moments when you act like they were dead right back in Gila City," he said. He'd better lay it on the line now; if he was making a mistake this was the time to find it out. It was just possible that she wasn't leading them to Siringo—they might be driving her to it. "I'd be mighty sore if we got to Siringo and I found out it was all for nothing."

She lashed out and slapped him hard with the back of her hand. His hand rose to the sting at his cheek and he thought of Billy behind them. And then he held Kit's face in a quiet, angry gaze.

"You just naturally do the wrong thing, don't you?"

"You're no different from the others. Why did you come? If you believe what you said—"

"Simmer down. I didn't say I believed it. I just wanted to make sure. I don't know any more about you than you got a mighty pretty face and a mighty fast temper. And not enough sense to get you to Siringo."

She seemed to wrap herself in a sudden iron-clad silence, turning him off with a final twist of loathing. "I simply don't care what you think."

"Then why did you slap me? Especially in front of Billy? I'm not forgetting the hurt I caused you and I'll never forget that boy of yours. But lady, you don't know me well enough to hate me as much as you're trying to do. Hating's a subject I know something about. You gotta be careful it don't bite you back."

She rustled the reins to urge the team on, but Yellowleg kept up. He wasn't sure why he kept talking except that there wasn't going to be room in the days ahead for anything but a working peace between them. Her green eyes squinted against the sun as if he had ceased to exist, but he went on talking anyway.

"I know a man who spent seven years looking for a gent he hated. Hating and wanting revenge—that's all he lived for." He glanced at Kit. "He was something like you. He hated hard and loved hard, with nothing in between. It took him all those years just to catch up with that gent. The day he did—that was the worst day of his life. He found out the man he'd been looking to kill wasn't worth—spitting on. All those years turned to alkaline and ashes."

Kit turned suddenly in a cold flash of exasperation. "Will you please shut up."

But now Yellowleg ignored her. "So he began putting it off. He knew he'd have to kill that man someday, but he just kept putting it off."

A horned toad lay sunning itself in the last light of day, luxuriating in its own ugliness, and it caught Yellowleg's eye. Then he slipped off into a silence of his own, knowing he had said these things more for himself than for her. And even at that he'd shaded the truth, for he'd never cared about killing the man. Death was a reprieve from life, and Yellowleg had no intention of being that generous with Turk. Their score would be evened with a few deft flashes of the Bowie knife.

He whirled the mare about as the crack of a lone gunshot split the desert quiet. He dug for his gun, not sure what to expect, for the explosion was so close behind; and in that instant of sudden reflex the sharp pain came to his shoulder. His fingers lost their feeling and in the next instant he saw his gun lying in the dust. He was struck with awe and amazement, and then stark humiliation.

When he looked up he saw Billy and Turk staring at him with faint grins, and Yellowleg knew his face had gone white. The wagon, too, had stopped, and even Kit was looking at it, as if it were some vile magician's trick —his .45 lying there, ingloriously, at the feet of his mare.

Yellowleg ignored the pain that was still in his shoulder. Billy's gun held a wisp of smoke, and then he twirled it and slipped it into its holster.

"There might be Apaches about," Yellowleg said. "There's nothing like announcing our arrival."

"Just a fat ol' horned toad," Billy said. "Got him right between the eyes."

Yellowleg gazed at Billy, thankful for the misdirection his anger could take. He refused to let his eyes fall again to the gun, as if it might disappear if they ignored it; how could he bring himself to get down and pick it up? "Don't shoot off that gun again unless it makes sense. Is that clear?"

"Just wanted to check my aim," Billy said, still grinning. "That makes sense, don't it?"

"All right. You checked it."

"Got him right between the eyes, too."

"Turk," Yellowleg snapped. "You and Billy ride on ahead to that saltbush. We'll make camp. Scout up beyond that outcrop and get the lay of the land."

Turk cleared his throat and sat there with his wrists crossed on the horn of his saddle and a conceited smile in his squinted eyes. He was just waiting for Yellowleg to dismount for the gun and make his humiliation complete. "Like you said, Yellowleg—there might be Apaches around and about."

"You go find out."

And then Billy said it, with his voice just this side of open laughter. "Ain't you goin' to pick up your gun, Yellowleg?"

Yellowleg felt himself bristle; his eyes burned into Billy's long, smug face. "I figured you might pick it up for me," he said.

"Come on, Billy boy," Turk said, as if it were an act of charity. "You gents is all horns and rattles."

They rode off toward the saltbush, but not before Turk delivered judgment in a voice meant to carry. "I've seen gunhands good, bad and cross-eyed, but never seen a leather slapper fumble quite so bad. Kinda scares a man to be in company like that, don't it?"

Yellowleg sat staring off at the darkening plain and then, slowly, he dismounted. He got hold of the gun and rubbed the dust off and realized that Kit was looking at him. He'd forgotten she even existed. He saw her now with a look of compassion on her face, and he resented it. He didn't want anyone's pity. He holstered the gun, picked up the reins and walked to the wagon. He tied the reins to the rear of the wagon and walked forward. He took hold, with one boot on the wheel hub, and pulled himself to the seat beside her.

"I'm taking those reins."

He wrenched the leather out of her hands, but she didn't really protest. She gave him room on the seat, as if to make sure their thighs wouldn't touch as the wagon jostled them, and turned her shoulder slightly. It was a kind of victory, he knew, but it didn't really mean anything to him.

"Git up!"

All that mattered was getting this wagon to Siringo and finishing his business with Turk. Did she think he felt like a king mounting the seat beside her? Well, she was wrong. He felt like a fool.

"Someone's got to keep you from killing this team. Once we get to Siringo we'll be leaving you. You'll have to find your own way back."

She turned, and their eyes met for an instant, and then he snapped the lines again.

"Ha! Git up!"

CHAPTER THIRTEEN

They dug around for dead roots and built a small fire in the lee of the outcrop. The first stars were out and a warm, sullen breeze had come up from the west. It rustled through the saltbush thicket, where Yellowleg had concealed the wagon, and brushed their faces in the last light of the sun.

Yellowleg dug out his bedroll and cleaned his gun beyond the light of the fire. He thought about the lame jack rabbit Turk had pounced upon in the rocks. He sat there now, skinning it with all the glory of a buffalo hunter, and for the first time Yellowleg wondered about his own survival. The lead plumb he carried in his flesh might disable him again, when it counted, and Turk had enough animal wit to adjust himself to unexpected odds. Turk, he knew, had a special sense for survival and with the proper odds would pounce on Yellowleg as eagerly as he had on the rabbit. It filled Yellowleg with a sudden inner fury that Turk might somehow escape his vengeance; in seven years the thought had never occurred to him before.

He looked over to the fire and saw Turk forcing a bent greasewood stick through the rabbit. He propped the spit over the fire and almost at once the fat on the animal burst into flames, flaring up and sizzling.

Tonight. I could get it over with tonight, Yellowleg thought. When his stomach is full of lame rabbit and he's dreaming of that redskin army of his.

And then Yellowleg put away his thoughts. Not tonight. Not until they had rid themselves of the girl.

"You goin' to cook for us?" Billy said.

Kit had come from the wagon with a frying pan, some bacon, and biscuit scald ready for the fire. She busied herself without looking up and Yellowleg saw that she had combed out her hair. She had spent a long time at the wagon, as if preparing for her entrance, and in the privacy of the night Yellowleg found himself staring at her.

She threw back her hair with a small movement of her head and settled on her knees at the fire. She looked almost squaw-like in the crackling, flickering light. Again he felt that earthy quality about her and a lessening of that cold, polished beauty she had brought from Gila City. The sun and the sky and the badlands were revealing her, he thought.

"I ain't never traveled with a lady before," Billy said, chewing on a match. "It kinda appeals to me."

She didn't bother looking up.

"Don't them biscuits look good, though," Turk said. "This here is going to be a meal."

"Here, let me cut that bacon for you," Billy said.

Kit's eyes flashed across the fire. "Just sit where you are."

"You sure rile easy, don't you, m'am?" He spit out the match. "You'd think we ain't been introduced. Kit. Now that's about the prettiest name I heard in a long time. I never did care much for them Bible names like Sarah and Ruth. But Kit. That appeals to me."

Yellowleg shot him a glance. "You're doing an awful lot of talking, ain't you?"

"It comes natural."

"Eat and get some sleep. You'll stand second watch."

"Where's the lady sleepin'?"

"That," Yellowleg said, "is up to her."

The biscuits swelled and browned and the bacon began to sizzle in the pan. Turk peered off into the darkness and then tested the flesh of the rabbit with the point of his knife. "Bet they can smell that bacon clear to Apache Pass. Wouldn't surprise me if we all woke minus our top-knots."

Yellowleg gazed at Turk and it was a moment before he realized Turk was holding the charred greasewood stick out to him. "Cut yourself a slab of jack rabbit."

Yellowleg flipped his cigarette into the fire. "No thanks."

"Ain't Yankees meat-eaters?"

Billy's glance turned back to Kit. "You like Yankees, m'am?"

"If it was up to me," Turk muttered, "we'd all be back in Gila City. Got so I kinda like that town."

Kit pulled the biscuits off the fire and set them on the ground to cool.

"Seen you arguin' fit to kill all afternoon," Billy went on. "Figured you must not like Yankees."

"Maybe she just don't like men." Turk glanced from Billy to Yellowleg. "And there are times when I can't say I blame her much."

Billy's eyes never left the girl. "Did you ever have your picture painted. You sure remind me of a picture I seen in a bar back in Dodge."

"Shut up, Billy," Yellowleg said.

Billy spat between his teeth and grinned. "Just tryin' to pay the lady a compliment."

"M'am," Turk said. "I don't like to tell you this, but you're burnin' the bacon."

She served it that way, burned black, and they ate it out of the pan with their fingers.

"Just the way I like it," Billy said. "Nothin' like a woman's cookin'."

"To ruin a man's stomach," Turk mumbled.

Yellowleg ate silently and without hunger, despite the day's hard ride. He wasn't fooling himself. His rule over Billy had lost its bite; the kid was only putting up with him now. Yellowleg hadn't only dropped his gun in the dust; he had dropped his reputation. The Yankee had fumbled his shooting iron as clumsily as a greener, and no one took a greener seriously. There would be trouble before the night was over, and he sat alert to every small change in Billy's voice. The kid's good spirits were only skin deep, he knew; Billy was enjoying himself at a game of patience.

Turk sat cracking and sucking marrow out of the rabbit bones, and the firelight polished his greasy face in a sort of primitive, gluttonous splendor. Billy lit the stub of his cigar and watched Kit clean out the frying pan with loose earth.

"You fixin' to sleep on the wagon?" he said.

Yellowleg peered at the kid, wondering if his patience had run out and the trouble would start. Kit went on scrubbing the pan, but her silence had no effect on Billy.

"Plenty of room down here with us," he said. "Might be safer, too. Can't tell what's out there in the black."

Yellowleg tossed his cigarette into the fire. "That's enough, kid."

But Billy ignored the quiet warning. "M'am, this is the way I size it up. There's the Apaches and there's us. Us is you, me, and these two. Turk here ain't much good—he's got the natures, you know, and he spooks easy. This Yankee ain't much good either, although I kinda take to him. There's somethin' haywire with that shootin' hand of his—otherwise that boy of yours wouldn't be layin' out there in the wagon."

"Shut up!" Yellowleg spat.

"No offense," Billy said, turning a bland smile on him. "Don't get your back up, Yellowleg. You're getting as touchy as a teased snake. Take it easy." He turned back to Kit. "That leaves just you and me, m'am. You and me and all them Apaches. The only way you'll get to Siringo is with me. I'm drivin' that wagon."

Yellowleg found himself on his feet. "I've been warning you to leave her alone. Now I'm telling you."

"Why, ain't you the limit, though. You'd think it was me that killed her boy. I'll bet she hates your Yankee guts. Why don't you ask her?"

"She hates my guts," Yellowleg said evenly. "You got anything else to say."

"I said it."

"Then shut up."

Turk paused with a broken rabbit bone in his mouth. Billy peered up at Yellowleg with cold, unblinking eyes and his long, Texan face set inscrutably. For Yellowleg it was an endless moment of suspended tension. He hadn't planned to goad Billy into a fight, and yet when a grin formed at the corners of the kid's eyes Yellowleg felt no sense of relief. Billy had to be cut down to size, but there wasn't going to be a fight. Billy was smiling now. Let the Yankee stew a while longer. He's looking to remake his reputation. Let him stew.

"No offense," Billy said. "Just tryin' to be sociable. What you so touchy about?"

The outcropping of granite commanded an open landscape of shadows, full of night hissings and rustlings and far calls. It was a black sky, blazing with stars that touched the badlands with a ghostly light, like a cosmic spindrift on a sea of night terrors. Yellowleg could see Kit below in the thicket, a slim shape on the wagon seat where she had wrapped herself in a thin blanket. But he knew she wouldn't sleep for hours.

Yellowleg heard Billy pour himself a final cup of coffee. He watched the two men below at their bedrolls and knew his muscles wouldn't ease until he saw Billy asleep.

The girl rustled, changing from one position to another and struggling with the blanket. It was going to be a touchy night for all of them, Yellowleg thought. He sat on a tilted shelf of granite, still warm to the touch, and waited for the hours of his watch to pass. And then he heard Turk begin to whisper.

"Billy."

Yellowleg peered down at them again.

"Look at this, Billy."

Turk held out a forage cap with gold braid that gleamed in the starlight. A general's hat, Yellowleg thought. A Reb hat.

"You gone off your rocker?" Billy said.

"I've had this with me for years. Stole it from a skinny general in Tennessee. I'll bet he's still lookin' for it."

"Go to sleep."

"Never showed it to you before, did I?"

Yellowleg watched Turk fix the hat on his head, like a whiskey sot with delusions of grandeur.

"A man looks like somethin' in one of these, don't he?"

"If you're waitin' for me to salute," Billy said in a bored voice, "you're gonna wait all your life."

"Here. See this paper. It's a map. I drew it. Unexplored country in the staked plains, only I explored it. That's where we set up. Get them slaves and uniforms and drill ourselves a little army, a raidin' army. And all this land to hide in. How does that sound now, Billy boy?"

"Fine, fine."

"We could pull out of here right now, you and me. You got the Yankee boogered."

"Go to sleep."

"Now's the best time—"

"Shut up!"

The two men fell silent and Yellowleg watched them a moment longer. Turk put away the forage cap, with all its gold braid, and Yellowleg wondered if his revenge would be sweet enough. Under the stars Turk seemed an insignificant fool, a pathetic lump of man following a strange vision, and Yellowleg wished it could have been different. It seemed a mockery to have spent seven years on the trail of a born chunk-eater, a cull, a cockroach. Where was the nobility in such revenge?

His thoughts passed and the dipper swung imperceptibly in its range of sky, holding its pointers on the pole star. His eyes kept returning to the figure on the wagon seat and he knew that she couldn't sleep. A rabbit shot out of the thicket and she rose in a moment of panic; and he felt sorry for her. When finally she covered her head with the blanket, as if to shut out the threats of the night, he was on the point of going down to talk to her. But he stopped himself. She was too exhausted, he knew, to stay awake, but too frightened to sleep. There was nothing he could do. Billy had already spelled it out. She hated his guts, and he'd only make more of a fool of himself.

He knew she must be aware of his eyes on her from above, and he supposed she saw him as hardly a different man from Billy. A little older, a little quieter, but with the same stirrings, the same temptations, the same hunger for a woman. And hadn't he, in the solitude of the watch, found himself remembering the scent of her perfume and the intimate rustle of her petticoats? He wasn't so different from Billy. He wondered about the touch of her flesh and tried to imagine her in a moment of laughter. And then he put away these thoughts, as he had so many others during the day, for Kit was beyond his reach. No woman, no beautiful woman would want a man, even for an hour, who carried the scars of a scalping knife.

Later, when he judged by the dipper that some four hours had passed, he climbed down and shook Billy's shoulder.

"Take the watch."

Billy shrugged off his hand and pulled the blanket more tightly around his shoulder.

"Come on," Yellowleg snapped. "Wake up."

Billy lashed out, a man who came awake fighting mad, and then his mind cleared. He grinned a little and shook the sleep out of his head. "Thought it was my old man," he muttered. "But it was only you."

Yellowleg rolled up in his blanket and watched Billy buckle on his guns and pull himself up the granite slabs. When Billy was gone Yellowleg pulled his hat down across the bridge of his nose and wondered if he should risk falling asleep.

It must have been an hour later when Yellowleg knew the trouble was starting. He heard the wagon creak, as if Kit were climbing down. The oak seat has got the best of her, he thought. Didn't she realize that Billy was watching every move she made?

She didn't approach the clearing. Yellowleg listened carefully and judged her to be in the saltbush on the far side of the wagon. She was too frightened to wander far, he thought, but too stubborn to join them in the clearing. When he heard Billy slip silently out of the rocks he knew he should head it off before it began. Instead, he lay there. Let Billy play out his hand.

He became aware of Billy standing not far off, probably staring at him in the darkness. Turk slept on, snoring off the disappointments of the day.

When Yellowleg was sure Billy was gone he pulled off the blanket and got his boots on. He stopped and listened and then headed for the wagon. He found the shotgun gone. He moved to the far side and saw Kit standing in the reflected starlight of a sand wash. She stood alone, a serene figure holding her face in the night breeze. He was surprised that she had gone that far, and he wondered if he was over-reckoning her helplessness and sense of fear.

She turned to start back and Billy stepped out of the shadows to block her way.

"Howdy."

She stopped short with the shotgun in the cradle of her arms. "What are you doing here?"

"Kinda restless. Just like you."

"I'm going back to the wagon."

"What's the hurry?"

"Get out of my way."

"My, but that red hair of yours is pretty stuff. And you got a temper to match, ain't you?"

"I'm warning you—get out of my way."

"Well, now, since you put it that way maybe I will—and maybe I won't."

She attempted to go around him, but he blocked her way. And then he wrenched the gun from her and tossed it aside, and they stood face to face. Yellowleg felt a surge of cold, murderous rage.

"Why don't you leave me alone?" she said in a hushed, hopeless voice.

"I always liked pretty things. And you're about the prettiest—Kit." Suddenly he clamped a hand over her mouth. "Wake him up and I'll kill ya both."

She began to struggle and he threw her to the sand and buried his knee in the fury of her petticoats. He ripped open the neck of her dress, exposing her breasts to the starlight, and then Yellowleg's hands were on him. He pulled the kid to his knees and drove his fist hard into that long, startled face. Billy's hands raised clouds of sand as he gripped the earth, and then he was on his feet and lashing out.

Yellowleg hit him again and was only dimly aware of Kit as she backed away with the torn dress clutched in her hands. He thought he heard a small sob and then Billy cut in with a jolting right and Yellowleg felt himself crawfish backwards. He tasted sand on his lips from the knuckles of Billy's fist, and then Billy leaped on him and they rolled over and over into the crackle of saltbush.

They broke, eyeing each other like animals, and then Billy rushed in again. It became a blind, groping combat fought in deadly silence, and yet it was no match. Billy had brute strength with no savvy, and Yellowleg whipped him back to his knees. He teetered there, only half-conscious now, looking out dully through a frozen face. The kid was beaten but wouldn't go down and Yellowleg drove a crazed, slamming right into that stuffed face. Billy crashed backwards through the saltbush like a calf with its legs roped out from under it. The wind left his lips in a moan that expired in the thicket. The night sounds of the desert had vanished.

Yellowleg stood catching his breath and holding his arm. The final blow had jolted his shoulder to the core of his old wound. He knew he had lost his hat when they rolled into the thicket and stood there now bare-headed. He hesitated to turn, fearing the girl was behind, watching in the starlight. He felt a rising panic when he did turn, but the girl was gone.

He tried to ease his shoulder and went groping through the brush until he found the hat. He dug his head into it and straightened.

He returned to Billy. His arm felt numb, but it would pass. It took him a long time to work Billy onto his left shoulder, and then he found the kid's gunbelt and carried him to the clearing. He passed Kit at the wagon and she lowered the shotgun. If it had been Billy, he knew, she would have blasted.

Turk roused as Yellowleg laid the kid out on the ground.

"Is Billy dead?" he croaked.

Yellowleg found cold coffee in the pot and threw it into Billy's face. After a moment the kid came to, dazed and bruised and running black coffee off the seams of his face. He sat up and tried to shake life back into his head. Yellowleg threw the gunbelt at him.

"All right. Now get out of here."

"Huh?"

"Clear out."

Turk perked up and reached for his boots. "I'm goin' with ya, Billy boy."

Yellowleg turned sharply. "You're not going anywhere."

"Huh?"

"You're sticking with us."

Turk was struck motionless, one boot on and one boot off. "Billy—"

But Billy didn't return Turk's glance. The kid was through backing him up. He ignored Turk, picked up his bedroll and saddle and moved quietly toward the horses. Turk licked his dry lips and peered hard at Yellowleg.

"The kid won't have a chance—alone in Apache country."

"That's his lookout."

"I won't be no good to you."

"Shut up."

Billy never looked back. He saddled up and mounted and rode out into the darkness and was gone.

"Awful dumb kid," Turk said. "But I was fond of him."

CHAPTER FOURTEEN

When dawn broke Turk was gone.

Yellowleg had taken the night watch and fought to keep awake. Even now, as the dawn light tightened his eyes, he didn't know he had been asleep. It seemed to him he had dozed for only a moment. He was reassured when he saw Kit asleep in her blanket on the wagon seat and then he glanced down to the foot of the outcropping. And he saw that Turk was gone.

He slipped down off the rocks and hoped he was wrong. Turk's bedroll was still there. Yellowleg scanned the saltbush.

"Turk!"

Not a sound. But his voice awakened Kit and their eyes met.

"Is he over there?" Yellowleg shouted.

She shook her head. "He's gone. I heard him leave."

Yellowleg stopped in his tracks. "You *what?*"

"It must have been a couple of hours ago."

Yellowleg saw her through a blinding rage. "You could have stopped him! Why didn't you yell out?"

"I was glad to see him go."

"I ought to break your neck!" Her cool, straight-backed poise infuriated him. "Haven't you any sense at all!"

"I didn't think you were asleep."

He swung the saddle to his shoulder and tried to restrain himself. He had no business falling asleep, but she could have.... No, how could she know. But still....

"You'll have to hitch up your team," he snapped. "I don't have time."

She had left the wagon and stood watching him saddle up his mare.

"I guess you're going back," she said.

"It sure looks that way, don't it?"

"Then goodbye."

"Lady, I spent seven years finding him, and I'm not letting him out of my sight."

"I said goodbye."

"I heard you."

He moved past her for his blankets, quickly rolled them, and strapped them behind the saddle. Then he mounted and paused only long enough to stare down at her. She stood there holding the neck of her dress together; there was a spark of resentment in her eyes. He was abandoning her, but that was what she had wanted all along, wasn't it? Now she was rid of them all. Still....

"They'll be heading for Gila City, both of them. I'll drive you back if you'll go."

She glared up at him and looked suddenly very small and helpless and icy. "Thanks, but no thanks."

"You're going on to Siringo?"

"Unless you think you can stop me."

"Lady, I haven't got time to try."

He swung around and dug in his spurs and carried off a final glimpse of her. Her lips had parted, as though she wanted to stop him, to exchange her words for better ones.

He galloped into the sun, but that final vision of Kit stayed with him. He rode back on the wagon trail, riding hard, to put her from his mind. Turk was his main business, not Kit. Turk belonged on his mind, not Kit. Turk had slipped away, but he could catch up by noon, and revenge would be sweeter. And long overdue. He would scalp Turk out in the desert.

Noon. By noon it would all be over.

The land began to rise under him and he found himself cross-whipping his mare almost as if he were whipping himself. The sun was already ablaze in his head, like a fever, and again the picture of Kit returned. Why had she had to look so fragile, with her bare feet in the dawn sands, so utterly hopeless in that last moment? What words had she held back? That she forgave him? Not in a thousand years. She had hated his company and his help from the beginning.

She could go to hell.

Noon.

Turk couldn't be too far ahead of him. A couple of hours. He wondered if Kit had the team hitched; he wondered if she even knew how. She was a stubborn, redheaded fool. He'd offered to drive that wagon back to Gila City, hadn't he? If the team bolted on her she could sit in the desert and bawl, and she'd be getting only what was coming to her. She shouldn't have let Turk slip out of camp. A mule would have had more sense.

He reined in and the mare reared on her hind legs. Yellowleg swung around with his eyes on the trail and stopped. He stared at cross tracks made during the night. Neither Turk nor Billy's horse had left that trail. He raised his eyes and peered at the silent lands around him. Unshod pony tracks. Indian, traveling north. Alone.

Bronco Apache, he thought.

Yellowleg peered around, but saw no further signs. The Indian may have gone on, crossing Kit's unseen wagon tracks in the night.

But maybe not. Yellowleg glanced back at the patch of saltbush in the distance, with the granite outcropping rising bold and gray out of the tilted landscape. Was the Apache aware of Kit too, from some far point of desert? Had he come by only hours before, just before dawn?

But still Yellowleg sat his horse and tried not to remake his mind and turn around. And yet.... What chance did Kit really have alone? Her wagon trail would be discovered. It was only a matter of time.

What was that to him, he asked himself broodingly. He had only gone along because of the boy, and getting the boy to Siringo wouldn't bring him back to life.

Yellowleg pulled his hat down tighter and reined back on Turk's trail. He spurred the mare and shrugged off the persistent burden of his thoughts.

He rode for another mile and then reared back again, a man drawn in opposite directions. He damned the woman and tried to force himself on into the sun, but in the end he spun the claybank around. Turk had waited seven years for his past to catch up with him. He'd have to wait a little longer.

CHAPTER FIFTEEN

It was past noon when Yellowleg drove the wagon out of the saltbush toward the west.

They sat side by side, in a brooding silence. Yellowleg's jaws were clamped hard. Earlier, when the thought first came to him, he had put from his mind the question of her horse savvy. But when he got back the team was gone. The blood bay had turned skittish as she tried to harness it and the other bolted with it. Yellowleg had lost more than an hour in the cutbanks and dry washes trying to find them, but it had turned hopeless. Either the badlands had swallowed them or they were still running.

He had harnessed his own mare to the wagon, which now creaked slowly over its own shadow.

"I suppose I should at least say thank you," she muttered finally.

He peered straight ahead.

"Thank you."

He pulled the hat tighter on his head.

"I never expected to see you again," she said. "You didn't have to come back."

He turned, giving her a slow glance. What was she trying to do, make him feel like more of a fool than he already was?

"I'm sorry about losing the team," she went on, avoiding his eyes. Her profile lay sharp against the far horizon, but he didn't let that soften his mood. Her beauty hadn't brought him back; her stubbornness had. "I know how you must feel seeing your fine mare hooked up to a wagon."

"Yes, m'am," he said quietly. She was getting like Turk; as full of talk as a general store. And what about Turk? How cold would the trail be when Yellowleg picked it up again?

"Hot, isn't it?"

He shook the reins. "Ha! Git up there!"

"You don't have to talk to me," she said.

"It ain't worth the effort."

He got a flash of her green eyes. "Seven years is a long time to turn your back on—especially for a woman like me. That's what you're thinking, isn't it?"

"Lady, I stopped thinking when I turned my horse around."

"Stop calling me Lady. My name is Kit."

"Lady, I don't plan to know you well enough to call you Kit."

"Don't think you're fooling me. You're not nearly as riled at me as you are at yourself."

"It looks like you're going to talk all the way to Siringo."

He could feel her bridle beside him, but it put an end to the conversation and left him alone with his thoughts. They rode for almost an hour, two strangers sharing the same wagon seat, each enveloped in a silent world of his own. The sun blazed against her face, fixing wrinkles in the corners of her eyes, and finally he turned to her.

"Where's that umbrella?"

No response.

"A woman like you ain't used to the sun."

She met his glance. "I'll get used to it."

Yellowleg felt around behind the seat and came upon the black umbrella. He snapped it opened and hooked it over her shoulder.

"Some folks is born mule-headed," he snapped. "Women, mostly."

They moved across the badlands all afternoon. The air was still and dry and heavily scented with creosote and sage. Kit sat concealed behind the big, black umbrella. Yellowleg ignored her and led the wagon along a wide dry wash. The sound of their approach flushed a red-tailed hawk out of a clump of hop sage. It rose to the sun with a dead snake in its talons. He was aware that Kit stiffened at the sight; she watched it in the sky until the hawk settled among the snubby buttes in the near distance.

Yellowleg unhooked the canteen and shook it and handed it over to her. She had already emptied the other canteen making noon coffee, and this one was low. He knew she had wasted water during the morning. Washing up, probably. But he let it go. There was a shimmer of green trees off in the distance, desert willows, he thought, and there would be water.

Toward sunset they were moving among the buttes and Yellowleg was having trouble staying awake. His eyelids smarted with the heat and lack of sleep. She must be dog-tired too, he thought. They were getting glimpses of water below, a large spring from the look of it, and he was glad the day's ride was over. They spotted the hawk, gorged and nerveless, on a high crag watching them go by.

When the gunshots came Yellowleg was almost too numb to react. Then he leaned back with the reins and brought the wagon to a standstill. The firing was at a distance. He listened and Kit stared at him from under the umbrella. The gunfire was somewhere on the flat below.

He turned the wagon into the base of a large butte, concealing it among the sandstone shadows, and grabbed up his Winchester. He left Kit on the wagon and started climbing along the spires toward a divide in the butte. He looked down on a sloping wasteland of boulders and cacti with water seeping through the rocks into a large, reedy pool. And almost at once he saw the stagecoach. It came bolting along a shallow rim to the north in a cloud of dust and Apaches. Yellowleg raised his rifle, and became aware of Kit climbing up beside him.

For an instant it looked as if the stagecoach was going to fly off the edge of the rim, but it swerved and righted itself and then careened down a wash toward the water hole.

Yellowleg counted four Apaches riding furiously, rifles in the air and whooping it up. Yellowleg was on the point of firing when he froze at the gunsight and then lowered the rifle. The stagecoach had gone into wild figure eights and the driver's slouch hat flew off revealing an eagle feather.

"Look at 'em ride," he said.

Kit had lugged the shotgun with her and looked at him as if he had gone mad. "Are you afraid to shoot!"

"They're savages. All of 'em. Showing off like a bunch of kids. Let 'em alone."

A whiskey bottle flew out of the stagecoach and it was shattered in the air. The race went on, around the water hole and through the willows and back again. Yellowleg was staggered by the pure horsemanship he saw, drunk as they were, and watched in a kind of grim fascination. A buck on horseback leaped onto the coach at full speed and then off again, just to see if he could do it. The shooting went on for the pure noise of it. The driver raced on daringly with savages crawling in and out of the windows like termites.

But Kit saw nothing but her own fear. "We ought to kill them while we have the chance."

"They're not bothering us."

"But—"

"We'll only give our position away. Sit tight."

The stagecoach burst out of the willows again with an Apache standing on the roof. Yellowleg could have picked him off, but the first shot from the buttes would turn their laughter into a war cry. He held his fire. The savages had themselves a stagecoach, a huge swaybacked toy, a prize of war. Yellowleg had never heard a savage laugh before.

And then it was over. Hurtling at wild speed the stage struck a boulder and seemed to leap into the air. The driver and his roof passenger were catapulted into the reeds. They picked themselves up, wet and laughing, while the others chased down the team, which was bolting with the coach on its side.

Yellowleg and the girl stayed hidden in the buttes until early dark. The savages spent a long time righting the stagecoach. They let the team graze and hunkered down with their bottles, tossing empties into the pool. When finally they rode away, back along the rim to the north, the echo of their laughter and high spirits hung over the spring.

Yellowleg pitched camp among the willows. He let the mare graze and brought coffee water from the springs. "I wonder where they ambushed that stage?" he muttered. He read a whiskey label in the light of the fire and then tossed the bottle away. "Pure snake-head whiskey. Come all the way from Texas."

"Anybody else would have killed them."

"Maybe."

"They'll find us."

"I don't think we have to worry until they run out of this happy juice, and they seemed to have a good supply. We'll stay alive longer minding our own business."

Kit dropped the subject and he wondered suddenly if she thought he was a coward. He spit and stretched out, waiting for the coffee to boil. What difference did it make what she thought? He didn't have to prove himself to her, and he felt no call to clear this desert of Apaches. At the moment he was hungry, tired and sleepy. And in need of a second horse. It wouldn't do to go on leaving a white man's trail.

The heat and dust of the day was still on them and she muttered suddenly, "I wish I could take a bath."

"Nothing stopping you."

She gave him a quick look. "Thanks, but no thanks."

"It was hardest on Mead."

He wasn't sure what started her talking about it. Maybe it was pure exhaustion or maybe she had to talk to someone—even him. They had eaten and sat now in the grip of a mutual loneliness. Her voice was low and full of the hesitations of bitter memory. "The church folks didn't want their children playing with him, as if some of the sin might rub off. He was a pariah... and never knew why."

Yellowleg gazed at her, etched against the darkness by the soft glow of the coals. A wisp of hair had fallen across her forehead and she brushed it away.

"It's strange," she murmured without looking at him. "I can hardly remember what my husband looked like."

"Yes, m'am."

"It seems so long ago. I wasn't quite seventeen. I'd got a job waiting table at a relay station west of Siringo. People were always going through to California or back east or somewhere far and wonderful. My husband was like that. They put him off the eastbound stage with fever and he stayed on for weeks. When he got better he asked me to go back to South Carolina with him. A parson came through on the stage, and he married us. On our first trip to Siringo to buy me some traveling clothes, my husband was killed. The Apaches."

Yellowleg said nothing. But he thought he understood now her urge to kill when they lay concealed in the butte. It wasn't a question of logic or cowardice. It was a surge of memory.

"I never had a wedding ring." She spoke very quietly now. "The nearest doctor was in Gila City, but when Mead was born talk started and no one believed me. They just smiled."

"You'd better get some sleep. We'll be moving on in a few hours."

She didn't seem to hear him. "Gila City put a brand on us both, and I just couldn't leave. Not until I'd made them know the sinning was theirs, with their talk and their jokes and their ugly little smiles."

"Sometimes," he said, "it's a sin to be beautiful."

It was toward midnight when he awoke. He hadn't meant to sleep even that long. He rolled a cigarette in the dark and lit it and glanced at Kit asleep in her blanket a few feet away. At least she had begun to trust him, he thought, and that would make the days ahead easier. But he tried not to deceive himself. She trusted him because she had to and she talked to him because there was no one else to talk to.

He rinsed out his mouth with cold coffee from the pot. He was saddling the mare when Kit awoke. "What are you doing?"

"We need a second horse," he muttered. "Those Apaches might not be far, and they've got more horses than they need."

She pulled off her blanket in quiet alarm and moved to the wagon. "You can't be serious. They'll kill you."

"Not unless they catch me."

"Please—"

He swung into the saddle and looked down at her. For the first time that icy calm had deserted her. She stood there in her bare feet, her eyes tight with sudden fear. He couldn't be sure whether she was frightened for him, or at being left out here alone.

"I shouldn't be long," he said. "They've got a lot of likker to sleep off. Be ready to leave when I get back."

He swung away and felt her eyes follow him as he rode out under the luminous night sky.

Once across the north rim an open flatland stretched to the ends of the earth. He followed a dry coulee until it played out. Less than an hour from the springs he saw the gray bulk of the stagecoach against the stars. It sat smack in the middle of nowhere with the horses still in harness, as if at a way stop, and the Indian ponies hitched to the rear.

Yellowleg left the mare ground-tied and approached on foot. When he saw the Apaches on the far side of the stage his muscles eased. They looked dead in the sand, but it was only from a stupor bottled in Texas. He saw that they had butchered one of the stage horses on the spot and gorged themselves. A broken leg had stopped them, he thought, and chosen their campsite.

He worked quickly now. He cut the driving reins at the lead team and chose a trim chestnut to take back. He was cutting it out of the doubletree when the Apache jumped him.

Yellowleg pitched him over his back and then leaped against him. It wasn't a fight. It was a battle of sheer, silent strength. Yellowleg pinned the Apache against the earth with a hand over his mouth, and then pistol-whipped him hard. It was only then, as he let up, that he noticed what the savage held in a dead grip. A scalping knife.

Yellowleg looked around, but saw no further signs of life. He found an army canteen still half full of sour whiskey. He uncapped it and wiped it off and took a long belt. Then he poured the rest into the sand. He set the empty tin under the coach and walked the chestnut back to his own horse. He fixed a line to the halter and got in the saddle. He pulled his rifle from the boot and came in just close enough to see the canteen waiting between the wheels of the stage. He took aim and began to fire.

The shots cracked out and the canteen went dancing and banging between the legs of the team. The horses bolted. Yellowleg swung around, touching his spurs to the mare's flanks, and led the chestnut toward the coulee. He looked around once. The stagecoach was stampeding across the night like a gray phantom and three or four Apaches had roused enough to wave their arms and give chase at a throbbing half-run. The stage looked like it wasn't going to stop running, dragging the Indian ponies behind it, until it crossed the Canadian line.

CHAPTER SIXTEEN

When dawn spread across the sandy wastes they had already been on the trail more than three hours. They had made bad time, even with the chestnut filling out the wagon team. Their way had been blocked by low, cavernous sandstone cliffs and Yellowleg had had to search out a pass. The sky had covered over during the night and now they could see rain falling to the northwest. But not even a passing rain would wipe out the fresh trail they were cutting in the red man's earth.

Yellowleg drove on for more than an hour before he saw a spot that would do. Gray, drifting sands had piled up against tilted outcroppings of rock. Yellowleg had made up his mind to bury the wagon.

The rain passed over them as they sat with their morning coffee. They had pulled in under the rock shelves and watched the shower move on.

"I don't know why I told you all that," Kit murmured.

Yellowleg looked at her absently. "All what?"

"My husband. About me."

"Forget it."

"It was really none of your business."

"Okay."

"I don't know why I told you."

"I said to forget it."

"I keep asking myself why you don't turn back."

"So do I."

"No matter what you do," she said, "we can never be friends."

"I know that."

"That first day I thought of killing you."

He spit and looked at her again. Her conscience is having a hangover, he thought. She'd begun acting civil toward him, even friendly, but he didn't look quite the same in the daylight. "If you're going to kill me," he said, "you'd better get at it while I'm still in season."

"Don't joke about it."

"Then start talking sense. I don't expect you to forget the pain I caused you. Shun me or hate me, but don't apologize for putting up with me. We're still strangers, not friends. If I'd thought you could make it to Siringo alone I wouldn't be here. Meanwhile, I'll go on drinking your coffee and listening when you want to talk, but don't keep reminding me that I'm the last man you want to talk to or have drinking your coffee." He tossed out what was left in his cup and got up. The rain had passed, leaving the sands pitted and the air close and muggy. "There's a shovel in the wagon," he snapped. "You can help by digging. I want to be out of here by noon."

She rose and followed him to the wagon. "Look, I didn't mean—"

"I said to forget it. We're burying this wagon. From here on out our trail had better look like an Indian's."

He handed her the shovel and left her standing. He climbed onto the wagon bed and began to unload. He was sorry he'd spoken out so sharply, but he had no patience with a shilly-shallying conscience. There was no denying that an informality had sprung up between them, but if that troubled her soul he preferred the open warfare of pure hatred.

As the hours passed he dismantled the wagon, and Kit dug. He buried the wheels and broke down the seat and wagon sides. He'd have use for the shafts, so he put them aside. He kept glancing at Kit sweating in the close heat at the shovel.

Her muscles would ache all the way to Siringo, he thought. He hadn't planned to put her to work shoveling sand, but he needed a pit, a big one; but now it seemed an act of punishment. Her petticoats were already heavy with wet sand and drifts of red hair fell across her forehead. She shook them back in absent-minded little tosses of her head and never once looked back at him.

"Getting tired?" he asked finally.

"I don't need any help."

"I wasn't offering it. I just asked if you were getting tired?"

Stubborn as a muley cow, he thought. She would drop in the heat if he didn't take that shovel out of her hands. But he went back to work, breaking up the planks of the wagon bed, dismantling the axles, but saving the tailgate. Finally he could stand it no longer and took the shovel. "That's enough."

She was too tired to argue back. She left him there without a word and he finished digging the pit. She walked off somewhere and he didn't see her again until he was dragging bits and pieces of the wagon into the pit. It was almost noon when he finished shovelling the sand back in and he could smell food cooking. Maybe the work had cleared her head, he thought. Or had she seen the way he found himself staring at the small pine box?

It would be so easy to bury the boy out here on the plains, and it would be for the best. This was a clean, silent land, open to the horizon and the night stars.

He tried to put the thought out of his mind and began prying the shoes off the horses. He planned to leave the trail of an Indian and his squaw, and the iron shoes had to go. He made a travois out of the wagon shafts and the tailgate, and hitched it to the chestnut. Then his eyes lit again on the pine box and he picked up the shovel. He had to try. If she let him bury the boy here she had good sense, but he doubted it.

His foot drove the shovel deep into the fresh earth and a sort of intuition brought Kit to her feet. "What are you doing?"

"What does it look like?"

"Get your foot off that shovel."

"Do you think the Apaches'll trouble to bury him if we don't make it to Siringo?" He took another spadeful of sand and when he looked up again she had the shotgun in her hands.

"I'll kill you," she breathed.

"You keep saying that."

"I mean it. I'll kill you right where you're standing."

Her eyes burned into his, and he stood motionless with his boot on the shovel. They wouldn't be going back. Slowly, he straightened and wiped his lips with the back of his hand. He knew sure death when he saw it. And he was looking right at it. "Just wanted to make positive," he said irritably.

They ate a silent dinner, and he packed their supplies on the travois, lashing the coffin down tight and covering it all with the tarp. When finally they were ready he pulled up a saltbush and wiped out all signs of their activity. He walked back along the wagon tracks to an exposed layer of sandstone, taking out the marks of the wheels as he went. When he was satisfied, he worked his way back to the horses and Kit. Anyone following their old trail would find it played out along the sandstone.

By early afternoon the sun broke through and they were on their way again. There was only one saddle between them and he let Kit have the mare. He rode bareback, dragging the travois after him.

In another day they ought to make Siringo.

CHAPTER SEVENTEEN

Yellowleg awoke just before dawn with the feeling that they were not alone. He lay still, listening. They had made camp that night under a heavy ledge and Kit had rolled out her blankets across the fire from him. They hadn't exchanged a word during the long afternoon and now a cold coffee pot separated them.

Yellowleg sat up in the bedroll, turning his head and listening. The wasteland lay in a pre-dawn stillness. He heard nothing, and yet the feeling persisted.

Yellowleg rose quietly, wondering about the horses, and checked the picket line. The two animals were still there. He turned and peered curiously at the ledge and at the rank on rank of cactus forms standing in the slate darkness. Nothing moved. Nothing stirred. He spat and decided the trip was making him jumpy.

He rolled a cigarette and lit it, shielding the light so as not to wake Kit, and went scrounging for roots. He collected enough fuel to warm the coffee. As he worked, he wondered about Turk and Billy. They'd have that bank money by now, unless they were dead. No, not Turk. Billy maybe, but not Turk. Turk had practiced the fine art of staying alive for too many years. Yellowleg refused to believe that providence would cheat him out of Turk. No, Turk was still alive, scuttling across the desert somewhere with that vision of himself in general's braid. Yellowleg laid the roots in under the coffee pot and set a fire going. He'd just as soon Kit woke up now; he'd like them to be on their way just after sun-up.

He hunkered there as the fire grew and found himself staring at Kit. She even slept stubborn, he thought, with the blanket close around her and a hand clutching it at her neck. She lay on her side and the firelight revealed the smooth, graceful rise of her hip. He'd never known a truly beautiful woman before; his life had been remote from anything beautiful or even lovely. And now he preferred to think of her as only an obstinate, willful female. They were qualities he understood and even admired. He was unsure about beauty.

She awoke almost at once and peered at him across the fire as if, suddenly, to assure herself that he was still there. When she sat up, she kept the blanket across her shoulders, and he decided to try an opening gambit. There was no point in going through the day in stony silence.

"Kinda chilly this morning."

She sat there, almost like an Indian, and he knew she wasn't fully awake yet.

"I'd have made the coffee," she said.

"I'm not making it. Just warming it up." That was that, he thought. At least they were on speaking terms again.

"I don't like apologies," she muttered obscurely.

"I'm not making any."

"I should. I was going to last night, but you fell asleep. I was impossible yesterday. I'm sorry."

"Okay."

The coffee began to simmer and dawn was breaking at Yellowleg's back. The firelight was losing its shadows and the color came out in Kit's hair and clear green eyes. Her skin was weathering and her hands, he supposed, were blistered from the shovel. She began undoing her night braids and he found her looking, at him again. "Yellowleg isn't a name," she said.

"I've been answering to it on and off for a long time. Someone should have told me before."

"Where are you from?"

"Ohio."

"Is it pretty back there?"

He hesitated. "It used to be."

Intuitively, she backed away from the subject. The coffee started to boil and she filled their cups. "I thought I'd go to California, someday," she said.

"Then why stick in Gila City? Maybe you care too much what people think."

"It would be like running away now. Like they licked me."

He nodded. "California is a good place. I've been there. Saw the ocean on a foggy morning once. Always stuck in my mind."

"You don't think much of a dance hall girl, do you?"

"I never gave it much thought at all."

"You don't have to pretend. Your friend took me for a parlor house girl."

"He's not my friend."

"I've been taken for that before. A lot of dance hall girls end up in the parlor house."

"I guess." It surprised him that she had been at all concerned with what he thought of her. Did it really matter? If they lived long enough to say goodbye they would never see each other again. She had had to defend her reputation for so long, he thought, that now her guard came up with the first glance anyone gave her. He supposed that accounted for the cold reserve she so easily slipped into.

Yellowleg finished his coffee, but remained there on his heels. She had kept the blanket around her shoulders and her eyes low, but now she looked up. "The dance hall was the only place they'd give me a job, and I had a baby to support. At first, I only planned to save enough to—"

She stopped, strangely, and he thought at first she was suddenly ill. Then he saw that she was looking past him, behind him, her eyes frozen, and he spun around.

He saw it too.

An Apache arrow exposed by the rising dawn.

It stood mute and ominous and almost close enough to touch. It had impaled the earth at an angle on the far side of Yellowleg's bedroll. His eyes, following the angle, whipped instantly to the ledge, expecting to see some savage standing there, but he saw only the endless, brightening blue sky. He snapped up the Winchester, remembering the uneasy feeling that had awakened him, and scrambled to the top of the ledge.

His glance swung over a silent, deserted waste—a vast emptiness. He cocked the rifle, his muscles tense and on the ready.

Kit stared up apprehensively, but the air of crisis seemed to pass from his face. "No one?" she muttered.

"Not even a jack rabbit."

He dropped off the ledge and yanked the arrow out of the ground. He examined it quickly and met her gaze.

"There's dew on the feathers," he said, and peered again at the surrounding badlands. "This arrow's been sticking here for hours, maybe."

The blanket had dropped to her feet and she stood motionless and silent, not troubling to conceal the fear that gripped her like a sudden chill.

"Some bronco Apache, I think," Yellowleg murmured. "Traveling alone. He may have been on that ledge watching us all night."

She gave a small shudder. "My God—"

"Yeah."

"He had the chance; why didn't he kill us?"

"If I find him I'll ask him!" He hadn't meant to snap at her; at the same time, how do you figure out a savage? What was Yellowleg to read into that feathered calling card? Either the Apache's curiosity had restrained him from murdering them in their sleep, or he had a cruel sense of humor. Yellowleg broke the arrow between his fists and tossed it aside. "Let's pack and get out of here," he said.

CHAPTER EIGHTEEN

The going was slow and agonizing. The day had started badly and now, with the travois dragging behind, Yellowleg had to keep the chestnut at a tedious, plodding walk. But the morning passed into afternoon with no further signs of the bronco Apache, and they began to speak of other things.

They had long ago lost sight of the old trail, and that was just as well, Yellowleg thought. Kit seemed to remember the dominant landmarks and they could keep to the concealment of faults and washes and cutbanks.

Ahead of them lay a salt flat and beyond that a hogback of eroded calico hills—raw humps and whirls of brown and red and yellow. Siringo, she said, lay across the hills and to the southwest. "Not more than twenty miles."

"Just a hop, skip and a jump," he said irritably. "Every step we take, Siringo seems to get further away." His mind had begun to dwell again on Turk and every mile seemed to double its length. Siringo was a luxury in time; vengeance lay somewhere behind him now. For the first time he'd begun to accept seriously the possibility that death might catch up with them. What about Turk then? If the Apache had chosen to kill them under the ledge, what happened to Turk? Was he to live out his existence, smirking and arrogant and unaware of his close brush with the man he'd tried to scalp near a Tennessee swamp? Did providence look out for the spineless and the depraved, the rag tag and bobtail, the treacherous? Turk. There could be only one reprieve for Turk—Yellowleg's own death, a maddening irony. If it were to happen that way Yellowleg would know, in that final moment, that life was without sense and order; it was all a stampede, a cunning practical joke of the fates and an entertainment of the Gods.

He decided the horses had better be Indian shod to cross the salt flat. The crust had crystallized into a jagged, blinding white terrain and they had to tighten their eyes against the heated glare.

Rawhide was the thing, but that was out of the question. He could spare a piece of the tarp, but that wouldn't be enough. He could use her other dress, but he had buried it with the wagon and all the other excess baggage.

"Do you need all them petticoats?" he said.

She looked at him sharply. "What are you talking about?"

"Just do what I say. Get over behind that clump of saltbush and strip 'em off. I need them."

She was too startled at first to react with any more than a blank stare. Then her temper caught up with the situation and her green eyes began to spark. She swung back her hair and let him have it. "You go straight to blazes."

"Let's not stand out here in the sun and argue about it. These horses have got to be shod with something, and that something is going to be your petticoats. They're in your way on the saddle anyhow."

"I'll be the judge of that!"

"Lady, these salt crystals will cut up the horses' hooves like they were walking on broken glass. Now either you get behind that saltbush like a lady or I'll take what I'm asking for as if you weren't."

"We can go around the salt flat."

"That's right, we could. But it looks ten, twelve miles long and not more than a mile wide. You might say I'm in a hurry. We're going across it—on your petticoats."

She stood there hating him, but the alternatives were clear. She turned and headed silently for the saltbush, and he set to work with what he could spare of the tarp. In the open silence he could hear the rustle of her clothing and he could almost count the petticoats as they came off. If he looked over that way, he thought, she'd kill him.

Only when he felt her standing behind him did he lift his eyes from his work. She threw the petticoats at the feet of the horses and retired somewhere behind him. From now on, he thought, she was going to keep him between her and the sun.

"Nothing personal," he said. "Pure circumstances."

"Don't apologize."

She was humiliated, he knew, but her voice had lost some of its earlier temper. She had calmed down enough to face reality.

Between the tarp and the white muslin he made up pads for each of the hooves, bunching the material up around the ankles and fastening it tight with thongs. It was a waste of pretty embroidery and ruffles and tucks, but she would ride cooler without all this excess dry goods. He was doing her a favor.

"You think about that man quite often, don't you?" she said suddenly, from behind him.

He said absently, "What man is that?"

"Turk."

He continued working at the hooves of his mare and said nothing.

"He was loathsome," she muttered. "But I'm sorry I let him slip away from you. I know he's the man you were telling me about—the one you trailed for five years."

"Seven."

"You can't forgive me for making you give up all those years, can you?"

He gave a sharp glance. "You didn't make me."

"But that's what you keep thinking about, isn't it?"

"It hasn't improved my humor any, if that's what you're talking about." And then he added softly, "I'll pick up his trail again."

"He hardly seemed worth the trouble."

"He's not. But a man needs something to live for, even if it's just to kill another man."

"That's not a very good reason."

"Maybe not. But it's the best I've got."

She hesitated. "Then you'll be going back to Gila City."

He met her eyes. "If we ever get to Siringo."

They started across the salt crust under a merciless sun. Yellowleg, on foot, led the chestnut and travois while Kit followed behind on the mare. It was like walking across the face of the sun. The salt reflection was a searing, white blast to the eyes and Yellowleg peered out through grimy, burning slits. He tried to pick his way carefully, but they had been at it less than half an hour when he knew he'd made a mistake. The footing was becoming more treacherous. Wedging had pushed up colonies of crystal into sharply embroidered ridges and ledges, and weathering had hollowed out grottos and chambers and spiked foottraps. He had been a fool not to take the longer way around, but there was no turning back now after commandeering Kit's petticoats.

He led the procession on in dogged silence. Occasionally one of the horses whinnied and the travois strained and clattered over the jagged crust.

But soon Yellowleg was unable to trust his vision. The intense, white landscape was blinding him to the faint, detailed shadows underfoot. He forced his eyes to focus, to search out the false crusts and sharp, filigreed crypts, but the close looking blinded him all the more. He stopped and looked back.

"Are you all right?"

"Yes."

He rubbed his eyes and blinked and peered at the hills beyond, a sanctuary shimmering in the heat. They had come too far to turn back. He took a fresh grip on the reins and forced himself on.

But now the hills seemed to recede with every step, a tantalizing landfall in a brilliant white sea. He was no longer choosing each step. He found himself blundering on and short of breath. His eyes ached and he was looking out through the merest, tortured slits.

And then it came.

There was the sudden explosion of crystal shattering close behind, and from the reins Yellowleg felt the chestnut lurch and fall to a knee. When Yellowleg turned a panic had already seized the animal. His left foreleg had broken into a razor-sharp trap and he was pawing wildly to free himself. Yellowleg grabbed the bit, but the horse tossed his head, whinnying and shuddering, and almost at once there was blood on the salt.

"Easy, boy!"

A moment later the leg was free, cut raw and hanging limp. It was broken.

Yellowleg worked almost without seeing. He unlashed the travois and fixed it to the mare. When he was finished he told Kit to move on ahead. He would catch up. He calmed and nuzzled the chestnut and when the travois had pulled forward and became only a dim shape in his mind, he drew his gun. The crack sounded loud and clear over the flat. He heard his mare's whinny in the distance, like an echo.

CHAPTER NINETEEN

The sun was still high when they started across the calico hills. Yellowleg never looked back, even from this distance, at the dark lump lying out on the salt flat. If he'd been in a touchy mood all morning, he was in a bitter, sombre mood now. Vultures had already risen up from the hills at the scent of carrion.

Kit walked in a silence of her own. They had stopped at the edge of the flat and he'd spared water from the canteen to wash off the salted cuts on the claybank's shanks and fetlocks. Then he had led the mare into the hills and Kit knew that he meant for her to walk.

But when they were coming out of the hills he waited for her to catch up and told her to get in the saddle.

"Can't we rest awhile?" she breathed. Her thin calico dress had gathered dust into its folds and clung to the heat of her legs. She was short of breath and her eyes had lost their green spark and luster. Her skin was weathering. The milky smoothness was a memory, and he saw in her face the merciless touch of the sun and its reflection. She was exhausted, he knew, and he was far from fresh himself, but they weren't stopping.

"You wanted to get to Siringo," he said. "You're going to get there. Today."

"It's too far."

"It can't be too soon to suit me. Let's go."

"Please. I've watched you. You're bone tired and feeling poorly about that horse back there. It won't hurt to rest."

He went to spit, but there was no saliva in his mouth. He wiped his lips anyway. "Lady, if there's anything I don't believe in," he said, "it's arguing under a hot sun. Now git."

She gazed at him hopelessly, then took a breath and went to the saddle. Even after she'd given up her petticoats she'd sat the horse side-saddle, holding onto the horn and making do; but now she hitched up her skirt indifferently and swung comfortably into the saddle. "You're a stubborn fool," she said.

"Git up!"

He tugged on the reins and led the mare down a rocky draw. They were almost out of the hills, with the travois scratching up a cloud of dust, when Yellowleg heard the whine of an arrow and saw it strike almost at his feet.

It stood quivering, like a death rattle of brown feathers.

Yellowleg grabbed the mare's bit to keep her from rearing and with the breath still caught in his throat he let his eyes range quickly over the hills above. He saw nothing, and it maddened him. He heard Kit cry, "Are you hit!"

Without answering he lurched around to the rifle boot and got the Winchester in his hands. He slapped the claybank's rump.

"Get outa here!"

The horse sprang forward and Kit let him race hell-bent down the draw. Yellowleg pumped a shell into the chamber and swung the rifle around looking for a target. But not a branch, not a blade of grass moved. He peered into every crevice, every shadow, but the hills only stared back at him in silent mockery. Yellowleg wet his lips and hardly breathed. It was the bronco Apache, and he was up there somewhere. The brown feathers had been the same and the attack had been hatched by the same brain. But it wasn't an attack at all, he knew. It was a savage game of death.

Yellowleg crept from rock to rock until a frenzy of anger and frustration came over him. He stood up and began to yell.

"Come out and fight!"

His voice drifted back to him from the empty shadows and rocks. His gaze swung around.

"What are you waiting for!"

He knew he was yelling like a madman, but he couldn't help himself.

"You yellow-bellied savage! Fight!"

His voice died out and Yellowleg stood blankly in the burning silence. How do you fight what you can't see? Had the Apache already slipped away, leaving him to yell like a fool.

"Come on!"

Yellowleg felt a blind surge of rage. He squared the gun at his shoulder and began exploding chips of rock, pumping and firing, all of them wild, until the frenzy within him subsided. The sounds faded away, like the ravings of a lunatic, and the late afternoon lengthened its profile among the rocks. And Yellowleg knew the Indian had made a fool of him.

Kit said, with an air of disbelief, "How could he have followed us?"

Yellowleg slipped the rifle back into its boot. He felt gaunt and incredibly weary. "He was ahead of us. Waiting."

She looked into his face, and he saw his own anguish in her eyes. "What does he want?"

"He's tantalizing me... before he gets down to killing me."

"Only you?"

Yellowleg picked up the reins and gave her a severe glance. "Even a savage knows what a woman's for. Especially a pretty woman. Let's go."

They plodded on through the last light of day. Only the sense of an unseen presence kept Yellowleg alert. At dusk they were crossing a mud flat, as dry as paper, and the world before his eyes became a sensation of browns and yellows. The spans of dried mud turned to dust under them, and whenever he turned he could see the tracks of the travois trailing off into a hazy infinity.

When the first stars came out he thought of stopping, of putting Siringo off until the next day, but a grim obstinacy forced him on and provided him with a rationale. To stop was to sleep and to sleep was death. The Apache would soon tire of his rituals and tortures.

But when Yellowleg felt mesquite grass under his feet a better rationale filled his mind. This was grazing grass and his mare had to be fed.

They made camp in the shelter of rocks, and ate a cold supper, without lighting a fire for coffee, and looked out over miles of luminous, quiet land. Siringo lay out there somewhere.

Yellowleg watched his mare grazing under the stars. He had trouble keeping his eyes open even as he lit a cigarette. The Apache, he thought, had figured out for himself that they were headed for Siringo. That's where the real trouble would start.

Not even an Apache could read trail signs at night, and Yellowleg felt they would be secure among the rocks once the moon set. Still, he would attempt to keep some sort of watch. It was impossible to second guess a savage.

But this one had already revealed himself. He would be still young, Yellowleg thought, young enough for daring and reckless gestures. But he had age too, with many scalp locks to his credit. Only a seasoned killer could afford the luxury of a brutal but exquisite sentence of death. His arrows had been finely made and Yellowleg was reminded of the matadors of Monterrey, goading and taunting their bulls with decorated instruments of death.

Siringo would be the bull ring.

Yellowleg fell asleep with the cigarette still burning between his lips. He thought he dreamed of Kit coming closer and removing it gently, a woman's touch, and he thought he could feel her breath on his face. And then he felt hands at his hat, loosening it from his head, and a vision of Turk charged into his mind. He grabbed out, neither asleep nor awake now, and caught a pair of wrists. There was a moment's breathless struggle and even as he wrestled over he knew it was Kit, not Turk. He held her against the ground and spoke fiercely. "What were you trying to do!"

Kit writhed under his grip. "You're hurting me."

"I ought to kill you."

"I only—"

"What did you think you'd find?"

"Please—I only wanted to make you comfortable."

But still he gripped her there. "Don't ever touch my hat again."

"I'm sorry."

He tried to quiet down his anger, and felt her breath against his face. "There are things about me you've got no right to know."

"Please—"

He had never known the close touch of her skin before and he found himself staring into her eyes. She had stopped struggling and there was a moment of suspended time, a quiet astonishment and a recognition. They could call themselves strangers, but it was only a deception. Day by day the ordeal had revealed them and bound them closer together until now she lay suddenly tight in his arms. Their lips met tentatively, softly, and then hungrily.

He felt her heart quicken under him and he knew that all the days they had been at horns and rattles they had been quietly falling in love with each other; and that was madness. He felt her lips, chapped but full of a desperate poignancy, and he put reality from his mind. And then, suddenly, as she raised in his arms, she froze.

She was looking at the small coffin, a silent reminder glinting in the last light of the moon. The real world closed around her with smothering force. She shook back her hair, and Yellowleg said nothing.

They sat for a moment, apart now, and then Yellowleg got up and went after the claybank. She had grazed far beyond the rocks; he brought her back and tied her to a greasewood stump. Kit was already curled up in her blankets. Yellowleg stayed awake another hour, but it was no use. He would have to back his notion that the bronco Apache would welcome them to Siringo. He lit a final cigarette and glanced at Kit, and fell asleep with the stub of the cigarette still between his lips.

CHAPTER TWENTY

The claybank was gone.

A dry storm had come up toward morning and when Yellowleg awoke drifts of sand lay across the blanket. He could feel it in the seams of his face. He rose, shaking out the blanket, and saw that the claybank was gone.

He went out into the storm, crimping his eyes to see, and half an hour later he found the mare toward the bottom of the slope where the mesquite grass was thickest and most tempting. An arrow had plunged deep into her hide and the wind was already beginning to bury her with sand.

The dry storm picked up, whipping through the rocks in long shrieks and gusts. Yellowleg stood with the wind at his back and his eyes seeing nothing. It was a long time before he was able to sort out his thoughts. His mare was dead. They were set afoot. And he had been wrong.

The Apache had no intention of going on to Siringo, that much was clear now. With great cunning he had cut the reins at the greasewood stump and waited for the mare to graze out of earshot. He had stood close and sunk the arrow deep. There had been great, savage strength in the arms.

He would be out there now, somewhere in the dirty winds, waiting. But Yellowleg would not sit still for him to strike again.

As the dry storm obscured them, Yellowleg moved Kit, together with the travois and supplies, into a low cave among the rocks. He made a small fire, enough to boil coffee, and then broke the shotgun to assure himself that it was loaded. Then he handed it to her.

"I'll be leaving," he said in a low, quiet voice. "I want you to sit with that shotgun looking out and if he shows up don't start an argument. Blast."

She looked up, hesitantly. "What are you going to do?"

"I'm through waiting. He's out there somewhere and I'm going to find him."

"Don't leave me."

"You'll be all right. You've got enough buckshot to stand off an army."

"Don't go. You're only fooling yourself."

"Maybe. But maybe I'll be lucky."

He wondered suddenly if this was what the Apache expected him to do—to separate and leave the girl unattended. But not even the Apache could have counted on the dry storm, and Yellowleg would try to make use of it.

He finished his coffee and loaded the Winchester and looked out. Almost as suddenly as it had come, the wind was spending itself. "Better put out the fire," he said.

He found Kit gazing at him when he turned. "Don't go yet," she murmured softly. "Can't you understand what happened to me last night?"

"Don't brood about it," he said crisply. "You hate my guts and that's just fine with me."

"Please—"

"We made a mistake. Forget it."

"What if you shouldn't come back?"

"You've got a shotgun."

"We may never see each other again."

"That's just possible."

She started toward him, but his harassed, scowling face stopped her. She threw back her hair in a small gesture. "I want you to know," she whispered, "that... I've fallen in love with you. No apologies. I love you."

She waited, clearly hoping for some sign that he would sweep her into his arms. But he stood cruelly still. This was not what he had wanted to hear. He'd told her it was all a mistake, and that's the way it would have to stand. She wouldn't be saying the same words if he took off his hat. He'd spare her that. "There was about as much love between us last night," he said, "as you'll find in a parlor house."

"Don't—"

"Smarten up. You're a mighty pretty little sage hen, and I ain't exactly blind."

"You're not fooling me."

"No, m'am. You're fooling yourself."

He was a rotten liar, and it made him angry that she just stood there without getting mad, and with the faintest of stubborn smiles tucked into the corners of her eyes. She saw through him, all right, and he had a furious impulse to wrap her up in his arms.

She whispered, "You might kiss me again before you go."

He pulled himself up straight, as if it were a burden. "Thanks," he said stiffly, "but no thanks."

The winds, when they passed, left a strange quiet over the land. The sun burned through a haze of suspended dust and overlaid the quiet with a cinnamon glare. Yellowleg worked his way to the west of the crags and rocks they had camped in. The Apache, he thought, would have chosen his bed ground to fall in the shade of a rising sun.

Yellowleg moved from rock to rock, obscure shapes in the haze. He became conscious of the sounds of his own breathing, amplified by the silence. The dry storm had either unravelled or covered every track of the night before, but he wasn't looking for signs. He was looking for luck.

He may have covered half a mile; he couldn't be sure. He kept his bearings by the sun, which burned a clear disc in the pall. He had a sense of crawling through some primordial wilderness of mist and shadow, a dead world. But he felt, with the awareness of instinct, that the Apache was out there too.

When he heard the whirr of rattles, off to his left, his blood ran cold. In the first split-second, unable to gauge the distance, he thought he had somehow aroused the snake, and now the dry hum of rattles were pinpointing him in the dust. But in the next second he heard a horse neigh, a soulful cry of pure terror, and Yellowleg rushed toward the sounds. Here was his Apache.

The dust seemed to open before him and he saw the Indian pony standing on his hind legs, his yellow teeth exposed in anguish; and with a tossing of its head a rope of dust came free and when it landed Yellowleg saw that it was a diamondback.

Yellowleg was already set with the Springfield, but now he lowered it. The Apache wasn't there. The pony was alone.

The air buzzed and Yellowleg saw that the pony had grazed into a den of rattlers that were now striking and coiling and lashing out again. The horse neighed, dropping helplessly to its forelegs and rearing up again, and then stampeded.

The diamondbacks, three of them, recoiled, rattling still, and Yellowleg half-expected to see the savage loom up out of the haze. Yellowleg pulled back and gradually the whirring of rattles cut out, one by one. He could hear the horse running wild, hastening his own death. There was no telling how many pairs of fangs had clamped into his hide.

And then, from somewhere behind the sun, the blast of a shotgun rolled out over the haze.

CHAPTER TWENTY-ONE

Yellowleg found the Apache almost on his feet, a young giant in bronze and blood, blown back into the spiked branches of a staghorn cholla and held there like a grotesque scarecrow. Yellowleg gazed at the torn figure with a mixture of consolation and regret. This had been no ordinary savage; even in death there was an air of defiance and nobility about him. His eyes stood open to the sun, gazing at the spirits that humiliated him, and a red harvester ant started across the ball of his eye. Yellowleg turned away and found Kit still in the cave, numb and silent, and later they started for Siringo on foot.

The brown haze thinned and visibility extended itself. Shadows began to form. Yellowleg trudged ahead with the short pine box on his left shoulder and carried the shovel and Springfield in his right hand. Kit kept close behind with all the water they had left in two canteens, a ration of coffee and dried apples, and a single bedroll. They left everything else behind, including the shotgun.

They had gone almost a mile when. Yellowleg saw the Indian pony rolling in the dust off to his left, as if to rub off the pains in his hide. Yellowleg stopped and set down the box and wondered if there was any use trying to catch him. It would be too late now to attempt to lance the snake bites: the poison would be well into his system. Still, he had to try. They needed that horse, alive or half-dead; it didn't matter any more.

Yellowleg had no rope to work with. He approached empty handed and the pony found his legs. He'd run himself into a lather and the loose earth clung to his buckskin hide. His nose was now hideously swollen where the diamondback had first struck and his eyes were glazed and his breathing came like that of a windbroken horse. Yellowleg stopped, hoping the pony would sense a friendly presence, but it sensed a white man instead. His great neck arched and he pawed backwards. A halter trailed on the ground and Yellowleg made a lurch for it. The pony swung away in a soft rattle of hooves and slowed to a stop. Yellowleg tried again, for he could tell the horse was dulled with venom and light-headed, but again the buckskin shied back. Yellowleg waited a long time before making another move. The halter came temptingly close and Yellowleg thought there still might be a chance of saving the animal, since an hour's running had not yet killed him. But as he waited, gauging his moment, the pony suddenly bolted and left Yellowleg standing.

Yellowleg watched him a long time race in a mad frenzy further and further out in the desert, until there was no use watching any longer. The horse would die somewhere among the rocks and chollas and greasewood.

They saw Siringo from almost two miles off. It stood out, as squared off as a matchbox, on the talus slope of a range of lavender hills. Yellowleg peered at it and glanced at Kit, but they said nothing. They exchanged a sort of smile that said it all. They were covered with dust, they were disheveled and burdened and tired, and the sun had seared their faces. But, suddenly, Siringo stood out there like some dusty promised land and Yellowleg felt his own blood quicken.

"Sure is a pretty sight," he said finally, and hoisted the box to his shoulder and plodded on across the hills.

They reached the sign in mid-afternoon. It had been nailed to an ironwood post and the sun had faded the paint, but still it said:

WELCOME TO SIRINGO
POP. 273

Yellowleg looked along the main street blossoming with bushes that had taken root. The clapboard stores and false fronts were weathered almost black and leaned with a strong prevailing wind. Some of the buildings had burst open from their studs, like overripe melons. Weeds had grown up through the chinks in the sidewalk planks, and as Yellowleg started into town a small antelope looked up from grazing and then went clattering off down the boardwalk.

They stopped in the broken shade of a wooden awning split and curled from its nails, and Yellowleg eased the pine box off his shoulder. The deep ache of the old wound had been a steady throb all day. He tried to work the numbness out of it, and then freed Kit of the canteens and blankets. She seated herself against an awning post with her head back and her eyes closed.

Yellowleg emptied the dirt out of his boots and left them off. His eyes surveyed the town once more. It was boarded up as if all those storekeepers expected to return, but the desert was already reclaiming the streets with its bushes and weeds and thorned plants. He looked at Kit.

"You all right?"

She nodded quietly. They lay there awhile and when the pain began to leave his shoulder he straightened and pulled his boots back on. "Where's the cemetery?"

"There's time. We can rest first."

"I want to get it over with."

"It's at the other end of town. In some smoketrees."

Yellowleg picked up the shovel and wiped the heat off his face. He looked at her again.

"What was your husband's name?"

It was a moment before she answered; he supposed a lot of memories had rushed in on her after all these years and he felt as if he were an intruder now. "Mead," she said, "was named after him. Mead Tildon."

"Don't get up. It'll take me awhile."

He left her there and walked through town. These last miles had seemed endless, like walking to the ends of the earth, but Kit had kept up. He'd never seen a woman like that, always walking straight as a poker, no matter what. She'd exposed her beauty to the sky without a thought, almost as if it were a thing despised and she wanted to destroy it. Her skin had roughened and seamed and her face had gathered a look of the hard, open spaces. She had changed, all right; the sun had taken a saloon painting and turned it into flesh and blood. The dirt and grime would wash off, but the beauty would still be there, a deeper, quieter thing, and it would be hard to put her out of his mind—ever.

He turned off thinking this way as he saw the long, mocking shadow of his hat traveling along the ground beside him. The hat. They could lay the boy to rest, but that hat would sit on Yellowleg's head for the rest of his days. He had an image of himself that no woman could accept, and there was no point in fretting about it. The sun had changed nothing. His future could be spelled out in the few letters of a man's name. Turk. And he'd better not forget it.

He passed up the stub of cigarette at first. And then it stopped him short. He went back a pace or two and there it was, lying in the dust. He bent down and picked it up thoughtfully. He broke it between his fingers and rubbed the fresh tobacco. Slowly, as he let the tobacco drift free, he began to scan the broken windows and the dead, shadowy doorways. A heavy silence lay over the town. He saw Kit rouse at the far end of the street and pick a few wildflowers at her feet. For the boy and his father, Yellowleg knew, and he thought it was fit and right.

He hunkered there a long time, his senses, casting about, but nothing stirred. Finally he straightened. Someone had come through town not more than a few hours ago.

The smoketrees shaded a flat about a quarter of a mile out of town. Weeds had grown up high across the graves, most of them with wooden markers, but a few of them stone. Even Siringo had had its big men, he thought, who lay in better graves. He tramped around, clearing weeds to read the markers. Most of them were at a lean, from the winds, and some of them had fallen over and been all but buried under moving sands. It was like tramping through a dry wilderness, and he came across many names: Bailey, Johanson, Lefevre, Smith, Bascom, Duncannon, Oldham, Wheatley. But he came across no Tildon.

When he looked up Kit was approaching. She had spruced up noticeably, tied back her hair, and she held a limp gathering of purplemat and white pricklypoppies collected from the street.

But as she came toward him he faced up to what had already begun to lurk in his mind. He had come a long way to make a fool of himself.

"Never mind the flowers," he said. "There's no Tildon here."

She gave him a small glance and walked past him. She brushed aside the gray filigree of a smoketree and seemed to know where she was going. He followed.

He watched. She stopped toward the edge of the flat, staring at the ground, but there was no gravestone. With a controlled reaction she looked around, as if to check her bearings after all these years. And then she glanced at Yellowleg.

"It's right here."

He didn't make a move. "Is it?"

"I don't know what happened to the marker."

"I looked at all of 'em."

"It might be buried."

"Maybe it was struck by lightning."

She gave him a sharp glance. "What are you trying to say?"

"I said it. There is no Tildon here."

She gazed up at him, her eyes green and steady and filling with temper. "Get out of here."

"Why didn't you tell me the truth?"

"I did!"

"Siringo would be a good place to bury a make-believe husband and give Mead a father. Do you think I'd have cared, if you told me the truth?"

"Stop it!"

"Do you know I actually told myself I was in love with the lady?" He wrenched the wildflowers out of her hand and pitched them into the weeds. "I wondered once if you really planned on coming all the way to Siringo. But once I was along, you couldn't turn back. And now you point to a patch of dry ground and say that's it, there used to be a marker, but it seems to have disappeared. Well, I've pried and poked over every foot of this place, looking at Duncannons and Smiths and Johansons and prayin' for a Tildon, but a grave don't get up and walk away, even if it is made of wood."

"Stop it! You're like all the rest!"

"No. They had more sense than I did. I had to come all this way to find out they were right back in Gila City."

Her hand lashed out, slapping him hard.

"Thank you, lady."

"Maybe there's no headstone here," she said, gazing evenly at him. "Maybe I didn't think anyone would be fool enough to come to Siringo, but you came and I was grateful. Now you can believe what you like, but leave me alone."

The sting of her hand lingered on his cheek. So this was how it was ending for him, he thought. Before, he hadn't known how he would be able to walk away from her when the time came. Now it would be easy.

"I'll bury the boy," he said. "Then I'll be going."

CHAPTER TWENTY-TWO

The sun was already behind the mountain peaks, shining through in great broken shards, when Yellowleg finished with the shovel. Then he headed back toward town, thinking all the while, and cut through with bitterness. Kit had left him to sit somewhere far off, alone, and he had cast around again among the ruins looking for Tildon. He might have been jumpy and too quick to judge. But he turned up nothing that he hadn't turned up before, and it was too much to believe that the winds would have chosen just one gravestone to cart off, and that one Tildon's. It had never existed.

There was nothing left but to fetch the pine box, and get it over with.

As he came to the edge of the town he realized that Kit was following him. He turned, his eyes defensive, but it was as if in an agony of loneliness she needed someone, even him, and the sight of her jarred him. For the first time he saw her broken, her mulish pride gone, a piteous gaze in her eyes; a slim figure moving dully after him.

"Well, come on," he muttered. "It's no good being at each other's throats now."

He waited for her to catch up and then started off again. She hurried a little to keep up, falling half a step behind, and he knew that he hadn't been able to cast her out of his soul with a few angry words. She possessed him still, like something devilish. The trek to Siringo had been a masquerade of fierce pride and she had almost brought it off. He'd known men to step onto a gunman's walk to make a reputation; he could forgive her trying to remake her own, but not for taking him in like some pilgrim in a frontier saloon. He had a mulish pride of his own.

They were passing outside the two-story hotel on the north side of the street when the voice broke out like a clap of thunder.

"Yellowleg!"

The yell stood in the air, suspended, and the two of them stopped in their tracks. Even before Yellowleg looked up he knew the voice and the man he'd see above at the hotel window. Billy.

"I'm aimin' at her!" Billy shouted. "Don't try for your guns!"

Yellowleg looked up slowly. Billy stood framed at a broken upstairs window, grinning over Yellowlegs own Winchester.

"That's it," Billy nodded. "Now raise up them elbows a mite."

Yellowleg peered up, his eyes hard and creased. "Where's Turk?"

"Right behind you," Billy said.

Yellowleg's face muscles eased: Turk was still alive. The squat-necked man came scuttling up to Yellowleg's back and lifted the guns from their holsters, and then stepped deftly away.

"Hello, Turk," Yellowleg said, and his voice sounded almost polite.

"Howdy. Howdy, m'am."

"What are you two doing here?"

Turk spit between the guns in his hands. "You know Billy. When he gets an idea, he just won't let go."

"What idea?"

"Her."

Yellowleg met Kit's glance and then Billy came down out of the hotel and onto the street. He ambled toward them, smiling, his hat at a jack-deuce angle and the Winchester loose in his hand.

"Welcome to Siringo," he said. "We seen you walkin' by."

"When did you get here?"

"This mornin'. You folks musta taken a detour. We almost give you up. Figured you might have got lost in that dry storm."

"Turk," Yellowleg said, "if I'd known you were here I'd have hurried."

"You was always fond of me," Turk said with casual sarcasm.

"Nice little town, ain't it?" Billy said, looking Kit over slowly.

"Dandy little town," Turk put in.

"You've got my guns," Yellowleg said evenly. "It looks like you're giving the orders, Billy."

"Don't it, though?"

"Well?"

Billy wiped his lips and looked around. His eyes picked out a boarded-up saloon. "That'll do. No point in keepin' the lady out here in the dust. We got the whole town to ourselves and nothing but time to talk it over."

"Sorry I can't offer you a drink," Billy said from behind the bar. "We're plumb out."

It was a hollow barn of a place, partly open to the sky where the roof boards had fallen in. There was a broken chair hanging on a wall gun peg, but everything else was gone. Sand had blown in along the cracks, wind-scouring the puncheon floor and piling up in drifts in the corners.

"Billy," Turk said from one end of the bar, "let's get it over with. You don't look right on the sober side of a bar, anyhow."

"Get the lady a chair."

"She ain't helpless."

"She'll stand," Yellowleg said.

Turk nodded. "The chair's broke anyway."

"M'am," Billy said. "M'am, I take off my hat to ya. I reckon you sure showed them folks in Gila City—"

"Shut up."

Billy's eyes whipped back to Yellowleg. "You still doin' her talkin' for her?"

"What did you do with the money?"

"Now what money is that?"

"There's only one thing that would bring Turk to Siringo. And that's keeping one jump ahead of a posse."

Turk chuckled under his breath. "Never saw folks so scared of Injuns. Worse'n Yankees."

Billy hunched his shoulders and looked levelly at Yellowleg. "Figured you might want a cut. That's why we took them guns of yours."

"I don't want a cut," Yellowleg answered. "All I want is my guns."

"It amounts to the same thing," Billy said. "She sure is pretty, ain't she? Awful quiet though. I saw her pickin' flowers to put on her ol' man's grave and I didn't have the heart to bother her. Some things is sacred."

Yellowleg stared at Billy, knowing his sentiments didn't even run skin deep, but it seemed important to let him go on thinking that all had gone right under the smoketrees. "Let her alone."

"I guess you two got to be real friendly," Billy said. "We noticed you only brought one bedroll."

"That's enough, Billy!"

"We couldn't help wondering about it, that's all." Turk spit. "All but drove the kid crazy."

Yellowleg's jaws were working hard and he didn't know how much longer he could keep his temper capped. "You going to stand there talking all day?"

"I had me a good sleep," Billy grinned. "I'm feeling right social. Turk, go get the money."

It came out so matter-of-factly that Turk didn't seem to get it at first. And then he peered at Billy narrowly, and Yellowleg knew that Billy was improvising a new plan. "You gone loco, Billy?"

"I said get it!"

Turk jerked to the sound of Billy's voice, but still he held back. "We ain't cuttin' that Yankee in."

"I didn't say we were," Billy snapped. "I just said get the money. And leave his guns right on the end of the bar. If he goes for 'em I'll have the privilege of shooting him. If he even looks at 'em, maybe."

Turk pursed his lips thoughtfully. "A nice fella like that," he remarked with wistful sarcasm. "We wasted too much time already."

"I'll bet the lady ain't ever seen so much money."

"We got plans, boy, you and me. Don't forget that."

"I might buy myself a pinch and a hug. Hurry up."

Turk started out and Billy's eyes held on his thick, soiled back. Yellowleg saw a flinty smile come into Billy's eyes. When Turk was gone Billy still stared at the open doorway. "I just don't have the heart to kill the old gent."

Yellowleg had all but seen it coming. "You were always the loyal sort," he said quietly.

Billy looked at Yellowleg under the low brim of his hat. "Your shootin' hand don't give me the colic anymore, Yellowleg. How'd you like to have your guns back?"

"You want me to kill him?"

"When he comes back through that door. He always said he wanted to die in a saloon. It's the least I can do for him."

There wasn't a true emotion in Billy's face, and Yellowleg knew he'd never misjudged the kid. Billy Short was born and bred a killer.

Yellowleg nodded toward Kit without looking at her. "And what happens to the girl?"

"We'll argue that out later. You and me."

Yellowleg's blood had quickened moments before. He watched Billy amble to the guns left at the far end of the bar, and their eyes met again. Yellowleg gave him a sign and Billy slid the guns down the bar, one by one.

"I'm goin' for a walk. But I'll be around when you're ready."

He turned his back to Yellowleg and sauntered with jangling steps toward the door. He looked out on the street, checking, and then half-turned. He glanced from Kit to Yellowleg with his chin lifted and his small eyes peering out under the brim, and grinned. "The lady's got to admit I got guts, don't she?"

Even after he was gone Billy's presence hung in the room. His cigarette still burned where he had dropped it and the air seemed fouled with a deadly presence. Yellowleg avoided Kit's eyes and picked his guns up off the bar. He checked each one and then slid them nervelessly in their holsters.

"You're not going through with it," Kit said.

"It's none of your affair."

"You can't kill in cold blood."

Yellowleg turned on her sharply. "I've waited seven years, and the waiting's over. Stay out of it." This wasn't the way he had wanted it, but it would have to do. "Now get out of here."

Her earlier despair was gone. She stood erect, her eyes crisp and withering. "No one's putting me up as the prize in a shooting match."

"I don't see where you've got much to say about it."

"Haven't I?"

"If you want to go with Billy, that's all right with me. But Turk is a different matter."

"You'll walk out of here a murderer. Don't do that to me."

"Don't do *what* to you? I told you it's none of your affair."

"But *you* are. Killing my son was an accident—I know that, even if I thought I could never forgive it. It doesn't matter what you think of me anymore—call me a parlor house girl if it makes you feel any better—but I love you. I have nothing else left. I love you. You're not like the others—

Billy and Turk—but you will be if you murder in cold blood. Billy's got you to do his killing for him—and I couldn't love that kind of man. A murderer."

"Get out. Do you think you were ever in love with me? That's almost funny. You don't even know me. I'm not the man you think I am; I'm just a face under a hat. Did you ever wonder why I wouldn't take it off in the preach house or even to sleep? I'll take it off for you—and then tell me not to blast Turk to some corner of Hell!" He bared his cropped head in a rage of self-contempt. "Have yourself a look and then tell me all about how you love me!"

He followed her glance as she looked up and time hung suspended in her clear, green eyes. But no spark of awe came into them, no quickly concealed wonder—nothing. And then her eyes lowered, almost unchanged, to his.

"You didn't have to do that," she said gently. "But I'm glad you did."

"Don't you understand? Turk tried to scalp me!"

"I saw you bare-headed. When you were fighting with Billy."

"You *what?*"

"That didn't keep me from falling in love with you. I thought you'd been scarred in the war, but you're the same man, with or without that hat. Leave it off. And what about me? My scars. Do you know how many I've let kiss me and pinch me because I'd lose my job if I didn't? Men with dirty clothes and smelly arms, but money to spend. Maybe I'll end up in the parlor house, like the others. Can I ask you to love a woman like that?"

"Shut up!"

"You're black-haired and graying a little and I love you."

No. Nothing had changed. Kit had been lying to him all the way from Gila City, and she was lying to him now. He remembered too much laughter, too many looks, too many silences. He put his hat on now, where it belonged. "I told you to get out of here."

But it was already too late. Turk came hurrying onto the plank walk and through the saloon doors, with a canvas money bag in each fist. In that instant, as Yellowleg drew, Kit swept against him and shouted. "Run!"

Yellowleg squeezed out the shot and Turk looked up, startled, but now aware of the ambush that had been set for him. He lit out and Yellowleg shot again, struggling to be rid of Kit's clinging arms. When Turk was finally gone Yellowleg threw her angrily to the floor.

She lay there a moment, looking up and accepting his hard glare of wrath. Then Yellowleg walked toward the door. The shots, he knew, would bring Billy back. Billy would take them as Turk's death knell. And now Billy would come lurking through Siringo with his arms slightly akimbo.

CHAPTER TWENTY-THREE

Dusk was gathering in the windows and doorways of the town. Yellowleg ducked across the street. A heavy silence hung in the air scented with dust and sage. Yellowleg's glance ranged over the boardwalks, the skinny false fronts, the broad street. Turk had disappeared.

It was like time suspended between heartbeats. Yellowleg reached the bedroll and dug out the Bowie knife. He slipped it under his gunbelt, at his back. He listened a moment and then straightened. Had Turk ducked into an alleyway?

Yellowleg walked slowly. His skin felt tight on his face. He passed doors and windows, boarded up and dead. The hotel. That's where they had passed the day, Yellowleg thought. The big window stood in great broken shards and there was fresh glass on the boardwalk. Yellowleg wondered if Billy had gone in there to sit out Turk's execution. He had an impulse to back away and wait. A great tiredness lingered in his muscles, and now the tension was moving up into his shoulders.

And then it was too late. He heard Billy's voice. Behind him.

"You lookin' for me?"

Yellowleg stood quite still, without turning, and the tiredness went away. "It looks like I found you."

"It's coming on dark. No sense in beating around the bush, is there? I'm ready any time you turn around."

"I told you before, Billy. My fight's not with you."

"There're only two horses in this town. You know as well as I do only two people are going to leave Siringo alive."

A shot cracked out through the broken awning overhead and thudded beside Yellowleg's boot. In that instant Yellowleg glimpsed the dusk sky between the wide cracks and saw Turk poised at the hotel window above. Yellowleg shot fast and saw Turk jump back. And then it was quiet again.

There was a grin of contempt in Billy's voice. "Three shots and you ain't finished him off yet."

"It looks that way."

"Like I said—anytime you feel like facing me."

Yellowleg peered up at the glimpse he had of the hotel window. It meant turning his back on Turk, but he supposed he would have to risk it.

"Come on!" Billy snarled.

"Easy, kid."

"You're long on bluff, ain't you? You don't think you fooled us dottin' the i's in that saloon sign, do you? We found out those slug-holes were sittin' there a year! Mister, I'm callin' your bluff. Now."

Yellowleg lowered his eyes from the hotel window. He felt tired and dry-mouthed, but he came about hard and tall, with his arms bowed and his eyes steady. He faced Billy across the split and weather-beaten sidewalk, and Billy stood like a young reflection of himself.

"Yellowleg," Billy muttered with a quickly fading grin, "what you been hiding under that hat? A tin badge?"

"Make your play."

Their gaze locked in a quickly mounting tension. Yellowleg saw Billy as two white eyes under a brim of hat. And then the bolt of pain struck Yellowleg's shoulder, a sharp, pulling ache that jarred his stance and Billy skinned his guns.

Yellowleg drew only one gun, his left, and nailed Billy's hide to an awning post. Billy curled around it, still on his feet, and then slid into the weed-grown street. A gun was still locked in his hand and his eyes were dazed and open and the gun exploded. Yellowleg felt his hat whip off, and saw it turning over into the street. The live matches kept tucked in the horsehair band had been scraped and set off, and they burned in the dust. Yellowleg felt open air at his head and a cold choke of rage in his throat.

Billy managed a grin. "I always wanted to do that."

Yellowleg watched him die that way, grinning.

Yellowleg's eyes tightened on Turk with the haunted look of seven years. Turk was bleeding. Yellowleg's third shot had chewed into his arm. Turk stood at the top of the broken hotel stairs with his hands raised and blood dripping down off the point of his elbow.

"Hold your fire," Turk said. "I've had enough. I'm coming down."

Yellowleg stood bare-headed with his feet planted in the dust of the lobby. Turk would know him now; Yellowleg waited for the shock of recognition.

"You and the girl take the horses," Turk babbled on desperately. "Just leave me be. I'll make out. Just leave me be."

"Hello, Turk."

"I never figured the kid to double-cross me that way. He was a mean one." Turk came down the stairs, hesitating at each step. "But you got good sense. I ain't worth killin'—you see that. Just a saddle tramp with the natures. Leave me go."

"Don't you remember me now," Yellowleg said tauntingly.

"The horses are hid. Stable behind the hotel. You and the girl help yourself. Don't worry none about me."

"Look at me!"

"I'm hit. You can't ask me to draw against you."

Yellowleg flung the Bowie knife and it struck and held a step below Turk's foot. Turk rose back and his hands elevated themselves.

"The money. I ain't askin' for a cut. You and the girl help yourselves."

"You've seen that knife before."

"I've seen a lot of knives."

"That one used to be yours."

"Anything you say, mister."

"Look at me!"

"Billy shot off your hat. I'm plumb sorry. You were right funny about it. That Billy was a mean one."

"You blind fool—"

But Yellowleg stopped himself. Turk didn't recognize the war scars for what they were. Yellowleg remembered now those words of Dr. Caxton in Gila City. The real wounds may have grown deep and out of sight. He had kept his hat clamped over a cropped head and a memory, as if to nourish it, to prime it and sustain it for seven years. A moment before Kit had accepted him on his own terms. All right. But the memory was still there. And the Bowie knife stood waiting in the stairs.

Yellowleg advanced slowly and Turk started backing up, mumbling anxiously. "We can talk this out. You're all riled up."

Turk lost his footing on a broken step and slid to his back. He held himself there, his head raised on his neck, and stared wide-eyed as Yellowleg advanced. "I'm hit. Can't you see I'm hit?"

Yellowleg pulled the knife into his palm. "You left this behind in Tennessee. During the war. When I'd been hit."

And then Yellowleg saw it. The deep shock of recognition.

"You...."

A slow horror came into Turk's eyes.

"Me."

Almost unseeing, Turk rubbed the old teeth scars in his hand. "Don't—"

Yellowleg took hold of Turk's boot and yanked him down to his own level on the stairs.

"This is what's kept me going," Yellowleg said. "This moment now."

"No!"

Yellowleg knocked off Turk's hat and grabbed up his sweaty hair.

"I was drunk," Turk cried hoarsely. "I hardly knew what I was about. Listen, I can help you. Don't. Listen, I know about the grave. Billy found the marker. It said Tildon, just like she said it would. Blown over from the grave. Billy hid it under the stoop of the hotel. It's there now. He had a mean streak in him. He wanted you thinking the girl had tricked you—"

Yellowleg heard footsteps below. He turned on a flash of blue calico and met Kit's glance a moment before she walked out. How long had she been standing down there? Watching and listening.

Listening. Under the stoop. And Yellowleg had been wrong. But in that hard glint of Kit's eyes that was forgiven, and something else said: It was

Turk or Kit. Turk or Kit.

Turk or Kit. Yellowleg stared at the sweat-soaked hair in his fist. There was a low sobbing in Turk's throat and the fear stood out on his face. And then Yellowleg unfisted his hand. Turk had filled his life for seven years. But Yellowleg had found something better to live for, and he made the choice quickly.

Kit was far down the open street when Yellowleg stood in the twilight. "Kit!"

She turned. They stood that way a moment, hesitating, and then she knew. They swept toward each other. When she was in his arms Yellowleg knew the vengeance was gone from his soul.

They were still in the middle of the street when the first hoofbeats sounded. Within moments a posse of Gila City faces stopped around them, and even Dr. Caxton was along.

"Howdy, Kit."

"We're trailin' a couple of bank robbers," the mayor said. He glanced at Billy lying dead off the boardwalk. "Looks like we found 'em."

"They figured you didn't have sand enough to come to Siringo," Yellowleg said.

"We don't as a rule. But you know how folks are. If it's their money, the gates of Hell wouldn't stop 'em."

"You're the parson, ain't you?" Yellowleg said, looking around.

"Says he is," the bartender nodded.

"Then Mead'll be getting a proper burial—next to his pa. We'll be needing the right kind of words."

All eyes turned on Kit and the parson finally cleared his throat. "I'll scratch up a right fine prayer. Come on."

Yellowleg found Kit's hand tight in his. And he wondered what kind of marriage ceremony the parson could scratch up. He'd ask him later.

THE END

AN INTERVIEW WITH A.S. 'SID' FLEISCHMAN
CONDUCTED BY GARY LOVISI

(reprinted from the pages of *Paperback Parade* #55, January 2001)

Gary Lovisi: How and why did you begin to write?

Sid Fleischman: I became a writer quite by accident. It was my intention all through my early years in San Diego to become a professional magician. At age 17, still in high school, I wrote up some original sleight-of-hand tricks into a short book, published for magicians only by the still active Abbott's Magic Company in Colon, Michigan. I didn't think of it as writing; I was just putting down sentences carefully explaining what to do with one's fingers. But when the book landed on my doorstep, with my name on the cover, it impressed the hell out of me. The thought of becoming a writer had never crossed my mind. But my aspirations took a shift. While I did Vaudeville once out of high school, I studied O. Henry and de Maupassant, and between performances tried to write trick-ending short stories.

When the Second World War came along, I was called up for active service in the US Naval Reserve. I went into the Navy a magician and came out, four years later, a writer. It was while on active duty that I sold a story to *Liberty* magazine, a popular weekly of those days, for a then bountiful $300. With the war ended, and before returning to college (San Diego State, now University), I took eighteen months to write full time. I sold to *Toronto Star Weekly This Week* (Sunday magazine supplement) and a slew of lesser fry. I also wrote two mystery novels, (*The Straw Donkey Case*, followed by *Murder's No Accident*), published by Phoenix Press, and for the first time used A.S. Fleischman as a temporary professional name on books. I didn't especially like initials, but I was undecided about exactly what to call myself.

Phoenix paid me an advance of $150 per novel, against royalties, but the publishers in an habitual oversight never sent me royalty statements—or subsequent checks. I was too naive to inquire about the matter, assuming that publishers were scrupulously honest and that the books must not have earned back their advances. Only years later did I discover that an agent got $500 advances from Phoenix for his authors—and royalty statements.

GL: How did you come to write for Gold Medal?

SF: Finishing up college in 1949, I got a job on the *San Diego Daily Journal* as a rewrite man and general assignment reporter. My byline was Sid Fleischman. When the paper collapsed a year later, and after starting up a local weekly news magazine, I had a letter from an agent I had met in New York, the unlamented Donald MacCampbell. He was searching me out to discover if I might be interested in doing something for Gold Medal, who was starting up and offering a $2,000 advance on print order, a fortune in those days.

GL: Can you talk about your earliest Gold Medal novel, *Shanghai Flame?* Any anecdotes?

SF: I sold out my interest in the news magazine and quickly wrote an adventure novel set in Shanghai, where I had ended up after the war. Dick Carrol, the salty but amiable editor, a former screenwriter and veteran of Gallipoli, accepted the novel almost instantly. I called the novel *The Man Who Died Laughing*. When my first copies arrived they blazed forth with a baffling new title, *Shanghai Flame*. Shanghai I could comprehend, but *Flame?* There were no fires in the yarn. Upon examining the text I discovered that to support his newsstand title, Dick had an underling go through the manuscript and change the name of my red-headed heroine (I've now forgotten what it was) to Flame. Gold Medal was no place for those who regarded their prose as chiseled in anything but quicksand.

GL: What were you paid?

SF: Gold Medal came up with a brilliant idea to eliminate all the usual royalty bookkeeping headaches, with the troublesome return of copies to be factored in, by paying the author on print order. While the publisher swallowed the loss on any returns, if any, it eliminated a legion of bean counters.

I received a cent-and-a-half a copy on a first print order of 200,000 copies—$3,000, less 10 percent agent's commission. Gold Medal was market wise on print orders. In my experience, the first printings always sold out within weeks and subsequent printings of 100,000 or so copies were ordered and paid for. With reprint following reprint, and check after check, I felt rich enough to pack up my young family and take off for Europe in the early 50s.

GL: Your earliest Gold Medal novels were, *Look Behind You, Lady* and *Danger In Paradise*. What possessed you to write them?

SF: As I had been a night club magician, before the war, I was naturally drawn to writing a novel about a magician in an exotic setting. I had never been to Macao, the setting, but the historic old place, off Hong Kong, was easy to research.

I had never been to Bali, either, so *Danger In Paradise* was a research job, too. As I don't plot my novels in advance, I begin with the background and the mere glimmer of an idea and a hope that something interesting might happen on paper. My starting point for this novel was a character idea—I wanted to work in an American woman who had gone native on the island of Bali, the island of bare-breasted women. This appealed to us prurient Puritans of that long-ago day, fresh from our copies of *Captain Billy's Whiz Bang*.

GL: Why the Oriental locales in most of your Gold Medal novels?

SF: After the war, I qualified as an Old China hand and since no one else was writing characters literate in pidgin English, I laid out a claim. The background seemed made for intrigue and mystery and suspense, the shadowy stuff that, as a magician, I found seductive. I still do.

GL: Some of your novels have a hardboiled edge. Comments.

SF: Really? I hadn't realized it. I suppose it comes from doing my literary teething on Dashiell Hammett and Raymond Chandler.

What's evident to me is the first appearance of laugh lines. This taste for wisecracks and slapsticks and putty noses flowered, much later, in my comic novels for children.

GL: Was *Blood Alley* your most successful Gold Medal novel?

SF: By far. It was bought for films, thanks to Dick Carrol, who had been visiting Monterey, California, where I was then living. Dick asked me for a carbon of the novel so that he might show it to his old friend Bob Fellows, John Wayne's partner in a film company, Batjac. Batjac bought it for the director, William A. Wellman. I was paid $5,000 for the film rights.

A few days later, Wellman phoned me and asked if I would be interested in writing the screenplay. I was, of course. That was in 1954. I have been a screenwriter ever since.

GL: *Yellowleg* is an excellent western, hardboiled in its own way. How did you happen to turn from the Orient to the American West?

SF: I think almost every writer wants to try his or her hand at the American classic form—the western. So I began reading western material and making notes. I began with the key idea of the story, a white man who had been scalped by another white man, and has caught up with him at last. The rest I improvised, day by day, at the typewriter. *Yellowleg* began life as a screenplay, immediately optioned by Marlon Brando. I then rewrote the script as a novel for Gold Medal, winning a Spur Award from the Western Writers of America.

After Brando let the option expire, making instead his western *One-Eyed Jacks*, I formed a film company with Maureen O'Hara and her producer brother, Charles FitzSimons, to make the film. We contracted for Sam Peckinpah, a television director, to lead the charge. This was his first feature length film, released under the title, *The Deadly Companions*.

GL: When referring to the agent, Donald MacCampbell, you used the adjective "unlamented". Why?

SF: MacCampbell was a small time literary agent when the original paperback revolution struck. He made deals with some publishers (Ace among them, or so he told me) to provide X number of action/ mystery novels per month. He then rounded up a lot of hungry writers, like Harry Whittington, like Wade Miller, like me, and quickly became known as the 'King of the Paperbacks.'

I first met him during the war when I had written a popular book of magic for the general public, which he placed with a publisher of craft books. When old college friends, Bob Wade and Billy Miller (Wade Miller) needed an agent for their first mystery novel, I passed along MacCampbell's address with some misgivings.

A photograph of Charles Lindbergh hung in MacCampbell's small Manhattan office, for MacCampbell was an American Firster, dabblers in the fascism of the day. I was in uniform when he told me the armed services were 'cannon fodder,' and openly told me how he had avoided the draft. Knowing that a Coke made his heart go haywire, he spotted a machine as he was about to take his physical. He dropped a nickel, drank his Coke, and an hour later was declared to be hopelessly 4F. I assumed he was telling me the truth.

I soon left him to go briefly with Sydney Sanders (who, by the way, was Raymond Chandler's agent), but by the time Gold Medal got underway I was agentless. Since Germany had lost the war and the American Firsters had been thoroughly discredited, and MacCampbell had taken down the picture of Charles Lindbergh, I chose to forget his political quirkiness. He was my agent from *Shanghai Flame* through *Blood Alley*.

I discovered something amiss when he phoned one day to say he'd had a film offer for *Counterspy Express* (Ace) for $3,000 from Willy Wilder (not to be confused with his hugely gifted writer-director brother, Billy). I asked him to negotiate the deal upward. He phoned back ten minutes later to say he'd been unable to improve the deal, so I accepted it. Wilder and I became good friends, and he told me that in visiting MacCampbell's office he was shown a film rights bookcase with shelves of $5,000 books, $3,000 books and $1,000 books. MacCampbell had made no agent-like effort to improve the deal for *Counterspy Express*. He had deceived me.

During those years he was selling many foreign rights to my novels, but I never saw a publisher's contract for any of them. On his own letterhead he'd typed a brief agreement of three or four sentences, providing a petty advance from Gallimard, say, against such and such royalty rate. As with Phoenix, I never saw subsequent checks and have no memory of receiving royalty statements. I was a slow learner. By the mid 1950s I was completely disillusioned with the grasping man Wade Miller had had to sue and whom Harry Whittington dubbed "MacCannibal". Harry told me that he was unable to write under his own name for fear of legal action from the King of the paperbacks, and for years had been obligated to conceal himself behind pseudonyms. Thus, unlamented.

GL: When did your second writing career as a children's novelist begin and why?

SF: I backed into this field when I was idled during the screenwriter's strike of 1960, and decided to write a novel to amuse my three children. I had finished researching the West for *Yellowleg* not long before, and I knew the magic world, so I put the two together in a story about a family magic troop in covered wagon days. The novel was hugely successful (and is still in print). I had had so much fun writing this novel that I decided to write another story for kids, the equally successful and still in print novel of the California Gold Rush, *By The Great Horn Spoon*! I said in my acceptance speech (for *The Whipping Boy*) that in the children's book field "...I found myself, and I didn't know I had been lost." I wrote only one more novel for adults, a 1963 Gold Medal, *The Venetian Blonde*, with the classy Knox Burger as editor. In the years since I have devoted myself entirely to children's books and screen work.

GL: Your autobiography, *The Abracadabra Kid: A Writer's Life*, was published recently. Can you talk about it?

SF: It was written for anyone, especially aspiring writers. I give a lot of the inside workings of professional fiction writing and track story ideas back to their lowly origins. For example, as a nine-year-old I got a crush on a carnival sharp-shooter named Wanda who, 60 years later, turned up in my novel, *Jim Ugly*. And, of course, I deal in some detail with my Gold Medal years.

GL: Is *The Abracadabra Kid* your last book?

SF: No. As I write this (August, 1998) a new novel is just out from Greenwillow Books, *Bandit's Moon*. This deals with Joaquin Murieta and the dark side of the California Gold Rush. First reviews, just in from *Publishers Weekly* and *School Library Journal*, are starred. Meanwhile, I mailed off a new book of tall tales a few weeks ago, *A Carnival Of Animals*. It pleases me immensely that, at age 78, I can still plot my way through a novel, and find the words.

GL: You were a guest at the 1998 Los Angeles Paperback Show. Does it surprise you that people worldwide now collect and cherish these now vintage paperbacks?

SF: I am astonished and delighted. I had no idea that there was so much enthusiasm for the fifties titles, so much scholarship, and magazines devoted to the field. Dick Carrol would be equally amazed at what he had wrought at Gold Medal. I saw mint copies of my novels in far better shape than I am. I was equally amazed that there were a few of us writing veterans still around, like Bob Wade, to sign books. I felt that I was among friends.

GL: Thank you, Mr. Fleischman.

—reprinted by permission of *Paperback Parade*

www.ingramcontent.com/pod-product-compliance
Lightning Source LLC
LaVergne TN
LVHW011932070526
838202LV00054B/4604